SOUL DRINKER

IT WOULD BE Sarpedon's first full command, and he knew there was a risk. If the Adeptus Mechanicus fought, there could be terrible bloodshed, and if that happened not all his battle-brothers would return.

But even if such an unthinkable thing happened, the Soul Drinkers would fight on, acquit themselves with honour, and win back the Soulspear. No matter what, there would always be hope that the insult would be redressed, that the affair would be put behind them and Sarpedon could return to the Soul Drinkers' flagship with the Soulspear in hand.

As Daenyathos wrote: *when all is darkness and every way out is lined with blood and lit with the fires of battle, there is still hope.*

SOUL DRINKER

Ben Counter

To Helen

A BLACK LIBRARY PUBLICATION

First published in Great Britain in 2002
This edition published in 2005 by
BL Publishing,
Games Workshop Ltd.,
Willow Road, Nottingham,
NG7 2WS, UK.

10 9 8 7 6 5 4 3 2 1

Cover illustration by Adrian Smith.

A CIP record for this book is available from the British Library.

ISBN 13: 978 1 84416 162 1
ISBN 10: 1 84416 162 5

Distributed in the US by Simon & Schuster
1230 Avenue of the Americas, New York, NY 10020, US.

Printed and bound in Great Britain by
Bookmarque, Surrey, UK.

See the Black Library on the Internet at
www.blacklibrary.com

Find out more about Games Workshop
and the world of Warhammer 40,000 at
www.games-workshop.com

CHAPTER ONE

IN THE SILENCE of the vacuum the corvus assault pod tumbled towards the star fort, the curved metal of its hull studded with directional jets that fired once, steadying the descent. The pod had been fired on a trajectory that took it halfway across the orbit of the planet Lakonia, which hung bright and cold below. The battle cruiser which had housed it, along with the half-dozen other pods glinting against the blackness of space, was on the other side of the planet. No one in the star fort would have any idea they were coming. And that was just how the Soul Drinkers preferred it.

Inside the drop-pod, Sarpedon could hear only the soft song of the servitor choir and the gentle hum of armour. The battle-brothers were quiet, contemplating the fight to come and the many years of warfare that had forged them into the pinnacle of humanity.

They were thinking of Primarch Rogal Dorn, the father of their Chapter literally as well as figuratively, and his noble example they strove to follow. They thought of the favour the Emperor had bestowed upon them, that they might travel the stars and play their part in a grand plan that was too fragile and vital to place in the hands of lesser men. They had thought such things a thousand times or more, readying their minds for the sharp intensity of combat, banishing the doubt that afflicted soldiers falling below the standard of the Space Marines; of the Soul Drinkers.

Sarpedon knew this, for he felt the same. And yet this time it was different. This time the weight of history, which refined the Soul Drinkers' conduct into a paragon of honour and dignity, was a little heavier. For there was more at stake than a battle won or lost. Soon, when the fight was over, they would have reserved a place in the legends that were taught to novices and recited on feasting nights.

The choir's delicate faces, mounted on brass armatures, turned to the ceiling of the corvus pod as the note from their once-human vocal chords rose. The Soul Drinkers Chapter used the mindless, partly-human servitors for all menial and non-skilled labour – those making up the choir were little more than faces and vox-projectors hardwired to the pod. Their presence was a tradition of the Chapter, and helped focus the thoughts of the battle-brothers on the battle to come.

They were close. They were ready. Sarpedon could feel the brothers' eagerness for battle, their concern for proper conduct and their scorn for cowardice, mixed and tempered into a warrior's soul. It shone at the back of his mind, so strong and unifying that he could receive it without trying.

The pod juddered as it encountered the first wisps of Lakonia's atmosphere, but the thirty battle-brothers – two tactical and one assault squad strapped into grav-ram seats, resplendent in their dark purple power armour and with weapons gleaming – did not allow their reverie to waver.

His brothers. The select band that lay between mankind's destiny and its destruction. The tune of the choir changed as the pod entered the final phase, almost drowning out the hiss of the braking jets. Sarpedon took his helmet from beside his seat and put it on, feeling the seal snaking shut around his throat. New runes on his retinal display confirmed the vacuum integrity of his massive armour. Every Space Marine had spent many hours on the strike cruiser observing the strictest wargear discipline, for they could be fighting in a near-vacuum before entry points were secured.

He activated a rune on the retinal-projected display and his aegis hood thrummed into life. Handed down the line of senior Librarians of the Soul Drinkers, its lost technology warmed up to protect Sarpedon as he led his brother Space Marines into Chapter history.

Close. Closer. Even if the choir and the corvus pod's alert systems had not told him, he could have felt it. He could feel the star fort's bulk rearing out of the darkness, its bloated shape creeping across Lakonia's green-brown disk as they approached. The braking jets entered second phase, and the grav-rams flexed to cushion the Marines' weight against the deceleration.

'Soul Drinkers,' came Commander Caeon's voice over the vox-channel, clear and proud. 'I need not tell you why you are here, or what is expected of you, or how you will fight. These are things you will never doubt.

'But know now that when the youngest novices or the most scarred of veterans ask you how you spent your time serving this Chapter, it will be enough to tell them that you were there the day your Chapter proved it never forgets a matter of honour. The day the Soulspear was returned.'

Good words. Caeon could tap into the hearts of his men, use the power of those traditions they held sacred to will them on to superhuman feats.

Lights flashed inside the corvus pod. The noise grew, the servitor choir matching its harmonies, a wall of sound growing, inspiring. The metallic slamming that rippled through the hull was the sound of the docking clamps forced out of their cowlings, ceramite-edged claws primed to rip through metal. Sarpedon could see the star fort fresh in his mind, planted there by the repeated mission briefings – it was ugly and misshapen, probably once spherical but now deformed. Docking corridors would be stabbing out from its tarnished surface, but the attack had been carefully timed.

There was no cargo on the star fort and no ships docked – no way out for defenders. The Van Skorvold cartel and its rumoured private army believed their star fort to be a bastion of defence, its weapon systems and labyrinthine interior protecting them from any attack. It was the Soul Drinkers' intent to turn the place into a deathtrap.

Long-range scans had only penetrated through the first few layers of the star fort. It had been difficult to plan an assault route when there could only be guesswork about what form the inside of the fort might take, so the mission was simple in principle. Go in, eliminate any opposition, and find the objectives. Where the objectives were, or what that opposition might be, would be discovered as the mission unfolded by the leaders of the individual assault teams. In the case of Sarpedon's squads, that was Sarpedon himself.

There were three objectives. Primary objectives one and two were means to an end – that end was Objective Ultima, and its recovery would emblazon the names of every Space Marine here on the pages of Chapter history.

Sarpedon checked his bolter one last time, and clasped a hand round the grip of his force staff, the psyk-attuned arunwood haft warm to the touch. Faint energy crackled over its surface. The other Space Marines were making a last symbolic check of their wargear, too – helmet and joint seals, bolters. The plasma gun of Givrillian's squad was primed, its power coils glowing. Sergeant Tellos's assault squad, stripped of their jump packs for the star fort environment, unsheathed their chainswords as one. Sarpedon could feel Tellos's face behind his snarl-nosed helmet, calm and untroubled, with a hint of a smile. All Soul Drinkers were born to fight – Tellos was born to do so with the enemy surrounding him at sword-thrust range, daring to take up arms against the Emperor's chosen. Tellos was marked for great things, the upper echelons of Chapter command had said. Sarpedon agreed.

The choir suddenly fell silent, and there was nothing in the Space Marines' minds but battle. The docking charges roared in unison, and they hit.

THE CORVUS POD's doors blew open and the air rushed out with a scream. The flesh on the servitor choir's faces blistered and cracked with the sudden cold. There was silence all around, save for the hum of the power plant in his armour's backpack and the almost-real sound of his brothers' minds, washing back and forth like a tide as they snapped through the orientation/comprehension routines that had been implanted on their minds during psycho-doctrination.

Sight – the swirling smoke through the blast doors, fragments of ice and metal spinning. Sound – nothing, no air. Movement – none.

The Space Marines unbuckled their harnesses, ready to rush the breach. Tellos would lead them in, his men's chainswords primed to rip through the first line of defenders. Sarpedon would be in the middle of the tactical squads on their heels, ready to unleash the weapon that boiled within his mind.

Sarpedon only had to nod, and Tellos bolted through the breach.

'Go! Go! With me!' Tellos's young, eager voice broke the silence like a gunshot as his squad followed. Then the sergeant's breath was the only sound. Every Space Marine listened with augmented ears for the first contact with the enemy.

The tactical squads were unbuckled.

'Clear!' called Tellos.

The Tactical Marines plunged into the smoky breach, their power armoured bulks dropping through into the darkness. Givrillian was in the lead, Brother Thax with the plasma gun at his shoulder. Sarpedon followed, bolter ready, force staff holstered behind his armour's backpack. As he ducked into the breach he caught sight of Lakonia, a glowing sliver of a world framed in the gap between the pod's docking gear and the star fort's hull. The pod had come in aslant and the docking seal had not adhered, the atmosphere within the pod and immediate environment beyond venting out into the thin near-void.

An assault craft of lesser forces would have been forced to disengage then and there, its blast doors clamped shut, to drift vulnerable and impotent until second wave craft picked it up. But the Soul Drinkers cared nothing for such things – power armour's sealable environment made a mockery of the dangers of vacuum. And there would be no second wave.

The smoke cleared and Sarpedon got his first look at the star fort's interior. It was low-ceilinged to a warrior of his superhuman height, dirty and ill-maintained – they had hit a derelict section, of which there were probably a great many in the fort. Oil and sludge had frozen on the pipes that snaked the ceilings and walls. They were at the junction of two corridors – one way was blocked by a lump of rusting machinery, but there were still three exits to cover or exploit. Two curved away into the dimness and one ended in a solid bulkhead door, guarded by half of Tellos's assault squad, ready to blow it with melta-bombs.

The lack of immediate resistance was explained by the two bodies. Probably maintenance workers, they were unprotected when the local atmosphere blew out. One had been thrown against a stanchion by the explosive decompression and had burst like a ripe seed pod, his blood bright like jewels of red ice on the floor and walls. The other was stretched pathetically along the corridor floor, mouth frozen mid-gasp, staring madly up at the breach with eyes red from burst blood vessels. Sarpedon's keen eyes caught the glint of an insignia badge on the body's grease-streaked grey overalls, a retinal rune flashing as the image zoomed in.

Stylised human figures, twins, flanking a golden planet.

The Van Skorvold crest.

The Tactical Marines fanned out around him, bolters ready, enhanced senses scanning for movement.

'Breach the bulkhead, sir?' Tellos voxed.

'Not yet. Flight crew, get that seal intact. I don't want any decompressions throwing our aim.'

'Acknowledged,' came the serf-pilot's metallic voice from within the corvus cockpit. Vibrations ran through the dull metal grating of the floor as the clamps edged the docking seal true to the breached hull.

Sarpedon contracted a throat muscle to broaden the frequency of his vox-bead. 'This is Sarpedon. Squads Tellos, Givrillian and Dreo deployed. Nil contact.'

'Received, Sarpedon. Confirm location and move on mark.' The voice was Commander Caeon's from his position some way across the bloated bulk of the star fort. Along with Caeon, Sarpedon and their squads, six more corvus ship-to-orbital assault pods had impacted on the spaceward side of the star fort and disgorged their elite Soul Drinkers complements. Three more were following carrying the remaining apothecaries and Tech-Marines, along with a platoon of serf-labourers kitted out for combat construction duty, ready to support their brethren and consolidate the landing site bridgeheads.

Three whole companies of Soul Drinkers. A battlezone's worth of the Emperor's chosen soldiers, enough to face any threat the galaxy might throw at them. But for the prize that shone deep within the star fort, it was worth it.

Sarpedon pulled a holoslate from a waist pouch and flicked it on. A sketchy green image of the corridors immediately surrounding his position flickered above the slate, with lines of data circling it. The star fort was based on a very old orbital defence platform, and the platform's schematics had been supplied in case any of the assault pods hit a section of the original platform.

'Subsection delta thirty-nine,' he voxed. 'Redundant cargo and personnel route.'

'Received. Consolidate.'

Sarpedon's fingers, dextrous even within the gauntlet of purple ceramite, touched runes along the holoslate's side and the corridor system was divided into blocks of colour, marking the different routes out of their position. Crosshairs centred on a point that flashed red, indicating the convergence of the three routes two hundred metres further into the fort. Barring enemy concentrations elsewhere, their immediate objective was the primary environmental shaft head, a grainy green curve at the edge of the display. Once taken, it gave the Marines an option for a larger thrust into the oxygen pumps and recycling turbines, and then through the mid-level habs into the armoured core that surrounded primary objective two. A messenger rune flickered on his retinal display, indicating the docking seal had achieved integrity.

'By sections!' he ordered on the squad-level frequency, indicating the holo to his squad sergeants. 'Tellos, the bulkhead. Dreo, left, Givrillian right, with me. Cold and fast, Soul Drinkers!'

The squads peeled off into the darkness, leaving two Space Marines from each of the tactical squads to hold the bridgehead and cover the arriving specialists assigned to Sarpedon's cordon. There was the thud of melta-bomb detonations and the whump of air re-entering the area as the bulkhead fell.

Sarpedon led Givrillian's unit through the side corridor into a cargo duct, broad and square, with a heavy rail running down the centre for crate-carts or worker transports. Thax swept beyond the entrance.

'Nothing,' he said.

'Unsurprising,' said Sarpedon. 'They weren't expecting us.'

No one ever did. That was how the Soul Drinkers worked. Cold and fast.

They felt the faint report of bolter-shots in the thinned air. 'Contact!' came Dreo's voice.

Sarpedon waited, just a moment.

'Enemy down,' said Dreo. 'Half-dozen, security patrol. Autoguns and flak armour, uniforms.'

'Received, Sergeant Dreo. Proceed to rendezvous junction.'

'Mutants, sir.'

Sarpedon's skin crawled at the mere concept, and he could feel the disgust of his brothers. The evidence of illegal mutant dealing had been damning enough, but there had been stories that the Van Skorvold cartel had skimmed off the most useful of their illicit cargo and formed them into a private army. Now it was certain.

'Move the flamer to the rear and burn them. Squads, be aware, mutations include enhanced sensory organs. Some of those things might see as well as you. And there will be more.'

Degenerate, dangerous individuals but cowardly at heart. His powers would work well on such foes. But first they had to find them.

'Heavy contact, cargo hub seven!' Luko's callsign flickered. Luko's squad was part of the strikeforce from another corvus pod, one which had come down nearby and just before Sarpedon's. Sarpedon knew Luko would be itching to tear into some miscreant flesh with his power claws, and it was right that he should the first into the bulk of the enemy.

'Sarpedon here, do you request support?'

'Greetings, Librarian! Come on over, the hunting is good!' Luko always had a laugh in his voice, never more so than when the foe dared show its face.

Givrillian led them down a side-duct, cutting across the unassigned sectors delta thirty-eight and thirty-seven. A flash of the holoplate showed Luko's auspex data – red triangles, unknown signals, skittering across the edge of delta thirty-five.

'Dozens, sir,' said Givrillian.

'I can see that, sergeant. Suggestion?'

'Tellos'll be there first, so their first line will be engaged. We go in with light engagement fire pattern, get in right amongst them. Don't let them get dug in.'

'Good. Do it.'

They all heard Tellos as he called upon his brother assault troopers to slay for the Emperor and for Dorn, and the familiar sound of chainblade into flesh. The bolter-fire from Luko's squad stitched a pattern of sound into the air every Marine had heard a million times before. Givrillian burst through an open hatchway into the cargo hub that made up sector delta thirty-five, picked a target and loosed off a handful of shots from his bolter. Thax was a footstep behind and a pulse of liquid plasma-fire burst white hot from the muzzle of his gun, power coils shimmering.

Sarpedon cocked his bolter and followed, and saw the enemy for the first time.

The hub had once been dominated by the tracks at ceiling-level, which moved huge crates of cargo around the immense room between the duct entrances and pneumo-lifters. The forest of uprights which had held up the system had mostly collapsed or fallen askew with age and poor maintenance, and it was these that the mutants were using for cover.

In that split-second Sarpedon picked out a hundred unclean deformities – hands that were claws, facial features missing or multiplied or rearranged, spines cruelly twisted out of shape, scales and feathers and skin sheened with ooze. They had autoguns, some las weapons, crude shotguns. There were implanted industrial cutters and saws, and some with just brute strength, all in ragged stained coveralls in the uniform dark green bearing the Van Skorvold crest.

There must have been a thousand of them in there, crowds of baying mutants behind their makeshift defences. Their leaders – those with the most horrific mutations, some with massive chitinous talons or vast muscle growth – had either communicators or slits at their throats that indicated crude vox-bead implants. This was an organised foe.

Tellos's men were vaulting the first barricades and laying in with chainswords – limbs lopped off, heads falling. The sergeant himself was duelling with something hulking and ugly that wielded a recycler unit's harvester blade like a longsword. If it wasn't the leader the creature would at least form a lynchpin of morale for the degenerates that crowded around it – Tellos was good, seeking out the target that would damage the enemy most if eliminated, using his duelling skill to the maximum. If he took a fine trophy from the beast, Sarpedon would put in a word for him to keep it.

It took Sarpedon half a second to appreciate the situation and decide on his plan of action. The enemy had overwhelming strength and the Soul Drinkers had to neutralise the threat before a proper line of defence could form. Therefore they would attack the enemy's prime weaknesses relentlessly until they broke.

He loosed a couple of shots into a crowd of mutants and workers that were sheltering behind mouldering cargo crates from Luko's pinning fire. The bolter's kick in his hand felt good and heavy, and somewhere in the heart of the enemy two red blooms burst – a stream of autogun fire crackled towards him and he ducked back into cover.

First blood. Sarpedon had made his mark on the battle and could join with his brothers in pride at its execution, according to the Chapter traditions.

'Givrillian, sweep forward and engage. Watch for Luko's crossfire. I will follow.'

'Yes, sir.' Sarpedon could hear the smile in the sergeant's voice. He knew what was coming.

Sarpedon slammed back-first against an upright stanchion for cover while he focused. The enemy's weakness was moral – there might be many hundreds of them but they were degenerates and weak in mind, not least those untainted by mutation's stain but who nevertheless stooped to associate themselves with the unclean. His augmented hearing picked out the grind of chainblade against bone above the gunfire, as Tellos wore down the mutant he had sought out. The beast's death would weaken the enemy's capacity to fight. Sarpedon would finish it off.

Givrillian's squad flowed around him and he heard the plasma gun belch a wave of ultraheated liquid into the enemy flank, skin crackling, limbs melting.

What did they fear? They would fear authority, power, punishment. That was enough. He shifted the grip on his bolter so he had a hand free to draw the arunwood force staff from its leather scabbard. Its eagle-icon tip glowed as its thaumocapacitor core flooded with psychic energy. He concentrated, forming the images in his mind, piling them up behind a mental dam that would burst and send them flooding out into reality. He removed his helmet and set it on a clasp at his waist, taking a breath of the air – greasy, sour, recycled.

He stepped out into the battlezone. Givrillian's squad had torn the first rank of mutants apart, and they were now crouched in firepoints slick with deviant blood as return fire sheeted over their heads. Mutant gangs were scuttling and slithering through the debris, moving to outflank and surround them. Tellos had the beast-mutant on its knees, one horn gone, huge blade chipped and scarred by the assault sergeant's lightning-quick chainsword parries.

Sarpedon strode through it all, ignoring the autoshells and las-blasts spattering across the shadowy interior of the hub.

He spread his arms, and felt the coil of the aegis circuits light up and flow around his armoured body. He forced the images in his head to screaming intensity – and let them go.

The Hell began.

The closest mutants, at least two hundred strong, were thirty metres away, firefighting with Givrillian's Marines. Their firing stopped as they stared around them as tall shrouded figures rose from the floor, carrying swords of justice and great gleaming scythes to reap the guilty. Some bolted, to see hands clawing from the shadows, hungry for sinners to crush.

Bat-winged things swooped down at them and the mutants ran screaming, knowing their doom had come to punish their corruption at last. They heard a deep, sonorous laughter boom from somewhere high above, mocking their attempts to flee. The waves of fire broke as the mutants fled back through their own ranks, sowing disruption amongst their own for a few fatal seconds.

Sarpedon leapt the barricade with the nearest of Givrillian's Marines and stormed across to the mutant strongpoint. Most of the enemy still gawped at the apparitions boiling out of the darkness. A swing of his force staff clove through the closest two at shoulder height – he could feel their feeble life-forces driven out of their bodies even as the staff tore through their upper bodies with a flash of discharging energy. The burst of psychic power knocked three more off their feet and they landed hard, weapons dropped.

The Hell. A weapon subtle but devastating, striking at the minds of his enemies while his brother Marines struck their bodies. In the swift storming actions that the Soul Drinkers had made their own, it bought the seconds essential to press home the assault. It worked up-close, in the guts of the fight, where a Soul Drinker delighted to serve his Emperor.

Three of Givrillian's Marines, more than used to Sarpedon's conjurations after years of training and live exercises, pointed bolter muzzles over the mutants' makeshift barricade and pumped shells into the fallen, blasting fist-sized holes in torsos. Several more Space Marines knelt to draw beads on the hordes of mutants thrown into confusion by the sudden collapse of their front line. Shots barked out, bodies dropped.

A tentacle flailed as its owner fell. Something with skeletal wings jutting from its back was flipped into a somersault as a shell blew its upper chest apart.

Sarpedon stepped over the defences and swung again, swiping a worker/soldier in two at the waist as he tried to scramble away. Givrillian appeared at Sarpedon's shoulder, his bolter cracking shots into the backs of fleeing enemies. Assault Marines leapt past them and sprinted towards the mutants ranged towards the back of the hub. Tellos's armour was slick with black-red gore.

A hand clapped Givrillian's shoulder pad – it was Luko. In an instant the two tactical squads had joined up to form a fire line and chains of white-hot bolter fire raked around the Assault Marines, covering them as they did their brutal work. Some mutants survived to flee – most died beneath the blades of Tellos and his squad, or hammered by the fire from Givrillian and Luko. Their screams filled the hub with the echoes of the dying.

The enemy had broken completely and the spectres of the Hell strode amongst the panicking mutants as the Marines slaughtered them in their hundreds.

It was how the Soul Drinkers always won. Break an enemy utterly, rob him of his ability to fight, and the rest was just discipline and righteous brutality.

Givrillian caught Luko's hand in a warrior's handshake. 'Well met,' he said. 'I trust your men are blooded?'

Givrillian removed his helmet, glancing around. 'Every one, Luko. A good day.' Givrillian had lost half his jaw to shell fragments covering the advance on the walls of Oderic, and he scratched at the swathe of scar tissue from cheek to chin. 'A good day.' He looked out to where Tellos's Marines were picking their way across the heaps of mangled dead. The kill had been immense. But now, of course, the whole star fort would know they were here.

'Sergeants, your men have done well thus far,' said Sarpedon. 'We must not give the enemy pause to recover. How are we for an advance on objective two?'

'The cargo ducts to port look better-maintained,' replied Luko, gesturing with his clawed hand. 'Enemy forces will be using them soon. If we bear to starboard we'll avoid contact and give them less time to form a defence around the shell.'

Sarpedon nodded, and consulted the holoslate on the speediest route to the sphere. As the other Soul Drinker units thrust deeper into the star fort their hand-held auspex scanners were piping information about the environment to one another, so each leader had a gradually sharpening picture of the star fort's interior. The holoslate display now showed a wider slice of the star fort, and several paths through the tangle of corridors and ducts were tagged as potential assault routes towards primary objective two.

Intelligence on the objective was slim. Its most likely location was a shell, an armoured sphere suspended in the heart of the station, two kilometres from their position. The star fort had once been an orbital defence platform, and the shell had protected its command centre – barely large enough for one man, the Van Skorvolds were probably using it as an emergency shelter.

Primary objective one was being dealt with by forces under Commander Caeon himself – responsibility for objective two fell to Sarpedon. This was to enable him to make command decisions regarding the use of his psychic powers, which were considered essential in an environment such as the star fort. Sarpedon absolutely would not countenance a failure to take objective two, not when the prize was so great. Nor when Commander Caeon had given the responsibility to the

Librarian when he could easily have picked a company captain or Chaplain for the role.

Once the two primary objectives had been taken, the information gleaned from them should be enough to allow for the final thrust on to the Objective Ultima.

And if it was Sarpedon who took the prize... He fought here for the Chapter, for the grand plan of the Emperor of Mankind, and not for himself. But he would be lying if he told himself that he did not relish the chance to see the true object of their attack first, to take off his gauntlet and hold it as Primarch Dorn had done.

The Soulspear. For the moment, it was everything.

'We pull Dreo's squad back from the environment shaft,' he began, red lines indicating paths of movement on the holoslate's projection. 'They are our rearguard. Tellos takes the lead into the starboard ducts and through the habs.' The holoslate indicated a series of jerry-built partitions, possibly quarters for lower-grade workers, possibly workshops. 'There's a channel leading further in, probably for a mag-lev personnel train.'

'We could take it on foot if we blow the motive systems,' added Givrillian.

'Indeed. There's a terminus a kilometre and a half in. Our data thins out there, so we'll meet up with the rest of the secondary force and work out a route from there. Questions?'

'Any more of those?' asked Tellos, jerking a thumb at the steaming, bleeding hulk that he had left of the mutant-beast.

'With luck,' said Sarpedon. 'Move out.'

The secondary elements – an apothecary, Tech-Marine and dozen-strong serf-labour squad – were already arriving at the beachhead near the hull. Sarpedon voxed the Space Marines left stationed there to join up with Dreo at the rendezvous point and follow his advance.

The Space Marine spearhead moved out of the cargo hub at a jog, leaving thousands of mutant corpses gradually bleeding a lake of blood across the floor. It had been slightly over eight minutes since the attack began.

NEITHER THE SOUL Drinkers' Chapter command nor the Marines in the assault itself knew anything of the Van Skorvolds save intelligence relevant to the strength and composition of any likely resistance. Everything else was beneath their notice. The Guard units transported by the battlefleet knew even less about their opponents, knowing only that they were part of a hastily-gathered strike force readied to act against a space station. But there were those who had been watching the Van Skorvolds very closely indeed, and through a number of clandestine investigations and carefully pointed questionings, the truth had gradually emerged.

Diego Van Skorvold died of a wasting disease twelve years before the Soul Drinkers' attack on the star fort. His great-grandfather had purchased the star fort orbital defence platform at a discount from Lakonia's cash-starved Planetary Defence Force, and proceeded to sink most of the Van Skorvold family coffers into converting it to a hub for mercantile activity in the Geryon sub-sector. Succeeding generations gradually added to the star fort as the manner of business the Van Skorvold family conducted became more and more specialised. Eventually, there was only cargo of one type flooding through its cargo ducts and docking complexes.

Human traffic. For all the lofty technological heights of the Adeptus Mechanicus and vast engineered muscle of the battlefleets, it was human sweat and suffering that fuelled the Imperium. The Van Skorvolds had long known this, and the star fort was perfectly placed to capitalise on it. From the savage meat-grinder crusades to the galactic east came great influxes of refugees, deserters and captured rebels. From the hive-hells of Stratix, the benighted worlds of the Diemos cluster and a dozen other pits of suffering and outrage came a steady stream of prisoners – heretics, killers, secessionists, condemned to grim fates by Imperial law.

Carried in prison ships and castigation transports, these unfortunates and malefactors arrived at the Van Skorvold star fort. Their prison ships would be docked and the human cargo marched through the ducts to other waiting ships. There were dark red forge world ships destined for the servitor manufactoria of the Mechanicus, where the cargo would be mindwiped and converted into living machines. There were Departmento Munitorium craft under orders to find fresh meat for the penal legions being bled dry in a hundred different warzones. There were towering battleships of the Imperial Navy, eager to take on new lowlives for the gun gangs and engine shifts to replace crew who were at the end of their short lifespans.

And for every pair of shackled feet that shuffled onto such craft, the Van Skorvolds would take their cut. Business was good – in an ever-shifting galaxy human toil was one of the few commodities that was always much sought after.

And then Diego Van Skorvold died, leaving his two children to inherit the star fort.

Truth be told, there had been rumours about old Diego, too, and one or two of his predecessors, but they had never come to anything. The new siblings were different. The tales were more consistent and hinted at transgressions more grave. People started to take notice. The rumours reached the ears of the Administratum.

Pirate craft and private launches had been sighted sneaking guiltily around the Lakonia system. The star fort's human traffic was conducted under the strict condition that all prisoners were to be sold on only to Imperial authorities; allowing private concerns to purchase such a valuable commodity from under the noses of the Imperium was not to be tolerated.

And there was worse. Mutants, they said, who were barred from leaving their home world, were bought and sold, and the cream skimmed off to serve the Van Skorvolds as bodyguards and work-teams. There were even tales of strange alien craft, intercepted and wrecked by the sub-sector patrols, whose holds were full of newly-acquired human slaves. Corresponding gossip pointed darkly to the collection of rare and unlicensed artefacts maintained by the Van Skorvolds deep in the heart of the star fort. Trinkets paid by alien slavers in return for a supply of broken-willed humans? It was possible. And that possibility was enough to warrant action.

Matters pertaining to the star fort fell under the jurisdiction of the Administratum, and they were concerned with keeping it that way. The Van Skorvolds had been immensely successful, but the persistence of the rumours surrounding them was considered enough to constitute proof of guilt. The accusations of corruption and misconduct indicated that the control of the prisoner-trade lay in the hands of those who broke the Imperial law, and so it was deemed necessary that the Administratum should take control of the star fort and its business.

The Van Skorvold siblings were not so understanding. Repeated demands for capitulation went unanswered. It was decided that force was the only answer, but that an Arbites or, Terra forbid, an Inquisitorial purge would do untold damage to an essential and profitable trade. The flow of workers and raw servitor materials was too important to interrupt. It had to be done as discreetly as such things can be.

In the decades and centuries to come, Imperial history would forget most of these facts when relating the long and tortuous tale of the Soul Drinkers. Yet nevertheless, it was there that the terrible chain of events began, in the drab dusty corridors of the Administratum and in the decadent hearts of the Van Skorvold siblings. Had the Van Skorvolds picked a different trade or the Administratum persisted with negotiations and sanctions, a canny scholar might suggest, there would be nothing but glory writ beside the name of the Soul Drinkers Chapter. But, as seems always the case with matters so delicately poised, fate was not to be so kind.

'EVERYWHERE... FRAGGIN'... EVERYWHERE...'

'...crawling all over the sunside... armour, guns... monsters, all of them...'

On board the Imperial battle cruiser *Diligent*, the transmissions from the Van Skorvold star fort were increasing in number and urgency. The tactical crews clustered around the comm consoles on the bridge were tracking a dozen battles and firefights, as a small but utterly ruthless force cut their way through the mutant army of the Van Skorvold cartel.

They were the sounds of panic and confusion, of death and dying and shock. There were screams, sobs, orders shouted over and over again even though there was no one left to hear them. He could hear them fleeing – they were the sounds of bolter shells thunking into flesh and chainsword blades shrieking their way through bone.

They were also the sounds of Iocanthos Gullyan Kraevik Chloure getting rich. It wasn't about that, of course – it was about safeguarding the economic base of this sector and rooting out the corruption that threatened Imperial authority. But getting rich was a bonus.

And, of course, most of them were only mutants.

Consul Senioris Chloure of the Administratum could see little evidence of the carnage within the star fort through the viewscreen that took up most of the curved front wall of the *Diligent's* bridge. Magnified inset panels appeared in the corners to pick out something the cogitators decided was interesting – plumes of escaping air and squat ribbed cylinders of large ship-to-ship assault pods emblazoned with the golden chalice symbol of the Soul Drinkers Chapter.

Space Marines. Chloure had spent decades in service to the Imperium and yet he had never seen one, confined as he was in the drudgery and isolation of the Administratum. Grown men talked of them like children talk of heroes – they could tear men apart with their bare hands, see in the dark, take las-blasts to the chest without flinching, wore armour that bullets bounced off. They were three metres tall. They never failed. And yet Consul Senioris Chloure, in charge of the mission to cleanse and seize the Van Skorvold star fort, had managed to engineer their presence here and let them do the job for him. Chloure had a three-cruiser battlefleet supported by one Adeptus Mechanicus ship, and if he played this right, he wouldn't have to use them until it came to cleaning up.

There was a moment of gloom as the screens and lights on the bridge dipped to acknowledge the figure arriving on the bridge. Chloure looked down from the observation pulpit to see Khobotov, archmagos of the Adeptus Mechanicus, enter flanked by an honour guard of shield-servitors, another gold-plated microservitor scurrying in front paying out a long sea-green strip of carpet for the magos to walk on. Three or four of those damned sensor-technomats droned in the air on hummingbird wings, trailing wires like cranefly legs – Chloure hated them, their chubby infant bodies and glazed cherubic faces. They were sinister in the extreme and he felt sure Khobotov affected them to inflict uneasiness on whoever had to meet him.

Chloure had spent long enough in the Administratum – that huge and complex institution which tried to smooth the running of the unimaginably vast Imperium – to know the value of politics. The Adeptus Mechanicus had wanted a part in the subduing of the rumoured heretics of the Van Skorvold cartel, and the representative they sent to join the battlefleet was Archmagos Khobotov and his ship, the *674-XU28*.

Chloure had been willing to suffer Khobotov's inclusion in the mission to grease the wheels between the Administratum and the Mechanicus, but he had begun to wish he hadn't. The Mechanicus was essential to the running of the Imperium, constructing and maintaining the arcane machinery that let mankind travel the stars and defend its frontiers, but they were so damn strange that their presence sometimes made Chloure's stomach churn. The *674-XU28* was almost entirely silent, so the first warning crews had that Khobotov was paying them a visit was usually when the archmagos swept onto the bridge.

Chloure rose from the pulpit seat, smoothing down his black satin greatcoat. He took the salute of Vekk, his flag-captain, as he trotted down the main bridge deck with its swarms of petty officers and lexmechanics. Khobotov himself was a complete enigma, swathed in deep green robes with ribbed power cables leading out behind him from beneath the hem. Tiny motorised sub-servitors held the cables in silver jaws and whirred around, keeping the cables from snagging on the rivets and consoles jutting from the deck of the *Diligent's* bridge. This caused the cables to slither like long artificial snakes, which was another thing that struck Chloure as gravely unpleasant.

He supposed he should be grateful it was the Mechanicus who had insisted on coming along. The puritans of the Ecclesiarchy or inflexible lawhounds of the Adeptus Arbites would have been more hassle and less use.

Chloure did what the Administratum had taught him to do many years before – grin and bear it, for the good of politics.

'Archmagos Khobotov,' he said, feigning camaraderie. 'I trust you have heard the good news.' One of the technomats buzzed past his head, a leathered tome clutched in its dead-fleshed hands, and he resisted the urge to swat it away.

'Indeed,' replied Khobotov, his voxed voice grinding from within his deep green cowl. 'It is of concern to me that neither your crew nor mine detected their approach.'

'They have fine pilots, as does any Chapter. And I hear this is the Soul Drinkers' speciality, rapid ship-to-ship swashbuckling and all that. I'd wager the Van Skorvolds didn't realise they were coming either.'

'Hmmm. I take it this indicates your intelligence was accurate regarding the artefact's location.'

'We'll see soon enough. Hopefully by the time they've finished our Guardsmen will only be fulfilling an occupational role. Save us assaulting the place ourselves.' Chloure remembered he was still maintaining a big false smile, and hoped the conversation would be over soon.

'My tech-guard would have been willing to take part in a landing action, consul.' If Khobotov had taken any offence it was impossible to tell. 'My forces are compact and well-armed. But yes, for them to attack would have yielded casualties amongst my resources that could be used profitably elsewhere.'

'Yes. Good.' Chloure wished he could see the archmagos's face – was he smiling or glowering? Then it occurred to him that the tech-priests of the Adeptus Mechanicus were notorious for the levels of bionic augmentation and replacement they indulged in, and that there was no telling if there even was a face under that cowl. 'I shall… keep you updated.'

'There is no need. My sensors and tech-oracles are far superior to yours.'

'Of course. Good.'

Archmagos Khobotov swept around and led his unliving entourage off the bridge, doubtless towards the command crew shuttle bay where he would return to the *674-XU28*. The rust-red Mechanicus craft was designated as an armed research vessel, but it was a damn sight bigger and more dangerous than it sounded. Within the hold was a regiment of tech-guard, although it looked like there was room for a lot more.

Had it come down to it, it would have been those tech-guards now piling into the Van Skorvold star fort alongside the Imperial Guard units transported by the rest of the fleet. Stationed on the cruiser *Hydranye Ko* there was a below-strength regiment from Stratix, the 37th, most of them mother-killing gang-scum who joined up for no better reason than that it would get them the hell off Stratix. The second cruiser, the *Deacon Byzantine*, contained elements of the Diomedes 14th Bonebreakers and, owing to an administrative error, a strike force of assault and siege tanks from the Oristia IV Armoured Brigade. The *Diligent* itself contained a regiment of Rough Riders from the plains of Morisha, deeply unhappy at being separated from their horses who were wintering several systems away.

Three cruisers, not of the highest quality but recently refitted and with well-drilled crews. It wasn't much compared to the immense battlefleets that scoured the void in times of crusade or invasion, but it had been all Chloure could muster through string-pulling and favour-calling in a short period of time. He had to secure the star fort and its lucrative trade before some other Imperial authority came sniffing around. And if it paid off he would be in charge of the star fort for the rest of his life, content and comfortable, as a reward for the seemingly endless drudgery he had undergone, pushing papers and running errands in the Emperor's name.

And now it seemed the Guardsmen and tech-guard would be more than enough, for his biggest gamble had paid off. The information that the Soulspear was on board the star fort had travelled exactly as he hoped it would, straight to the ears of the Soul Drinkers Chapter. Judging by the displacement of the small Astartes fleet anchored on the far side of Lakonia and the number of corvus assault pods, their number was estimated to be above three hundred.

Three hundred. Smaller Marine forces had conquered star systems. Of course, officially their presence here was fortuitous and Chloure didn't have the authority over them that he did over the battlefleet. Space Marines were famous for their autonomy. But the Soul Drinkers were so honour-bound that their reaction to the information on the Soulspear could be predicted exactly. Chloure had known they would ignore his fleet and make their own attack, sweeping through the star fort as they searched for their antique trinket. When they found it they would leave as quickly as they had arrived, leaving the star fort filled with bodies and ripe for occupation by the Guardsmen.

Warming as these thoughts were, Chloure couldn't stop his skin from crawling as Archmagos Khobotov's technomats droned past. Soon the star fort would be taken in the name of the Administratum, the risk would be over, and his future would be secure. And he wouldn't have to talk to that Mechanicus spectre again.

* * *

YSER HAD HIDDEN as soon as the first shooting started. At first it had been relayed over the cull-team's communicators – scratchy, distorted screams and dull crumps of bullets spattering into flesh. There was confusion and anger, but for a change none of it was directed at Yser or his flock. Something new had appeared, something terrible. Giants, they said. Giants in armour, with guns and swords, swarming without number from the sunward side of the star fort. They were everywhere at once.

Yser peered between the mouldering packing crates where he had hidden in the corner of the maglev terminus. He had hoped to steal some food from the lumbering supply carts as they hummed down the maglev rail towards the heart of the star fort, but the cull-teams were out and he had been cornered. He had felt sure they would take him this time – they were brute-mutants, afflicted with a semi-stable strain of uncleanliness that let their muscles bulge out of control. They stomped across the sheet metal of the maglev deck, beetling eyes peering into the shadows, shotguns and spearcannon clutched in their massive paws. Yser hadn't minded that much – it was a worthy way to die, trying to keep his flock alive, striving to continue the dutiful worship of the Emperor. What else did he have?

Then the reports came in. Word was that Mirthor was down, which was in itself impossible – the Van Skorvolds had appointed Mirthor the chief of their close-knit mutant bodyguard solely because it was reckoned absolutely nothing could kill him. He was an immense horned monster, twice the height of the tallest man, and yet they said he was dead, cut to pieces by armoured giants who bled from the shadows and had the spirits of vengeance on their side.

Impossible. But for Yser to have gone from violent petty thief to a priest ministering to the faith of a flock of escaped slaves was also impossible. Yet Yser had done it, praise to the Architect of Fate. Yser wondered if there was a miracle unfolding in the depths of the star fort – or, indeed, if the Emperor would let him live long enough to see it.

The brutes began to select fire points as the reports put the attackers closer and closer, and suddenly the crump of gunfire was real, echoing from the cargo ducts and recycler shafts snaking away from the terminus.

More arrived. Danvaio's lot, mostly with minor mutations that made them ugly and bitter, and a bunch of unaltered humans from the dock work-gangs in the dark green uniform of the Van Skorvold army. Yser could hear the voices ugly in their throats – they had tooled up with whatever weapons they could find and mustered here, because the attackers were heading this way and they were damned if that bitch Veritas Van Skorvold was going to have their heads because they ran instead of fighting.

They were still arguing over what to do when an explosion ripped into the side of the great maglev platform.

Yser reeled in shock and slumped onto his back, ears screaming, a white patch blotting his vision. As it cleared he could see the wash of blood spattered over the platform where Danvaio's mob had caught the worst of it, their incomplete bodies slumping over the plasticrete rubble.

And he saw them. Clad in purple trimmed with bone, holding heavy squat guns or whining chainswords almost as long as Yser was tall. He thought there was some trick of the light, but no, these men really were that tall – they topped out as tall as the bigger brutes, and their armour gave them immense bulk. There were a dozen of them perhaps, sprinting across the terminal space to rush the makeshift defences. Someone fired back but the few shots that hit spanged off their armour. Guns opened up in reply and tore through plasticrete and flesh alike, a half-dozen normals shredded in a second.

He had seen them before, in the waking dreams when the Architect had first come to him and answered his plight. They were His chosen, the warriors of justice, whose unending battle would redeem humanity's sins and lay the foundations for His great plan. Could it be? He had thought it a legend, something that would come to pass long after he had died. Was it happening now? Was the Architect of Fate really sending his warriors here, to save Yser's flock?

More of them were pouring in at a sprint as the first wave slammed into the defenders, mutant and normal alike sliced or riddled with explosive shells. The warriors dived over barricades into the teeth of blades and work-axes. Amongst those now arriving was one without a helmet, shaven-headed with a battered, yet volatile face, around whose skull played a blue-white corona echoed by that around the top of the mighty staff he carried. The chalice symbol on the shoulder pad of every man's armour was echoed on this warrior, but chased in gold. Sparks flew as his feet hit the floor and he raced with his brothers into the fray.

As Yser cowered he saw more and more mutants pouring from the maglev tunnels. He knew the voice of Veritas Van Skorvold herself would be stinging the ears of those with communicators, demanding they make their lives worth something by giving them to defend her star fort. He saw crews from the hunt gangs, who tracked runaway slaves through the star fort with their stalked eyes or sensitive antennae, running right into the teeth of the warriors' gunfire and being shredded to bloody rags. He watched the bare-headed warrior raise his staff and unleash a storm of power, which coalesced into shadowy shapes that descended on the hordes of arriving mutants and put them to flight.

Yser had never seen such slaughter. Those of his flock who had been caught by the cull-teams had been surrounded and butchered or killed while they slept, and Yser had seen many of them die – and now it seemed they were being paid back a thousandfold by the righteous warriors of the Architect of Fate. It was the deliverance of justice as Yser had dared to believe it would be, swift and merciless. The screams of the dying and the stench of blood washed over his hiding place, and when he dared peek out again he could see mountains of mutant corpses piled up against the maglev platform. The warriors, not pausing to gloat over the dead, moved swiftly on into the maglev tunnels, the bare-headed one shouting orders. Yser caught his words – they were to press on, strike fast before the defenders could get properly organised and meet them a third time, find the objective and link up with their brothers.

Then they were gone, leaving only the dead.

THE EDUCATED GUESSES had been correct. The maglev line led deep into the star fort, past cavernous generatoria and parasitic shanty-towns, right onto the doorstep of the shell. Mutant strongpoints dotted the square-sectioned maglev tunnel, but the energy weapons to the fore had cracked open gun emplacements and grenades had blown apart huddling bands of mutants. Some had communicators, and the Space

Marines on point had reported a screeching female voice yelling orders through the headsets.

The Soul Drinkers had kept moving, posting pickets to guard the route into the heart of the star fort as the Chapter serfs moved in behind the Marine spearhead. With the mutant army scattered and broken, the Soul Drinkers had passed through the increasingly intact command sector of the ancient orbital defence platform, and reached the shell.

It was thirty-nine minutes since the attack had begun.

Sarpedon checked the vox-net for Caeon's progress. The larger force of Soul Drinkers had advanced on a broader front, for primary objective one was believed to be located in the Van Skorvolds' lavish private quarters – four floors of garish decadence that were well-defended and had required an assault from many angles. There were injuries, some disabling, but no deaths. Caeon had thrown a ring of Marines around the private quarters and was in the process of squeezing the defenders – fewer mutants, and more well-armed mercenary guards – to death inside.

Good, then. Caeon would get the job done – he was an experienced and trustworthy commander. Sarpedon himself, with what was his first true command, could concentrate on his own part of the mission. The part that concerned primary objective two.

Sarpedon watched the dozen-strong work-serf gang hurrying past, one of them carrying a needle-nosed melta-saw. They were some of the thousands of Chapter serfs maintained by the Soul Drinkers for tasks too menial for the Space Marines themselves. They were stripped to the waist and covered with a sheen of sweat from their work rapidly shoring up the assault pod breaches, and from the quick march along the trail of destruction the Soul Drinkers had blazed before them.

The serfs passed into the Marine perimeter – fifty of the Imperium's finest warriors had formed a cordon of steel around the exposed section of the shell. The rest of Sarpedon's hundred-strong command either formed rings of defence further out or were organised into hunting parties to eliminate knots of mutants skulking nearby.

There had been casualties – the sheer numbers of the opposition had made it inevitable – but every one hurt when each Space Marine was so valuable. Koro and Silvikk would never see another dawn, and Givlor would be fortunate to survive, his throat transfixed by a metre-long speargun bolt. There were scores of minor injuries, fractures and lacerations, but a Space Marine could simply ignore such things until the mission was finished. It had been cold and fast. Chapter Master Gorgoleon himself would be proud.

Sarpedon watched as the serf gang prepared to bore a hole in the shell. The exposed section of the shell was surrounded by crudely wired data-consoles, charts and maps, detritus of the Van Skorvold business. Doubtless the Administratum would make much of the information in the scattered files and cigitator banks, but Sarpedon cared nothing for it. Once the Soul Drinkers had secured Objective Ultima they would leave this place and let the Imperial battlefleet outside take it over and do what they willed.

There was one way into the one-man command module housed within the shell. It was sealed, and Sarpedon knew it would take time to crack the encryption locks. That was why they had brought the serfs.

One of the work-serfs, his arms replaced with articulated tines to fit the melta-saw, hefted the huge cutting device and let a thin superheated line bore into the smooth metallic surface of the shell. Slowly a red tear dripping with molten metal was scored across the metal as an entrance was carved.

The work-serf strained to drag the cutting beam the last few centimetres, black smoke coiling from where the bionics met his shoulder. The Chapter apothecaries and serf-orderlies often practised cybernetic surgery on the work gang augmentations, and they weren't always of the highest quality. But they sufficed here, for a large section of the shell wall fell away with a loud clang.

Sarpedon stepped forward, projecting a crackling aura of power around his head. It was a simple trick, but it worked surprisingly well in cowing the weak-willed. Several of Givrillian's Marines followed him in.

Inside, the shell was clean and well-kept. It was small, enough for one or two men, but it had been stripped of the command mind-impulse units and cogitator readouts, and kitted out as a luxurious bedroom. There was a four-poster bed, deep carpets, and a dressing table with a large mirror that doubled as a holoprojector. Antique porcelain decorated the shelves running around the room, and several original paintings lined the walls, along with a finely-decorated sword that had almost certainly never been drawn from its scabbard. It was evidently intended to ensure the notable forced to shelter here did so in the comfort he was accustomed to.

That notable lay cowering on the bed, trying to hide under sheets although he was fully clothed in a powder blue velvet bodysuit with gold lace trimmings. His periwig had fallen off and lay beside the bed. His face was thin and youthful, with a weak chin, watery eyes and lank blond hair dusted with powder. A faint odour of urine rose from him, plain to Sarpedon's enhanced senses.

Primary objective two: Callisthenes Van Skorvold.

Sarpedon was a transmitting telepath, not a receiver – a rare talent, and one that was of little use in dragging thoughts out of a man's mind during interrogation. But Sarpedon suspected he would not need such trickery here in any case.

'Callisthenes Van Skorvold,' he began, 'doubtless your crimes against the Imperium are many and grave. They will be dealt with later. For now, I have but one question: *Where is the Soulspear?*'

HALFWAY ACROSS THE star fort, amongst the tapestries and chandeliers of the garish inner sanctum of the Van Skorvold cartel, Commander Caeon's force closed in on primary objective one. The assault had been near-perfect, storming the hastily prepared defences of the Van Skorvold private chambers from a dozen directions at once, isolating pockets of defenders and annihilating them with massive firepower or lightning assaults before sweeping on to the next opponents.

Hard, fast, merciless. Daenyathos, the philosopher-soldier of Chapter legend, might have written of such an assault when he laid down the tenets of Soul Drinker tactics thousands of years before.

Bolters blazed their way through the last few chamber guards. The guards were professionals, picking defensive points with care and trying to relinquish them in good order when they had been overwhelmed. But their quality as soldiers meant only that they were compelled to die to a man in the teeth of Caeon's advance.

Commander Caeon strode past Finrian's tactical squad, whose two melta guns had burned great dripping holes through the partitions between the drawing rooms, audience halls and bedchambers. His feet crunched through the glass of the shattered chandelier and the splinters of priceless furniture the defenders had tried to use for cover.

All around smoke coiled in the air and flames crackled around the wooden panelling. The opulence of the chambers was in ruins, strewn with bodies and riddled with bullet holes. The Soul Drinkers were rising through the gunsmoke as the echoes of bolter fire died away, sweeping the muzzles of their guns across the bloodstained corridors and hunting for survivors.

'Clear,' came Finrian's voice over the vox, as twenty sergeant's icons flashed in agreement on Caeon's retina.

Caeon was an ancient and grizzled man, three hundred years old, and he kicked the bodies of the fallen guards aside with the contempt appropriate to a Space Marine hero. He had fought some of the sharpest actions in the recent history of the Soul Drinkers and taken trophies of the kraken, the ork, the Undying Ones and a dozen other species besides. He peered through the wreaths of bolter smoke, searching for primary objective one.

A couple of parlour slaves were wandering about stunned, ignored by the Marines. A thin, aged woman whimpered as she stumbled over the wreckage, seemingly oblivious to the two hundred-strong Marine force stalking through the area. A pudgy child scampered here and there, as if trying to find a way out. A couple of others were huddled in corners, seemingly catatonic. They barely registered with Caeon.

The place was desolate. There were no reports of the objective being sighted, and he was running out of time. He wanted to secure his goal and get off the star fort before he had to deal with the Administratum minions who considered themselves to be in charge here. He wasn't about to waste time having his Marines chase around like children.

There was a sharp pain in his leg, where the greave met the knee armour. He thought it must be one of his older war wounds, of which he had a score – but glancing down, he saw the pudgy bat-faced girl withdrawing her hand, something long and glinting in her palm.

How had she crept up on him? A child! A heathen serving-girl! He would never hear the end of it – not to his face, of course, but every Marine would know...

He knocked her flying with a backhanded swipe, but though she landed hard she sprang up again, her ugly little face filled with hate.

'Filth! Hrud-loving groxmothers! This is my business! Mine! How dare you destroy what is mine?'

The pain in Caeon's leg hadn't gone. It was a spreading heat winding its way deep down into the muscle.

One of Finrian's Marines – Brother K'Nell, the bone and purple of his armour blackened with melta-wash – grabbed the child by the arm and held her up so she dangled, squealing. The thing in her hand was a heavy ring, chunky gold with a thin silver dagger jutting from it. 'Digital weapon. Xenos, lord.'

A needler. The child had a digi-needler. Where the hell had she...

'Butchers! Bilespawn! K'nib-rutting gorebelchers! Look what you've done!'

The pain had turned cold and Caeon felt himself beginning to sway. He had passed out from massive wounds on the battlefield more than once, but this was different. This time, he wasn't so sure he would get back up.

Before the eyes of Finrian's squad Commander Caeon's massive frame teetered like a great felled tree and slammed to the ground.

'Ninkers! Thug-filth! My home! My life!' screeched primary objective one, Veritas Van Skorvold.

CHAPTER TWO

IT WAS A massive inverted cone of compacted superconductor circuits that speared down from the room's ceiling like a vast stalactite. Though the hall took up a sizeable proportion of the Adeptus Mechanicus ship it somehow felt low-roofed and close, such was the presence of this most ancient of machinery.

Archmagos Khobotov paused a while before beginning the ceremony, as he always did before dealing with a hallowed device such as this, to appreciate its beauty and intricacy. His bionic eyes, faceted like an insect's with scores of tiny pict-stealers, picked out magnified images particularly pleasing in their intricacy and logic. To think that the hands of mere men had made this machine! It was such wonders that inspired the magi, and the tech-priests below them, to prepare the way for humanity's capacity to create them again. It would take many thousands of years of painstaking and dangerous work, but time and hardship were beneath the notice of the Omnissiah and so they were beneath that of the truest magi.

One day the Omnissiah's great masterpiece of knowledge would be complete at last. And this time, it would not be misused as the ancients had done, for it would be protected by the expertise and secrecy of the Adeptus Mechanicus, who did not feel the capriciousness of petty emotions. This was the dream – and a fragile dream it was, for with every scrap of knowledge that slipped into eternal obscurity, humankind stepped a little further from the Omnissiah's vision of a galaxy whose great and terrible forces were controlled by man through his machines.

Yes, there was much to do. There was so little time, it seemed, and he was so busy…

The chronometers reached the appointed hundredth of a second and the one hundred and ninety-eight ceremonial servitors snapped to attention, their puckered dead skin glowing amber in the warm halo of the machine. Khobotov's artificial joints whirred as he drifted to the gap in the deck floor where a section of plating had been removed to reveal a web of cogs and gears. Khobotov knelt – he felt nothing as he moved, for he had long since cut off nerve-responses from the motive parts of his artificial anatomy – and took a small pot of six-times-blessed engine oil from within his robes. With a finger of matt-grey synthalloy he placed a symbolic smear of oil on the teeth of the uppermost cog. The mouths of the servitors dropped open and from within their throats came a rasping, clicking sound – the sound of the Omnissiah's praises being sung in binary, the language that it was said most pleased the Machine God.

Khobotov straightened and glided over to the sub-control console wired into the floor. He made the sign of Mars over its verdigris-stained casing and depressed the large flat panel in its centre. The panel lit up and printed prayer-tapes began to chatter from twin slots in the casing, ensuring that the running of even this minor part of the machine was imbued with sacred gravity.

The cogs began to grind and an expectant juddering sound came from the large power conduit running around the edges of the room and into the root of the machine's conical projector. Such was the energy required by the machine that the conduit was to pump plasma into it directly from the Mechanicus craft's engine reactors. Once the coupling system was warmed up, the machine itself could be activated.

The servitors formed a line, then a triangle, then a square, with perfect geometry, as they had been programmed. This machine was old and could not be replicated with the current expertise of the Mechanicus, and so the Omnissiah's favour had to be sought before using it. Geometric shapes and meaningful numbers were pleasing to Him, for He loved the abstractness of logic above all things, and it was right that His pleasure be sought before using His most hallowed devices.

Now, a servitor with its exposed mechanical sections inlaid in gold approached from the shadows in the corner of the hall. It entered the sacred square and handed the control sceptre it carried to Khobotov. The sceptre was a solid rod of carbon inscribed with machine-code legends in delicate scrolling lines, topped with a perfect sphere in which spun twin hollow-centred cogs, symbolic of the Mechanicus and its work. Deep inside the cylinder was a tiny filament of silicon in which were set threads of an as yet unidentified element, which were as old as the machine and formed the key which allowed its activation. How it worked was a mystery to the tech-priests – doubtless this and all other mysteries would be revealed when the Omnissiah had judged their labour to be sufficient.

Khobotov pointed the sceptre at the activation rune on the surface of the machine's cone, and a gentle choral hum filled the air. The servitors stepped swiftly into a hexagon, then an octagon as the machine charged up. Faint gold and silver shimmers flickered along the superconductor circuits, and the coils deep inside the cone began to thrum. It was these coils, it was believed, that generated the shield against the warp.

Khobotov made a gesture of command and servitor hands three decks below slammed the plasma seals open, sending torrents of energised plasma coursing through the conduit. It was newer, this technology, far less refined than the machine itself, and there were alarming howls and rumblings as the plasma surged on. Drips of plasma oozed from overstressed joints in the conduit and landed hissing on the deck. But the power coupling held and delivered its payload into the heart of the machine.

The sound was a song – a beautiful harmony of coruscating power. The machine was alive.

Khobotov turned and walked towards the ramjet elevator that would take him to the crew muster deck. It was time to fetch the Machine God's servants-at-arms and prepare them for His purpose.

The teleporter was ready. By the end of this day the Omnissiah's masterpiece would be one step closer to revelation.

THEY SAID CAEON was going to die. Looking at him, Sarpedon was forced to admit he believed them. The apothecaries had done all they could but the needler had been loaded with a cocktail of viruses and neurotoxins. Caeon's mighty constitution had held off most of them but there were xenoviruses that had latched on to his nervous system and wouldn't let go. Caeon's immune system was fighting so hard it was beginning to reject the commander's augmentations – soon his replacement organs would fail, the apothecaries said, and Caeon would fail with them.

Caeon lay in a side chapel leading off from the Van Skorvold private quarters. It was a little-used place, for the Van Skorvolds were anything but pious, and it was considered unsullied enough for Caeon's deathbed. Sarpedon had taken Givrillian and Tellos's squad and headed across from the shell as soon as the news of Caeon's injury had hit the vox-net. The other units of his command were holding position around the shell, and guarding a broken Callisthenes Van Skorvold. Elsewhere in the fort the situation was good, considering Caeon's injury had forced a pause in the assault – the mutant army, robbed of Veritas Van Skorvold's caustic leadership, was pinned down in knots between the two Soul Drinker positions of the shell and the private quarters.

The boldest of them had led raids against the Space Marine defences. The boldest of them had died.

Inside the small, sparse chapel the commander had been stripped of his bulky armour, which had been arranged respectfully in the corner. Mighty arms that had torn at the battlements of Quixian Obscura lay immobile at his sides, the veins standing out purple-black with venom. Hands that had broken the neck of Corsair Prince Arcudros were curled into claws of gnarled flesh. His mighty face was sunken-featured with strain. The black carapace implanted just under his skin was livid and red at the edges.

The Soul Drinkers had been on the star fort for one hour and thirty-seven minutes.

'What are your orders, commander?' Sarpedon knew the time for sentiment and mourning would come after. For now, it was cold and fast and nothing else.

'Librarian Sarpedon, I am unable to discharge my duty to the Golden Throne.' Caeon's voice should have been a low rumble of authority, but it was faint and cracked. 'I cannot fight. I am dying and I must submit myself to Dorn and the Emperor for judgement. You will recover the Soulspear.'

The Soulspear. Truth be told, Sarpedon had entertained thoughts of the circumstances that could lead to him being the one to finally hold the sacred weapon. But he hadn't wanted it to happen like this. Caeon was too great a man to lose. 'I shall fulfil your wishes and my duty to this Chapter, commander.'

'I know you will, Sarpedon. This is an unkind way to discover whether you are suited to command, but I believe you will serve your Emperor well.' The corners of Caeon's mouth were flecked with foamy blood. 'May I ask that you commend my soul to the ancients?'

Sarpedon hesitated. Caeon was great and he was suffering, and everything should be done to let him know he was dying with honour. But…

'Yours was… yours was not a warrior's death, commander.'

'Hmm. Indeed it was not.' A hint of colour flared into Caeon's face as he recalled with anger the child who had mortally wounded him. 'A treacherous slay. A moment's distraction. Be vigilant always, Sarpedon. As you cannot pray for me, learn your lesson from this. What appears to be a wretched girl-slave may be more. What seems innocent may be deadly. Do not fail as I have done here, for if it costs you your life, too, the prayers of your brothers cannot accompany you to the Judgment Halls of Dorn.'

It was a sad fate. Caeon would be at the Emperor's side in the legion of Rogal Dorn when the final battle of the endless war took place, of that there was no doubt. But he would not enter their ranks with the glorious fanfare that was his due, for he had died not by the hand of a deadly foe, but through a second's lapse of concentration. Veritas Van Skorvold was not a worthy enemy to have killed any Space Marine, let alone a Soul Drinker, and still less one of Caeon's rank, and it had been Caeon's lapse far more than Veritas's needler that had felled him. It was a measure of the man that Caeon did not argue, but accepted the results of the insult done to him in death.

Apothecary Pallas entered the side chapel. With Pallas were two orderlies, Chapter serfs carrying racks of unguent jars which Pallas would use to ease Caeon's journey into the next world. Sarpedon took his leave and stepped out into the remains of the Van Skorvold's private chambers, in which the Soul Drinkers' headquarters had been set up. His headquarters now, he realised.

Veritas Van Skorvold was forty-seven years old. She had a rare and subtle mutation that inhibited her growth and gave her the appearance of a particularly spiteful eight-year-old child. Veritas was as ruthless as her brother was weak – she placed efficiency and profit far above morality and the laws of the Imperium, and had masterminded the many illicit dealings that had made the Van Skorvold business both very rich and destined for conflict with the Administratum. She was reaping the terrible harvest of her earlier sins – her punishment would doubtless be grave indeed, and she was in considerable discomfort at that moment, locked as she was in a small side pantry. Her screamed curses were of such venom and inventiveness that her guards had to be changed hourly to prevent their moral corruption.

Outside the chapel waited Sergeant Tellos and Brother Michairas, whom Sarpedon had requested attend upon him for the Rites of the Libation. Tellos was there by virtue of acquitting himself admirably with the slaying of the mutant behemoth in the operation's first stages. Michairas, as a novice, had been attendant upon Caeon for many years before his elevation to the status of full battle-brother, and so brought a measure of Caeon's honour and authority to spiritual matters. Michairas had fought as well as his brothers in the thrust into the Van Skorvold chambers, but it was his connection with the dying commander that caused Sarpedon to seek him out.

Wordlessly, the three strode into a small cartographic chamber, where a large star map glimmered beneath the glass top of a table. Other hand-drawn maps were displayed on the walls or rolled up in racks, for Callisthenes Van Skorvold had counted such things amongst his collecting passion.

Onto the star chart table Sarpedon placed the ceremonial golden chalice that hung at his belt. It was old and despite his dutiful care of all his equipment there was a cordon of tarnish building up around the deep carvings. It had been presented to him upon his ascension from scholar-novice to Librarian, more than seventy years before – a time that felt so distant that Sarpedon sometimes wondered if he had been the same man at all. It was as if he had always been a Librarian of the Soul Drinkers, his life a cycle of battle and honour-reaping, his driving force a fierce devotion to the eradication of the enemy and an unbreakable code of martial dignity.

Michairas took a canister from his belt, the type used by the apothecaries when transporting samples of unusual xenos the Soul Drinkers had fought. In it was a mass of pulpy tissue, taken from the brain stem of the huge mutant Tellos had fought and slain. It would have been improper for Tellos to carry it himself for he had already taken one trophy – a massive horn shorn from the beast's brow.

The bloody, pulpy matter was poured into the chalice and Sarpedon took it in his gauntleted hand.

'Know your enemy,' intoned Tellos. They were the only words permitted to be spoken in this ceremony, an ancient and hallowed one, yet one kept small and simple to ensure clarity of mind.

As commander, it was now Sarpedon's right to observe the soul of the vanquished foe. He tipped his head back and poured the semi-liquid mass down his throat. Swallowing it, he placed the chalice back on the table and ran through the mental exercises that would begin the rite.

There was a spirit's eye inside him that saw what the physical senses could not. He imagined it opening, drinking in the light after so much darkness, careful not to blind it with the glare of knowledge. There was a warm electric sensation in his stomach and he knew it was working.

He felt a film over his body like dirt that wouldn't wash off. His limbs were clumsy and ungainly – there was an unclean taste in his mouth and a dull churning in his ears. He glanced around the room and saw his two brother Marines as if through a gauze, their faces distorted, the room's many maps shifting and untrue. His organs were tight and ill-fitting – he felt wrong, completely wrong, like a picture of a man drawn by a child, ugly and crude. A pressure bore down on him – the rest of humanity, this whole universe, that felt such revulsion at him that it had imprinted itself on his very soul and pressed like a weight on his shoulders. He was human, but less. He was alive, but didn't feel it.

He was unclean, bathed only in shadow where the light of the Golden Throne should be. He couldn't get out – he was trapped here in this tainted existence, trapped forever. He felt panic rising in him, for he would be like this forever until death, and after death there was nothing. Nothing, just the blank finality of knowing that he was not even supposed to have been born...

With a start, he slammed the eye shut again and his vision lost its dirty tint. Michairas looked worried, for he had not witnessed the ceremony of the chalice before and Sarpedon must have appeared weak and scared in a way not proper for a Space Marine. But it had been worth it. He knew his enemy that little bit more, and knowledge was power in war.

Due to the Soul Drinkers' gene-seed the omophagea, the organ implanted in every novice during his conversion to a Space Marine, was different to that of most other Chapters. Its purpose was to absorb racial memories and psycho-genetic traces from ingested organic matter – allowing the Marine to gain intelligence on how to use the enemy's weapons, into their beliefs and morale, sometimes even battle plans and troop locations. The Soul Drinkers' omophagea was overactive compared to those of other Marines, delivering an experience both more intense and less precise. It was one of the cornerstones of the Soul Drinkers' beliefs that they could experience the thoughts and feelings of their enemies and come out sane and uncorrupted, furnished as much with disdain for their inhumanity as with knowledge of their behaviour.

And it had served well here. Sarpedon had felt the mutant's uncleanliness, the sin inherent in its existence. Huge and mighty it had been, but without duty or purpose. It believed in nothing and survived only for the sake of existing. They were better off dead – he and his Marines had done them a favour this day by sending so many of them to the inky blackness of death.

'I am well, brothers. My gratitude for attending upon this ceremony. But though the victory has been won it is not yet complete.' He flickered a retinal icon and his vox-link switched to the all-squads frequency. 'Soul Drinkers, withdraw patrols and muster inside the primary defences. It is time.'

CALLISTHENES VAN SKORVOLD had not held out for long. Once Sarpedon had picked him up by the throat and held him up against the wall of the shell, he had told them everything – the many and various crimes committed by his sister in maintaining her profits, the illicit dealings made to assemble his collection, and many other things that Sarpedon would rather not have heard. Callisthenes had proven himself to be that particular type of criminal who commits wrongs through boredom and idle curiosity rather than the urge to survive, and whose depravations become gradually worse until he is no better than the heretic in the gutter.

Sarpedon wasn't interested in any of this. But in the middle of his garbled confessions Callisthenes Van Skorvold had mentioned the star fort's brig dating from its days as a PDF orbital defence platform, which had been refurbished and expanded by generations of Van Skorvolds into a solid vault for keeping prized valuables. It was this brig that eventually became the home to Callisthenes's collection of tech and alien curiosities. This was what the Soul Drinkers had come for. And though it had cost them the life of the commander, it was where they would enter the annals of the Chapter's glorious deeds.

Sarpedon had led a strike force through the tangle of conduits and machinery and into the location of the brig. The Chapter serfs went with them, cutting gear at the ready, along with Tech-Marine Lygris. The mutant defences were, as suspected, non-existent, but they were closing in on the location of the Objective Ultima and there was no excuse for laxity. The Soul Drinkers approached the great metal slab of the brig cautiously, and in strength.

When they arrived, the things they saw were enough to take even a Space Marine's breath away.

'Do you think we could take a prize of conquest, sir?' It was Luko's voice, breaking the hush as only he could. This was only the first vault of the star fort's brig and with one glance they had seen enough decadence to elicit horror and admiration in equal measure. There was no denying it – some of this was beautiful, and that was what made it dangerous.

The floor was carpeted a deep blue and the walls hung with tapestries. Spotlights in the ceiling picked out glass display cases in which glimmered some of Callisthenes Van Skorvold's beloved collection. One case held half-a-dozen antique pistols, one an extraordinary compact melta-weapon, another with multiple barrels and a chunk of glowing crystal for ammunition. There were statues of women with insect heads and semi-humanoid figures made from petrified vines like bundles of snakes. There was a composite bow of horn and matt grey metal as long as a Marine was tall, with a quiver of arrows tipped with barbed reptilian teeth, and a suit of armour made with sheets of diamond and silver links.

The Marines waited for Sarpedon's lead. He stepped through the massive brushed metal vault door and into the room, his psychically sensitive mind fairly humming with the cold, sharp resonances of rarity and high technology. He felt uncomfortable – there was too much unknown here, too much forbidden. He decided that much of this would be taken to the flamer as soon as they were done, and that Luko would be castigated for suggesting the Chapter sully itself with xenos tech and forbidden devices, even in jest. They were no experts in archeotech, and they had no way of knowing what was dangerous. Better destroy it all than risk impurity.

'Librarian Sarpedon?' came a voice over the vox-net, crackling with distortion as the signal passed through the massive bulkheads of the star fort's inner structures. 'Squad Vorts. We're encountering civilians here.'

'Civilians?'

'Cargo, sir. Slaves or prisoners.'

'I thought there was no cargo on the star fort. There were no transports docked.'

'Must be runaways, sir, escaped from the transports. We've got a civilian named Yser, seems to be some kind of priest for them. Sounds like they want to help.'

Vorts and about half the Soul Drinkers were deployed in concentric rings of mobile defence around the vaults. There was little danger of the shattered defenders mounting a concerted counter-attack but the Marines had already lost a commander to a treacherous slay and no more chances were being taken. The assault had taken place when there were no large prisoner transports docking to avoid cargo humans getting in the way, but it seemed like there were some on the station anyway – runaways who had made their homes in the guts of the station.

Sarpedon didn't have time for this. He wanted to end this now, before the dark clouds gathering over the mission began to rain further misfortune. 'Relay to all defensive units. Keep civilians clear. We shall be gone soon and we can ill afford complications. Leave any dregs for the Guard to deal with.'

A sequence of acknowledgement runes flickered. A troop of serf-labourers and Tech-Marine Lygris had filtered through the exhibits and were working on a couple of massive techno-locked doors at the far end of the first hall.

The labourers kept their eyes from the exhibits, knowing that undue curiosity would earn them the severest of reprimands. They were a good example of what even lesser-quality humans could do, thought Sarpedon – owned by the Chapter from birth and schooled to respect their superiors in all things. A crypto-drone skimmed behind Lygris and settled like a fat insect on the glowing runepad of the first door, bands of light across its curved metal body flickering as it worked on the door code algorithms. There was a beeping sound and a deep thunk as the restraining bolt drew back.

As the serfs attached chains to the door and prepared to haul it open, Sarpedon glanced again at some of the objects Callisthenes had assembled. Beside him hung a banner seemingly woven from hundreds of shades of human hair, and a perfect replica human skull carved from deep crimson stone the lustre of jade. Callisthenes Van Skorvold had collected an astounding range of forbidden objects in his lifetime – how many alien slavers and noble degenerates had he dealt with to do it?

Sarpedon could not deny many of these things were beautiful, but he could feel the corruption that surrounded them.

These trinkets would not deceive the Emperor's chosen warriors as they had Callisthenes Van Skorvold.

The door was open. At Sarpedon's signal the closest tactical squads stalked carefully through the vault, wary of traps or ambushes. He would not put it past the Van Skorvolds to sacrifice some of their prized possessions just to spite the Emperor's servants.

The door opened on a corridor lined with cages in which scuttled a small alien menagerie, hooting and chittering. Sarpedon stopped the tactical squads and waved forward Brother Zaen, flamer-bearer in Luko's squad. Zaen stepped carefully into the corridor past eight-legged monkeys and birds with feathers of glass. Sarpedon saw a pair of servitors trundling along the carpeted floor of the corridor, simple waist-high automata designed to deposit pellets into feed bowls and scrape the cage floors free of excrement. It had doubtless pleased Callisthenes Van Skorvold to have a private zoo beyond the doors of the brig, maintained by servitors, where even servants would not be permitted.

'Threat nil,' voxed Zaen.

Sarpedon followed him and felt the crude thoughts of the animals. He could not receive any impressions from intelligent creatures, for he was a transmitter rather than a receiver and intelligence was too complex and fluid for him to pick up. Nothing here had enough cunning to do them harm from within their cages. He considered flaming them anyway, but that would slow them down and he wanted the objective recovered as quickly as prudence would allow. A tiny pair of sapphire-blue eyes glared at him from within a symbiotic knot of snakes and something half-plant whumped at him dolefully. Callisthenes had strange tastes.

The corridor opened up into a room with walls of brushed steel, large but shadowy and sparse. A single spotlight shone down on a simple table in the centre of the room.

On the table was the Objective Ultima: the Soulspear.

THE STORY WAS carved into the walls of the chapels and meditation cells throughout the fortress-monastery that was spread out across the Soul Drinkers' fleet. It was the first thing the recruits learned before they were ground down by punishing training and volatile chemo-engineering until there were but a handful left fit to become novices. In the origins of the Chapter could be found the seed for the fierce martial pride that became a fundamental part of every Marine. Without it, they were less than nothing. With it, they could not be stopped.

Rogal Dorn, the perfect man created by the Emperor as the greatest of his primarchs, gave his genetic blueprint to the Imperial Fists legion that followed him like sons into battle. Ten thousand years before Sarpedon first shed his novice's habit and took up the armour of a full Soul Drinker, the Imperial Fists had fought on the very battlements of the Emperor's Palace on Terra against the besieging forces of the Traitor legions under Horus. Abbots taught children the tales of that terrible conflict in the schola progenia, and it became legend to the untold billions who swore fealty to the Imperium.

When Horus was slain and the rebellion broken, the remaining loyal legions were broken up into Chapters so no man would have power over so many Space Marines at any one time. Dorn knew the pride his sons took in the glory of the Imperial Fists, and fought to have his legion left intact. But he bowed to his fellow primarchs, and his Marines became a multitude of Chapters, one retaining the name of the Imperial Fists, the others taking on new names and heraldry, ready to forge new paths into Imperial history.

Crimson Fists. Black Templars... Soul Drinkers.

To each of them was given a symbol of their sacred purpose, gifted by Dorn himself so they would remember that his spirit was with them always, that his glory was theirs also. The Soul Drinkers, formed from the fleet-based shock attack elements of his legion, received the Soulspear. Dorn himself had found it on a dark and lonely world during the Great Crusade – with it he had speared great warp-beasts and from it had hung his banner on a hundred worlds reconquered in the Emperor's name.

Such a tale was taught to the recruits brought in by the Chaplains before they were put through the savage meat grinder of selection, so they would have some inkling of the ideals for which they were suffering.

Sarpedon had been taught it himself, as had all the Marines under his command. He had come through the fire and the agony of selection and training, received the Space

Marine's new organs and psycho-doctrination. Through it all, the Soulspear had been a symbol to hold on to – and for his generation, something more: a reason for vengeance, a catalyst for the sacred hatred that served a Marine so well in the fires of battle.

For the Soulspear had been lost for a thousand years, since the Soul Drinkers' flagship *Sanctifier* had been lost on a warp jump. Now it had been found in the collection of a degenerate who had no comprehension of its true significance. With their commander dying, it was Sarpedon who would bring it back to his Chapter's embrace.

THE SOULSPEAR WAS as long as a man's forearm, gloss black, and inlaid with intricate circuitry that shifted and changed before the eye. There were smooth indentations where fingers far larger than a normal man's would fit, each one with a laser-needle surrounded by a ring of gene-sensitive psychoplastic.

Even Callisthenes had seen enough in its simple elegance to give it a chamber to itself. But to Sarpedon it shone like a beacon of hope, rage and righteousness, as if everything he had fought for – his Emperor, his primarch, the place of mankind at the head of the galaxy and the sacred plan that would lead to humanity's ascendancy – was embodied in this one sublime artefact.

Zaen froze beside him, and Sarpedon could sense he was holding his breath in awe. The Tactical Marines following were similarly dumbstruck.

'Prep the corvus pods to disengage,' he voxed quietly. 'We have found Objective Ultima and are ready to withdraw.' Then, on the local frequency – 'Squad Luko, Squad Hastis, with me. Honour guard duty.'

Then, the world turned black.

HE SHOOK THE darkness out of his head and tried to get his bearings – he was down on the floor, half-lying on his back with Zaen beneath him. He heard confusion welling up around him as his inner ear recovered from the massive shockwave of noise that had washed over him.

A bomb? That would be just like the Van Skorvolds. But the Tech-Marines had swept the place. It was possible but unlikely. What, then?

His vision returned and the dimness sharpened before him. Then light, bright and sudden. He hauled himself further upright and saw he had been thrown halfway back up the corridor – the cages were smashed and any alien creatures still alive were scampering about in confusion. He could hear the pinking of breaking glass as Marines picked themselves up from the glass-strewn floor of the first chamber, where they had been blasted back through the display cases.

There were figures moving ahead. Dark, cloaked, a dozen of them crowding the Soulspear room. Rust-red with hooded faces.

Not a bomb then… a teleporter – but how? Teleporter technology was rare in the extreme, and the Soul Drinkers' own such devices had not worked for centuries. Not only that, but this was a small, precise target in the heart of a large and complex space station. It was madness, no one could do it.

There was a greasy reek in the air and Sarpedon spotted knots of twitching flesh on the floor of the room, tangled with scraps of dark red fabric and twists of metal. Some of the arrivals had not arrived intact: whoever had activated the device had been willing to lose some men in getting them here.

Sarpedon was quickly on his feet, bolter in hand. Zaen had landed heavily and Sarpedon could hear Marines clambering over him to follow – the thrum of a plasma pistol sounded as one of Hastis's Assault Marines prepared for action.

'You!' yelled Sarpedon, rage boiling inside him. 'You! By the Throne, identify yourselves!'

The nearest figure turned. Blank augmetic lenses met his gaze. A wide ribbed cable snaked from a dead-skinned mouth, ferromandibles spreading out from the upper chest and neck like insect legs. Around the hood's edge was embroidered the cog-toothed motif of the Adeptus Mechanicus, and a black-panelled heavy bolter jutted from one sleeve.

Siege engineers. Mechanicus elite. They must have been stationed with the Mechanicus ship in the battlefleet, which had not seen fit to tell Chloure's intelligence of its teleporter array.

But why?

'Nobody move! We are Space Marines of the Soul Drinkers Chapter, the Emperor's chosen, and we are here to do His will.' Sarpedon levelled his bolter, and all the Marines crammed into the corridor behind him did the same.

The engineer's heavy bolter whirred level, pointing at Sarpedon's chest. Twelve others had survived the teleporter jump and as one they took aim with lascannon, multi-meltas, and stranger weapons besides, all fitted to hardpoints wired into their bodies. If they fired, Sarpedon and the Marines around him would be shredded.

But firepower had never decided a fight. It was strength of mind, and nothing else, that won victory. Sarpedon had known this all his life. He would not fail here.

'You will return to your ship,' he continued. 'This station is under our control now, and you will be permitted to enter once we have retrieved what is ours and left. I shall assume this is a misunderstanding. Do not prove me wrong.'

Could he use the Hell, if it came to that? What did these people fear? Were they even people at all? What he knew of elite Mechanicus troops had given him an impression of emotionless, cold-blooded warriors, who could march on unconcerned as their numbers were decimated or lay down a curtain of fire for weeks without rest or respite. Did they fear anything at all in the normal, human sense?

The nearest engineer turned away again. At the centre of their number dextrous mechadendrites slid from three engineers' hoods and wrapped around the Soulspear, lifting it from the table.

They had the most sacred relic in the Chapter's history in their cold, dead, wretched grasp. This was dangerously close to blasphemy.

A crackling corona of blue light flared and contracted around the room, covering the engineers with a layer of ice-cold fire. Then, with a thunderclap so loud it was felt rather than heard, they were gone.

IOCANTHOS GUILLYAN KRAEVIK CHLOURE was asleep when he was woken with the news. For a depressing moment he thought he was back in the Administratum habitat on the agri-world he had served for fifteen years, and that he would have to drag himself through another mindless day reviewing production quotas from the continent-sized grox farm that formed the planet's reason for existing.

Then he saw the glint of Lakonia's bright disc through the porthole of his well-appointed but dingy cabin, and remembered he was on the *Diligent*, trying to secure a future and serve the interest of the Imperium. And someone was knocking very loudly on his door.

'What is it?' he shouted, hoping he didn't sound too groggy. He had decided he didn't like space travel – sleep was disturbed by the peculiar metabolic uncertainties created by constant half-light and the random vibrations from the *Diligent's* guts.

'Captain Vekk's orders, sir. Something's come up on the scanners. It's really big.'

Chloure struggled into his plain black Administratum uniform and threw his greatcoat over the top of it. He probably looked disgraceful, but it would be worse not to bother turning up. Vekk seemed a flag-captain of reasonable competence and if this was something important he wanted to know about it. Chloure was in command of the battlefleet and he had to make sure that he was there if decisions were to be made.

'Take me to the bridge,' he told the lad outside his door, one of those young men in a petty officer's uniform who had been suckered into running errands for Vekk's crew in return for a nominal rank.

'They're in the sensorium, consul.'

'Then take me there.'

The lower crew of the *Diligent*, gangs of rope-muscled conscripts and tarnished servitors, seemed rather more busy than usual, and petty officers barked orders at every turn. They seemed to be gearing the ship up for some kind of defensive station – gun gangs were to stow munitions and the engine crews were pulling another shift off rest to open up the coolant channels. Chloure began to get nervous.

The sensorium was a transparent dome bulging from amidships, braced with gothic ironwork. The view into the void outside was distorted by the many layers of filtration to protect observers when the ship was in the warp, and the stars outside were just grey smudges against the blackness. But there was something sharper – a blue-white blossom boiled sunwards. Even Chloure could appreciate it must have been something major.

Vekk was standing in full dress in the centre of the sensorium deck, surrounded by chattering knots of lexmechanics and logisticians. One of the ship's Navigators was there, looking worried, and Chloure wondered if he had seen the anomaly with his genestrain's warp-eye before the ship's sensors. Two of the ship's complement of astropaths brooded in their robes, sightless eyes wandering. A leisure-servitor, waist height with a broad flat cranium for serving drinks, was trundling around in the mistaken belief that the important crew gathered here represented a social engagement.

'Chloure,' called Vekk. 'Good job you're here. This might be rather important.' Vekk's voice was clipped and alert. Chloure wondered if he ever slept at all. 'We picked up this little curio twenty minutes ago.' He pointed at the anomaly above them. 'It's not on the visual spectrum but the warp-reactive layer lights it up like a firework.'

'What is it?'

'A rift.' It was the Navigator who answered. He was a tall, thin man as all Navigators were. Chloure had not seen him before as, again like most of his kind, he kept himself firmly cut off from the rest of the crew in the armoured shell of his private chambers. 'It's localised, not big enough for a ship. It is also centred on the craft of our Mechanicus allies.'

'Are they damaged?' Chloure didn't want to start losing ships now, not when he was so close.

'You misunderstand, consul. The rift was deliberately created. The archmagos himself caused it to come into being.'

'How?'

'Interesting you should ask,' said Vekk. 'DiGoryan here and I were discussing the same thing. We thought it might be a subspace propulsion rig at first, those solid-state numbers they had docked at Hydraphur a few years back.'

'But that, of course, would cause infra-quantum fluctuations far beyond the range of what we are currently acquiring,' said the Navigator, DiGoryan, folding his long, intricate fingers into a steeple below his chin.

Chloure nodded. He had no idea what they were talking about. He could organise the details of an entire planetary economy, but the vagaries of warp science were simply beyond him.

'We believed it was a psychoportive weapons system powering up,' continued DiGoryan. 'But, of course, the astropaths have detected nothing that might suggest such a thing.'

'Then we realised,' said Vekk conversationally. 'It was a teleporter. The Mechanicus have brought a teleporter along with them.'

Arcane technology might not have been Chloure's area of expertise, but he had some idea of the kind of influence required to acquire a teleporter, even within the Mechanicus. Emperor's throne, what was happening? Was Khobotov attacking? Was he being attacked?

'We've got the fleet on code amber,' continued Vekk, 'just in case. But it very much looks like the archmagos has plans of his own he's not telling us about.'

'I… I shall contact him. We'll find out what he thinks he is doing.' But Chloure didn't get where he was without being slightly sharper than the average wage slave, and in truth he had already guessed.

THERE WERE TWO kinds of operation in which Space Marines might be employed. One was much more common than the other – a surgical strike. A small but – in terms of quality, equipment and leadership – vastly superior force would be sent in, perform a particular task, and get out again. The enemy would be struck hard and the weapon withdrawn before they knew they had been attacked. A foe cannot retaliate if he does not know he is fighting.

Space Marines excelled at such operations – they could deploy in an instant, move with skill and confidence through any terrain, take fire and dish it out. They were the best assault troops in the galaxy. The Soul Drinkers specialised in ship-to-ship and drop-pod actions of this kind, and soem even said there were few Chapters amongst the Adeptus Astartes that could claim to match them. Their tactics were based on their own speed and the enemy's confusion, and as the attack on the star fort had shown, they were savagely effective.

The second kind of operation was far rarer, and a far more serious undertaking. Sometimes in the thousands of wars the Imperium might be fighting at any one time, there was an objective so vital that it had to be achieved at any cost. A strongpoint that absolutely had to be held to keep the

Imperial line from breaking. An enemy-held spaceport that could not be allowed to function one minute longer. A fortress that had to fall before the armies of the Emperor were bled white at its gates. These were times when the odds were grave and the enemy undaunted, but the might of the Imperium had to prevail, when strength of mind and faith in the Holy Throne were as decisive weapons as the chainsword and the bolter. Times when Space Marines took their stand and prepared to die to the last man if necessary.

Marines were trained for the first kind of mission. But they were born for the second.

It was this thought that prevented Sarpedon's rage from turning to despair. They had done everything they could have been asked – an assault of surgical precision, far beyond the clumsy posturings of lesser Imperial forces, cutting through the mutants and criminals the Van Skorvolds had put in their path. Caeon had been lost, and a terrible loss it was, but they had secured every objective in rapid time. The warfare tenets of the philosopher-soldier Daenyathos had been followed to the letter – they had been cold and fast, fearless and merciless, just and proud and deadly.

But it had not been enough. Their prize had been snatched from them by those who dared call themselves allies. And now what had been the first kind of mission was in real danger of becoming the second.

'The insult is not done to you.' Caeon's voice was no more than a whisper, for he was slipping away. 'You are the Emperor's chosen. An insult to you is an insult to Him, and is a heresy in itself.' It pained Sarpedon to hear him like this, when once his voice commanded Marines to superhuman feats.

Chaplain Iktinos was also at his side, watching his commander dying through the impassive red eyes of his permanently fixed rictus-mask. When Caeon died – and it was when, not if – Iktinos would help administer the rites due to any Soul Drinker in death while Apothecary Pallas removed Caeon's gene-seed for transport back to the Soul Drinkers' fleet.

Iktinos did not speak. In a moment of crisis, when not battling the Emperor's foes with the crozius that hung at his side, Iktinos was required to observe and silently judge. It was he who would report to the Chapter's upper echelons on the quality of morale and leadership shown here.

'They shall suffer for it, Lord Caeon,' said Sarpedon. 'They will know how the Soul Drinkers answer to slighted honour.'

'This is no place for a final stand, Sarpedon, here amongst the filth and mutant-stench. Do not let them trap you here, and threaten you until you back down. If you must fight, remember what we are born to do, to strike hard and fast and never look back.' Caeon spoke as if with his last breath, and his eyes slid closed. His chest heaved with laboured breathing as the jagged red lines on the pict-screens of Pallas's monitoring equipment jumped alarmingly. The poison had already robbed him of movement, and Pallas said the old hero's lungs were next.

It would not be for nothing. Sarpedon vowed then, to himself and to the ever-watching Dorn, that the Chapter would prevail and honour would be satisfied. They were but a few thousand strong, substandard Guard and Mechanicus troops, and they would quail before the threat of the Soul Drinkers.

Stop. What was he contemplating? Fighting the forces of the battlefleet? There would be little honour in that. He and his Soul Drinkers had to acquit themselves with honour here, for they were Space Marines, the best, and had to act like the best in all things. He could not just fight to get the Soulspear back, like a common soldier. There had to be another way.

The philosopher-soldier Daenyathos, the greatest hero of the Chapter save Rogal Dorn himself, had written of the strength the Soul Drinkers could have by virtue of their mere presence. They did not have to charge into the fray to win wars – sometimes the legend that had grown up around them was enough, and the threat implicit in their existence could force an enemy's surrender without a shot being fired. Such occasions were rare – the Imperium's foes were usually too degenerate and corrupt to countenance backing down. But the Adeptus Mechanicus and Chloure's battlefleet were led by Imperial servants, who would surely understand how dangerous an angry Space Marine would be.

It would not have to be a massive threat. The Administratum, who controlled the battlefleet, wanted the star fort and little more. The Soul Drinkers would hold the fort and demand the Soulspear, relinquishing the fort only when it had been returned to them. They would have to make sure the threat was real, of course, manning the star fort weaponry and preparing defensive positions. But the Guard units and the Mechanicus troops would never dare assault, not when they realised that the Soul Drinkers held the upper hand. There would be some posturing and red tape, but the Administratum consul in command – Chloure, Sarpedon recalled from the mission briefings – would never for one moment contemplate actually facing the Soul Drinkers.

Yes, that was how it would work. They would recognise their folly and give back the Soulspear with obsequious blandishments and the Marines could travel back in triumph, with Caeon's body in state. That was how the Chapter had maintained its place at the head of mankind, by refusing to back down or kneel before the weaknesses of lesser men. They were the Emperor's chosen, and to the Emperor they would answer, not to some half-machine tech-priest tinkerer or desk-bound Administratum bureaucrat.

There had been enough fighting here. All the real enemies were dead and the Soul Drinkers' losses, though few in number, had included one of the best of them. Now it was time to resolve the threatened conflict without bloodshed, and in a way that would ensure the Soul Drinkers retained their honour and returned with their prize intact. This place had cost them enough, and once this unfortunate matter was resolved they could leave as soon as possible.

Sarpedon saluted Caeon and left the chapel, leaving Iktinos to his vigil.

He had defences to prepare.

CHAPTER THREE

THOUGH MANY OF the fleet's officers gathered on board the *Diligent* were of old naval aristocracy stock and would never admit weakness in front of the lowly logisticians and petty officers, in truth they were quietly terrified.

A holo-servitor in the middle of the bridge, its torso opened like fleshy petals to reveal a pict-array, projected a huge image in front of the viewscreen.

It was the first Space Marine most of them had actually seen outside the stained glass windows and script illuminations of the schola progenia or cadet school chapels. His face was scarred, not with obvious wounds such as the sort many naval officers wore like badges of office, but with dozens of tiny wounds accumulated over the years to form a face battered by war like a cliff face battered by the waves. It was impossible to guess his age, for there was youthful strength there alongside the wear of a lifetime, eyes brimming with both experience and childlike fanaticism. The head was shaven and from the high collar of his massive purple-black armour curved an aegis hood. The chalice symbol of his Chapter could be seen on one shoulder pad, echoed in the cup emblem flanked by wings proudly emblazoned in gold across his chest.

'We have the star fort,' he was saying in a voice that filled the bridge like thunder. 'We can defend it indefinitely. I do not have to tell you how unwise any force on your part would be.'

He had called himself Commander Sarpedon, and though his booming voice was coldly disciplined, he was clearly beyond rage. His eyes burned out from the viewscreen, pinning the assembled officers to the deck, and the corded muscles of his neck strained with anger. 'If you want your prize, consul, you have two choices. You can come and get it, in which case you will fail. Or you can return our prize to us, which was taken as our victor's right.'

Consul Senioris Chloure was a diplomatic man. He had spent a lifetime negotiating the most delicate deals where a whole planet's economy might rest in the details. He hoped it would be enough now. 'Commander Sarpedon,' he began, trying and failing not to be awed by the huge image glowering down at him, 'you must understand that the Adeptus Mechanicus are but nominally under our–'

'Our attempts to communicate with the Mechanicus have failed!' boomed Sarpedon. 'They stole what was ours, fled to their ship and jammed all contact. This falls to you, consul. If you cannot control the elements of your own fleet, that is your problem, not mine. Return the Soulspear to us or return to port without your star fort. This communication is over. Do not make us wait for a reply.'

The image winked off and the holo-servitor whirred closed. For a few seconds there was silence on the bridge of the *Diligent*, the after-image of the huge grizzled face still bright in the officers' minds.

'Sir?' asked Flag-Captain Vekk. 'Your orders?'

A Space Marine. Chloure had been so proud that he had managed to engineer their presence here. It was to have been the crowning achievement to justify the comfortable future he sought. And now he was forced to accept the possibility that it was going very wrong, very quickly.

But that did not mean he had to let it all fall apart. He had dealt with conflict and stubbornness before, for many years. He had spent decades negotiating the Emperor's share. He told himself he would just have to do it one more time.

'They hold the star fort. But they have nothing else. Their fleet is tiny, probably only a couple of strike cruisers. We have more, and a blockade should be simple. They will be without supplies and support, and they cannot leave the place without our permission. If it comes to a blockade they will have to back down eventually.'

'They are Space Marines, sir. They don't need supplies…' It was Manis, Vekk's Master of the Ordnance, who spoke.

'We have all heard tales of how they can survive on nothing but thin air and faith, Manis. But the Emperor has chosen not to make men who do not need to eat or breathe – the fort is based on an old-pattern orbital defence platform that requires new recycling filters and liquid oxygen supplies to maintain a survivable atmosphere. If we must we will simply wait until they see sense and ask to be allowed to return to their fleet.'

'It would be simpler by far, dear consul, if we were merely to return this trinket,' said Kourdya languidly. Kourdya was the captain of the *Hydranye Ko* and had, allegedly, won his ship with a particularly dazzling hand of five-card raekis.

'I am assuming that will be the solution we arrive at, Captain Kourdya. But I don't think any of us here can truly guess what these Marines are thinking, and there is no shame in planning for all eventualities.'

THEY WERE STILL there when a petty officer – the same flustered-looking lad who had woken Chloure several hours before – scurried up to the knot of officers in front of the holo-projector.

'Officer on the bridge, sirs,' he said. 'Archmagos Khobotov.'

The bridge blast doors opened apparently of their own accord and Khobotov swept in. He was flanked by a dozen tech-guards, in rust-red flak-tabards and toting weapons of exotic design. The drones were drifting above like fat loathsome insects.

'I trust,' said Chloure, interrupting Khobotov's entrance, 'that you heard all of that.' Chloure gestured at the space where Sarpedon's face had hung an hour before.

'Indeed,' droned Khobotov.

'Then you are aware we have some questions.'

Vekk, seeing the tech-guard, had silently summoned a squad from the *Diligent's* naval security battalion, who were

silently filing onto the bridge. Chloure knew enough about
the Imperial Navy to appreciate that captains didn't like anyone lording it on their bridge. Vekk might be insufferable
sometimes, but Chloure was glad then he had the man on his
side.

'We monitored the transmission,' said Khobotov. The tech-
guards around him were tightening their formation as the
black-armoured naval security troopers formed up. 'Commander Sarpedon's views have been noted.'

'Do you plan to do anything about it?'

'Commander Sarpedon's force is small and ill-supplied.
They are not equipped for defence. It is unlikely they can
hold out against a concerted assault from the Imperial Guard
and Adeptus–'

'We are not going to *attack* them, Khobotov,' said Chloure
sharply. As ever, he couldn't tell if Khobotov was serious or
just stalling. Would he really throw the battlefleet's combat
units against Space Marines? They said tech-priests started
thinking differently when there was more machine in them
that human, but surely Khobotov wouldn't throw away so
many lives. 'We're going to give them what they want and
then forget all of this. You are still under the command of
this battlefleet, archmagos, no matter how you may wish otherwise. The next time Sarpedon contacts us I want to tell him
where the Soulspear is and how long it will be before we give
it back to him, so I ask those questions to you now.'

Chloure had dealt with awkward customers before. He had
negotiated his way through whole planets full of hostiles. But
he had never had to gauge the reactions of a man who might
not have been a man at all in the physical sense. Chloure had
gained a feel for the tone of voice and body language that
very few could conceal, but Khobotov betrayed none of those
things. He would have to be firm and direct, and hope that
Khobotov's view of the situation approximated Chloure's
own.

'Very well.' Khobotov looked right at Chloure, who could
just pick out the gleam of a lens deep within the cowl. 'The
Soulspear is currently on board a high-speed heavy shuttle
within warp route 26-Epsilon-Superior.'

'Destination?'

'Koden Tertius.'

Koden Tertius was a forge world, a planet owned and run by the Adeptus Mechanicus as a centre of manufacture and research. Specifically, Koden Tertius was half a galaxy away and famed for the robustness of the war engines it supplied to the Imperial armies of the Segmentum Obscura. It was also the name stencilled on the side of the *674-XU28* and from which Khobotov's tech-guards were recruited. Archmagos Khobotov was sending the Soulspear to his home world.

'I see,' said Chloure coldly. 'Would it be pointless of me to demand its return?'

'It would, consul senioris. Communications are impossible with the vessel in the warp. Once at its destination the contents will fall under the jurisdiction of the Archmagi of Koden Tertius, not your battlefleet.'

'That's why you were here in the first place, isn't it?' said Captain Kourdya from somewhere behind Chloure. 'Sly dog. You only showed up so you could steal your little toy.'

'I had imagined Consul Senioris Chloure would have deduced this for himself and hence would not need informing of the fact.' Somehow the tech-priest sounded mocking even with his monotone voice.

Chloure couldn't keep the chill out of his blood – the Soulspear was gone and this situation was dangerously close to being more than he could possibly handle. The truth was that Khobotov could do pretty much anything he liked – Chloure could not monitor his communications or exert direct authority when the *674-XU28* possessed unknown but probably superior capabilities.

It would probably be beyond even Chloure's abilities to magic the Soulspear back from Koden Tertius. But he was here to do a job, to secure Administratum control of the Van Skorvold star fort. He would see it through to the end, no matter how long it took. And then, he told himself, he would truly deserve his reward.

'I don't think we need to know anything more,' said Chloure. Flag-Captain Vekk gestured and the security troopers took a step back as the tech-guards stomped off the bridge. Khobotov was already on his way out, moving deceptively fast. He didn't walk – he glided, his robes swishing along the floor behind him. The pudgy corpse-drones followed him, attentive cherubs trailing wires.

A heavy hand was laid on Chloure's shoulder, and he smelled stale smoke and age.

Druvillo Trentius, hoary and generally disagreeable captain of the *Deacon Byzantine*, glared down at him with liquor-shrunk eyes.

'Complete gak-up this, Chloure.' They were the first words he had spoken on the bridge that day.

As the fleet's officers gathered their lackeys and headed towards their respective shuttles, Chloure fought off the feeling that Trentius was right.

YSER DIDN'T LOOK like much. The man was on the wrong side of middle age, thinned and harrowed by malnourishment. His hair and beard were matted rats' tails, his nails blackened. He had evidently made some effort to keep himself clean, but the effect had been merely to highlight the pallor of his skin. He was dressed in rags, almost bare-chested. Yet around his neck was a heavy pendant, doubtless from some decoration scrounged and punched to accept a chain – an Imperial aquila, with an eye drilled through each of its two heads so it stared out in two directions. Forward and back, the past and the future. The icon lent the man an air of holiness and purpose that Sarpedon couldn't shake from his head.

They were standing in what Yser called his church. It was a supply hopper, a massive round-ended cylinder set into the very guts of the star fort, where light was sporadic and breathable air hung in pockets around recyc-line leaks. The place had once held towering stacks of food and other supplies which would be winched up by means of an enormous cargo crane, but the supplies had long been used up or reduced to a level of detritus that filled the bottom third of the hopper. The great four-clawed metal hand of the crane, fallen from its mountings, formed the church itself, and cargo containers had been salvaged for pews and side chambers. Tattered banners, frayed wrappings sewn together and daubed with simple symbols like children's drawings, hung from the plasteel girders. The place was strangely serene, lit by the twilight of halogen work-lamps high above them, and with the soft breeze of convection currents tugging at the banners all around.

'You are Yser?' said Sarpedon. He stood in the shadow of the makeshift church and towered over the scrawny man, who seemed to show little of the fear that men normally did when confronted by a Space Marine.

'I am.'

'A priest, you say?'

'Yes, ministering to my flock. We are few, but the Architect turns His light upon us all.'

The Architect of Fate – the Emperor, it seemed. Aspects of the Divine Emperor were worshipped all over the Imperium, where He might be the god of the seasons on a primal agri-world or the Chooser of Warriors in a gang-infested underhive. Such things were tolerated by the Adeptus Minis-torium as long as they acknowledged the primacy of the Imperial cult. To Sarpedon, such fragmentation showed the inability of lesser men to comprehend the true majesty of the Emperor and His primarchs. But this man did not seem at all feeble-minded.

'Our church is not much, I grant you,' continued Yser. 'It is all we could do to survive in the depths of this station, when the cull-teams were sent down. But no longer… you have come and swept them away in turn.'

Vorts's squad was searching through the church and debris piles. As the squad who had been approached by Yser in the first place, they had been given the church and its immediate area to search and appraise. There were many useful – if derelict – recyc-lines and cargo ducts radiating out from the supply hopper that made it worth fortifying. Most of the other Soul Drinkers were prepping and manning the many macrolaser emplacements and missile clusters that were still operational, and Sarpedon wanted to ensure that routes through the station were open and secure for redeployments.

It wouldn't come to that, of course. They were up against Administratum pen-pushers and Guardsmen, who would soon back down when they considered the quality of soldier they were daring to cross. But if the star fort was to be made ready for a battle, it was worth doing properly.

Givrillian's squad were in guard positions covering the many exits to the hopper. They were functioning as Sarpe-don's command squad as he moved from one part of the star fort to the other – over the last few hours he had overseen preparations on the sunward and orbitside firing arcs, and in the maglev terminal where Tellos was in command of a mobile assault company to react to any boarding actions.

Not that it would come to that. But it was worth being sure.

'I have long known that He would send His chosen to save us, to complete His plan,' Yser was saying. 'I had never thought I would see it my lifetime – but the things I have witnessed in my dreams are coming to pass.'

'How many of you are there?'

'Perhaps four dozen. We make our homes in the dark corners of this place, and gather here to worship.'

'Escaped prisoners?'

'Mostly. And one or two Van Skorvold men who grew sickened by toil in the service of corruption.'

'Ah, corruption. It is good that you and I see it in the same places here. My men are to fortify this station and we need to know of any defences we may have missed. If you wish to serve your Emperor, you will share your knowledge of the star fort's layout.'

Yser smiled. 'You are the Architect's chosen, Lord Sarpedon. I have seen you when He places His visions in my mind. Anything you ask shall be delivered as far as we are able.'

Visions. Normally talk of visions and prophecy was dangerous – Sarpedon had seen the darkness of the psyker-taint when it ran unchecked in the weak-willed and malevolent. He had seen the arcs of green lightning spearing down from the heights of the Hellblade Mountains and heard the gibbering screams of a hive-city driven mad, and known that renegade witches were responsible. Such men claimed visions and voices from their gods.

But it seemed Yser was different – thrust into the belly of this dark place, he had responded by clinging to his faith until it granted him visions of holiness. Perhaps the years here had taken too much of a toll, or perhaps he really was blessed by the Emperor's light. For now, Sarpedon was glad only that he seemed to have an ally here at last.

'I shall consult with my flock. We should be able to divert power back to some of the guidance domes, and uncover some of the servitor emplacements. There may be more – you shall know shortly, Lord Sarpedon.'

'Good. Sergeant Vorts will send his men with you.'

Yser nodded and smiled, and hurried away through the debris. It was as if he had been expecting the Soul Drinkers, and was at last able to fulfil some goal now they had arrived. Sarpedon wondered for a moment what would happen to Yser when the Marines had reclaimed the Soulspear and left. He would probably be consigned to the fate he had tried to escape – mind-wiping and incorporation into a biologically-powered servitor. A shame? Perhaps. But he was only one man, and protocol forbade anyone to set foot on a Soul Drinkers' ship who was not a member of, or owned by, the Chapter, so he could not come with them when they left.

A thought occurred to Sarpedon. 'Yser!' he called out. 'You were a prisoner. What was your crime?'

'I was a thief,' replied the prisoner-priest.

'And now?'

'I am whatever the Architect of Fate makes of me.'

THE ADEPTUS MECHANICUS ship *674-XU28* was just under one thousand years old. Every hundred years to the day it was refitted in the dockyards of Koden Tertius with the latest rediscovered and re-engineered archeotech and machine-spirit augmentations. A fighting force was maintained on the craft of tech-guard, siege engineers and other, more exotic forces, that needed constant upgrading and replacement of parts if it was to operate at full potential.

For some time this work had been done under the supervision of Archmagos Khobotov, for he was three hundred years old.

He believed in the primacy of the machine as the building block of human civilisation. Machines were efficient and tireless, and possessed cold, analytical, unfalteringly loyal personalities of the kind that Khobotov himself was proud to rejoice in. Their dedication to the completion of the Omnissiah's lost masterwork of knowledge was the equal of his, and through their example he would create a microcosm of human perfection.

Apart from the tech-guard units, the *674-XU28* was crewed entirely by servitors and tech-priests whose industriousness and knowledge-obsession reached Khobotov's exacting standards. Between them the Mechanicus magi that crewed the ship had barely enough flesh on their bodies for a single man

– the rest was augmentation and improvement. Khobotov himself had lost track of how much of him was real and how much synthetic, and he was glad, for it was one less distraction from the Omnissiah's work. In the massive crypto-mechanical entrails of the ship, in the corridors of gleaming glass where the ancient machine-spirit dwelt and amongst the forests of rail driver cannon and sensorium tines, the map of human knowledge was rebuilt. Between the magi and the servitors, Khobotov's own rigorously disciplined personality and the dark throb of the ship's machine spirit itself was built a web of learning that would grow and mature until the Omnissiah saw in it a part of Himself. The critical knowledge mass would be reached, a point where the learning contained in the ship would render it capable of unlocking any secret, fearing nothing, travelling beyond the prison bars of the real universe. One day, one day, when the ship and the crew and the knowledge within it would be as one, that distant day when all that had been lost in the perversions of the Dark Age of Technology would be regained…

The ship was still young. A thousand years was not nearly enough to begin such a task. And he was always busy, so busy. Sometimes it seemed too far off to even contemplate.

But then, that was just the human in him.

Khobotov glanced across at the huge muscular piston array that stood poised to wrench a vast section of hull off the underside of the 674 and cast it bleeding into space. Sometimes he was sorrowful for causing such a wound in the craft of which he was an essential component, but he knew it was for the good. The machine-spirit agreed with him, rattling the hydraulic rams and breach-charges in eagerness.

There were few servitors in the area for the near-vacuum caused their tissues to degrade, and so it was tech-priests and more senior magi who performed the rites required. This was not as delicate an operation as the most holy teleporter's activation had been, but a job was still worth doing well. Some were dark, robed figures, hunched or inhumanly shaped. Others were bright and gleaming, with the bodies of young men and jewelled decorative attachments of glass and chrome.

Let it not be said that Khobotov was an unfeeling man who had lost contact with his human instincts. He knew well the ways of ordinary men – like children or animals, they were quick to anger and quick seek comfort. They needed encouragement to commit acts of logic, and in some cases, they needed fear.

They said the Space Marines knew no fear. But they were still human. Khobotov was a man of such immense knowledge that he had no doubt he could read their actions and resolve the situation they had stubbornly created. It was simple. Give them no option but to back down. They believed themselves to be the elite of the Imperium, and so the logical way to determine their path was to give them only one option that would not require them to take up arms against that same Imperium.

He could let it go. He could return to Koden Tertius to study the Soulspear, and leave Chloure to deal with the Space Marines himself. But that would leave the Adeptus Mechanicus looking like cowards to the Soul Drinkers, and like thoughtless thugs to the Administratum. These things were not important in themselves, but Khobotov understood that they were important to other Imperial authorities. He was not a politician but the ways of humanity were simple enough for him to grasp – if he forced the Space Marines to back down they would respect the Adeptus Mechanicus as brave and powerful. The Administratum would welcome the possibility of future alliances. But these results would be beneficial to the Adeptus Mechanicus overall. It was almost childlike the way they acted, but Khobotov had to remind himself that one day, before he had trod the path of the Machine God, he had been motivated by similar concerns of politics and saving face.

So he would not let it go. The Space Marines would relinquish the star fort and the Administratum would take it over, and Khobotov would help them do it, because that it what would be to the greatest benefit to the Omnissiah's servants.

His plan was simple. The Soul Drinkers would have no choice but to give up the star fort and return to their fleet under terms of truce. Any other course would require they fight Chloure's battlefleet or Khobotov's forces themselves. They would not choose these options. They would back down.

It was simple.

Satisfied that the necessary rites and preparations had been made, Khobotov impulsed his desire to return to the archivum and continue his manifold researches. This problem, having been set up to resolve itself, would require no more of his attention. And he was so busy…

'SENSOR SWEEP TURNED up something,' said Brother Michairas. 'What do you think that is?'

Michairas was one of the Soul Drinkers manning the sensoria that studded the surface of the star fort. For the past few hours he had pulled a shift in the tiny transparent bubble looking out onto the star field and great glowing disk of Lakonia. The Administratum and Mechanicus fleet was formed of glinting silver shapes hanging in space. The object of his concern was a bright burst of white against the black.

Brother Michairas had voxed for the Tech-Marine as soon as he had seen it. A flare, again centred on the Mechanicus ship, but different this time – purely physical, like an explosion.

'How long?' Tech-Marine Lygris clambered up into the cramped sensor shell, assisted by the clamp-tipped servo-arm reaching up from his backpack.

'Three minutes.'

'Hmm.' Lygris tapped the large curved surface of the clear bubble. 'If it is a secondary explosion from attack, it is catastrophic. But these are deliberately vented gases. Not air. Pneu-retros, or air rams. And a spray of ice crystals, there are hydraulics in there too.'

'Meaning?'

Lygris glanced down at the many tarnished instruments and readouts, noting figures that confirmed his suspicions. 'Meaning they are launching something. Something big.'

CAPTAIN VEKK HAD a habit of yelling at the servitors on the bridge of the *Diligent*. They didn't answer back, so it didn't matter that the blank-eyed thing was merely delivering the best guesses of bridge logistician corps.

'I need more than that!' he shouted. 'Is the 674 hit?'

The explosion was bright on the viewscreen above him, the image inset with different views from the fleet's other craft. The Adeptus Mechanicus ship was spewing a white cloud of vapour from its hull, a huge mass of gas and liquid growing

by the second. Then he saw it. First a tiny sliver in the brightness, then growing and gaining shape. Something huge and
flat – a section of the hull? A huge, intact hull section, just
ripped off by an internal blast? Or…?

'I want specs on that thing, now! Size, orientation, class!'

'It looks like wreckage, sir…'

Vekk glanced at the petty tactical officer who had spoken.
A glare was all it took. 'It looks like nothing of the sort. I was
at Damocles Nebula, boy, I know what it looks like when you
blow a chunk off a ship. I want it scanned and classed, and I
want it double-quick. Move!'

It was growing more defined now. Yes, he was sure. It could
be good, it could be bad. It all depended on what that cyber-
freak thought he was doing.

'And somebody wake Chloure!'

THE GERYON-CLASS orbital artillery piece found brief favour
amongst the forge worlds bordering the halo zone, given that
the form of warfare there often involved opposing or
unknown forces blundering upon one another in the depths
of space. In such a situation confusion and disruption are
potent weapons with which a withdrawal can be covered, or
a potential enemy can be stalled while more information is
sought. The Geryon-class was conceived from the start to take
advantage of this with the rapid and forceful deployment of
electromagnetic and magna-frag weaponry alongside conventional munitions.

It was an ordinatus-level macro-artillery piece, a huge cannon that lobbed disruption shells through the depths of
space to detonate in the midst of attacking spacecraft. When
mounted on an orbital platform it was the size of a small
spacecraft itself. However, the Geryon-class sadly lacked any
edge in conventional engagements compared to similarly
sized, less specialised pieces. Its use gradually declined with
the increased tendency of commanders to simply blast their
way out of uncertain situations and concern themselves with
niceties only after the enemy was drifting and ablaze.

It seemed that Archmagos Khobotov, however, had some
fondness for the Geryon-class. Because that was what had
detached itself from the *674-XU28* and was now descending
into geostationary orbit several thousand kilometres from

the star fort, riding on a standard artillery platform as big as a medium-sized island.

Sarpedon speed-read this information from the data-slate handed to him by Tech-Marine Lygris, and brooded. They had been at an impasse – that was bearable, because he knew his Space Marines could hold out for as long as it took. But this changed everything. This meant the Administratum fleet had the upper hand.

They knew they couldn't take the star fort, not against the Soul Drinkers. So they were going to lob macro-shells into the station until the Soul Drinkers were broken and scattered before ramming hordes of Guardsmen in to take the place. They knew they couldn't face the Emperor's chosen, but they were so petty and preening that they couldn't back down and lose face – they would rather massacre humanity's finest than admit they were wrong.

'An insult to us is an insult to the Emperor, for we are His chosen and Dorn was His foster-son,' said Sarpedon.

'Agreed, commander,' replied Lygris.

'Then these men have insulted the Emperor.'

'Indeed they have, commander.' Lygris talked in the curt, clipped way of most Tech-Marines, his voice echoing slightly in the maglev terminal which was now cleared of mutant corpses. 'Have you spoken of this with Caeon?'

'Caeon is dying, Lygris. I cannot trust him to be in full possession of his faculties.'

'A bad death.'

Sarpedon snapped the data-slate closed. 'There are too few good ones.'

But what to do now? Their ships were was on the other side of Lakonia, and would never survive an engagement with the sub-battlefleet and the Ordinatus. Extraction was simply not possible – that, of course, was the plan the Administratum and Mechanicus had doubtless concocted, to trap the Soul Drinkers like rats and butcher them from afar. Curse them, that did such evil in the Emperor's name! The Soul Drinkers were the best men of the Imperium, and yet the Administratum and Mechanicus had first stolen from them, then dared to threaten violence to keep their prize. What could they be thinking? Didn't they know what the Soul Drinkers were, what they stood for?

Was the Imperium truly the instrument of the Emperor's will, when it was peopled by such lesser men? When the battleships and fighting men were wielded in the Emperor's name, to humiliate those who most closely followed the Emperor's plan? Sarpedon had long known there was corruption and indolence in the very fabric of the Imperium, but rarely had he seen it so starkly illustrated, and never had it put his life and those of his battle-brothers at such immediate risk.

When the Geryon-class ordinatus cannon spoke, the Soul Drinkers could be lost, all so the Administratum and Mechanicus could save face. It couldn't happen. It wouldn't happen. But how would Sarpedon find a way out? They were effectively trapped on the star fort with a massive orbital artillery piece bearing down on them and several thousand Imperial Guard waiting in the bellies of the battlefleet.

There was little doubt that Consul Senioris Chloure and Archmagos Khobotov intended to do violence to the Soul Drinkers if they did not relinquish the star fort, Soul Drinkers would not back down, not while Sarpedon still breathed.

Would they have to die, to prove that they would not accept an insult unanswered? Was that as petty as stealing the Soulspear and refusing to return it? That was not the issue here. The Soul Drinkers were the superiors of anyone the battlefleet might boast. They expected to be treated like the elite that they were.

If the Soul Drinkers had to die to show the galaxy how seriously they took the martial honour that made them what they were, then so be it.

Yet there was hope. Not because he had hit upon a plan, but because a Space Marine is a stranger to despair. There would be a way, even if it would only let them face death as warriors. The legends were true – Marines never failed, even in death.

Givrillian, who was maintaining the terminal perimeter, jogged up to Sarpedon, breaking his thoughts. 'Commander, we have a communication from Squad Vorts.'

'Routine?' Sarpedon had better things to worry about.

'No, sir. The priest, Yser, was showing them some of the orbitside workings and... well, he remembered something.

Something old. He suggests you and Lygris come immediately and see for yourselves.'

WHEN SARPEDON ARRIVED he found Tech-Marine Lygris surveying what Yser had shown the Soul Drinkers. Given the decadence and ill-maintenance of the star fort it was almost the last thing Sarpedon would have expected to find. It was a fully functional, fully stocked, flight deck.

Lygris was primarily an artificer, overseeing the maintenance of weaponry and armour in the forge-ships stationed with the Chapter fleet. But like every Tech-Marine he had been appraised during novicehood as possessing a certain skill with all manner of technology, and had been thoroughly schooled in myriad branches of combat tech. He therefore knew a thing or two about attack craft.

'Hammerblade-class,' he was saying, mostly to himself. 'And Scalptakers. Throne of Earth, these should be in a museum…'

And the place could have served as a museum – a flight deck within the orbital platform architecture, like a thin horizontal fissure through several decks of the star fort, low and broad. There was very little air here and Yser had been given a rebreather array by the serf-labourers, while the Marines wore their helmets.

Where breathable air had seeped in the metal was corroded and treacherous, but most of the flight deck was intact, scorched comfortingly black with blast scars that were still there after centuries. Vivid black and yellow strips marked out complex taxi routes across the gunmetal deck, and islands of refuelling equipment surfaced here and there, hoses coiled, some with tanks still marked full.

And all around stood the craft. Some were hulks of rust, others had been stripped of anything that could pried off the fuselage. But there were plenty that looked intact – sleek and noble compared to the blunt killing weapons of more recent times, with ribbed superstructures and swept-forward wings tipped with lascannon. The Hammerblade boasted a great underslung plasma blastgun while another variant bristling with close-quarter megabolter turrets was a Scalptaker-class superiority fighter. These marks had been flagged as obsolete more than a thousand years before, when the Soulspear had yet to even be lost, and had been relegated to patrol duty around Lakonia before the platform was acquired by the Van Skorvolds.

'There was some talk from the Van Skorvolds of using them again,' Yser was saying, his breath misting against the rebreather mask. 'But it would have cost too much, I suppose, and who amongst them could have flown one of these? I and my flock used this place as a shortcut sometimes, when the air was good.'

There were other variants, too – a bloated nearspace refuelling craft, a fighter-bomber with a single-shell payload bolted to its back. Great chains of ammunition were racked at intervals across the deck, and the noses of warning-marked missiles poked up from pods below decks. Ships, fuel, ammunition...

Sarpedon had thought they were trapped, and had been ready to defend every metre of the star fort against attack. But here was another option, and suddenly he saw the possibility of his Soul Drinkers doing what they did best. The philosopher-soldier Daenyathos had written that the surest way to defend a place was to attack the enemy until they were incapable of attacking what you wanted to defend. On the flight deck was the means to put Daenyathos's words into actions.

Sarpedon turned to the Tech-Marine, and saw he was thinking the same thing. 'Lygris? Can you do it?'

The Tech-Marine gazed at the mechanical playground to which Yser had led them. 'Not on my own. Pull the others off the weapons systems and give me all the serf units, and I'll see about making some of these spaceworthy.'

'It shall be so. Vox for what you need.'

'Yes, commander. May I ask what you are planning?'

'The obvious.'

As Sarpedon was assembling his force and the serf-labour units were breaking backs in the halogen glare of the fighter deck, Commander Caeon died.

Chaplain Iktinos delivered the death rites all but alone. There were few required to attend when the death had not been a glorious one, and there were preparations elsewhere that had to be made. Michairas was there, and Apothecary Pallas. The rites were simple given that they were on an active battlefield – a recitation of Caeon's condensed chanson in Iktinos's monotone, detailing the moments of Caeon's fine life that had been judged fit to be recorded in the epic that every Marine compiled to record his deeds. The ceremonial taking of Caeon's gene-seed, and the reclamation of his weapons to be sealed and archived in the armoury until it was their time to enter the hands of a novice. The weapon's history would be revealed to this novice when he ascended to the position of full Marine, and would serve to emphasise the gravity of his calling which bore him on his way into Chapter history.

There was nowhere Caeon could be buried, so a cairn of rubble and wreckage was erected, blocking the door to the chapel. There they left him, and returned to their posts.

Less than twenty minutes after Lygris had given his word that the fighter deck would be operational within hours, Tellos and a full hundred Soul Drinkers were assembled around Yser's church in disciplined ranks. There was an air of reflection about them, for every one of them was fully aware of the star fort's situation and the lengths to which they would have to go to protect themselves.

But the death of Caeon and the loss of their prize had steeled their minds, and he could see the pride in their eyes. Perhaps they felt distaste at raising arms against those they had once fought with – but they were all certain that honour, and in this case their very survival, were paramount. Sarpedon felt they all hoped, as he did, that once the assault began the Adeptus Mechanicus would realise the gravity of their folly and relinquish their grip on the Soulspear. Then the Soul Drinkers would take their prize and return to the fleet, honour satisfied.

Sarpedon was grateful for Sergeant Tellos's presence. His exultation in battle was infectious, and he was a talisman for the assault squads who formed the core of this force. Givrillian, too, would accompany Sarpedon, a solid dependable voice at his shoulder in case the madness started. Most of the Tactical Marines would maintain the defences of the star fort – the attacking force, consisting of most of the assault squads and a handful of specialists, was amongst the most swift and deadly Sarpedon had ever seen.

And it was his force. He was in command. That Caeon had to die was a tragedy, but now he was gone and such things should not be dwelt upon. These were his brothers and he was leading them even if only to provide the threat of force, and he was proud. He had felt the swell of pride when he first joined the ranks of the Soul Drinkers, and to think that such men were now looking up to him as he had looked up to Caeon, and to Chapter Master Gorgoleon himself, was more than he could describe.

His psychic talents were not tuned to receiving from the minds of others but he could still feel that the men standing before him were eager to put the fear of the Emperor into their opponents. They had all felt the slight of the Soulspear's loss and wished nothing more than to send the Mechanicus crew quailing before them. And if a tech-guard or machine-priest dared resist them, they would use every ounce of force at their disposal to teach them what happens when you raise arms against the Soul Drinkers.

'Lygris here, commander.' The Tech-Marine's voice crackled in Sarpedon's comm-bead. 'The fighters are old but space-worthy, and there's enough fuel for a one-way trip. We can take about one hundred and twenty Marines if we strip out most of the weapons systems.'

'We'll have about a hundred, spread out across the craft, so don't skimp on the firepower. And select pilots if you haven't done so already. How long do you need?'

'Two hours.'

In two hours borer shells could be gouging their way through the star fort's hull to explode, or magnacluster bombs could be raining frag torpedoes across its surface. 'You have one.'

'Yes, commander.'

'Sergeant Tellos!' barked Sarpedon, turning to the assembled Marines. 'I want squads of eight, at least one plasma weapon in each and as many melta bombs as you can carry. I leave squad organisation to your discretion. You will be prepared within the hour.'

Tellos saluted and began carving the assembled squads into self-contained fighting formations, each with its leader and many with a Tech-Marine or apothecary. They were facing possible combat in a largely unknown and unpredictable environment where each element had to be able to survive on its own unsupported.

It would be Sarpedon's first full command, and he knew there was a risk. If the Adeptus Mechanicus fought, there could be terrible bloodshed, and if that happened not all his battle-brothers would return.

But even if such an unthinkable thing happened, the Soul Drinkers would fight on, acquit themselves with honour, and win back the Soulspear. No matter what, there would always be hope that the insult would be redressed, that the affair would be put behind them and Sarpedon could return to the Soul Drinkers' flagship with the Soulspear in hand.

As Daenyathos wrote – *when all is darkness and every way out is lined with blood and lit with the fires of battle, there is still hope.*

But it wouldn't come to that. The Mechanicus wouldn't fight. These were Space Marines, the best of the best, no one would dare actually fight them face to face.

It wouldn't come to that.

IT WAS A man's life in the Sixers. The regiment's proper name was a twelve-digit string of letters and symbols that indicated its size, composition and base camp location on board the *674-XU28*. It was only the tech-priests and magi of the crew, and the senior officers who might one day be accepted into the tech-priest ranks, who could remember the whole thing in full. The logic-string happened to begin with the number six, and so it was as the Sixers that they knew themselves.

Kiv had been a Sixer all his life, as had most of the tech-guard. On his rare forays out onto inhabited worlds he would be alarmed and dismayed at how so many people seemed to have nothing around which they built their life. He had his grenade launcher, entrusted to him as a child when the neurojacks were first sunk into the back of his skull and he was upgraded to a member of the tech-guard. He had learned its exact rate of fire down to tenths of a second, and the range at which the electromagnetic pulses and photon glare would be effective. He knew that at that particular angle he could lob a haywire grenade over two partitions on the Geryon platform's muster deck and drop it right down the throat of an attacker. It had been stripped and repaired so often that none of the original components remained, yet it was the same because it was bound by the weapon's spirit, to which Kiv spoke thrice-daily as the Rites of Maintenance decreed. He knew that the shadowy figure of Archmagos Khobotov had a similar affinity with the unimaginably vast and complex ship itself, which must have given him a deep and holy understanding of the ordered universe the magi laboured to create.

It was something that tied him to the great spirit of logic that stood against the random chaos of the universe – the Omnissiah, Machine God, the defender of reason and knowledge. He assumed that the Omnissiah and the divine Emperor were different sides of the same coin, although the magi he had asked found some way of avoiding the question. The answer must involve concepts beyond his understanding, he guessed.

'Heads up, Sixers! Combat protocol ninety-three, defence in depth and repel!' Colonel-priest Klayden's voice was artificially amplified so every Sixer on the muster deck woke from their reveries. 'Action stations, dogs, action!' The klaxons started up a second later – Klayden's rank allowed him access to the simpler levels of the ship's own machine-spirit, and he was able to anticipate the more important decisions it made.

A whole Sixer battalion had transferred to the ordinatus platform before it had been launched. Every one of them was suddenly up and aware, throwing open ammo trunks and pulling on their quilted flak-armour. There were even units stationed on the Geryon itself. The huge barrel of the cannon was high above, jutting above the upper hull of the platform, but the immense recoil-dampeners and ammo feeds were housed in the centre of the muster deck and it was on this steel mountain that tech-guard squads were preparing defensive positions.

Combat. Kiv had seen it many times, and was chilled by the randomness of it. It was something akin to righteous determination with which the tech-guard and the other forces of the Adeptus Mechanicus would take up arms and strive to win the fight, so that the supreme logic they built could be preserved and the disordered tide of battle turned back. Kiv shrugged himself into the heavy flak-tabard and strapped up the knee-high boots that would protect his feet and legs from the backwash of haywire chaff released from the disruptive grenades he could fire. He hefted the cylindrical metal bulk of the grenade launcher that was as familiar to him as another limb. He drew the jack-lines from the targeting array and pushed them into the sockets in his skull, feeling the orientation of the launcher through his own sense of balance, the barrel temperature through his skin, the ammo count through the fullness of his stomach. The augmentation was a simple one compared to the near-total prosthesis of the tech-magi, but it gave Kiv a taste of how it was to be truly at one with the Machine.

'Subsystem nine! Muster and deploy!' came Klayden's amplified voice. Subsystem nine was Kiv's unit, a mobile defence squad, equipped to hunt down attackers and expel them.

The other tech-guard of Kiv's unit hurried past bearing melta-guns, plasma rifles and hellguns. Each one would fulfil a particular role in the fight, where the confusion of Kiv's haywires, destruction of the energy weapons and precision of the hellguns would combine to form an efficient combat machine.

There was fear. But it was a good fear, like a diagnostic rite, running through his mind and checking for flaws of cowardice. There were none. He had been a Sixer all his life, and Sixers never died. They just broke down.

'Multiple signals, tracking,' boomed the machine-spirit voice. The machine-spirit on the platform was a part of the *674-XU28* itself, and spoke with the ship's authority. 'Approach vectors confirmed. Prepare for boarding on platform twelve.'

The enemy, whoever they were, would probably think they were making a surprise attack. But the sub-spirit that controlled the Geryon platform was as cunning as its parent on the *674-XU28*, and no one could approach without the platform, and then the tech-guard, knowing about it. The attackers would be met by a fully-prepared tech-guard battalion and the weapons system of a fully-aware orbital platform.

High above the muster deck other tech-guard units were scrambling over the vast loading rams and ammo cranes, prepared to sell their lives rather than have disorder infect a masterpiece like the Geryon.

CHAPTER FOUR

THE GERYON ORDINATUS platform was a silver diamond against the star field, bright with light reflected from the planet Lakonia. Sarpedon watched it growing closer through the age-grimed glass of the porthole, the Hammerblade fighter-bomber juddering around him as the Chapter serf-pilot flew Sarpedon's Marines towards their objective.

Sarpedon's craft held eight other Space Marines under Sergeant Givrillian. There were eleven other craft like it, Hammerblades and Scalptakers, speeding in scattered formation towards the Geryon platform. They would land all over the upper surface, and the Soul Drinkers would enter the upper decks of the platform from a dozen different entry points. Once inside they would link up as they swept through the structure, with the ultimate objective being control of the Geryon itself. Once they had the platform the Soul Drinkers could be sure the Adeptus Mechanicus would have no choice but to return the Soulspear. Then the two Chapter cruisers could swoop in unmolested and pick the Soul Drinkers up from the platform, along with the nearly two hundred Marines remaining on the star fort.

'Taking fire!' crackled a serf-pilot's voice over the vox – Sarpedon glanced at the holomat set up in the centre of the Hammerblade's cargo bay and saw the rune that flashed was that of Squad Phodel.

'Squad Phodel, give me details.'

'Magnalaser turret fire,' replied the serf-pilot, voice warped by sudden static. Sarpedon peered through the thick porthole glass and saw ruby-red lines of laser flashing out from the platform, lancing past the silver glimmers that were the Soul Drinkers' makeshift assault craft.

In spite of everything, of all honour and tradition and basic loyalty, the Adeptus Mechanicus would resist. This should have been little more than a show of strength, a lightning raid that would leave the Geryon platform in Soul Drinker hands and convince the Mechanicus to return the Soulspear – but instead, the tech-priests had seen fit to turn this into a battle.

Deep down, Sarpedon had feared this. Those willing to steal the Emperor's finest could have it in their hearts to fight them for it, too. He had thought it hardly possible that sane men would dare take up arms against the Soul Drinkers, and now it seemed that this enemy was not sane after all.

There was a sudden flash of sparks against the black of space and the vox-link to Squad Phodel filled with static. A glint of silver sheared away from a magnalaser beam and tumbled towards the fast approaching Geryon platform. Six good Marines died as the Scalptaker hit at an angle, its scything wingtip catching on the edge of a hull plate and flipping it over and over until it smashed into a support stanchion. It burst, spilling its guts of fuel and machinery against the structures supporting the gargantuan ordinatus barrel above.

Two of the runes were still lit – an Assault Marine from Squad Phodel and an apothecary. They clung to the hull, hard vacuum against their backs as the fuel evaporated around them, watching the rest of the attackers come down.

Sarpedon watched the half-dozen life-lights winking out on the command holo.

They were the first he had lost as a commander.

The Hammerblade juddered violently – Givrillian and the six Marines of his squad clung to the beams and struts of the cargo-passenger compartment. Through the porthole

Sarpedon could now pick out the great metal plain of the artillery platform and the mountainous bulk of the Geryon cannon itself. The wide mouth of its squat main barrel could have swallowed a whole flight of attack craft, and Sarpedon had seen cities smaller than the web of recoil dampeners clustered around its base. He saw three more Soul Drinker craft swoop in low, aiming for the wide expanses of flat hull between sensorium arrays and thruster jet columns.

The Adeptus Mechanicus's apparent treachery had cost the lives of Space Marines, better men by far than any tech-priest. Every Soul Drinker would know it, in the star fort and the attack force. Their hearts would be steeled by the loss of their battle-brothers even as they whispered prayers to Dorn for the souls of the lost.

Sarpedon could feel their anger, for it was inside him, too, channeled into cold determination. This was war, it had been all along. The Mechanicus would have to kill to keep what they had stolen. Honour demanded that Sarpedon ensure they died for it, too.

Defences opened up all across the platform's surface, lasers and missiles. Bright bolts of power streaked across the port-hole as servitor-emplacements took aim and fired. But there was nothing like the forest of fire they would have encountered had they gone for the platform's underside, where bombing runs would target the main thruster columns and ammunition holds. The Soul Drinkers weren't trying to blow the platform up – they were trying to get in.

A near-miss and the craft lurched violently, the Marines struggling to keep stable in the zero gravity. The platform loomed up ahead of them – they were heading for a wide expanse of metal with two craft going in beside them. Below the whine of the engines Sarpedon could hear the zips and crackles as las-bolts passed close and scored the hull.

Another Hammerblade was hit, one wing sheared off, and it angled sharply down towards the platform. Sarpedon didn't see how it impacted, but another eight lifelights turned cold.

Then the serf-pilot dipped the craft's nose and they were on their final run, hills and valleys of metal speeding by, explosions stuttering blooms against the blackness of space above them.

They hit shallow and belly-first, the pilot using the impact to slow the craft down given the Hammerblade's lack of retrothrust power. The noise was awesome – a screech of metal that felt like it would never end, stanchions snapping, hull peeling back like shredded skin. The floor buckled and ruptured, and the platform's hull plates could be seen scudding past below their feet as the compartment was shaken as if grabbed by a giant fist. Sarpedon glanced through to the pilot's compartment and spotted the Chapter serf wrestling with the attitude controls, void shield splintering in front of him. The atmosphere had gone by then and his rebreather hood was misted with perspiration.

They stopped. The lights had failed and the command holo was just a glowing green smudge in the air.

'Report!'

The squad counted off. They had all made it intact. The serf, should he survive, would be suitably decorated upon their return.

'The cargo door's jammed,' said the serf-pilot breathlessly.

'Get us out,' said Givrillian, glacing at Trooper Thax at the tail-end of the hold.

The gravity was normal now they were in the platform's gravitic field, and Trooper Thax stepped forward holding the las-cutter with which each craft had been issued. The only sounds as he carved a wide arc in the side of the craft were the tingling vibrations through the Hammerblade's hull, and the faint background hiss of the vox-link.

They needed to get into atmosphere soon. The Mechanicus were undoubtedly capable of jamming their vox-net and the Soul Drinkers needed the option of verbal communication.

The hull section fell away and Sarpedon looked out on this new battlefield. A rolling expanse of riveted hull plates, punctured by mechanical outcrops and bulky mech-shed hills. The mighty peak of the gun soared above them, brooding and dark, picked out in reflected light from the glowing disk of Lakonia and hung against the backdrop of stars.

Givrillian was at his side, bolter levelled as the squad deployed from the wrecked Hammerblade. 'Looks like a munitions supply tunnel half a kilometre west, commander. Good for an entry point?'

'Take us in, sergeant.'

The Marines moved swiftly across the platform deck, forming a cordon around Sarpedon. Thax and his plasma gun were on point and two Marines jogged backwards to cover the field of fire behind them. The munitions tunnel was a large square opening in the platform deck covered with metal slats of a shutter – there was a good chance the tunnel shaft led somewhere useful. There was an equally good chance the place had been marked as a likely entry point by the enemy and would be well-defended.

Good. Let them try. Let them find out what happens when they cross swords with the Soul Drinkers.

Sarpedon opened the command channel of the vox-net. The too-familiar broken chatter of battle flooded into his head.

'Squad Phodel down, I've got visual…'

'… hit hard, we have wounded and are heading into the secondary intake…'

'… pressure suits and energy weapons, taking fire…'

They were losing men already. But that was to be expected in such a high-risk deployment. When they were in the thick of the enemy and could fight back, it would be a different story. If there was another way, he would have taken it. But there was not. They had forced him into this, these thieves not fit to wear the Imperial eagle. And now they had shown the depths to which they would sink.

He held that thought and cherished it. Purity through hate. Dignity through rage. The words of the philosopher-soldier Daenyathos, written eight thousand years before in the pages of the *Catechisms Martial*, were a rock in the sea of war.

Purity through hate. Dignity through rage. Let the fire within you light the fires without.

The vox-net picture built up. The first craft had landed unmolested, with only a few injuries reported. The next flew into the defensive fire and two of these had been lost, with at least fourteen Marines dead and probably more. Amongst them the six members of Sergeant Phodel's assault squad and one of the Tech-Marines. There were no reports from the other two.

Tellos's squad, inevitably, was already inside, emerging in a main thoroughfare and blasting a great wound in the defenders they found with melta-bombs and bolt shells. In the background of his vox-frequency was the unmistakable thrum of chainblade through bone.

Las-fire stuttered soundlessly overhead as Sarpedon and Givrillian's squad reached the lip of the cargo-feed. Krak grenades blew off enough slats to provide an entrance, their small armour-piercing bursts imploding strangely in the vacuum.

'Go! Go!'

The Marines vaulted into the shaft in quick succession, Thax first, with Givrillian and Sarpedon in the middle. The shaft twisted alarmingly into the body of the platform and the Marines struggled to keep their footing. Sarpedon visualised their position – the shaft curled down alongside the massive machinery of the Geryon's loading and recoil mechanisms, right down to the muster deck where the Soul Drinkers would be able to move around the platform and secure it. They were heading in the right direction.

'Auspex is not transmitting,' said Givrillian from somewhere in the darkness. 'Interference.'

Deeper, through the guts of massive machinery. Through grilles in the shaft's side Sarpedon's enhanced eyes glimpsed immense cogs turning slowly, pistons thudding out a rhythm. The vox-net was fragmented – he could tell there were combats breaking out all over, but no more. Tellos's voice cut through for a second, bellowing triumphant.

'Contact!' came a yell from beneath, a split-second before a wall of air whumped up the shaft. An atmosphere. Somewhere for the tech-guard to fight.

The bright wash of Thax's plasma gun rippled up from the bottom of the shaft. Fire from both sides crackled. Sarpedon tore off his helmet, felt the oily air in his throat, and leapt downwards.

'For Dorn!' he yelled, force staff raised to stab and thrust.

Contact.

THE AIR HOWLED into the shaft when tech-guard Grik slammed the intake lever down. The *674-XU28's* machine-spirit spoke to the platform, which breathed atmosphere in the cargo feed so the Sixers could fight there without fear of vacuum-death. As long as they fought on this platform, the Sixers knew the very battlefield was on their side.

The loader shaft the enemy was entering through emptied into the throat of an ammo shifter, all huge blocks of brushed-steel machinery chased with bronze icons and inscribed machine-prayers. The great cogs beyond would move and the machinery would form a great swallowing gullet, dragging shells down to be slammed into the Geryon's breech. The shifter had reversed flow and brought the Sixers up here, to meet the attackers forcing their way in from above.

The twenty-strong tech-guard fire-team drew up around the feed exit, torchlights darting up into the twisted shaft. Klayden held up a metal hand flat and they waited for a second or two, listening.

A voice, shouting from inside the shaft. Panic, without a doubt. The attackers knew they had been found and they would probably be scrambling back up, trying to find a way out of their trap.

The fist closed. *Advance*.

Both flamer-bearing Sixers hurried forward and aimed the spouts of their weapons into the feed. After they had washed the feed with flame the hellgun and melta-gun guard would follow, picking off those fleeing from the firestorm.

Suddenly a plasma blast, a great bolt of white-hot liquid fire, vomited from the feed with a brash roar, drenching the flamer troops and dissolving one in an instant. The reek of burning metal swept over Kiv, and his launcher racked a grenade to echo his revulsion.

Kiv caught a glimpse of the attackers – a sheen of purple ceramite picked out in haloes of gunfire, the glint of jade green eyepieces, the shine of bone.

The second tech-guard had lost half his body, dripping skeleton's arm fragmenting, ribs burned clean. He had caught sight of the attackers just as the plasma gun opened up.

'Space Marines,' he gasped, and died.

'Give me haywires!' yelled Klayden as bolter fire spat from the feed, punching holes through tech-guard and ringing around the shifter equipment.

Kiv knew he was their one hope – his haywire grenades could remove the Marines' advantage of armour and auto-senses. He would shout and his launcher would shout with him, sending electromagnetic waves billowing up into the

Marines, shorting their senses, locking the joints of their armour. Tech-guards were dying, one decapitated as a round punched into his throat and blew his head clean off. Rounds snicked through the edges of Kiv's flak-tabard and cracked around his ears as shrapnel spun and gunsmoke coiled in the air.

He took aim, ready to fire a haywire grenade through the shaft entrance and into the massive purple-armoured figures crammed into the metal throat. The launcher willed his finger to the trigger.

For order. For logic. For the Omnissiah.

A crackling shaft of arunwood speared out from the shaft and stabbed Kiv through the eye.

IT WAS SARPEDON'S first glimpse of the enemy here – a pale-skinned and shaven-headed tech-guard, clad in red-brown quilted flak-gear, his skin punctured with wires and interfaces. The determination on the face contrasted with the youthful features as the tech-guard slid off the force staff with a flick of Sarpedon's wrist.

There were about a dozen tech-guard still fighting, and Sarpedon wished for the hundredth time he had a better idea of the total tech-guard numbers on the platform. A hundred? A thousand? Five thousand? How many enemies would the Soul Drinkers have to fight before they could secure their honour and their lives?

He told himself it didn't matter. The tech-guard were just men. No more.

Sarpedon was now in the thick of the fighting, Marines spilling out around him with bolters blazing. His own weapon fired off three rounds into the chest of the nearest guard, whose left arm fell sheared at the elbow along with the hellgun he was carrying.

Givrillian barrelled forward into their half-bionic leader and crushed him to the floor, bolter stock slamming into the man's head. The bionic hand grabbed the sergeant's shoulder pad and began tearing handfuls out of the ceramite, deep enough to draw blood, before Givrillian drove a fist through his sternum.

Another brother Marine dragged Givrillian off the enemy's body so Thax could get a clean shot into the backs of the tech-guard now retreating between the massive steel buttresses. He caught one of them full on, the bolt boring right through him before spattering others with gobbets of superheated plasma. They fell, screamed, and caught fire. The Marines now advancing through the machinery picked them off before they could even start to scream.

Sarpedon despatched a wounded tech-guard with the butt of his staff. He was the last.

'Secure the entry point, commander?' said Givrillian.

Sarpedon pointed down the wide, dark metal tunnel that stretched downwards. 'No time, sergeant. Press on, remember the objective.'

A noise vibrated through the floor like thunder from a steel sky. Flakes of rust flittered down from the juddering walls and the huge chunks of machinery began to shift. Gaps between them opened up and Sarpedon could see those cogs slowly turning.

The machinery had activated. They were being swallowed by the offspring of *674-XU28*.

NIKROS, THE SINGLE Marine who remained of Squad Phodel, along with Apothecary Daiogan who had also survived the crash, somehow managed to find a way into the platform's secondary magazine chambers and set krak grenades to destroy the caches of macrocannon ammunition. Then their luck ran out, however. Pinned down by a siege engineer unit, Daiogan died under a hail of heavy bolter shells and Nikros was severely wounded.

Then the magazines went up, incinerating Nikros along with everyone and everything within a two hundred-metre radius, taking a huge chunk like a bite mark out of the platform's surface. Several dozen tech-guard were killed as the local atmosphere depressurised, failing to get their pressure-masks on. When the bulkheads closed and the leak shut down, Nikros and Daiogan had personally accounted for almost three hundred tech-guard.

ASSAULT-SERGEANT GRAEVUS linked up with two other units, one assault and one tactical, and threw a cordon around a huge docking emplacement that sprung from the platform's sunward corner. In a textbook move of which Daenyathos would have been proud, he stormed the emplacement as if it was a fortified town. Sweeping in and downwards half his troops cut their way through the tech-guard to reach the massively complex building-sized knot of wires and readouts, which contained the portion of *674-XU28's* machine-spirit. Several squads of tech-guard, their weapons silenced to avoid accidental damage to the sacred cogitators and knowledge-conduits, attacked with bare hands.

Graevus was a stone-cold killer with little time for such amateurish antics. He dealt with most of them personally with his power axe while Tech-Marine Lygris went to work on the link between the machine-spirit and the control systems for the Geryon.

TELLOS'S SQUAD HAD broken through the upper surface of the platform with melta-bombs, and leapt from the rafters straight into the heart of the tech-guard prepping for combat on the vast, high-ceilinged muster deck. His squad carved out a beachhead in the shadow of the Geryon's recoil-rams, and was acting as a focal point for the assault units making it through the hull and onto the platform's muster deck.

Tellos stood on a mound of tech-guard corpses, energy and las-fire like a halo playing around him, with Marines scrambling up to fight beside him, firing, slicing, dying. The tech-guard fed more and more· men into the maw of the killing zone he was creating – he had taken upon himself the vital task of draining the tech-guard manpower and morale while the other scattered Soul Drinker units closed in on the real prizes.

THE MACHINERY DISGORGED Sarpedon and Squad Givrillian into the intake for the lubricant ducts. They came out halfway up the gargantuan recoil dampeners that dominated the muster deck. The metallic mandibles opened up before them and they tumbled into the slick trench of the intake, green-black lubricant sluicing over them. Brother Doshan was sucked into the yawning black oval of the intake before Givrillian dug the boots of his armour into the stained metal and halted the slide.

Sarpedon hauled himself up so his eyes were level with the edge of the intake trench, and looked down.

They were easily a hundred and fifty metres above the cavernous muster deck. From one corner billowed a great hemisphere of flame where the magazines had gone up minutes before. Smoke was thick in the air and straggling groups of tech-guard on the Geryon structure were trying to co-ordinate supporting fire. Below them the deck, partitioned into roofless rooms and corridors, was swarming with tech-guard streaming towards the centre.

Towards a charnel house. Bodies lay so thick the attacking tech-guard had to clamber up a slope of their own fallen just to get into sight of the Marine position. The tactical squads who had made it this far were sending sheets of disciplined bolter drill-fire down towards the tech-guard, scattering charges so they would break uselessly against the counter-charging Assault Marines.

Tellos was at their head, of course, his armour black with blood and his hair thick with it. It streamed down his bare face and rained from the whirring teeth of his chainsword. In the sharp relief of his augmented senses Sarpedon watched him take down two men with one swipe, ignoring the hell-gun blast that raked channels into his armour like claw marks.

'Voxes coming in, sir!' called Givrillian. 'Lygris reports contact with the spirit-link!'

'Tell him to keep me updated. We're buying him time here.'

'Aye, commander!'

Lygris was good. He would know what to do.

Every battle was tough. The star fort was tough. This was tougher by far. The Van Skorvold mutants had been determined but ill-trained and of varied competence. The tech-guard, meanwhile, were quality troops equipped with some of the best weaponry the Mechanicus could forge. The star fort had been a rehearsal – this was the real fight.

'With me!' Sarpedon called, and Squad Givrillian clambered out beside him as the closest tech-guard stragglers spotted them and moved to fire.

THIS WAS WHY he had been born. This was why the Emperor had looked upon him and marked him out as a warrior, so the year-long Great Harvest of the Soul Drinkers had found him a strong and valiant youth, driven to excel, fearing not even the armoured giants who strode from their spacecraft to judge him.

To fight. To bathe in the blood of his enemies, to know that every cut and stab and bullet fired was for the good of mankind and the glory of the Imperium.

This was why Tellos had been born.

They were learning fast, these tech-guard, as does anyone who must learn to survive. Their advantage was the quick-firing high-impact energy weapons and they were sending fire-teams around all sides of his makeshift position to assault from many directions at once. Tellos, like any Soul Drinker, knew the power of psychology in the thick of combat – he picked out one enemy front, annihilated it totally, and left the others gazing into the gaping hole in their attack. They faltered, they turned. Then they died, for turning to flee is the most dangerous thing a warrior can do.

He dived in – literally, blade-first over the heads of a tight knot of tech-guard, two of their number manhandling a bronze-chased autocannon. He hit shoulder-first, buckling one man's ribcage underneath him, chainblade lashing out at the legs of another. His other hand held his combat knife and it jabbed up beneath the jaw of one of the autocannon crew. Tellos twisted it, felt the gristly wrench as the jaw came loose, and withdrew it in a fountain of blood.

Hot pain punched through his knife arm – a hellgun shot, thin and powerful. It went through the muscle and painkillers shot into his veins. The offending gunman was bisected with a wild upwards stroke, a novice's cut that would have left Tellos wide open to counter-thrust from any foe not shell-shocked and panicking.

He knew they would be defeated even now, nerves in tatters, unable to counter the most base of attacks. Elegance and duelling had its place in war – but the need here was for butchery.

He loved them both alike. The fine art of noble combat, and the glorious rush of righteous carnage. He had loved them both even before the ships of the Great Harvest had come to his world. It was why he had been chosen.

Behind him his squads followed up, firing bolter shells into fleeing backs and quickly slaying anyone still close. The Tactical Marines further back sent volleys of shells over their heads to explode against the partitions and machine-stacks, keeping tech-guard heads down.

A few energy bolts lasered down from a hidden position and a Marine was cut nearly in half by a thick crimson melta-beam. Another took a bad-looking abdomen shot from a lasweapon and had to be dragged as the assault squad regrouped before they were surrounded.

They were dying here. Tellos's squad was already down to half-strength. Only a couple of their fallen would ever fight again, for the formidable tech of their enemies inflicted grievous and unhealable wounds. Pallas, the apothecary who had made it to the position with some of the Tactical Marines, was busy collecting gene-seed from the fallen as well as patching up the brothers' wounds.

But they had taken down hundreds, maybe thousands between them, and there were only so many tech-guard on this platform. Marines were hard to kill and harder to beat, and though Tellos himself bled from a dozen wounds he was more eager for the fight than he had ever been. If they had to die, they would. But they would win.

Someone screamed, and Tellos was shocked to realise it was a Space Marine, for Squad Vorts was suddenly under attack. His auto-senses blocked out the flare but the shower of sparks was still spectacular, cascading from the sundered body of one of Vorts's Assault Marines. Attackers were storming the rear of the position, leaping from wall to console to corpse like inhuman things.

There were half-a-dozen of them and their skin was covered in swirling designs glowing blue-white so brightly the glare would hurt a normal man's eye. Flashes of lightning burst from their fingers and eyes, and rippled across their bare torsos. They were moving so quickly that Vorts's men hadn't had the chance to counter-attack.

Electro-priests. Tellos had never seen a real one – few in number but famously deadly, fanatical dervishes of the machine-cult. He faced them and readied that charge. This was why he had been born.

One was cut down by bolt pistol fire before he got there. Another was speared neatly by a chainblade as he landed. The others were suddenly in the middle of Vorts's squad – a helmet exploded under an electrified hand, a Marine was hurled twenty metres in the flash of energy discharge, trailing smoke from a ruptured chestplate.

Tellos picked out one and drew his assault, parrying blows from bare hands stronger than plasteel. The electro-priest's eyes were silvery and blank. He jerked and spasmed quicker even than a Marine's reflexes would allow. The priest whirled, one hand chopping low and clipping Tellos's knee, and the sergeant barely kept upright as the shock ripped through his leg. He felt the charred muscle and skin soldered to the inside of his armour. This thing would die.

He dodged, sliced, drawing a shower of sparks off the priest's torso. But the priest was still alive and grabbed the chainblade with arcing fingers. The mechanism shattered and teeth flew everywhere like shrapnel. Tellos countered with the knife, aiming for the space between the ribs where a heretic heart dared to beat, but the priest's other hand grabbed his wrist with inhuman reactions.

The power sliced through him. He couldn't get his hand away, the grip was too strong, like a magnet. He tried to slam the wrecked chainsword into the priest's face but it caught his other hand and the circuit was completed, power coursing free through him for a split-second before with one final effort he wrenched himself free.

Tellos landed heavily on his back and spotted the priest falling, recovering, standing again. Smoke coiled from the chainblade wounds. Tellos noticed that from somewhere it had picked up two purple gauntlets.

Then he looked to see if he still held his knife, and saw the charred stumps of his wrists. His hands. It had his hands.

The world was turning white around the edges and there was a thin keening in his ears. Something grabbed him and he caught the white shoulder pad out of the corner of his eye, knowing it was Pallas who was dragging him away by the collar of his armour and pumping bolt pistol shells into the electro-priest's face.

His hands.

This was it. He would die here. Just like he had been born to fight, he had been born to die here, maimed and broken, surrounded by his brothers and the corpses of his foes.

It wasn't bad. He would be remembered. But there was so much more he could have done, so much…

Something huge and dark dropped down in front of him. Power arced from its staff and around the aegis hood raised from his collar. And Tellos was glad, for as long as their commander was watching, he knew his death would be glorious.

SARPEDON DECIDED TO give the tech-guard what they deserved. He decided to give them the Hell.

What did they fear? Too simple. Go back a stage – what did they want? They wanted order and logic and a plan to the universe, a galaxy where the machine god's rules governed reality. And fear? They feared disorder and anarchy, confusion and madness, bedlam, impulse and rage.

That was *their* hell.

Somehow, the fact that these men had once called themselves his allies made it easier. Treachery felt worse that the mark of the xenos or the pollution of the mutant – it was more immediate, a thing of pure malice. Those who allied themselves with the foulness of Chaos were traitors too, against the Emperor and the rightness of the universe, and so it was treachery that Marines were raised to loathe more than anything else.

Put like that, it was simple.

He let the Hell boil up from the mound of corpses beneath his feet, and flood down from the shadows of the platform's superstructure high above. It was the screams of the dying changing to howls of bloodlust, the reek of brimstone and blood. Insane loops of colour coursed through the air and deathly stains of rust spread from the hands of great shadowy spectres of corrosion.

The tech-guard ran but the electro-priests just convulsed in confusion and anger, too far gone to flee but unable to fight on with sounds and smells and images of disorder surrounding them. The battered remainder of Vorts's squad took one down at chainsword length, sparks flying as the chainteeth bored through its skin and into its hyperactive organs.

Sarpedon went deeper. Groans of breaking machinery, like ice caps in thaw, rocked the muster deck, and the half-glimpsed shadows of falling cogs and masonry plummeted through the darkness.

'Advance!' The voice was that of Pallas, taking charge of the surviving forces in the strongpoint. Squads Volis and

Givrillian levelled bolters and swept out, storming the surrounding positions of tech-guard now thrown into sudden disarray by the Hell. Walls of bolter fire tore through flak-tabards and augmetic torsos. Some way distant Squad Graevus arrived, dropping in from the overhanging ventilation channels onto the heads of reinforcing siege engineers. Graevus's axe blade could just be glimpsed, a bright blue diamond flashing up and down surrounded by crimson mist.

Sarpedon joined the three survivors of Squad Vorts as they sprinted after Volis and into the heavy weapons emplacement the tech-guard had been trying to set up. Two lascannon and an autocannon with six crew and about thirty tech-guard were crammed into a flak-board emplacement built around columns of cogitator-memory blocks.

'Lygris!' voxed Sarpedon as he ran. 'Does this platform run from the ship's machine-spirit?'

'Yes, lord.'

'Find out how it communicates with the crew. If it's verbal, I want a sample. You have twenty seconds.'

'Yes, lord.'

It took him fifteen.

By the time Sarpedon had vaulted over the flak-board behind Squad Vorts, he knew how the machine-spirit sounded over the vox-casters scattered throughout the platform and the Mechanicus ship itself. It was a cultured male voice with a hint of the aristocratic – reassuringly confident, calm and intelligent. Perfect.

He went deeper still. He hardly registered his force-staff swiping off the arm of a heavy weapons crewman about to fire. He was occupied with the Hell, going deeper still.

What did they fear?

'Die,' boomed the voice of the machine-spirit. 'Die. Die. Die.'

Most of them probably knew it was a trick. It didn't matter. They froze anyway, shocked to the core by the possibility that the beloved machine, the one thing in the universe that they could trust without question, was turning on them.

'Die.'

And they did. Volis's bolters chewed through dozens, the chainswords of Squad Vorts cut down more. Sarpedon must have bludgeoned and carved up a score of tech-guard as they fired blindly into the air or ran screaming. In the thick of the fighting they linked up with Graevus to form a body-strewn corridor into which Soul Drinkers poured and spread outwards, surrounding knots of panicking tech-guard and butchering them.

But even if they killed every single one of them, the battle-fleet surrounding the platform could destroy them as soon as it was apparent the platform had been taken. It was time they were buying, nothing more.

ABOVE THE MUSTER deck, in the dark and cold mem-bank complex Graevus had captured in the assault's opening minutes, Tech-Marine Lygris and a dozen-strong Marine guard were pulling a cogitator stack apart. The complex was a tangle of cogitators and mem-banks, linked by metal-clad conduits and endless snaking lengths of cable. The moans of the dying and sharp cracks of gunfire filtered up from the muster deck below, echoing and eerie in the dim shadows of the complex. The Marines' hands tore a tarnished metal plate away from the four metre-high obelisk of the cogitator stack, revealing a multicoloured tangle of cables. Lygris reached in and hauled a bundle of them out of the housing.

'We'll do this the old-fashioned way,' he said grimly, and the shears of his servo-arm cut through the waist-thick primary cable.

Electricity flashed violently and a hundred lights on the tangle of wires and cogitators above him went dark. The machine-spirit was cut off from the Geryon, for now at least.

Lygris drew the interface from his backpack – a snaking bundle of cables tipped with a sharp silver spike. He used it rarely, but knew it intimately. It was difficult to explain for someone who had not seen the machine-cult's teachings – this was something only the higher echelons had the right to do, and though he was a Soul Drinker and the best of men, he still recoiled at the horror the tech-priests would feel at his transgression. But it was the surest way. The only way.

He pulled down a likely-looking knot of mem-cables, pulsing with the information than ran through their filaments. He found a socket and snapped another cable into it, feeling it come to life in his hand.

'Cover me,' he said, glancing at the Tactical Marines. 'I'll be unconscious for a couple of minutes.'

'Yes, lord.'

Lygris took the interface cable and jammed the spike into the back of his head. His eyes must have rolled back and his arms flopped by his sides, but he didn't notice. His mind was full of the white light of knowledge – a standard mind-impulse unit link would disorientate an untrained man but this was anything but standard. The information from the Mechanicus craft and the platform was coursing through him, too much to filter, too fast to read.

He knew he couldn't interface directly. No one could – if such technology had ever existed then it had been lost tens of thousands of years ago. He had to focus, find the systems he was looking for, do his work and get out.

Remember what you are fighting for. For the Emperor. For Dorn.

He thought he would drown in the torrent of information. Finally he found a shape – a great shape of power and brutality, massive and terrible. Lygris could feel its intelligence burning as it loomed out of the hot white overload of information, could hear the deep throb of its virtual heart, taste its reek of old iron like blood in his mouth.

He looked for a name, and found it: *Geryon*.

He knew the machine-spirit would be furiously seeking a way through its secondary and redundant systems, trying to find a way in to challenge the interloper. Already a black beam like a searchlight was scouring the depths of the platform's mem-systems, hunting. Lygris had a few seconds here before the massive amorphous darkness of the machine-spirit found him, and knew also that it would all be over if it did. No one outside the Mechanicus had any idea of what a truly ancient and powerful machine-spirit could do to an intruder in its systems. Lygris could only be sure that he would be lucky if he got away with his mind wiped.

The Geryon yawned before him, huge and dark. Lygris scrabbled faster through the pale crystalline thought structures he had made to depict the mem-bank files, tore through the endless loops of cables that were control interfaces, battered down the plasteel doors his mind made from the hard-wired barriers. He sank imaginary fingers into the hard metal of the command program, forcing it to yield beneath his hands, feeling the vast machinery as great thrumming shapes against his skin. He felt immense ammo-haulers and forced them to move, slamming disruptor shells the size of tanks into the breech. The coolants, the recoil compensators, the propellant tanks – he rammed them all into position.

It was too late. The Geryon was upon him, powering up an information burst of such magnitude it would fill Lygris's mind to bursting and then drain away, leaving a brain scoured of all memory and intelligence. It was over. He was effectively dead.

He did the last thing the machine-spirit would expect. He dived right into it, down the black-smoke throat of the Geryon, feeling its reeking hot breath blistering his skin. He had to be quick, quicker than anyone could reasonably hope to be, before the Geryon caught him and crushed him with coils of information.

Lygris swept through the darkness of the Geryon and hurtled upwards, skimming the roiling black madness of the neural circuits that formed its brain. He sought out the tiny pinprick of light that was the link between the machine-spirit and the platform's sensoria, the conduit through which information about the outside void poured into the Geryon's brain.

Faster, so fast Lygris thought he would die of the effort. But the Geryon was behind him, breath hot on his back, teeth gouging at him even as he dived into the glowing portal and into the sensoria systems.

Lygris looked out onto space through Geryon's great eye. He spotted something, focused. The definition grew: conning towers and gun emplacements, the aquiline prow, the bright wash of its engines. An Imperial battleship, proud and strong, a large and tempting target.

He was locked. He was loaded.

He fired.

THE GERYON-CLASS had several classes of ammunition. One was a single titanic shell that had an immense starburst area, which would create an instant zone of interdiction through which attack craft and even lighter cruisers would be unable to travel.

Another contained a half-dozen void charges, which would spread electromagnetic chaff and pulse waves in all directions and create the equivalent of stellar minefields across a wide area.

Still another contained over a hundred disruption canisters, which would rain interference over an entire battlefleet, causing a temporary sensor-blackout. It was one of these that belched from the huge metal throat of the Geryon and burst just orbitwards of Chloure's sub-battlefleet.

One canister struck the underside of the *Hydranye Ko* and its momentum barged it through a full seven decks before it exploded, sending rivers of chaff-filaments rushing through corridors and pooling in cargo holds. More than thirty crew died in the explosion, and a further seventy or so from inhaling the filaments and fragments that flooded the lower decks. Half the light cruiser's air filtration system was clogged and the ship issued an all-points life support alert.

Several erupted between the star fort and the ships of the battlefleet. The *Diligent* and the *Deacon Byzantine* were in themselves relatively unaffected, but their view of the star fort was covered in a thick gauze of interference. Two scout craft on routine patrol from the *Deacon* became hopelessly lost as their unprotected servitor-guidance and comms failed completely. Several hours later they finally ran out of fuel and their crews froze to death.

The *Deacon* was quicker to respond to the sudden attack, firing several fragmentation torpedoes into the mass of interference discharge. The warheads malfunctioned as soon as they entered the electromagnetic fields and detonated piecemeal, adding more wreckage to the mess.

On the bridge of the *Diligent*, massive electrical feedback tore through the command systems and sent sheets of flame rippling up from the navigational consoles. For a few minutes all was black and hot and deadly – the screams of the dead and the roaring of flames mixed with the hiss of emergency saviour systems flooding the burning areas with fog and foam.

The damage control crew were there within three minutes, musclebound ratings with crowbars and rope hauling petty officers and nav-servitors from the burning wreckage. When the bridge was ordered enough for effective command, it had been established that the small craft tracked near the ordinatus platform were not obsolete fighters being used as maintenance craft after all, and that the platform was now under the control of the Soul Drinkers Space Marines.

It was also apparent that the Soul Drinkers had acted in a far more violent manner than Chloure had predicted. Chloure chose not to mention this.

Only the *674-XU28* was relatively unaffected, positioning itself to have a clear shot at the star fort and using its own jamming systems to counter the disruptive electromagnetic waves. Unfortunately its primary armament was currently under Soul Drinker control several thousand kilometres distant, and it had little more than defensive turret fire to boast in the way of firepower.

The tech-priests on board the *674-XU28* noted the puzzling fact that the defences on the star fort were powering down.

'GET ME DAMAGE reports! Now! And sensors!' Givo Kourdya hated letting things out of his control, and jumped from the deep leather upholstery of his captain's chair to bawl at the hapless petty officers and logisticians stumbling in the half-light of the bridge. Most of the lights had blown and the cogitator screens were flickering. Plumes of white smoke spurted from ruptured conduits and the viewscreen was full of ghostly static. The only sounds were sparks and steam, and the shouting of orders and curses. Otherwise there was silence, and this was significant because it meant the engines had stopped.

Lines of glowing green text chattered along the pict-slate set into the arm of the command chair. Damage reports – structural damage from the disruptor warhead was confined to a relatively small area, but the control systems for half the ship were haywire.

The engines had gone into emergency shutdown. Kourdya knew they wouldn't be back on-line for several hours, because priority for the damage control crews was the switching back on of the coolant systems before the plasma reactors overheated.

There were still no sensors. Sensors were the most delicate things on any ship and, annoyingly, the most useful. The *Hydranye Ko* was almost entirely blind. The most effective

means of navigation, targeting and close manoeuvring was
currently to look out of a porthole.

'Front sensorium's down, sir,' said the tech-adept whose
unfortunate task was to liaise between the Mechanicus personnel and the command crew. 'But the rearward facing
arrays are in some kind of shape.'

'And?'

'We've got energy signatures, sir, from the planet's far side.
Two of them, cruiser strength, heading–'

'How fast?'

'Very fast, sir. Faster than our top speed.'

'Space Marine cruisers,' said Kourdya, mostly to himself.
Wonderful. His ship was temporarily blind and crippled, but
it didn't matter.

The real effect of the Geryon shell had been to prevent
co-operation between the three cruisers of the sub-battlefleet. Between them they could have taken on the strike
cruisers, which were probably light on weaponry to make
room for attack craft bays. But one-on-one, the *Hydranye Ko*
wouldn't have stood much of a chance even in full working
order.

Kourdya sank back down into the command chair and
pressed a control stud on the arm. If it still worked it would
ring a bell somewhere below decks to indicate that a valet
servitor should trundle up to the bridge bearing a decanter of
eighty year-old devilberry liqueur and a shot glass. The
Hydranye Ko wasn't going anywhere for a while, and in such
situations Kourdya always tried to allow himself some little
luxury to make sure it wasn't all bad.

'I wish I'd never won this ship,' he mused as he waited on
the darkened bridge for his drink.

SARPEDON GLANCED AROUND him – he was in the flak-board
corridor they had carved through the middle of the muster
deck, daring the tech-guard around to attack, sending out
counter-assault parties when they did. The Hell still burned
all around – chains of glowing numbers formed equations in
the air that fragmented and dissolved, and snakes of rust
slithered along the bloodsoaked floor. The shock was
dimmed by now but tech-guard still lost it here and there,
screaming for machine-spirit's mocking voice to shut up. And

the ordeal was taking the edge off even the stoutest of them, their aim thrown by shaking hands.

A voice came over the vox, strangled with static. 'Commander Sarpedon, this is the *Unendingly Just*. We are clear for pick-up.'

It had worked. Lygris had done it. If the Tech-Marine survived – and the Marines set to guard him said the interface had a taken its toll on him – he would be rewarded.

'Acknowledged, *Unendingly Just*,' replied Sarpedon, raising his voice to be heard above the static on the vox-net. 'Preparing to move out.'

Sarpedon had the majority of the Soul Drinkers with him, with the rest around Lygris's position. He loosed off a snap shot at a head that poked above a heap of wreckage, missed, guessed the position of the rest of the body and fired through the cover. Something screamed.

Treachery can never hide.

'Soul Drinkers!' he yelled. 'Prepare for withdrawal! Graevus, Vorts, meet up with Lygris's position and secure a route. The rest, fall back with me!'

THE GUNDOG AND the *Unendingly Just* swept in from the other side of Lakonia's orbit, where they had hung in the planet's sensor-shadow while the star fort and, later, the platform had been won. Their engines, overcharged for speed, were tagged as a larger-than-cruiser signal by the sensors of the closest ship, the *Hydranye Ko*.

The *Ko* made no move to intercept as they swept over the battlefleet, through fire arcs that would have destroyed even the tough Marine strike cruisers had the battlefleet been able to see them. Only the Adeptus Mechanicus craft tried to stop them, offering token turret blasts from its macrocannon batteries. The dark purple paint on the *Gundog's* hull was slightly scorched, nothing more.

The strike cruisers were run by serf-crews under the command of small Soul Drinker retinues who knew when to let their charges make the decisions and when to rein them in. Both ships had been refitted extensively for close-order manoeuvre and they tumbled elegantly towards the top of the platform, which was still wreathed in propellant wash from the Geryon's firing. Few of the defensive turrets were still functioning – the close-range lance batteries and light torpedo waves ensured that none continued to do so.

The *Unendingly Just* launched a wave of twenty Thunderhawks towards the docking emplacement that Graevus had assaulted less than an hour before. Marines were already gathering amongst the docking clamps and refuelling junctions, holding the landing sites against attack.

The *Gundog's* belly was empty, having held the corvus pods now dotting the hull of the star fort. Lacking a means of moving large numbers of troops it docked directly with the star fort, latching on to a wide ship-to-station thoroughfare through which millions of shackled feet had marched in the decades before. Chapter serfs made the docking secure and the Soul Drinkers withdrew from the star fort's weapons emplacements and muster points onto the strike cruiser.

Chaplain Iktinos, nominally in command of the two hundred Soul Drinkers left on the star fort, ensured that as per Sarpedon's standing orders, the personnel embarked upon the strike cruiser *Gundog* included the prisoner-priest Yser and the three dozen members of his flock.

WHEN THE SOUL Drinkers withdrew into the waiting Thunderhawk gunships from the ordinatus platform, it turned out there was more than enough room in the transports. Only sixty-three Marines of the original hundred were still alive.

The *Unendingly Just*, receiving its brood of Thunderhawks back into its flight decks, turned gracefully and gunned its primary engines, sprinting towards the system edge where it would meet up with the *Gundog* and escape into the warp. It left behind nearly forty dead Soul Drinkers, and uncounted thousands of Mechanicus tech-guard.

BY THE TIME the *Diligent* had recovered its wits and managed to focus its sensors beyond the interference field, the two strike cruisers had long since disappeared with the three company-strong Soul Drinkers' force. Chloure could do was sit back in his command pulpit, and watch the star fort die. The viewscreen was full of the ugly swollen bulk of the Van Skorvold star fort. It flashed like lightning as the first charges went off across its metal skin.

'Tertiary fuel stacks,' said Manis, the *Diligent's* master of Ordnance, as a blossom of fire burst against the scorched metal shell. 'They knew what they were doing.'

Chloure guessed the Soul Drinkers had planted bundles of grenades, or maybe explosives salvaged from the Van Skorvold arsenals, equipped with timers. Every Space Marine, he guessed, would have had extensive demolitions training and would know exactly where to plant a charge to hurt that star fort the most.

'Can we save it?' he asked.

'Not a chance,' said Manis.

Even Chloure could tell that the star fort was already tilting alarmingly towards the pale orb of Lakonia. The gravitic stabilisers, Manis informed him, had been the first to go. Probably melta-charges, but again bundles of standard grenades would do the trick if you knew what to look for.

Another explosion, the largest, tore a massive section out of the side of the star fort. The flaming wreckage scattered from the hull as if in slow-motion before winking out in the vacuum. It was moving quicker now, turning over ponderously as it fell into a terminal orbital decay.

His mission had been to apprehend the Van Skorvolds, dismantle their empire, and take it over in the name of the Administratum. He had thought he had done an extraordinary job, using just the right rumours to bring the Soul Drinkers into the operation, saving valuable resources and casualties by having the Space Marines clear the fort of resistance. But instead he had failed in his mission as completely as could be imagined – the fort was destroyed, his fleet damaged, the possibility of an Administratum-controlled human cargo business in flames. He might as well have left the Van Skorvolds in charge – the Administratum would have been far better off.

He tried to tell himself the worst thing was the billions of credits burning up before his eyes. But in truth, Chloure knew there were whole Imperial organisations devoted to publicly punishing men who had failed as totally as he had.

'Your orders, sir?' Vekk stood proud with his arms behind his back, as if nothing had happened.

'I suppose we'd better follow them,' said Chloure wearily. 'We'll lose them but there will be questions if we don't try.'

'Aye, sir.' Vekk turned and started barking out orders as if they were important.

All that revenue, he told himself. Bloody Khobotov. Bloody Marines. All that revenue.

CALLISTHENES VAN SKORVOLD never found a way out of the old defence station's command centre, let alone the star fort itself. When the friction with Lakonia's atmosphere melted the outer hull and sent flames gouting through the star fort, he died screaming as the skin and muscle was scorched from his bones. Finally he was reduced to a fine ash and scattered over Lakonia's rolling green countryside along with several million tons of flaming wreckage.

Veritas Van Skorvold found and launched one of the few saviour pods she had bothered to keep maintained on the star fort, and got far enough clear of the station to avoid being dragged down into its orbital decay. She drifted for three days and was picked up by the *Hydranye Ko*, which was stationary in high orbit while repairs were carried out. She was promptly arrested and thrown in the brig. The security systems had failed along with rest of the ship and keeping her incarcerated proved very tiresome, especially when she began biting whoever was assigned to guard her. Captain Kourdya was heard to voice on several occasions the suspicion that the Soul Drinkers had let her live deliberately for the sole purpose of annoying him.

Every warrior needs a funeral pyre. Commander Caeon got his when the flames roared through the hull of the star fort as it broke up in the atmosphere. Caeon was, perhaps inevitably, very difficult to burn. But by the time the star fort had disintegrated, this proudest of Soul Drinkers was nothing but dust.

CHAPTER FIVE

THE GUNDOG AND the *Unendingly Just* had been fleeing for six months, the last five of which had been spent hidden in the depths of the Cerberian Field. From a distance it was beautiful, a scatter of glowing dust clouds and sparkling asteroid fields, lit by the stars being born in its heart. Up close it was hideous – the outer regions were composed of chewed-up lumps of rock that span in random patterns, the largest the size of moons, the smallest still enough to degrade engine intakes and speckle portholes with cracks.

It was in this outer region that the *Gundog* and the *Unendingly Just* hung, powered down, hull paint almost stripped away by micrometeorite impacts. The sensor fuzz of the dust and rock clouds hid them from view and meant that monitoring their communications was worse. In fact, the only way the besieging battlefleet knew their quarry was there was for their crews to look out into the field and spot the tiny slivers of reflected starlight gleaming off the metal of their hulls.

It was a grim situation. Fuel was low and supplies were more so.

* * *

APOTHECARY PALLAS HAD been worried about Sergeant Tellos for some time. He had requested that he be the one to care for Tellos's grievous wounds, for he felt a strange sense of responsibility for the man. He had dragged him out of danger and hauled his bulk up to the platform surface, and duty had insisted he finish the process by seeing to Tellos's recovery.

That had been then. Now, many months on, it was concern and not a little curiosity that spurred his interest in the mutilated assault sergeant. Of course, to allay his concerns about Tellos, he would first have to find him, for Sergeant Tellos had once more absconded from the secure infirmary bay where he was being kept until Pallas had worked out just what was happening to him.

Tellos would be hard to find, as he had been the last half-dozen times he had escaped. The *Gundog* was not the largest of the Soul Drinkers' ships – their faraway main fleet included immense battle barges and bloated supply craft – but its crew were elite and few in number, and hence there were whole decks completely deserted. Here, in the monastery wing where no brother Marines had dwelt for centuries, the footsteps of his heavy ceramite armour echoed through the cells and chapels. The place was kept spotless by the maintenance servitors which were occasional glimmers of movement in the long shadows, but somehow that made it seem more like a ghost town.

Pallas checked the auspex. Nothing. That in itself was worrying – Tellos's life-signature had been showing less and less on the auspex screen in the past few weeks. Pallas glanced around the high vaults of the ceiling and dark, matt-grey walls of the cells lining this thoroughfare. Lots of places to hide, if you knew what you were doing. Was Tellos treating this as a challenge? If so, he could evade detection for weeks down here. Maybe more – he was eating and resting less according to the latest data, and seemed to be existing on energy alone.

The thoroughfare opened into a librarium annexe. In years gone by some of the Chapter's Marines and novices had dwelt here, before the *Gundog* was refitted for ship-to-ship assaults. In the librarium they had maintained some of the Chapter's records, from the newest battlefield statistics to the aged chansons written by long-dead heroes to ensure their legends were not forgotten. Heroes had been made there, and new ones rediscovered.

Now the ceiling-high shelves were mostly bare with only a handful of texts. One was still perched on a lectern, from which a Chaplain would have berated the novices or inspired them with tales of their betters. Pallas had to take care not to crumble the yellow paper with the fingers of his gauntlet – the book was an elaborate epic of some crusade into a sector long since benighted.

One wall of shelves was not empty, but still packed to bursting with slim volumes – they were all copies of Daenyathos's *Catechisms Martial*, each one illuminated and annotated by the owner, each one recovered from his body after he had died in battle. This librarium had been designated their final resting place, and their removal had not been permitted when the *Gundog* was reassigned.

The auspex bleeped, and a warning sigil flashed up in the corner of Pallas's vision. A life-sign. It was faint, but it could still be Tellos.

Pallas backed up against a wall, knowing the shadows cast by the dim light would not mask his bulk from the senses of another Marine. One hand was encased in the injector/reductor gauntlet which would administer drugs or remove the gene-seed of the fallen. The other grasped his bolt pistol.

Not that he thought Tellos would attack. But Tellos had never been a predictable man and Pallas couldn't be certain.

He saw something moving some way off, across the wide space of the librarium, edging through the archway leading in from a side-chapel. The figure's raw muscles were twined around chunks of stained metal, twin glowing lenses jutted from a stripped-down head of sinew and bone. A drum-fed autogun was held in one hand, and a twin-bladed halberd in the other. It trailed bunches of wires and servos whined as it moved.

A combat servitor. As a novice, like any Soul Drinker, Pallas had despatched scores of the things with boltgun, chainsword, knife, bare hands, and all manner of weaponry he might use or find on the battlefield. They were designed to die hard, giving almost as good as they got – novices who failed combat assessments did not, by definition, survive.

Its artificial eyes scanned the librarium. Pallas knew the things had a limited range and it would not have seen him yet. Pallas hadn't even known there were any training facilities left on the *Gundog* – it must have been left here, like the books, when the monastery facilities were relocated.

The faint snick he heard was an autogun selector flicking to full auto.

Pallas raised his bolt pistol, drew a bead as the servitor's glinting eyes swivelled to fix on him.

A second figure, human this time, dropped all the way down from the ceiling, blocking Pallas's aim. Something long and silver flashed and the half the servitor's head flopped to the ground, wet and gleaming fresh-cut meat. The autogun drummed out a second's worth of shots in a fan that rang around the massive architecture, paused to re-acquire the target, fired again.

The attacker was quick. They all missed.

The servitor's halberd lashed out – it didn't have a power blade, of course, but that blue crackle of an energy field meant it was a shock weapon that would lock muscles and addle minds before the weapon's wicked point found its mark. There was a loud clash as the newcomer parried, whirled, drove his own weapon home.

Suddenly the servitor had been opened from throat to groin, cables and muscle loops spilling out. Then its gun arm was gone, then one foot. Then the remaining half of its head.

The pieces slid down the servitor's metal casings and flopped to the floor. There was the faint thrum of servos powering down, and the sound of the newcomer's breathing as it regained composure.

Stripped to the waist, broad-backed and pale, the man stood over the shreds of the servitor. His skin was translucent and Pallas could see the overdeveloped muscles of his back and upper arms slowly untensing as the battle-rage died down, and pick out the stark black plates of the carapace under the surface.

The weapons were blades from an air intake fan, a metre long and sharpened lovingly. They had been polished to a mirror silver, and thrust into the cauterised stumps where his hands had been.

'Greetings, Sergeant Tellos,' said Apothecary Pallas.

Tellos turned. The skin on his face was the same – Pallas could pick out the muscles of his jaw as he spoke. 'Apothecary. I didn't expect you to follow me this far in.'

'You are under standing orders, Tellos. You must remain in the infirmary. You have much healing to do.' Pallas could smell Tellos's sweat as he walked towards him. Pallas indicated the quietly oozing remains of the servitor. 'Practice?'

Tellos smiled. 'Re-training, apothecary. If the Chapter wishes me to fight on, I must learn to do so again.'

'Sergeant Tellos, you cannot fight. We have told you this, many times. The shock damaged the nerves, the augmeticists cannot connect any bionic–'

'I don't need bionics, Pallas. Just because I cannot hold a chainsword doesn't mean I cannot give my life to my Chapter as I have always done.' Tellos held up his home-made blades, edges shining in the half-light. 'I need more practice, I know that, but I was a novice once and I can be again.'

'No, Tellos. It is over. Talk to the Chaplain if you have difficulty accepting it. My concern is your physical well-being, for you are a brother and though your days in battle are over, I still have a duty towards you. We do not know enough about what has happened to you, Tellos. We are concerned that you are changing. Whether this is your gene-seed reacting to the trauma, we do not know. Until your condition has stabilised we cannot let you wander as you please.' He looked down at the servitor again. 'Where did you find that?'

'I went exploring. I've never done that before. All these years on one or another of our ships and I never thought to find out what lay beyond the next bulkhead. Why do you think that is, Pallas? Are we afraid? Under orders? Or does it just not occur to us to question?'

'These are matters for the Chaplain, Tellos. Let me examine you again and you can discuss them with him.'

'I will fight again, Pallas.'

'I know you will, sergeant. Now, will you come with me?'

The apothecary led the sergeant out of the librarium and back towards the *Gundog's* infirmary, where the serf-adepts and Chapter apothecaries would puzzle over what was happening to Tellos, and decide once again that they didn't know.

* * *

THE VIEWSCREEN IN the lecture theatre on board the *Diligent* showed the same unmoving image it had done for months – the scattered asteroids of the Cerberian Field lit by a glow from far within. Somewhere in the thick mass of floating rock were the two Soul Drinker cruisers.

The asteroid field blocked all but the most basic scans from the battlefleet. So far all the intelligence they had gathered told them only that the *Gundog* and the *Unendingly Just* had scarcely moved for the last five months. As to what the Soul Drinkers were doing, how many there were left, what they were planning, the state of their ships and remaining armaments – all they had was guesswork.

The Cerberian Field was a nightmare. Trying to engage the Soul Drinkers was suicide, for the cruisers would just coast deeper into the field while the Imperial battleships were torn up by the asteroids as they tried to pursue. But equally, the Soul Drinkers couldn't escape from their hiding place, since the battlefleet was now far larger than they could hope to evade, large enough to bring numbers to bear wherever the Space Marines tried to break out.

Consul Senioris Chloure never thought he would be glad to lose control of the most important mission of his life, but now he felt a curious strained relief that he no longer commanded the battlefleet in any meaningful way. His name might be tagged onto official communications to mark his nominal command, but his opinion was no longer worth anything.

It meant he was a passenger, an observer, unable to alter the events around him. It also meant he could absolve himself of any responsibility for what might yet become another bloodbath.

If Vekk hadn't suddenly decided to go all dashing and efficient they would never have picked up the warp-trail of the two strike cruisers. There would have been no astropathic communication with the sub-sector admiralty and the sub-battlefleet would not have swollen with every light year to become a mighty flotilla of the Emperor's Navy. The *Hydranye Ko* had stayed at Lakonia for repairs but there were now cruisers, escort squadrons, several fighter-bomber wings, a Departmento Munitorum hospital ship and innumerable support craft swarming around a stationary position outside the Cerberian Field. They had even been joined by the *Penitent's Wrath*, a Ragnarok-class that had seen better days but was nevertheless an immense capital ship bristling with more destruction than Chloure could comprehend.

'Five months,' he said to himself.

'Consul?' came a questioning voice from behind him.

Talaya must have been standing there for some time. She was a naval tactician, one of several dozen sent by the admiralty who had gradually eroded Chloure's authority until they were running the battlefleet by committee.

'Tactician. I thought I was alone in here.' He indicated the giant viewscreen of the amphitheatre – normally used for training lectures, it had been rigged to mirror the view from the screen on the bridge. 'Sometimes it helps to take stock of the situation away from all the noise and bustle.'

'Indeed. You do not have to explain. Your position must be one of great stress and tension.'

Chloure couldn't tell if she was being subtly critical, or if she simply wasn't much of a people person. She had a sharp, pale face that didn't seem designed for expressions and stood out spectrally against the dark blue of her uniform. 'You were saying, consul?'

'I was just thinking... they've been out there five months. Nothing has come or gone. We've had whole fleets of supply ships in and out, but they haven't had anything. Not one shuttle. What are they doing for food? Or fuel?'

'Our data regarding Space Marine resistance to privation is grievously lacking,' said Talaya. 'It is entirely possible they do not need food or water at all in the conventional sense. Even their life support requirements may not be the same as those of a normal naval crew given their resistance to hazardous battlefield conditions.'

'Maybe. Hardly encouraging if we're trying to starve them out.' It was the only way he could see to break down the Soul Drinkers and bring them in for disciplinary procedures. All offensive strategies had been ruled out given the density of the asteroid field and the probable attack capabilities of the strike cruisers themselves, not to mention the horror of another boarding action by the Soul Drinkers.

Of course, quite who would conduct the courts martial of three hundred Space Marines wasn't certain given the number of Imperial authorities that could claim wrongs done to them at the star fort and ordinatus platform. It wasn't even clear if there were brigs on the ships of the battlefleet secure or numerous enough to hold troops who they said could tear through bulkheads with bare hands and take hellgun shots to the chest and laugh. No one had thought that far ahead.

'A blockade is only one strategy. There may be others. It is being suggested that the arrival of further attack-configured craft would make a conventional attack feasible. A Golgotha-class factory ship has been requested, to be refitted for clearing a path through the field.'

'Talaya, that would take months. Years.'

'If that is what it takes, consul. These are renegade Space Marines of a famous and battle-proven Chapter. I am unable to name a more dangerous foe.'

She was right, of course. Somewhere within the grainy mass of the Cerberian asteroid field were two shipfuls of soldiers so deadly and dedicated they could hardly be called human any more. Whatever had driven them to stab their allies in the back – had it really been that freak Khobotov and their Soulspear trinket? – he knew enough of what was said about Marines to realise they would not give up on their treachery now, not ever. He could not imagine the Soul Drinkers forgetting their grudges.

'We'll have to kill them, consul. All of them. There is no other way.'

He looked at her. The woman's face wore no emotion. 'You understand what you're saying, Talaya. I mean, these are…'

'You cannot comprehend anything worse, consul. Renegades, free to do as they will. Banditry, idolatry, secession. All with the prowess and self-sufficiency of a Space Marine Chapter. If it took a century and led to the losses of all the ships of this battlefleet, it would still have to be stopped. We are fully aware of the consequences the extermination of such warriors will have. But we are also aware of what they will do if we are unable to act with complete ruthlessness.'

'I know, tactician, I saw what they left of the Geryon. But… in all my life, I never thought it would come to this.'

'Of course not, consul. And you should not blame yourself for the loss of the star fort and the treachery of the Soul Drinkers. You could not have been expected to cope.'

Evidently satisfied with her morale-boosting, Tactician Talaya walked neatly up the auditorium steps and back into the arteries of the *Diligent*, where officials and adepts from a dozen Imperial authorities combined to form the nerve centre of the mission. It even had a name of its own – the attempt to hunt down and capture – or, more likely, kill – the renegade Soul Drinkers was officially labelled the Lakonia Persecution.

Iocanthos Gullyan Kraevik Chloure wished very much that he was back on a backwater agri-world, pushing pens and drowning in a sea of boredom in the name of the Emperor.

YSER HAD A strong voice for such a weak-bodied man, and it filled the chapel of the *Unendingly Just*. The room was entirely carved of stone, from the lectern in front of him to the pews on which his flock sat, and the echoes of his voice were cold. It was a good place for inspiration, and they had needed it.

'You have all seen what can happen when the Emperor's name is taken in vain,' said Yser. 'When He becomes nothing more than an excuse for men to lay down laws which gain them power and riches, or He is used like a monster in a children's tale to frighten the weak into obeying the corrupt.

'You have seen it, for you have all lost brothers and sisters to such blasphemy, both Marine and the low-born of my flock. Now we are sorely tested – so great are the machineries of corruption and self-service built by such men that even the greatest of warriors, the chosen of the Emperor himself, are driven hard by their aggression.

'But the Emperor, the Architect of Fate, has seen these things and acted upon them. Has the true abuse of the Imperium been made clear to your eyes? Have the self-serving apostates not shown their hand by tarnishing the name of the Soul Drinkers and moved to do violence upon them? For though we are few and the enemies of the Emperor surround us even now, we know that knowledge of the Architect's true plans are a sounder weapon than the mightiest fleet of starships.

'Perhaps these words will be of little comfort to those of you who have lost much, or who are dying yourselves. But to be enlightened, even in death, is a thousandfold greater than to live for centuries in ignorance. We are few, and we are beset on all sides. But we are free.'

Yser looked across at the gathered flock. There were barely thirty of his original followers left – so many had been wounded or simply misplaced in the fall of the star fort, others had died of weakness or disease accelerated by the rationing. But alongside those few survivors were new worshippers welcomed to the light of the Architect of Fate – Space Marines, Soul Drinkers, over a hundred of them, kneeling giants in full armour repaired and gleaming.

It was daunting to think that such men were hanging upon his words, when he had once been a thief and lower than the low. But he knew he was right. He had heard the Architect calling to him, assuring him he had a part to play in the sacred plan, steering him from the debauched and idolatrous church of the Adeptus Ministorum and the superstitious oppression of its many cults. Now the Soul Drinkers had seen first-hand how the Imperium treated those who truly tried to follow the Emperor's path, they were open to Yser's teachings. Every Marine without immediate duties on the *Gundog* or the *Just* was here, silent, contemplating, gradually letting Yser's words mingle with the decades of teaching they had undergone. Even their Chaplain, Iktinos, who never removed his skull-faced helmet in their presence, listened to Yser, and found truth in the priest's words.

Yser could feel the power here. He had seen in his waking dreams the legion of warriors in purple and bone, who would take the plans of the Architect of Fate and make them real at last. That Yser should be there when it happened, that he should help show them the way… it would be pride, if he did not feel the Emperor's own hand guiding his thoughts.

'Be strong, brothers and sisters. Refuse to fail in His sight. Fill your veins with faith, disdain the foe, and prepare yourselves. For He will be our salvation, whether they take our lives or not.'

When the sermon was over the flock went about their duties – some to the sick, others to the ship, many of the Marines to their proscribed periods of contemplation when they would reflect upon the principles by which they lived. One approached him – Yser did not have to look up to know his name, for he could feel the power welling up inside him.

'Yser, I would speak with you,' said Sarpedon, the one the other Marines addressed as commander. 'Some of us are… changing. You have heard of Tellos.'

'I am ashamed that some rumours have reached my ears. My few followers hold your warriors in awe, Commander Sarpedon. They are curious, and they talk.'

'We do not know what has happened to him, or quite how he is changing. The details are complex but the chemistry of his body has altered and he refuses to accept his fighting days are over, crippled though he is. And there are others, but more subtle. The bone structure of Sergeant Graevus's hand is changing, and Givrillian says his eyesight is being altered. These are just two of many.'

'If you wish an explanation from me, commander, I must disappoint you. I can feel the presence of the Architect of Fate and, on occasion, I catch glimpses of what he wishes to tell us. But I know nothing more.'

Sarpedon turned to leave, but paused. 'Yser, there is something else.'

'Commander?'

'We have turned our backs on much that we once learned was sacred. We have seen the threat the Imperium itself presents to the right order of the universe. I think that when we realise just how little we know, and how different now are the reasons we fight… it will be much for us to deal with. I am not certain myself what will become of me. The whole universe will change for us.'

'Faith, Commander Sarpedon. There need be nothing more. But I think you know this already.'

'Of course, preacher.'

After Sarpedon had left, his image was burned onto Yser's vision for many minutes. He had never felt such power. Did Sarpedon himself realise what he could become? Could even the Emperor's own chosen warriors ever be truly prepared to do His will? He had seen, in his visions, what they must do – he had seen the world built from corruption, with a terrible intelligence at its heart, which must be cleansed to prove the warriors' worth. Would they be ready? Would anyone?

All his questions had the same answer. *Faith.* There need be nothing more.

* * *

No SUNLIGHT STRUGGLED through the purple-grey clouds on the forge world of Koden Tertius, but they were lit from beneath by the fires of the factory pits. Huge columns of flame, kilometres high, licked out from the exhaust ports bored into the rocky round, scorching the habs and control complexes, roaring with the fury that burned in the forge world's belly below. Most of the planet's habitable structures were set within mountainsides or underground, and the spindly metallic webs that stretched between pylons and mountain peaks were support struts and sensor mounts. A thick gauze of smoke hung in front of everything, making it washed-out and grey, punctuated by the great columns of fire gouting up from the planet's geothermal core.

Tech-priest Sasia Koraloth looked out on this scene through a porthole in the side of her laboratory annexe. She knew that one day she would not think the darkness and fires of her forge world so ugly – such minor aesthetic distractions would be far beneath her when she was so occupied with the masterful logic that was the tool and creation of the Machine God.

Gradually she would be augmented and improved until there was so little of her original body left that her mind could become detached from the outside world and contemplate only the mechanics of reality.

She longed for that day, for this universe was a dark place and only the Omnissiah could make sense of it.

The stillness of her laboratory stirred and a servitor drifted soundlessly in. It was little more than a suspensor unit and a voice box. 'To Tech-priest Koraloth, the wishes of Archmagos Khobotov are to be known. One: that Tech-priest Koraloth is to commune with him on matters vital on the Route Cobalt. Two: that her laboratory and associated facilities are to be cleared and made ready for an examination temporal. Three: that he expects and will receive complete discretion on matters discussed and discovered. Awaiting reply.'

'I shall be there,' she said, and the servitor buzzed away. The idea that Archmagos Khobotov himself should have chosen her... her work here must have been noticed after all. The painstaking reverse engineering of trinkets brought by explorator parties took up all her time, as witnessed by the rows of disassembled and polished components on the work benches of her lab. But she had not thought she had discovered anything worthy of note, or that her diligence and dedication had been seen by any of her superiors.

Perhaps this was it. Perhaps this would mark the beginning of her ascent. Or perhaps it would end in nothing.

The data-mat set into the skin on the back of her left hand flashed up the location of Route Cobalt. She left her dingy lab and hurried through rock-walled streets populated by servitors of all sizes and functions, their only common link the presence of recycled human tissues to form their nervous and muscular systems. There was the occasional tech-priest too – recent initiates like herself and more venerable magi, some with small crowds of apprentices in tow.

Already she was beginning to see humans as machines of meat and bone. Already the underlying logic of the universe fascinated her, and she was increasingly repelled by the patina of corrosion that she had to clean off her technoclaves and data-thief probes every day. One day she would sweep through these rock-warrens with her own apprentices, enduring their unending questions and not caring about any of them. She would at last understand.

Route Cobalt was a little-used channel cut through the mountain to reach a shuttle terminus on the surface. A phalanx of servitors stood shoulder-to-shoulder across the street, before parting to reveal Khobotov himself, lens-eyes glinting within the shadows of his hood.

One day, she would be like that.

'Tech-Priest Koraloth,' said Khobotov in his wonderful metallic drone. 'I give you leave to select your research coven and conduct the rites of reverse engineering as you see fit.'

Something hummed behind her – a cherub-drone, dead-skinned face locked in a serene smile, arms replaced with dextrous mechadendrites that handed her something with great delicacy.

It was a scroll-case, simple and plain, rather longer than her forearm. Then she opened it, and saw what she had been summoned to investigate.

It was a cylinder, the surface of which gleamed with intricate golden circuitry, and which had what looked like impossibly miniaturised gene-encoders set into the hand-grip. A small enough thing, but her experience with pre-Imperial technology told her it was something much more than it seemed. She could feel the power of its complexity flowing through her hands as she touched it.

'Archmagos, what…?'

'It is known as the Soulspear. There was considerable trouble involved in its acquisition. I will expect your preliminary data-sermon within the year.'

Koraloth couldn't take her eyes off the object, even to acknowledge the archmagos. What was this thing – a weapon, a shield, a transportation device – that by its mere presence could project such certainty in her that it was a masterpiece? And could she ever do such a creation justice?

She forced herself to look at Khobotov. 'Why have you chosen me, archmagos?'

'Your lack of status means few will care for your research, and your veneration of me and the values of the Omnissiah I represent mean you are unlikely to betray me. When much is at stake, it is always prudent to make use of the lowly.'

Khobotov swept away and his servitor-guard closed around him, striding away down the Route Cobalt and leaving Koraloth holding the Soulspear.

Lowly? She knew that. But not for long.

There were things not even Khobotov knew about her. The depth of her determination to do the work of the Omnissiah, the brightness with which her goal burned within her. And more besides.

Much more. There were others on Koden Tertius with the same devotion as her, and they shared a bond beyond their common calling. They would be her coven, and with the Soulspear they would begin their ascent to the ranks of the magi.

THE BATTLEMENTS OF Quixian Obscura had burned. The artillery had shelled for a solid week before the assault had begun, and the chemical fires they had lit raged across the crenellated stone of the cyclopean fortress wall.

Sarpedon had clambered from his drop-pod and saw theirs was one of the last pods to fall. Commander Caeon was already dragging his great armoured body over the lip of the nearest gate house, spraying bolter shells into the alien defenders below as energy bolts melted the stone around him. Squad Kallis, to which Sarpedon had been attached, hunkered down into a defensive position ready to cover the attackers who had landed before them. Fifty-strong, they had to take the gatehouse and force open the vast gates below so the storm units in the vanguard of the Imperial army could put these alien heathens to the sword.

Fire swept over them, fanned by the shrieking wind, but they had ignored it. Kallis took stock of the situation – hoary and old with a face that looked as if it had been stitched together out of battered leather, it was his calling to lead the newly-initiated into battle, to test what they had learned as novices. They had all taken part in the brutal live training regimes and fleet patrol duties, but few of them had been thrown into action as thick as it was there.

'I want plasma cover east! Flamer, Librarian, take down that weapons post!' Kallis had pointed towards an emplacement built into the stone where once a defensive lascannon or launcher had stood, but which was now being used by a half-dozen slender-faced aliens to fire a monstrous energy weapon into the backs of the Soul Drinkers ahead.

Vixu had led them in, flamer gouting, Sarpedon behind working up the energy for the Hell. Some within the Chapter's librarium could have cracked open the emplacement with telekenesis or psychopyretics, but Sarpedon's way was to crack open the minds of its crew.

And yet… what had been the point?

The thought in his head was like an intruder. He remembered Quixian Obscura in every detail, as he did every battle in which he had seen action, yet he had never thought any of it pointless. No, he had tried projecting every horror the aliens might fear, and lashed them with gunfire along with the rest of his brother Marines, all the while feeling righteous hatred coursing through him.

But really, what had been the point? After Quixian Obscura was claimed, what had become of it? It was probably just one more vacuous husk of a world run by the greedy and power-mongering, populated by underlings who never knew the futility of their lives. To exterminate the aliens, that was a worthy thing – but when it was done to satisfy the whims of corpulent merchants and lying priests, was there anything truly noble in it?

The thoughts were new and strange. Suddenly, it was brought home just how much the universe had changed around Sarpedon – the deeds which had made him proud now seemed empty and futile, the heroism that propped up a regime of corruption. He tried to shake it out of his head, but it wouldn't go – the nagging voice at the back of his head stayed, bleating that it was all meaningless, that he had fought at the whims of the same self-serving bureaucrats that had tried to butcher his battle-brothers.

He tried, as he sometimes did when he needed to look long and hard at himself, to relive the battle and not just watch it played out in his head. He imagined the sharp-edged wind across the battlements and the reeking sulphuric clouds from the shelling below, the low rumble of shouted orders from a million Imperial Guardsmen and the flickering in the air of a hundred shuriken rounds from alien guns shearing towards him.

Suddenly he was there as the Marines had burst into the emplacement and the energy weapon was a fiery shell, power cells crippled by a krak grenade. From just below the edge of the wall the ambush sprung, aliens with masks and bodysuits carrying glowing power-scimitars, cartwheeling and somersaulting with unholy speed.

It was no good. Sarpedon didn't care – gone was the warrior's rage at the enemy's deceit that had sent him wading into their midst, pumping bolter shells into their unarmoured bodies, cracking necks and splitting open heads within jewel-eyed masks.

A bolter blast caught the closest in the stomach and almost blew it in two – its grace dissolved instantly as it flopped to the ground. In the time it took the bullet to find its mark two more had come too close to draw aim – he slashed at one and it ducked, the other struck back and the tongue of its blade licked deep into his thigh. He stabbed at the head of the first, let it duck, stamped down on the back of its neck with a ceramite boot, felt it crunch beneath his foot.

But this time, living it all again, Sarpedon didn't care. He might as well have been breaking an eggshell or kicking an obstacle out of his way.

When the third staggered backwards, left arm torn off and still held in Sarpedon's hand, he felt none of the holy triumph that had filled his soul that day. When it fell from the lip of the battlements to land, hundreds of metres below, as a shower of bloody fragments, he did not cheer in victory, though he remembered doing so all those years before.

It had been the moment he had truly proved himself on the battlefield. The junior Librarian with the strange psychotransmitter power, whose inclusion in the force had been little more than an experiment, had slain three of the treacherous xenos in close combat and held the rearguard of the assaulting force. He had been clapped on the back and saluted in the victory feast as the fortress burned, and known that he had finally earned his place at Dorn's side. Now it didn't matter. None of it did.

The Chapter archivists had even given him a line in the saga of Quixian Obscura. It had been only his third action since novicehood – Daenyathos's words must have impressed the Marine deeply, they said, for him to follow his creed so exactly. It had been an honour afforded few Marines of his status, but somehow, he just didn't care any more.

He knew that he would look around to see Sergeant Kallis slain by heathen power-blades, and would rally the squad's survivors to butcher the surviving aliens before they could carry their attack into the advancing Soul Drinkers. He knew that he would hear the earthquaking rumble of the gates opening and the cheer as ten thousand Guardsmen poured through to flood the fortress with vengeful steel and las-fire. He had been there, and recalled it all a hundred times over. But it felt different now, and he was distant and uncaring. Brother Marines lay dead – what had they died for? Alien vermin were slain beside them – why waste good Marine lives on them? And the swarming, idiot hordes of Guardsmen below – was there anything for them really worth fighting for, when the Emperor whose name was on their lips as they charged was thousands of light years away, His will distorted and ignored by the men who ruled in His stead?

All this waste. It was a hollow deep within him where his pride should have been.

Caeon, high on the battlements of the gate house and slick with alien blood, turned and fixed Sarpedon with war-honed eyes.

'Die,' he said in the voice of machine spirit *674-XU28*.

Sarpedon shook his head violently and the inside of his cell swam back into view. While Marines never truly slept, in their half-waking rest period they could dream, and there Sarpedon had visited the battlements on Quixian Obscura many times. But it had never been like this. He had never felt such emptiness in the face of battle, where a Soul Drinker should revel in the glory of the fight.

The fires of Quixian Obscura finally died down and he was alone in the cell. The walls were bare aside from the pict-slates for reviewing briefings and reports, and the shelf on which stood his volume of the *Catechisms Martial*. His armour was racked neatly in one corner and his bolter and force staff hung on a weapons rack. There was nothing else in the room, for what need had a Soul Drinker of anything else?

There was so much troubling him that he didn't understand. Seventy years a warrior, and yet what did he really know? He had lost himself in such a cycle of honour and battle and holy anger that he had nothing else. Seventy years, and a hundred battles burned bright in his memory, but somehow they did not fill him with the pride they had done many months before. He looked down on his bare torso and saw the scars from surgery and wounds – a score of scalpel cuts around the edges of his implanted carapace, an ugly tear from an ork's chainblade, the slight colour mismatch of a skin graft and the dozen pockmarked memories of lucky shots. All these and more, and yet he felt that in gaining them he had earned nothing.

A tiny green cursor was blinking in the corner of the ship-comms pict-slate. Sarpedon focused on a retinal icon and the image of Tech-Marine Lygris appeared. He had suffered considerable neuro-trauma during his brush with the machine-spirit, and his facial muscles had been fixed into place with medical staples to stop them from spasming. It looked as if someone else's face had been nailed to the front of his head.

'Commander Sarpedon, we request your presence on the bridge. The serf-crew have picked something up.'

'Something?'

'We have some guesses, but none of us have the necessary clearance. These are some of the highest-level codes we have ever encountered.'

'Enlighten me.'

'Carmine, commander. Level carmine.'

'NOT EVEN OUR most senior tacticians can open level carmine encoding – we'll have to wait for them to come to us, consul, if we are to know who they are.' Vekk was getting the chance to be important for the first time in some months and had his chest puffed out and hands clasped behind his back accordingly. The long-service medals on his chest were probably kept polished just for chances like this.

Talaya looked up from the mostly meaningless data streaming across the screens in front of her. 'Agreed. Preliminary scans suggest a considerable power output potential. I suggest we prime the shields as stated in the standard fleet procedure for the approach of an unidentified ship.'

'And roll out the red carpet in one of the shuttle bays,' continued Vekk. 'Could be a visitor.'

'Very well. Do it all.' Chloure was under no illusions that the decision had been made already – he was barely a rubber-stamp any more. Two fighter wings from the *Epic* were even now showing as tiny tagged blips on the main viewscreen of the bridge, fanning out to surround the new ship and run guard-dog duty. Just in case.

'Comms down!' shouted someone and suddenly the dark blood-glow of the warning lights strobed painfully across the bridge. 'We've lost comms control!'

The security troops at the rear of the bridge stomped into the alert formation as several emergency tech-teams, lower-grade tech-priests and attendant servitors bristling with servo-tools, scuttled out of maintenance alcoves and began prying the panels off comm-consoles.

'They've hijacked our vox-casters and transmission network,' said Talaya tonelessly. 'Interdiction and exploitation patterns.'

'Why? Are they hostile?' Chloure had so far avoided participation in a proper pitched space battle and had no intention of breaking the habit.

'Unknown,' said Talaya predictably, the deep red lights picking out her sharp, precise face.

Vekk jumped down into the sensorium readout pit, sunken into the deck of the *Diligent*, which was populated by a gesticulating gaggle of tech-priests and petty officers trying to interpret the signals pouring in from the ship's sensors. Streams of printouts were spewing from data outputs. 'Here!' yelled Vekk, pointing at a stream of coordinates. 'Get this on screen!'

The ship appeared on screen. And what a ship it was. A bright swell in space, warping the light passing through it so the stars were drawn into long white streaks. The few sensorium traces that Chloure could understand implied the *Diligent* didn't believe there was anything there at all.

'Are they Imperial?' he asked.

'Probably,' called back Vekk from the sensorium pit. 'It may not be entirely good news for us if they are.'

The vox-casters screamed and Chloure tried to cover his ears, too late. He imagined the same sound screeching through every 'caster on every ship of the fleet, but fleet comms were still out and he couldn't be sure.

'Helm control lost,' said Talaya just before the lights went out completely.

The crew were silent. Only the viewscreen still lit the bridge of the *Diligent*, washing the faces of its crew with faint blue-white light.

'In the name of the Immortal Emperor and all His dominions,' spoke a sonorous, throaty voice from every vox-caster in the ship. 'This battlefleet is now under the command of Lord Gorgo Tsouras of the Ordo Hereticus. Your ships are mine, as are your bodies and minds, as tools with which to execute the Emperor's will.'

Chloure could hear the whispers from the petty officers below. In truth, he thought, he had known this would happen all along. Given the nature of their foe, and the principles at stake, it was perhaps inevitable that this would happen. Chloure would have given anything at that moment to be back managing the sector's largest grox farm, anything to get away from the organisation now claiming command of his fleet.

The image on the viewscreen swam as layers of sensor-shielding puffed away from the newcomer ship in layers of shimmering light. Below them was revealed dark, slick metal, beaten into sensor-deflecting triangular plates, with shiny black viewports like slitted eyes and sharp blades of projector weapons stabbing forward from its sleek bat-shape. The twin engine cowlings flared out behind it like fans of steel feathers, and from its sleek belly tiny gunmetal flakes broke off and sprang to life – drone-ships, tiny blue engines flaring as they formed a shimmering necklace of guard ships around their parent.

The ship was completely bare of paint save for one symbol carved in crimson onto its side. It was a simple image, but it was enough to confirm Chloure's fears and freeze the breath in the throats of the bridge crew. Few of them had ever seen it for real, but every one of them knew what it meant, even if only from stories that preachers told them as children to scare them into obedience.

A huge stylised letter 'I', with a sleek-toothed skull at its head.

The Lakonia Persecution was now officially under the command of the Holy Orders of the Emperor's Inquisition.

CHAPTER SIX

A SINGLE SHUTTLE, of the same bare angular metal and with the same sigil of the Inquisition emblazoned on its hull, weaved dextrously through the tumbling rocks of the Cerberian Field. It was unarmed and transmitting a truce-signal, keeping a respectful distance from the Thunderhawks the *Unendingly Just* sent out to escort it.

Sarpedon watched the shuttle approach from the bridge of the *Just*, knowing as soon as the visual became clear that it was an Inquisitorial craft. Chapter-serfs in vacuum gear hauled the docking clamps into place as the sleek craft alighted in the shuttle bay, and hurriedly backed off as its occupants emerged.

Sarpedon waited in the audience chamber, where tapestries of Chapter heroes hung on the age-darkened walls and the flagstones were worn smooth by generations of power armoured footsteps. He watched a holomat image as the shuttle's passengers emerged, always looking with an eye to evaluate potential opponents.

Though the shuttle had come under truce, there was no doubt that the Inquisition's representatives here believed in conspicuous strength. A phalanx of twenty Ordo Hereticus troops marched down the gangplank of the shuttle, clad in glossy dark red combat armour and armed with hellguns. Their faces were masked with veils of scarlet-linked chainmail and bundles of grenades hung at their belts. Towards the back of the group was a figure entirely shrouded in dark grey robes, a large shoulder-mounted hypodermic array pumping murky fluids into its neck.

An astropath, guessed Sarpedon, for rapid psychic communication with the main Inquisitorial craft. Probably an aged and experienced one judging from its stooped, laboured gait.

Flanking the Hereticus troops were two mercenary gunmen. One was a man dressed in battered leather with muscles swarming with gang-tattoos, carrying a shotgun and bearing a bionic eye worth rather more than him. The other was a woman in bulky padded armour, with three pistols at her waist and a burn-scar taking up half her face. Sarpedon had heard tell of the rag-tag miscreants that some less orthodox inquisitors could assemble as field agents and bodyguards, and these two low-lives were in stark contrast to the ordered ranks of Inquisitorial troops alongside them.

At the centre of the phalanx was a man in armour of brass, the barrel chest and gauntlets of his armour imposingly huge. His face was incongruously youthful, sleek-featured and dark-skinned. There was a sword slung at his back with an immense blade, nearly a metre and a half long and half a metre wide, surely too large by far for anyone to wield?

Around his neck hung a solid silver Inquisitorial symbol, a simple and definite badge of office.

There were protocols for this sort of thing. Sarpedon stood at the centre of the audience chamber with Givrillian and his tactical squad at the back of the room, to observe proceedings. The Hereticus troops waited at the opposite end of the room and the visitor strode up to meet Sarpedon.

The man's armour gave him almost the bulk of a Space Marine. The sword at his back still seemed impossibly huge – Sarpedon looked over the man's body and saw there was nowhere another weapon could be concealed.

'Librarian Sarpedon,' said the visitor, his voice slick and cultured. 'I am Interrogator K'Shuk, envoy of Lord Inquisitor Tsouras of the Ordo Hereticus. My master has sent me to convey his demands to you and your men. You have been accused of treachery, heresy by action, and the mutinous killing of the Holy Emperor's servants in the person of tech-guard stationed on the *674-XU28*.

'You will surrender your ships immediately to me. We shall bring in a containment team who will receive all your weaponry and armour. You will be incarcerated and sub-jected to an Interrogation Martial and full Oculum Medicae while you are transported to an Inquisitorial fortress-world for processing. You will co-operate with us in all these mat-ters, and failure to comply in any particular of these demands will be considered an admission of guilt.'

K'Shuk folded his hands behind his back, waiting for the answer.

It was as Sarpedon had expected, as soon as it was clear the Inquisition were now involved. Tsouras would take the Soul Drinkers' weapons away, shut them up in a prison-ship, and use all manner of techniques old and new to get them to con-fess. No matter what the result of the Interrogation Martial, Sarpedon and his Marines would be taken to a planet con-trolled by Inquisitor Tsouras, tried, and executed. A verdict of guilty and the deaths of his men were inevitable, but that was not the worst. To be disarmed and rendered harmless while they were examined and tormented, unable to fight back and defend the honour that was stripped from them, would be worse than death for any Soul Drinker.

The insult was appalling, worse by far than anything the Chapter had ever suffered before. Tsouras and K'Shuk would be well aware of the reply they would get. But still, there were protocols for matters such as this.

'Interrogator K'Shuk,' began Sarpedon, 'The Soul Drinkers do not recognise the authority of Inquisitor Lord Tsouras or any agent of Imperial authority. The Imperium has been shown to be corrupt and self-serving, its actions a mockery of the most blessed God-Emperor's will. It has robbed this Chapter of its due, then moved to destroy us when we took steps to redress the slight, then pursued us in its anger and sent its agents to demand our humiliation.

'Your demands are refused, Interrogator K'Shuk. The Soul Drinkers submit only to the will of the Emperor, and you act only for yourselves.'

'Very well.' K'Shuk's face was impassive. 'Commander Sarpedon, it is my duty to inform you that the Soul Drinkers Chapter is hereby declared Excommunicate Traitoris, to be struck from the annals of history. The Chapter's name will be deleted from the scrolls of honour in the Hall of Heroes and wiped from the memories of the Archivum Imperialis. Your gene-seed will be destroyed and your bodies incinerated so that no more will your blood taint mankind. The Imperium of man turns its back on the Soul Drinkers.

'Confess now, Sarpedon, repent your misdeeds, and it shall be quick for your men. Either way, your lives will end for your sins against the Emperor.'

Sarpedon said nothing. He had known deep down it would happen, but somehow had never accepted it as a possibility. Excommunicate Traitoris. Banished from the human race, cast from the light of the Emperor. Though he and his Marines had learned the true sickness of the Imperium and refused to be a part of it any longer, the concept still filled him with horror. He was Excommunicated from mankind. For so long, there had been no graver fate.

He was horrified, but was also angry that the Imperium would pass such a judgement on those no one was fit to judge. Use that anger, he told himself. Use it, let it keep you sharp, do not turn numb with shock or cold with fear. Stay angry, because you will need it.

K'Shuk reached up the the hilt of the huge sword slung at his back. 'You understand, Commander Sarpedon, your conduct here has revealed you to be a dangerous man and a threat to the stability of the Imperium. The Inquisition cannot allow your sins to multiply with your continued existence. I am empowered by Inquisitor Tsouras to perform your immediate execution.'

Sarpedon had known they would try to kill him, just as they had tried before by launching the Geryon to shell the star fort. It was only logical – he had realised what the Imperium really was, and they would do anything to silence that truth. But now it had come to it, here in the age-hallowed audience chamber of the *Unendingly Just*, he let the anger grow in him again. That anyone would think themselves not just Sarpedon's equal, but his superior, that they could pass a sentence of death on him – that was an obscenity. Daenyathos had written that emotions are the enemy of the common soldier, but for a Space Marine, they were an ally. Use the hate, channel it, turn it into strength.

K'Shuk drew the sword. It seemed impossibly light in his gauntleted hand and Sarpedon's enhanced hearing picked out the faint hum of tiny gravitic motors as the immense blade swung over the interrogator's shoulder. Suspensor units, one in the pommel, one at the tip of the blade. The sword would be light enough to lift with a finger, but utterly unbalanced and so difficult to use that most martial treatises considered such weapons to be useless in combat.

But K'Shuk had been sent here as an executioner, and would be skilled beyond comprehension in the arts of the blade. The interrogator stepped forward, and lunged.

Squad Givrillian and the Hereticus troops didn't move. This was a duel between accuser and accused, and such things were not to be interfered with.

The blade thrummed past Sarpedon's ear, and he could feel the keenness of the edge as it cut through the air. He ducked back and drew his own force staff just in time to parry the blade's backswing.

K'Shuk was skilled to a near-supernatural level, with the kind of speed and finesse that comes from being trained from birth. Tsouras probably had a stable of infants he could have raised as interrogators, and every now and then, he would find one like K'Shuk.

Sarpedon was on the back foot, the blade slicing at him like an arc of lightning, K'Shuk's movements swift and slick. A cut down towards Sarpedon's throat was turned onto his shoulder pad and the blade bit deep through the ceramite, slicing through it as if it wasn't there. K'Shuk dropped a shoulder, span, lashed a reverse cut towards Sarpedon's torso which was parried with a wild swing that left Sarpedon wide open.

K'Shuk span again and this time the sword hit home, the massive broad blade carving up into Sarpedon's abdomen. Red pain stabbed up from the wound, but Sarpedon knew he would survive, knew he would go on fighting. He had taken a thousand wounds, and knew which ones would slow him down.

What was more, he knew how he could win. K'Shuk was lightning-quick and his sword was a weapon of a type

Sarpedon had never faced before, but his skill came at the expense of variety. Whatever ancient fighting system the interrogator followed, it was one which relied on intricate set patterns to allow its adherents to wield the suspensor-blade in anger. There must have been a million variations on a thousand patterns, but they were there in the movements of K'Shuk's feet on the worn flagstones and the bright shapes made by the lashing blade. A half-step back was a cue for a lateral cut, an overhead strike from the force staff was met with a broad circular parry leading into a counter-thrust to the solar plexus. There were basic principles built into every movement, and if Sarpedon could learn them...

Gradually, as Sarpedon met K'Shuk's blows, he saw the fundamentals of the suspensor-blade art. On an upward cut the blade could take flight thanks to its anti-grav units and spiral out of the wielder's hands, so K'Shuk's upward swings were limited. It was difficult to change the direction of the blade suddenly, so every sequence of attacks had to be made up of strikes that flowed into one another – it was fast and no doubt pretty to watch, but it cut down K'Shuk's options. The interrogator compensated with speed, but Sarpedon was fast, too.

Sarpedon reminded himself that though he had never fought anyone like K'Shuk, the reverse was also true. K'Shuk had probably killed hundreds of skilled opponents, heathen aliens and warp-strengthened heretics, but he had never faced anything as deadly as an angry Space Marine commander fighting for his honour.

The wounds were opening fast – a deep thrust right through the meat of Sarpedon's forearm, a lunge that put the blade's tip dangerously close to his secondary heart. The blade was broad and wounds bled terribly in spite of the Marine's rapidly-clotting blood, and K'Shuk could win simply by wearing Sarpedon down with debilitating cuts. Sarpedon's time was limited – he had to break the code of K'Shuk's skill soon, or he would be too slowed by his wounds to stand a chance.

Sarpedon blocked a blow to the side and knew what would follow – K'Shuk had the option of an upward cut that promised a killing strike up underneath the jaw. Sarpedon ducked back and sure enough the blade swept up a hair's breadth from his face.

K'Shuk needed a precious fragment of a second to arrest the blade's upwards motion, turn it and bring it swinging down. In that fragment of time he was open, and Sarpedon struck.

The hit to K'Shuk's stomach didn't penetrate the massive bronze armour, but the butt-end of the force staff left a massive dent that must have ruptured K'Shuk's organs. He was sent him stumbling backwards, blade dragged down to guard. Sarpedon followed up with a lunge over the blade ringing off the armour above K'Shuk's collar bone.

Sarpedon stabbed again, and struck home. The end of the staff passed right through K'Shuk's throat, spearing out through the back of his neck. Sarpedon stepped to the side, reached behind the interrogator, and grabbed the blood-slick end of the staff. He pulled, drawing the whole length of the staff through K'Shuk's neck, until the eagle-winged head of the staff ripped through the throat in a shower of blood.

K'Shuk tried to turn but his spinal cord was in tatters. His legs collapsed and he sent one final accusing glance at Sarpedon as, nearly decapitated, he clattered to the ground. The suspensor blade escaped his grasp and fluttered like a leaf to the floor where, with delicate slowness, the monomolecular blade sunk up to half its length in the flagstones.

There was only a faint oozing sound as K'Shuk's blood flowed. The rest was silence.

Sarpedon holstered the force staff at his back. He looked around the Hereticus troops and K'Shuk's warband, and the Marines of Squad Givrillian, arrayed around the room. This, it occurred to him, could be awkward.

'Cut the fuel lines of their shuttle,' he said. 'Set them adrift.'

He could hear the fingers easing off the triggers of the Hereticus troops' hellguns.

Squad Givrillian moved to surround the troopers and acknowledgement runes flashed in Sarpedon's vision to confirm that serf-labourers were heading to cripple their shuttle.

He could have killed them there and then, with the guns of Squad Givrillian chattering against the wall of the audience chamber as the Hereticus troops and scum of K'Shuk's warband died for daring to set foot on a Soul Drinkers' ship. But they would have shot back and Sarpedon could have lost good Marines.

And, besides, there were protocols for this sort of thing.

IN THE LECTURE auditorium on board the *Diligent*, a holo display projected a room-filling image of the Cerberian Field, the asteroids a grainy haze of orange specks. The battlefleet of the Lakonia Persecution was represented by a host of blue icons at one edge of the large circular room. Between the fleet and the edge of the asteroid field were two dagger-shaped purple icons, the *Gundog* and the *Unendingly Just*, heading rapidly through the air towards the field.

Many of the *Diligent's* bridge crew were seated around the room, watching the display as it re-enacted the scene several months before as the Soul Drinkers had first been chased to the edge of the Cerberian Field.

Well separated from the crew was Inquisitor Tsouras, watching impassively from the back of the room. The inquisitor was grudgingly admiring of the skill the Soul Drinkers showed in keeping their cruisers ahead of a large and well-provisioned battlefleet for so long. Very grudgingly.

Twin shockwaves burst at the nearest edge of the cloud, sending the tiny orange specks tumbling out of the way. The daggers flew into the space created as the obstacles closed again behind them, just as several blue squares pulled up suddenly as the field knitted itself back together around the Soul Drinkers' cruisers.

'Gravitics torpedoes?' asked Inquisitor Tsouras.

'We do not believe so,' replied Senior Tactician Talaya, pausing the holo display. 'We suspect the torpedoes the Soul Drinkers used were improvised. Probably assault torpedoes loaded with munitions – the blast would spread in all directions.'

'Their flying was reckless indeed, then.'

'Insane,' agreed Talaya. 'It is likely they suffered minor damage once within the Cerberian Field but it is impossible to verify. The extremely hazardous nature of the manoeuvres evidently reflects the desperation of their flight.'

'Presumably your forces have been unwilling to replicate such hijinks, consul?'

'Their strike cruisers are much more athletic than any of our craft, my lord inquisitor,' said Chloure, with a touch of nervousness he couldn't hide from Tsouras's sharp ears. 'It would have been suicide for us to follow them.'

'Of course.' Tsouras didn't like Consul Senioris Chloure. He was wet, gutless, and utterly out of his depth. A decent commander, being aware of what was at stake here, would have sent an expendable ship in to test the waters and make sure there was no way a direct assault could have been carried out. There were enough captains and crews here that were only good for sacrificing.

It was good he had arrived when he had. An operation like this was more than capable of disintegrating completely. He had seen it happen, and incompetence had been the most common justification on his lips as he gave the order for execution.

Not this time, though. This time it had been treachery in the extreme, Grand Treason Imperial. And for the first time, his order had not been carried out. His executioner, Interrogator K'Shuk, had not returned or made any communication of success. It was a shame, for Tsouras had harboured some hopes for K'Shuk, who was as cold-blooded a killer as Tsouras had ever come across. But at least there was no doubt now as to what Commander Sarpedon and the Soul Drinkers really stood.

'As you can imagine, inquisitor,' continued Talaya, 'our current tactic is to enforce a blockade while exploring alternative options. It is very probable to our tactical corps that privation will eventually render the enemy defenceless, allowing us to begin a campaign of pioneering through the Cerberian Field to reach them.'

'And in this time there will be no actions taken by the enemy that could possibly catch you by surprise?' said Tsouras. 'No way in which they could bring the fight to you? Perhaps when your crews were so dogged by fatigue and indiscipline that their threat reactions will be slow and confused? Such things have happened to fleets far greater than this. They become lazy. Indecisive. Space Marines, on the other hand, do not. They will be razor-sharp right up until the end, when they are exulting over the burning corpses of your ships.'

Talaya was silent. Chloure squirmed uncomfortably, and Tsouras reflected that he had little reason to let the consul survive. 'We act now, and decisively. No matter how many we lose, every second we wait gives them further advantage. They do not sleep, gentlemen. They need to eat or drink only rarely, and even if for whatever reason they have no supplies they will have the underlings of their Chapter to live upon if necessary. They are not an ill-led rabble. They will not decide to break for your benefit. We must break them ourselves.'

'It is debatable,' said Talaya, apparently unflapped, 'whether entry into the Cerberian Fields will even be possible for either main craft or assault waves.'

'There is no debate, tactician. The Marines had to blast their way in without gravitic warheads. We do not have to suffer that hardship. My ship carries more than enough gravitic weaponry for our present purpose. In any case, having seen the quality of leadership here I shall be taking command of the operation personally. Every captain on this fleet will have every available assault wing fully bombed up and ready to launch. Perhaps you can claw back some semblance of dignity by refraining from screwing it up this time.'

Heresy. Why did they not understand? It was like a plague of vermin, near-impossible to eradicate unless you were prepared to destroy much of what you were trying to save. Once a world was tainted by unchecked heresy you could cover every square metre in smouldering craters a man's height deep, and still there would be some dark-thinking traitor ready to poison what was left. Inquisitor Tsouras knew this because he had tried it himself.

And now there was a Chapter of Marines that had fallen from grace, and these officers dithered here like nervous children while the cancer grew. At least the sentence of Excommunicate Traitoris had given him free rein to do whatever he wanted to bring the Soul Drinkers to the Emperor's justice.

He stood, drawing himself up to his full augmented three metre height. All of it, the skeletal elongations, the bronze ram's head shoulder pads, the thick studded leather cloak and tabard and the blank yellow-grey eyes, had been affected solely to intimidate weaklings like these. They were simple, cosmetic augmentations, far from the complex bionics that the Mechanicus were rumoured to have developed – but they seemed to work. Only Tactical Officer Talaya seemed unperturbed, from which Tsouras concluded she was a rather more stupid woman than her codex-quoting speech suggested.

He swept out of auditorium dramatically, leaving the tactical holo display frozen with the battlefleet's blips impotent outside the orange sparks of the asteroid field.

Marines. Soul Drinkers, no less, who by all accounts had never been the most genial of the Emperor's servants. He couldn't wait to see the faces of his allies and enemies when he brought a thousand grizzled heads back to the Ordo Hereticus conclave-sermon. This would make him. They would teach his example to interrogator pupils as how one man might defy a legion of the galaxy's most murderous warriors, if only he has faith and justice on his side.

But there was still much to do. He had to ensure the gravitational warheads were loaded and primed. They were delicate and ancient technology, not to be trifled with. He would not let carelessness rob him of his finest moment, not when the loss of his executioner had already illustrated the venom of the foe.

Even now, his astropathic choir would be transmitting the sentence of Excommunicate Traitoris throughout the Imperium, and not one inquisitor would be ignorant of the importance of Tsouras's mission. Behind him, the battlefleet's useless officer class would be watching him and quaking, knowing that to obey his every word might just be to secure their lives. They would be lost, frightened, disposable. Those few who knew anything of the Inquisition would have only heard tales of implacable crusaders, prepared to torture and kill whole populations at once, who let nothing stand in the way of the moral purity of the Imperium.

Most of those tales were true.

Inquisitor Tsouras smiled.

THE ORDERS WENT out immediately, with the highest Inquisitorial authority. The attack craft of the Lakonia Persecution were fully armed and fuelled within three and a half hours of Tsouras's declaration, ranked up with engines idling and crews on board, ready for their call signs to be broadcast.

The first bomber wing launched from the flight decks of the *Penitent's Wrath*. It was not anticipated that there would be any interceptors to oppose them, but they went with full fighter escorts anyway, just to be sure.

They were followed by dozens of other swarms, from Avengers and Praetorians with their bellies swollen with bombs, to control craft trailing salvoes of semi-smart torpedoes, to the delta-winged gloss-black nightmares that swept from the flight bays of the Inquisitorial ship itself. The flight assets of the Lakonia Persecution had not been accurately totalled, and the number of fighters and bombers launched was uncertain. Estimates made it a thousand, give or take.

The first waves, though they did not know it, were to test the density of the Cerberian Field. Their engines clogged with micrometeorites and their hulls were punctured by ice fragments or buckled by the gravitational forces of superdense ferrous asteroids. The fleet logistitians under Tsouras's orders used the data of their death throes to calculate where best to strike. When a hundred had been sent crashing against the wall of broken rock, the gravitational salvo erupted from the wedged nose of the Inquisitorial ship.

The torpedoes' size indicated their age, for they were ancient indeed, to the degree that the secrets of their manufacture had long since been lost. They had cost much both in funds and favours. But Tsouras had known they would be worth it.

Slowly, with the nearest bomber wings banking wildly to avoid them, the shoal of impossibly valuable torpedoes detonated and the edge of the Cerberian Field began to collapse. Ripples of electromagnetic power drew the tumbling rocks closer and closer in a gravitational trap. Clumps of asteroids dragged into the epicentres in turn drawing in more matter until a chain reaction had begun, the field contracting into single lumps of rock.

More warheads exploded further in and the effect travelled deeper, melting a path towards the Soul Drinkers' position in the heart of the asteroid field. Attack craft followed in their wake, and many had to sight their target visually as their navcogitators broke down amidst all the interference. To them, the *Gundog* and the *Unendingly Just* were barely visible, picked out by the sharp-eyed as twin patterns of silver against dark purple against black. They were both on all-stop so there was no engine flare to lock onto – the bombers would have to get in close and do things the old-fashioned way.

'WE ARE HERE for a reason, children.' Yser's voice was inspirational as ever, this time quieter and more reflective. 'The Architect has seen to it that all we do for good or ill has led us to this point. If we are to die here, we know it is because He has chosen it as our punishment or reward.'

It was first lesson of the Architect of Fate. Any who dedicated their life to following His plan would be sent through the Architect's weaving of fate to the end they deserved. Yser knew he had done his best, for the Architect had spoken to him and he had done all He asked – founded his church, protected his flock, enlightened His chosen warriors. If he was to die here, it was for the good. It was what should be.

The first bombs that hit sounded like rolls of thunder deep in the heart of the *Gundog*. The men and women of the flock shook with both fear, and with the cold caused by the reduction of life support to give the ship the lowest possible energy profile. Vapour steamed off them as they huddled in the armoury chamber, Yser at their centre, the focus of their faith.

The armoury housed no weaponry any more, and it was one of the toughest parts of the ship. But that would not save them if the ship's reactors went critical or there was a massive structural failure. Or the power could shut down completely and they would be entombed here, to freeze or suffocate.

And if, by some miracle, the ship was lost but they survived, they would each die a thousand heretic's deaths. Their crime, of associating with Space Marines declared Excommunicate, would doubtless require the ritual purification of their flesh before they died. They would be unlikely to remain sane under such punishment.

Could he bear that? Yser had undergone many privations as a poor man, a thief and a prisoner, but was there a point when he would give up on his faith again? Would he renounce the Architect of Fate and admit to the foulest of treacheries under the torturer's blade? He honestly didn't know. It was said that a man would be known by the manner of his death – Yser hoped his was quick and sudden, in a flare of nuclear light or the lethal shock of the void.

The child closest to him was crying quietly. A tough one, this, because she had to be to make it this far. But this was too much.

'It's alright,' he said, hoping he sounded like someone who could be believed.

'It's because she can't do anything about it,' said the child's father, who had buried her mother in the garbage spoil of the star fort a year earlier. 'You can deal with anything if you can fight it. But this… we all feel so small.'

'Faith,' said Yser quietly. 'There is nothing else.'

Another hit, and was followed by the huge crunch of an explosion which seemed to boom from everywhere at once. The shockwave threw many people to the floor and for a minute there was no sound, only a ringing white noise.

They were going to die. They were all going to die.

'THAT'S IMPOSSIBLE.' TALAYA'S face was lit by the ghostly green glow from the screens of data arrayed in front of her. Chloure had begun to think of it as her natural appearance. 'The route's been Interdictus for six hundred years.'

'Then what is that?'

Half the bridge viewscreen was taken up with the best image they could bring up of the *Gundog*, a blurry fractured purple-black shape pocked with tiny orange-white explosions as the first waves of bomber swept over it. The other half was full of complicated wavelength readouts that fluctuated violently. Chloure wasn't an expert in these things, but every officer on the *Diligent's* bridge had told him the same thing. It was the signature of a warp route, the entry/exit point of a rare and relatively stable path through warp space. It was pulsing with the energy of a large volume of shipping hurtling through it. This was unusual because all the charts said there was no warp route there.

'I don't know,' replied Talaya. It was the first time Chloure had ever heard her say those words. Perhaps she was human after all.

'Alright. Will Tsouras know about this?'

'Probably more than us,' said Vekk. 'Of course, you know what it is.'

He paused for effect. Chloure glared at him.

'Six hundred years ago they closed warp route 391-C after

something woke up inside it and ate a transport convoy. They lost about three hundred thousand souls. Their astropaths tried to get a signal out but all was left were a few echoes. Walls of flesh, they said. Walls of flesh closing in.'

'Why wasn't anybody told?'

'The route's been dead for centuries, consul. Besides, it's just some mariner's tale.'

'Only now it's got hungry again?'

'Could be, consul.'

Then one of the logistitians screamed and a shower of sparks burst from the mind-impulse link plugging him into the sensorium banks. He spasmed violently before the mind-jacks were thrown free and he convulsed to the ground. Petty officers barked orders and a couple of menials hurried forwards to drag away the smoking body. The rest of the logistitian corps did nothing, locked into the world generated by the sensor arrays.

'What now?' asked Chloure, trying not to gag at the wafting reek of charred skin.

'Feedback,' said Talaya. 'Something big.'

For the first time in six hundred years, warp route 391-C opened.

FIGHTER COMMAND ON board the *Penitent's Wrath* was a vast sheer-sided circular pit of iron in which rows and rows of flight controllers, lexmechanics, statisticians and tech-adepts were arrayed along rows of sensor screens and holo displays. Most of them never left. Some of them had been born there.

Snatches of comm-link transmissions from the fleet's attack craft rang through the air. The attack wings were in a ragged state – some were executing attack runs on the Soul Drinkers' cruisers, others were on their way into the maw of the Cerberian Field or limping half-strength back towards the fleet carriers. Every crew out there had been thrown into shock in the last few seconds as an immense warp rift had opened up just outside the Cerberian Field and started disgorging starships.

'–out of nowhere... starboard retros out...'

'Claw leader to all points! Break formation and bank fleet-ward, Now!'

'–down, going down, going...'

Tsouras strode between the mem-bank columns and star maps. All he heard were the sounds of a crisis beginning. Naval Chaplains intoned the death-rites over comm-links to crews who were bombed-up and burning. Vacuum seals popped, men screamed, igniting fuel ripped through hulls. Where there had been heartless efficiency just a few minutes ago there was now confusion and desperation.

Every display showed the same thing – a ship, yet to be identified – had emerged from warp route 391-C insanely close to the edge of the Cerberian Field, and charged into the waves of fighters heading for the Soul Drinkers position. Close-range ordnance and turret fire had torn through several bomber wings before they had the chance to break and scatter. Now the forward wings were trapped in the field, enclosed in the tunnel of rock created by the gravitic warheads, with a swift and well-armed ship blocking their path. Tsouras could hear the weapons battery-fire scything through them as they died. The attacking ship was huge – bigger than the *Penitent's Wrath* itself. It was fast, too, and loaded with close-range weaponry. Its pilots must be maniacs and its gunners trained to the point of inhumanity.

A hundred stories of heroism and disaster were unfolding at the edge of the Cerberian Field. Tsouras didn't care about any of them. The *Unendingly Just* and the *Gundog* were still intact. All other considerations were secondary.

'Lord inquisitor!' Hrorvald, captain of the *Penitent's Wrath*, emerged from the clouds of incense. He was a large-jowled man of greater bulk than had been allowed for in the naval uniform he wore. 'Disastrous! That route had been closed for hundreds of years! Hundreds! I have briefed my command crew on a full attack craft withdrawal followed by a fleet action…'

Tsouras held up a taloned hand to stop him. 'I want everything in space, captain. Everything. These could be pirates or opportunists, but they could also be heretics come to aid the enemy. If the Soul Drinkers escape then all is for nought. When the targets are confirmed destroyed, then they can regroup.'

Hrorvald looked around at the officers following him like pupils, looking for support. 'Our men will be butchered, inquisitor! We cannot just–'

'You know, Captain Hrorvald, it almost sounded as if you were questioning my authority. I do so hope you can prove me wrong.'

A satisfying wave of fear passed over Hrorvald's red, flustered face. 'Of course. Just for information, you see. They won't survive.'

'That has been allowed for. Now, I assume you are here to tell me the identity of our newcomer.'

'They're jamming us, lord inquisitor, and most effectively. But… well, the visuals are very sketchy, but our tactical officers have hazarded a guess. It's rather far-fetched, you see, and I… well, the long and the short of it… it's the *Carnivore*, inquisitor.'

There was silence, broken only by the faint background of prayers and screams.

'I see,' said Inquisitor Tsouras at length. 'My orders stand. Destruction of the *Gundog* and the *Unendingly Just* supersedes all other concerns. Including survival. Get to it, captain.'

THE CARNIVORE WAS followed by the *Sanctifier's Son* and the *Heavenblade*, both smaller but still deadlier than any ship of the battlefleet. The *Heavenblade* swept out towards the battlefleet, which was hastily organising a defensive line. Out of position and with attack wings already out, there was nothing they could do to prevent the *Heavenblade* closing. It drove an arrow-straight course towards the *Deacon Byzantine*, ignoring the nova cannon shot from the heart of the battlefleet that almost clipped it to starboard.

The *Son* launched a fighter wave of its own and the tract of void where the battlefleet's assault waves were regrouping became a seething cauldron of combat. The *Son* itself dived in, taking bomber hits all over, swatting fighters aside like insects.

'TARGETS, SIR?'

Captain Trentius paced the bridge deck of the *Deacon Byzantine*. 'Nose. Underside, around the cargo ports.'

'It's increasing speed, sir. Close to ramming velocity. Should we…'

Trentius glared at his master of ordnance. 'Your job is to acquire the targets I require, Bulin. Not tell me what I should and not shoot at. Nose, underside, cargo ports.'

'I just thought that a hit on the engines might...'

'Do a lot of thinking, do you, Bulin? It doesn't suit you. Get me targets and load torpedo tubes for a tight spread.' Trentius rounded on his chief of the watch. 'You, get those lazy buggers out of the boarding parties and get them on damage control detail.'

The *Heavenblade* loomed large, head-on, her bone-coloured prow like the point of a knife stabbing towards the *Deacon*.

'Perhaps,' came the slickly educated voice of Flag-Lieutenant Lriss, 'we should consider our options. Given the nature of the enemy and their known tactics, it might be the case that–'

'They are not going to board us, Lriss,' growled Trentius. 'They are not going to ram us or do any of the things they would normally do.

'Imagine, Lriss, your mission was rescue and not destruction. You want to get in and out as fast as possible. You are facing a numerically superior but low-quality enemy already in disarray. None of their ships are worth anything to you so there's no point boarding. You're not desperate to bash up a good ship with ramming. What do you do?'

Lriss knew better than to venture an answer.

'No?' Trentius took a thick cigar from the pocket of his nicotine-yellowed uniform. He lit it with a flourish. 'A fire ship, Lriss. You send a fire ship.'

The *Heavenblade* slewed sideways suddenly, presenting the side of its armoured hull.

Trentius saw it was painted dark purple, with the huge chalice symbol emblazoned in gold.

The torpedo spread hit and a tide of fire billowed from the underside of the *Heavenblade*. The entire lower decks must have been filled with nonoxidising fuel, the kind that didn't have to react with air to burn. A cloud of flame boiled off like the outer layers of a dying star, sprays of structural debris stabbed out through the massive rents opened by the torpedo blasts.

'Burn retros, and I mean now,' ordered Trentius as his bridge crew observed the spectacle. 'She's going to go critical.'

And she did. The screen was pure white for half a minute, the plasma cores hitting critical temperature and expanding catastrophically, before they collapsed to leave a shattered husk of a spaceship.

'Reload ordnance, move to engage, sir?' asked Lriss with a smile.

'Don't be bloody stupid, Lriss. You think we can actually fight them?'

THE BATTLE BARGE *Carnivore*, along with the strike cruisers *Heavenblade* and *Sanctifier's Son*, were more than enough. But they were joined by more – the interceptor cruiser *Animosity* scattered the battlefleet's flank merely by driving forward with its lance arrays charged. The carrier-fitted battle barge *Mare Infernum*, meanwhile, sported so many assault boat docks that they covered it like scales – the prospect of the ship launching a boarding action was so truly ghastly that the battlefleet fell into general retreat, Tsouras be damned. With the flaming wreck of the *Heavenblade* in their midst and the highest-quality ships now bearing down on them, the ships of the battlefleet were in utter disarray.

Only the *Deacon Byzantine* held its nerve, refusing to follow the rout though it was alone and effectively surrounded – as if it knew the new fleet had no intention of attacking it.

It was the *Mare Infernum* that fell back to escort the *Unendingly Just* from the Cerberian Field, battered but unbowed. Sarpedon watched from the porthole in his cell as the battle barge's near-inconceivable bulk gradually slid past against a backdrop of debris. The *Gundog* would be limping alongside the battle-scarred *Sanctifier's Son* – the first bomber wings had blown two of the main engines clean off the *Gundog*, but it was a tough cruiser and it would make it with help.

The communication flashed through the comm-systems of both cruisers.

'Fleet command orders to Librarian Sarpedon. Return to fleet ground immediately. Conclave Iudicaris to commence. Out.'

Simple and blunt. But it told him everything he had expected.

BY THE TIME the Lakonia Persecution's attack craft had begun to regroup at the edge of the Cerberian Field, the *Gundog* and the *Unendingly Just* were far out of their attack range, escorted by a vast and dangerous phalanx of ships into a warp route from which no bomber wing could hope to emerge. The Lakonia Persecution was scattered and useless, its attacking assets milling in confusion, its cruisers and battleships hopelessly out of position.

Warp route 391-C was contracting even as the *Animosity*, the rearmost of the fleet, slid through its shimmering gate and into the maelstrom of the immaterium. With dangerous rapidity the warp gate closed behind the cruiser, sealing off the new fleet from realspace.

This new fleet – two battle barges and three strike cruisers, enough to fend of the mightiest fleet – had been sent by Chapter Master Gorgoleon of the Soul Drinkers Chapter. Sarpedon had under his command three companies of the Soul Drinkers. Now the other seven had sought them out to get some answers.

CHAPTER SEVEN

SARPEDON LOOKED OUT into space, seeing for the hundredth time the blackness that hid the Soul Drinkers from prying eyes. He knew they were far to the galactic north-east, past the Qisto'Rol system and the warp storm they called the Emperor's Wrath, on the indistinct boundary where Imperial space gave way to the Halo Zone. But he knew this only from his memory, for there was no frame of reference in sight.

It was a dark sector. Nebula clouds that could swallow whole systems formed a featureless backdrop through which only the brightest stars could shine. It was abandoned and quiet, and it could take decades for anyone to find the Soul Drinkers here. It had been marked by the Chapter millennia ago as somewhere they could lie low in case of emergency. An emergency such as this.

Closer was the Soul Drinkers' fleet, the size of a sector armada, formed almost entirely of lightning assault craft – some pregnant with pods and boarding torpedoes, others weighed down with lances and nova cannons. The *Leuctra* was hanging in the blackness beside them, and on the other side was the *Carnivore* still bearing the scars of the Cerberian Field.

A battle barge was one of the most deadly creations that mankind could wield. And there were two of them here, detailed solely to guard the darkship on which Sarpedon and his Marines were being held. It was with a curious pride that Sarpedon realised what important prisoners they were. The rest of the Chapter considered them rebels whose conduct had brought a stain of suspicion to the name of the Soul Drinkers, and rogue Space Marines were not to be trifled with.

The rest of the fleet could be seen glittering further out. A silver diamond was the immense training platform on which novices and Marines made practice drops and dummy assaults, live ammunition and hard vacuum combining to force combat discipline into the brothers. The strike cruisers looked like a shoal of fish in the distance – amongst them would be the *Gundog* and the *Unendingly Just*, undergoing flame-cleansing by the servitor purge-teams in case Sarpedon's Marines had brought the stain of corruption back with them. Furthest away yet huge and bright, was the *Glory*. Immense: half as big again as a standard battle barge. Its hull was smothered in gold and the great gem-chased chalice on its side was visible even from the darkship.

For good or ill, Sarpedon's fate would all be decided on the *Glory*, in the hallowed gathering hall of the Chapter elders and the chambers of Chapter Master Gorgoleon. Perhaps Sarpedon and his Marines would be exonerated, perhaps they would be killed. But it would be easier now either way, for they were at least amongst brothers at last.

Sarpedon turned from the porthole and headed back towards the light of the autosurgeon, bright on the dim infirmary deck. The stained metal slab on which Sergeant Tellos lay gleamed with new blood as the sanguiprobes peeled back the skin of his abdomen and sunk thin shafts into his organs. Apothecary Pallas, standing over him with two serf-orderlies, watched the complex readouts on his holoslate flicker with the flow of information. The orderlies both had their mouths and ears sutured shut – they had been supplied by the Chapter infirmary and were not permitted to speak or to hear tainted words.

'Will he live?' asked Sarpedon.

'I am beginning to suspect that life and death are relative terms, commander,' replied Pallas. 'He will probably soon cease to be alive in the normal sense. But I do not think he is about to die, either.' He pressed a finger into the skin of Tellos's chest – it was greying and translucent, and beneath it could be seen the twin hearts beating and the tough third lung rising and falling. The skin puckered and rippled, like something gelatinous. 'His body chemistry has changed and his biorhythms are very erratic. He has sudden floods of energy.'

'And his mind?'

Pallas shrugged. 'As far as Iktinos can tell, he is convinced he will fight again. No matter what we do, he keeps training. A Marine with no hands is like a mockery of a warrior, but sometimes has me convinced. I don't pretend I can know what he is thinking.'

The probe array, spindly like a skinny metal hand, rotated and a finger with a long transparent tube leading from its tip stabbed down into Tellos's stomach. A thin line of red ran up the tube as the blood was drawn out. 'The gene-seed itself shows no abnormalities, so the source of the changes is a mystery. I would endeavour to find out just what was causing all this but our facilities here are limited. We've given samples to the Chapter apothecarion in case they can help, but they won't.'

'They wouldn't. Not while there is chance they would be aiding traitors.'

The probe withdrew and began knitting Tellos's skin back together. But the blades of the tiny manipulators kept slipping through the altered tissue and the join was left ragged. Slowly, the ripped skin began to flow together, as if melting, until there was no trace left of a wound.

'The other battle-brothers are the same,' Pallas was saying. 'There is no obvious cause for those who are changing. Yourself included. You haven't eaten for weeks now – there should be some degradation in energy levels or muscle mass. But there's nothing.'

'I feel stronger.'

'It's hard for us to judge.'

'I mean psychically. I felt it on the Geryon platform. The Hell has never gone that deep, Pallas. It has served us well, but never that well. Yser says it is strength born of faith, now we have seen the truth. The Architect's blessing.'

Tellos stirred on the slab. The anaesthetics couldn't even keep him under for an hour at a time – as if something had woken inside him that struggled and fought any attempt to make him lose control. Sarpedon had forbidden him to be imprisoned, as he had committed no crime, and it was all Pallas could do to keep track of the assault sergeant. Several attempts had been made to take the twin blades Tellos had jammed into the stumps of his wrists, but he had always found new ones. It was eventually decided that it was best to leave them as they were.

'In any case, commander,' said Pallas, 'it can hardly put us in good stead. There will doubtless be an investigation of great thoroughness and any abnormalities will be noticed. But without facilities or power, there is little I can do.'

Power. The dim light and lack of working equipment on board the darkship was deliberate – no simple brig existed that could hold a Soul Drinker against his will, and so a whole ship was set aside for incarcerating Marines under investigation. Its plasma reactors were crippled so it could only travel latched on to another ship, preventing its use for escape, and the weapons systems had been torn out. Power was limited to the most basic life support requirements. This darkship had once been the strike cruiser *Ferox* – now it had no name.

A vox-icon flickered at the back of Sarpedon's eye.

Chaplain Iktinos's dour voice sounded in his ear. 'Your Chapter Master requests the presence of Librarian Sarpedon. A shuttle will be sent. You will come alone.'

'Tell him I will be ready.' Sarpedon switched to another channel. 'Sergeant Givrillian, make ready for diplomatic escort duty. We are going to the *Glory*.'

CHAPTER MASTER GORGOLEON adhered to one rule in war: the rule of despair. If an enemy despairs, if he does not believe there is any hope left, if he has seen his comrades dead and maimed by the hand of invincible foes, he has lost. When he is in such a state he cannot resist – whether he is to be captured or killed, or merely broken, there is nothing he can do. Battles are won when one side is rendered incapable of fighting, and that is best achieved by the massive and unrelenting infliction of despair. This was one of Daenyathos's prime tenets for the conduct of war, and it was one Gorgoleon had turned into a science. It was why he was Chapter Master. It was why he so rarely failed.

Despair was usually created by inflicting fatal or mutilating damage on an enemy, but there were other ways. That was why the walls of his private chambers had been stripped out and replaced with carved marble slabs depicting his life as a warrior – here he was, kneeling on a pile of tau dead, back-to-back with the long-dead Chaplain Surrian as the pulse shots blazed down at him. Here he strode into the halls of the Archfoul and looked it in the eye as bolter-fire poured into its corrupt flesh. Again, in the jungles of Actium, and again, in the shattered streets of Helsreach. Gorgoleon's entire chanson had been carved out here, an epic of his life chiselled into the stone.

He didn't really care for it personally. There had been careers more glorious than his in the long history of the Soul Drinkers, and he needed no picture-book to remember it all. But it inspired a measure of awe in those who saw it and, in the right circumstances, he had hoped it would inspire despair.

A servitor shuffled along the long gallery that led to Gorgoleon's chambers, past the carvings of his early heroics. 'The shuttle approaches,' it said in its the thin, feeble voice. The servitor had once been a Chapter serf, who had become too aged and decrepit to be of further use and had been rebuilt as Gorgoleon's personal valet. Gorgoleon took pains to make the menials in his presence especially wretched.

'Convey permission to board the *Glory*. Have Sarpedon leave his escort squad in the shuttle bay and send him to my presence immediately. Ensure he is not rested or fed.'

'Yes, Lord Gorgoleon,' lisped the wizened servitor, and limped off across the gilded tiles of the chamber.

Gorgoleon settled his armoured bulk into the ivory chair. Pict-slates set into the hardwood of his desk flashed images of Sarpedon and the officers now apparently under his command. He called up the Chapter command citations from Quixian Obscura, Karlaster Bridge and the Haemon Forest. Sarpedon had turned battles, buying time when all was lost, sowing confusion to crack open impenetrable positions. Gorgoleon switched to a list of active commands. There was only one – Van Skorvold Star Fort, joint command with Caeon. Librarians rarely took such roles in the Soul Drinkers, where combat-hardened regular officers were favoured to lead from the front. Caeon must have trusted Sarpedon's competence and integrity to have selected him. But everyone, even veterans like Caeon, can make mistakes.

He went further back, calling up Sarpedon's earlier record. Sarpedon was something rare – possessing both the mental qualities needed for selection as a Marine, and the great psychic potential required to use his powers without danger of possession. The unusual nature of his talents had not dissuaded the Librarium from taking him on, almost as an experiment.

As a novice his adherence to the tenets of Daenyathos had been something of note. As a new Marine he had proven capable of using his psychological advantage to take on opponents far superior in number. His should have been a fine career, an example of Daenyathos's teachings applied exactly to the practice of war. But instead, something had gone wrong.

Gorgoleon could find nothing that suggested instability or incompetence. In other circumstances he would have considered Sarpedon a good model for novices – an ideological soldier who wielded the beliefs and traditions of the Chapter like a weapon.

Yet he had rebelled. He had spilt the blood of his allies. His words to the Inquisitorial envoy he had slain were the most damning of all – it seemed Sarpedon had turned his back on the very Imperium the Soul Drinkers were supposed to shepherd towards greatness.

Gorgoleon was good at his task. He had rarely had cause to bring a fellow Marine into his chambers and subject them to that same despair he believed in, to see if they would break down and confess to some sin. And this time, the whole Chapter was at stake – nothing really scared him, but even he had felt the tension in his gut as he heard the ugly words of Inquisitor Tsouras grinding from the astropath's throat.

He had heard the stories – Astral Claws, Thunder Barons, Chapters who had fallen from grace and become everything they feared. The Soul Drinkers would not be added to that list. Not while he still lived.

The brass-banded doors slid open and a protocol servitor thrummed in. 'Into the presence of Dorn and the Emperor's sight, announcing Librarian Sarpedon.'

Sarpedon did not look like a man who had suffered months of privation. The darkship had been stripped of all supplies, and the few the Marines had brought with them had been squandered on the filthy rag-tag prisoners they had insisted on bringing with them. As Sarpedon strode along the gallery, Gorgoleon saw he seemed as healthy as he had been on the eve of battle.

The chambers were designed to force anyone entering to walk past the great galleries of Chapter history and Gorgoleon's own deeds. Sarpedon was not distracted. He looked utterly determined.

Gorgoleon, still seated behind the desk, waited for Sarpedon to reach him, letting the silence last as long as possible. 'Librarian Sarpedon,' he said at length, 'there are matters we must discuss.'

Sarpedon stood proudly, hands behind his back, no fear in his face. 'Indeed there are.'

'Perhaps you have not yet been made fully aware of the consequences of your actions. Several months ago I received a communication from Inquisitor Tsouras on behalf of the lords of the Ordo Hereticus. We were commanded to down our weapons and submit ourselves to an Inquisitorial purge. We refused, as Dorn himself would have done. And then we ran.'

'My Lord Gorgoleon, I too have had dealings with–'

'We *ran!*' yelled Gorgoleon, standing and slamming his fist into the desktop. 'Do you understand what you made us? We were fugitives! Us! The best the Imperium can produce, and we ran like criminals! They would have taken our weapons, Sarpedon. They would have stripped us of our armour and entombed us in some prison-rock until they had decided not to kill us. We would have been treated like vermin, Sarpedon! They forced me to order this fleet to flee, as if we were nothing more than cowards. I cannot begin to describe the humiliation – to run when every word Daenyathos ever wrote extols us never to retreat. But that was not the worst, Sarpedon. That was not the worst.'

'It is a complex matter, lord–'

'No, Sarpedon, it is very simple indeed. After the insult of demanding we hand over our guns and walk in chains, I received a second communication far worse than any I have seen.'

Sarpedon paused, perhaps struggling to force out the unholy words. 'We were declared Excommunicate Traitoris.'

'Excommunicate!' Gorgoleon spat out the word. 'We are the lowest of the low, Sarpedon. We are the worst of the worst of the worst. I sent you out with Caeon to restore a terrible injustice, and you return bearing only dishonour such as this Chapter has never beheld. They can kill us on sight, Librarian! They can remove any trace of us! They can end our existence!' Gorgoleon stood suddenly, stopped for a moment, let his rage boil down. 'What happened to you, Sarpedon? What could have made you so abhor the beliefs you held dear that you let your brothers fall so far? Why did you fire upon your allies, and defy the highest authorities of the Imperium? Why did you stain us all with your taint?'

'Why?' said Sarpedon evenly. 'Because I believe, Lord Gorgoleon. I believe in justice and dignity, and in the will of the Emperor. I believe in the best of men being given their due. I believe that those who would deny us that due are our enemies, because they defy everything that makes us great. I am accused of shedding the blood of my allies. But the Imperium is no ally of mine.'

Gorgoleon shook his head, 'No, of course not. Because that vagabond preacher says so. Dorn's flesh, even your Chaplain kneels at his sermon! Sarpedon, you had such strength of mind. But now you have brought foulness upon us all. You understand, there is only one option left open to me.'

Sarpedon was silent. There was no trace of repentance in his face – he knew full well what Gorgoleon would have to do.

'The Ordo Hereticus want me to hand you over,' said Gorgoleon. 'With your head on a spike and your brothers burned to ash, they would rescind the order of Traitoris. I would be rid of a traitor and the Inquisition would have their heretic to burn. After enough purging and sacrifice, we might be free of the taint again. Hand you over, and we would eventually be free once again.'

'But you have not, Lord Gorgoleon.'

'No. Why would that be, when you have committed the gravest sins a Marine ever can?'

'Because only my brothers may judge me.'

Gorgoleon would have dearly loved to have thrown the Librarian to the wolves for the dishonour he had wrought. But he could not. Though his hate was cold in his veins, there were certain principles that made him a Soul Drinker and not just another man. 'Only your brothers. The Inquisition knows nothing of the standards a Marine must maintain, or the beliefs he holds dear. We are but one step removed from the Emperor, Sarpedon, for His blood ran in the veins of Dorn, and Dorn's in ours. No one can judge you but a fellow Marine, before the eye of the Emperor.'

'Such were the words of Daenyathos, Lord Gorgoleon.'

'And I intend to follow them. You have led us into a terrible place here, Sarpedon, but there is no excuse for failing to honour our traditions. The trial shall be in the Chapel of Dorn, in three days. The Emperor will lend strength to the arm of the righteous man.'

'I am ready, Lord Gorgoleon. I do only the Emperor's will.'

'So will I, Sarpedon. For the greater the sin, the greater the judge. And I am the greatest man of this Chapter. For your crimes, you must face me.'

'So it shall be.' Sarpedon was impassive. Was it denial of his treachery? Or was there genuine belief there? Had he really convinced himself that stabbing his allies in the back had been a right and honourable thing? Impossible. It was either mendacity or delusion.

'No fear? You know what I have done. You can see it carved into the walls of this chamber. You heard the tales when you were just a novice. I need just to think it, and you will be dead. You are tough, Sarpedon, but you're not that tough.'

'I have faith, Lord Gorgoleon. There need be nothing else.'

Gorgoleon fixed the traitor with a hard stare – but there was no fear there, or even anger at his imminent death. What had happened out there? Had the loss of the Soulspear really done so much to addle his mind? They said he was having visions, and there were even hints of physical corruption amongst them.

It was the only way. He had to die, and justice had to be done.

'Three days,' he said quietly. 'Hope that Dorn will forgive you, for I will not.'

Sarpedon turned and left, ignoring the intricate carvings of Gorgoleon reaping fields of the dead and pouring bolter-rounds into hordes of xenos.

He could have been so much, thought Gorgoleon. Something unique. And in a way he was, for the Chapter had never known shame such as Excommunication.

But the Soul Drinkers would not fall from the Emperor's light. Not while Gorgoleon was still alive. But before he could begin to heal the wound of dishonour, Sarpedon would have to die. And though he was a brother Marine, Gorgoleon would enjoy pulling him apart.

THE SHIELD-RITES TOOK many hours if they were unabridged. Normally a cut-down version of the rites was conducted in battlefield conditions, when time was at a premium on the eve of battle. But before a warrior set off on a crusade, or when he had ample time to contemplate the task ahead of him, they were to be observed in their entirety.

Sarpedon had nearly finished. In the half-light of the dark-ship his eyes picked out the sheen on the ceramite of his armour where he had scrubbed off the grime that had built up over the last months. It was easy to miss where it was ground into the seals and plate joins, and the gold was worse – it took so much care to keep it from tarnishing, and each bullet scar needed delicate reworking.

Sarpedon took a breath of the incense as he fitted the lens back into the eyepiece of his helmet. He wouldn't be actually wearing it, of course, but these rites were about preparing the spirit of the armour and every piece had to be included. He always felt strangely raw out of his armour, as if the armour was his skin and without it he was naked and bleeding. The faint stirring of the circulated air rasped against his back, and even when he breathed it seemed cold and harsh.

He placed the helmet to one side, satisfied that it was ready. Every piece of the armour – the greaves and kneepads, thigh-pieces, gauntlets, backpack, and all the rest had been checked by Lygris and cleaned by Sarpedon. At last, before the fight, it was a sacred thing again.

The door of his cell hissed open. Sarpedon heard the padding of bare feet and knew who it was.

'Father Yser. Thank you for coming.'

'Anything for the flock, Lord Sarpedon. There must be many things troubling you.'

Sarpedon turned to face the priest – without his matted beard and layer of grime he looked healthier in spite of the conditions. 'Yser, there is every chance I will die today. This has been the case for me many times and I have no fear of it, but… there are things I would like to know.'

'Ask.'

'I have seen things, Yser. In my dreams. I have seen a world steeped in filth, with something terrible at its heart calling out to me. My body is changing, too. I do not eat, and things have begun happening to my bones that Pallas cannot explain. I have never been afraid of anything, Yser, but this is different. I need to know what all this means. Why am I receiving these visions, and why am I changing?'

Yser smiled. 'Lord Sarpedon, we have all felt it. This is the hand of the Architect of Fate. The Emperor is preparing you. He has shown you the world you must be overcome to prove your worth. The trial you must undergo today is the same – the Architect saw the injustice done to you and turned it into a test that will make you stronger.'

'I have followed the will of the Emperor for many years, Yser,' said Sarpedon. 'I have never felt anything like this.'

'Because you never knew the truth, Sarpedon. You followed a lie. But now you know the truth, and you are at last truly doing His will.'

If it was true… the idea that he might actually feel the touch of the Emperor was more than Sarpedon could really comprehend. How many had been done such an honour in the ten thousand years since the Emperor ascended to the half-life of the Golden Throne? None?

'But none of this will matter,' Yser continued, 'if you are dead. Can you win this fight?'

'Gorgoleon is the finest warrior this Chapter has produced for centuries, Yser. Before, I would have said I had no chance of defeating him. But everything is different now.'

'No, Sarpedon. Everything is the same as it ever was. The only thing that has changed is you.'

Sarpedon stood and picked up the massive barrel chestplate, with its winged chalice wrought in gold and the collar where the aegis hood would lock. 'Thank you, Yser. Tell my brothers I shall be armed and ready, there is no need to keep them waiting any longer. And Yser?'

'Lord Sarpedon?'

'They will bring me my force staff. Bless them for me, father, and wish me well.'

IT WAS WHISPERED between the brothers, and spoken aloud only by the Chapter's higher echelons, that Dorn was the inheritor of the Imperium.

There had been twenty primarchs created by the Emperor as templates for the superhumans that would conquer the galaxy in His name. But there were dark forces watching Him and meddling through mortal tools, and the primarchs were born flawed. Fully half would be revealed as traitors in the fires of the Horus Heresy. The others were tormented vampires, hot-blooded butchers, barbarian thugs, power-hungry tyrants. All passed on their flaws to the Chapters who bore their gene-seed, and inflicted them with some stain of dishonour that was never spoken of, yet which had started wars.

All except Dorn. For the Emperor was wise and just, and outwitted the dark forces to make one of His sons the true model of perfection He had intended. Though Marines carrying the gene-seed of other primarchs would die rather than admit it, Dorn was the best of them all. He did not crave power, only justice. He fought not with savagery or malice, only with honour. His legion excelled in all things – doughty defence, merciless attack, cunning stealth and everything in between, skills which existed to this day in the many Chapters formed from the Imperial Fists.

Yes, Dorn was the best man who had ever lived save the Divine Emperor himself – by following only Dorn's example, the Soul Drinkers could ensure that they, too, would be nothing but the best. At the heart of the Chapter was Dorn, his words and deeds burning as bright as they had when he was alive. Matters of the greatest gravity were conducted before the gaze of Dorn, who watched from his halls of judgement in the afterlife, so he might see how his sons followed his example of justice and righteousness in everything they did.

And so it was that the Chapter Master and the traitor met in the Cathedral of Dorn in the heart of the battleship *Glory*, to settle the Chapter's greatest crisis in the only way they saw fit.

GORGOLEON IN FULL battle-array was as fearsome as Sarpedon had remembered. His armour was polished and gleaming in the light of a thousand candles, the crest of Rogal Dorn bright on one shoulder pad, the golden chalice glinting on the other. Gorgoleon still wore the bone-carved crux terminatus around his neck, from the days long before when he had worn one of the Chapter's few suits of terminator battle armour. The ceremonial armour he wore now was the same bulk as Sarpedon's, but shone with artificer's craftsmanship and the constant attention of the Chapter's Tech-Marines. One hand was massive and pendulous with the power fist he wore – the fist had a built-in power field which, when switched on, would let the Chapter Master punch through walls and tear through tanks, and certainly dismember Sarpedon with one good shot. The field could be flicked on and off at Gorgoleon's whim, leaving his hand dextrous one second, destructive the next.

In the centre of the vaulted cathedral, Gorgoleon waited as Sarpedon was marched in flanked by a six-Marine guard. Sarpedon had left his bolter for the ritual combat did not allow for guns – his sole weapon was therefore the force staff which would have to serve its master well one more time.

The Soul Drinkers were arrayed all around the cathedral, exercising their right to witness the honour-combat that was a tradition as old as the Chapter. Rogal Dorn himself looked down upon the scene, a titanic figure in stained glass rendered on the window above the altar. A faint gauze of incense hung far above, and the whole cathedral was bathed in the warm, pulsing glow of candlelight.

The place was quiet, the assembled Marines hushed to respect the few moments before the fight. This time was dedicated to the watching Emperor, because that was why this combat held the central place it did in the traditions of the Soul Drinkers. Now, more than ever, He would be watching, because He would be the true judge here, and His will decided the victor.

Then the moment was over. Sarpedon's guards stepped back and joined their battle-brothers around the cathedral. An ancient Chaplain, one of the very few who had survived long enough not to end his days on the battlefield, stood forward on servo-assisted limbs and intoned the ritual words.

'Lord High Emperor, to whose plan our brothers are bound, and Rogal Dorn, he whose blood is our blood. Observe with us this tradition, lend Your strength to the arm of the righteous, and through victory show us Your way.'

The Chaplain stood down, Gorgoleon activated the field of his power fist, and the fight had begun.

Sarpedon ducked Gorgoleon's first blow, but he realised too late he was supposed to. Gorgoleon's kneepad soared up and into the side of his face, snapping his head back. The cathedral's interior whirled as Sarpedon staggered – the vaulted gothic ceiling, the stained glass face of Dorn looking down fiercely, the rows of purple-armoured Marines that turned the nave into an arena.

He could feel their eyes on him, watching every move, fascinated and appalled by the magnitude of what would be decided here. Even a non-psyker could have tasted the tension in the air.

A lesser man would have flailed blindly. A Marine could think the world into slow-motion and see the next blow before it was struck – and so Sarpedon caught Gorgoleon's follow-up strike on his forearm, felt the ceramite buckle under the Chapter Master's strength, stepped sideways and brought his force staff up to parry the power fist uppercut. The power field and force-circuit clashed and a great shower of sparks erupted, pushing both men onto the back foot.

Gorgoleon was smiling. He knew he would win. The massive power fist flexed its fingers and Sarpedon could see the hundreds of golden rivets struck into its surface – one for every foe of note it had despatched.

'Give in, traitor,' said Gorgoleon, not even out of breath. 'We could make it quick for you.'

Marines in the crowd were yelling – demanding a fast end or a long and bloody one, making claims to parts of the dead traitor's corpse. Disciplined as they were, there was nothing like a good honour-scrap to get their blood rising. They said it was older than the Chapter itself, as old as Mankind – two men settling a matter of the deepest honour, armed with their favoured weapon, in holy combat ended only by death. So sacred an act was it that the Emperor himself would give strength to the fighter who was in the right, and the transgressor would be struck down by righteous power.

The Emperor knew. The Emperor was watching. And through this honour-combat, the Emperor would act.

Sarpedon stabbed with the butt-end of his force staff, aimed deliberately wide so Gorgoleon would dodge into the strike – but Gorgoleon had fought a thousand foes on a hundred worlds and turned the blow aside. Sarpedon realised he was left wide open as Gorgoleon shifted his weight, barged forwards, caught Sarpedon full-on and bowled him backwards.

The Soul Drinkers cheered as Sarpedon tumbled down the steps, down amongst the hardwood pews. All cheered save the separate section of the crowd – Sarpedon's Marines, brought here to watch their treacherous leader die.

When he was dead, they would follow.

No. It would not end this way. If Sarpedon lost here they would parade the few remaining body parts through the *Glory*, so the serfs and novices could see what happened to traitors, even as the Marines of Sarpedon's three companies were put to the sword. That would not happen. No matter how impossible it seemed, Sarpedon would survive.

Time slowed. Gorgoleon's bulk bore down on him, framed by the stained glass window at the far end of the cathedral and the crowds of watching Marines all around. The power fist's field was a halo of lightning, Gorgoleon's eyes flashed with triumph.

They would kill his battle-brothers, and Yser's flock alongside them. The Architect of Fate would be forgotten. The truth would die out and the Soul Drinkers would return to serving the whims of evil men.

Again, something deep inside him spoke. It would not end this way.

With a speed he didn't know he possessed, Sarpedon grabbed the nearest pew and wrenched it from its fittings, swinging in into the falling body of Gorgoleon, swatting him aside like a fly. Wood splintered as the Chapter Master crashed through the pews and hit a pillar.

They were shouting with anger now. They were hissing and yelling for his head.

If they wanted it, they could damn well come and get it.

Gorgoleon was quick but Sarpedon was quicker now. He strode over Gorgoleon's prone form and grabbed him by his arms, lifting him up and slamming him into the pillar at his back. Shards of stone flew and Gorgoleon's head snapped back and forth with the force.

'You dare call me traitor?' shouted Sarpedon. 'I am the only true man here!'

Gorgoleon's body slammed into the pillar again and a fracture ran up the stone surface.

'You are slaves to corruption! You are puppets of greed!'

Suddenly Gorgoleon's free hand was at Sarpedon's throat, and the two men's eyes met – frenzied, fanatical, all semblance of discipline gone. They were the eyes of men fighting for the survival of everything they believed in.

'Wretch!' snarled Gorgoleon. The power fist's energy field roared into life and Sarpedon dodged backwards as the fist's gauntleted fingers threatened to tear a chunk out of his torso. Gorgoleon grabbed the collar of Sarpedon's breastplate with his other hand and headbutted him square on the eye.

Sarpedon reeled. He sensed the battle-brothers had broken ranks and were swarming closer now, a baying crowd just metres from them, a wall of huge purple-armoured bodies. They would tear him apart.

Ha! They could try.

Gorgoleon's backhand swipe could have ripped Sarpedon in two – he turned just in time and it caught him on the back, throwing him into the crowding Marines. Armoured bodied pressed in on him as he clambered to his feet, expecting the pendulous weight of the power fist to tear through his body any moment.

Sarpedon recognised the men around him and realised he was among his own battle-brothers now, if only for a second. Dreo and Givrillian helped Sarpedon to his feet and spoke a few encouraging words. They had been stripped of their weapons, but they could still help him for their very presence gave him strength. He would survive.

His brothers. They had fought all these years, only to find they were fighting for a lie. He felt their anger, as the same anger raged inside him. He would use it, as Daenyathos had taught.

Purity through hate. Dignity through rage.

Gorgoleon hurled Dreo aside and the crowd parted to give the combatants room to fight.

Both were bruised and bleeding. Neither would ever give up. Gorgoleon's fist would be death if it got a good hit in – but Sarpedon's force staff could punch through even Gorgoleon's artificer armour if the Librarian timed his mind's focus with the blow. They ducked and struck, parried and dodged, the crowd following them as the fight flowed across the cathedral's flagstones. The ancient place, its peace usually broken only by the Chaplains' fiery words, echoed to the crunch of cracking ceramite and the cheers of the assembled Space Marines. The stink of sweat and blood mingled with the incense, and the candles guttered with the shock of the might brought to bear.

Sarpedon could feel the blood crusting around his eye, and knew the hit to his back had cracked his rib-plate and ruptured at least one of his lungs. Gorgoleon was bleeding from a gash to the cheek, but if he was suffering internally he did not show it.

Sarpedon's anger. That was the key. What had set it all off? Why had there been such bloodshed on the Geryon? Why had the inquisitor's executioner met with such a savage refusal? Sarpedon had been willing to meet death rather than back down, and his battle-brothers had followed him. Why had they done that? What had made their actions so extreme?

It had to be anger. It was the only force strong enough. But was it just the loss of the Soulspear that had driven them to such excesses? To tell the truth, Sarpedon had hardly thought about the Soulspear at all in the last few months. Its loss felt more like one thread of a whole web of injustice.

What could he tap into that would give him anger enough to win? He had to think quickly, for Gorgoleon would surely kill him soon.

Sarpedon realised his concentration had slipped when Gorgoleon suddenly jinked behind him and there was an arm around his throat.

Gorgoleon hauled Sarpedon into the air, hoisting him high above the heads of the cheering Marines. The soaring vaults of the cathedral ceiling span before him as Gorgoleon ran towards the altar end of the nave.

Sarpedon struggled. It didn't work. Gorgoleon reached the altar and lifted Sarpedon high above his head.

'For Dorn!' he bellowed, and hurled Sarpedon through the stained glass window.

The world turned into razor-sharp shards of colour. An iron floor slammed into him and Sarpedon felt something else rupture.

No. Don't go under. Not yet. Not when there is still hope.

He saw startled, young faces staring at him, their scalps newly-shaved, implants raw. Novices.

He was in the Hall of Novices, where the Chapter's new recruits gathered to contemplate the traditions of the Chapter and the magnitude of their task in becoming full Space Marines. Sarpedon had spent untold hours here as he was honed into someone fit to wear the chalice of the Soul Drinkers. Statues of saints and Chapter heroes glared sternly down from alcoves in the grey walls and fat prayer-drones hovered, belching incense from their bulbous bodies.

The purple-robed novices scattered, clutching copies of the *Catechisms Martial*. They must have gathered to pray for their Chapter Master – but they had never thought they would be blessed with witnessing the combat itself.

Sarpedon grabbed his staff and hauled himself to his feet. He could feel he was bleeding internally and his inner breastplate of fused ribs was shattered. His system was cutting out the worst of the pain but he knew he was badly hurt.

And for a second he was back on Quixian Obscura, an alien neck snapping in his fist, feeling a terrible futile emptiness...

He had fought across a hundred planets and been savagely wounded dozens of times. He had seen battle-brothers dead by the score and killed enemies by the thousands.

Why? Why had they died? Why had he killed?

Gorgoleon vaulted through the frame of the shattered window and landed nearby. The other Marines were swarming into the Hall of Novices, eager to watch the kill.

The servants of the Emperor had died on Quixian Obscura, on the star fort and the Geryon platform. And all across the Imperium – on Armageddon and Ichar IV, through the depths of the Sabbat Worlds, Tallarn and Valhalla and Vogen. At the Cadian Gate they had died, in the hives of Lastrati, on the plains of Avignon, and on sacred Terra in the final acts of the Heresy – millions of Space Marines and untold billions of men had given their lives to protect the sanctity of the Imperium, and yet the Imperium was built of lies.

But that was not the worst of it.

Gorgoleon's strides seemed slow and loping. Sarpedon could feel it, the power Daenyathos had written of – the sacred anger that drove a man's feats beyond the limits of possibility. It was filling him, coursing through his body and the aegis circuit. Sarpedon could feel the light of the Architect of Fate shining on him, and knew that there really was hope.

Because he knew what had been boiling at the back of his mind, something so terrible that he had not dared contemplate it. At the heart of all that futile death and meaningless war, the Soul Drinkers had fought braver than their brothers, kept purer than anyone, striven to be the best there was.

But they had won only shame, for they had held the decadence and corruption of the Imperium together. They had thought they were following Dorn's example with fanatical zeal, little knowing that all this time...

Gorgoleon's fist swung in a massive uppercut. Sarpedon caught it with the staff, turned it aside, and ripped the staff's head deep into Gorgoleon's torso.

'All this time,' yelled Sarpedon, 'we were nothing!'

He grabbed Gorgoleon by the arm and threw him through the wall of the Hall of Novices, sending him tumbling into the dormitories and study-cells beyond.

Had he ever been this strong? No, it was the Emperor, the Architect of Fate, filling him with such power that it felt like he could hardly contain it. Sarpedon strode through the shattered wall and saw Gorgoleon, battered and bleeding, pulling himself to his knees. The spectre of panic crossed the Chapter Master's face. He had never faced anything like Sarpedon. No one had.

What did Gorgoleon fear? He feared *failure*.

And so, the Hell.

Barren, scarred rock lay beneath their feet. Above was the pure black of space, the stars swollen and dying. Deformed alien craft streaked across the star field and warp storms opened immense weeping wounds in reality, bleeding form-less hordes of Chaos out into the universe. It was a galaxy lost to the alien and the daemon, cold and evil, sucked dry by the foes of humanity. It was an image calculated to horrify the stoutest Imperial servant, a place where all their efforts had failed.

The sound was the worst. The cackling of alien slavemas-ters. The gibbering of mindless daemons. The distant scream of a dying mankind. Even Gorgoleon's face registered shock at the horror around him.

Sarpedon had never gone this far, never constructed a whole world of fear out of the Hell. But he knew that noth-ing less would serve against Gorgoleon, and he felt the Emperor's strength inside him, fuelling him until his psychic power was a white-hot star inside his mind, its power stream-ing out into the Hell. All that power was focused on Gorgoleon himself – the Hell was for him and Sarpedon only, utterly real to them but only a faint haze to the battle-brothers watching them.

'You can't win with witchcraft, Sarpedon!' shouted Gor-goleon against the din of a suffering universe.

Sarpedon could feel the power growing, building up inside him so he felt fit to burst. It pushed against his skin and the bones of his altered skeleton. He was full of fire. The power was ready to explode out of him.

Gorgoleon clambered to his feet and swung again with the power fist, gouging great rents from the ground. His face streamed with blood and his teeth were gritted – his was the face of a man confronting death, as he had many times before. Every last gramme of the Chapter Master's strength went into the assault, battering at Sarpedon, swiping the stabbing force staff away, desperately trying to keep the Hell around him out of his mind by letting himself fill with rage. But Sarpedon couldn't be beaten back – there was a boiling sea of fire in his veins, and the hand of the Architect of Fate was upon him.

The two Marines ducked forwards and locked, face to face, for a split second. Gorgoleon's face was lit from beneath and Sarpedon realised that light must be streaming from his own eyes, such was the massive build up of power within him. It rose impossibly high as the ceramite of Gor-goleon's armour fractured within his grasp – it was too much for him to contain, the screaming in his ears too great to stand, the fire inside him too vast to bear.

There was a shriek of tearing armour and the cracking of bones. A great burst of light erupted all around as energy discharged from Sarpedon's body. There was a bolt of pain through his legs and then something he had never felt before – growing, splitting, changing.

Suddenly they were back in the wreckage of the study-cells. Gorgoleon lay where he had been hurled against the cell wall, unable to disguise his horror. There were thick lashes of blood up the walls and scraps of purple ceramite scattered all around.

Eight segmented arachnoid legs jutted from Sarpedon's waist, chitinous, jointed, and each tipped with a wicked talon.

The pain was gone. The Hell was gone; he didn't need it any more. Here was the blessing of the Architect of Fate – a new form, swift and deadly, a symbol of how he had thrown aside all that had imprisoned him. Sarpedon reared up on his hind legs, fully four metres high, and crashed down onto Gorgoleon. The two front talons speared the Chapter Master through the chest and lifted him high into the air. Sarpedon hooked his fingers into the shoulder joints of Gorgoleon's torso armour, stared up into the glazing eyes, and pulled.

The power. The majesty. Sarpedon had never felt this strong before.

Gorgoleon's body tore in two above him, raining blood and coiled organs. Sarpedon cast the flailing remains down onto the floor of the cell, breath heaving, ears ringing.

The din in his ears died down. There was silence, broken only by the steady drip of the blood spattered across the ceiling and running off Sarpedon's shoulder pads.

He looked around and saw the Soul Drinkers were crowded in a circle around the bloodstained wreckage that remained of the cells. Gradually Sarpedon's hearing returned and above the dripping of the blood and the coiling of the smoke, a thousand voices grew louder and louder, filling Sarpedon's soul.

They were chanting.

They were chanting his name.

CHAPTER EIGHT

THE WARP WAS a dark and terrible place, a realm where fears and emotions were made real, where the nightmares of men found form, and evil things lived. There were malevolent forces that called themselves gods, and mindlessly violent predators. There were no safe paths through the warp, and only the guiding light of the Astronomican beacon and the skills of the Navigator caste could bring a ship home.

The risks of travelling the shifting ways of the empyrean were offset by the vast distances that could be travelled in a matter of hours, so that ships which sailed the warp for a few days could make several years' worth of distance in real space. But inevitably, when ships departed the safety of reality and ploughed the waves of the warp, some did not return.

Worse, some returned changed.

Ghost ships. Prodigals. Craft which had been gone sometimes thousands of years, suddenly spat back out into real space. The terrible forces of the warp could twist their structures or weld lost ships together, and sometimes – the worst times – they brought something back with them. Their original names forgotten, these ships were known as space hulks.

Sarpedon couldn't tell how old this particular space hulk was, but it must have been older than any he had heard of. It was not the first he had seen, for the Soul Drinkers were suited to storming hulks and destroying them before their inhabitants could pose a threat. But it was the most ancient, and by magnitudes the biggest.

His half-arachnid form let him clamber along the walls and ceiling, so any foe he found would suffer a moment's disorientation in which Sarpedon could strike. This particular part of the hulk was Imperial, as witnessed by the aquila and devotional texts on the bulkheads. It had been an Imperial Guard hospital ship, with wards running its whole length and a huge quarantine and decontamination sector in the stern. It was also in a sensor-shadow, a part of the hulk which had been veiled from the fleet's intensive life-sign scans. Which meant it had to be searched the old-fashioned way.

Sarpedon rounded a corner and looked down from the ceiling at the ward. It was perhaps a kilometre and a half long. Centuries ago the rows of beds and equipment stations had been lit by unforgiving strip lights, but now the lights were dim and the beds were mouldering. Shadows gathered too dense for even Sarpedon's eyes to pierce.

He dropped down onto the floor and flipped the closest couple of beds with a talon. The layers of grime had built up over the centuries – which was good, for it meant nothing had been here to disturb them.

'Sarpedon to control, waypoint nine reached.'

'Acknowledged, Lord Sarpedon,' came Givrillian's voice over the vox. Sarpedon had been happy to appoint Givrillian as the mission's tactical co-ordinator, where his level head would be put to best use. Givrillian was back on the *Glory* with the HQ, while Sarpedon led the search on the hulk.

Sarpedon recalled the four extra eyes that had opened in Givrillian's facial scar since the victory on the *Glory*. If they had bothered him, he hadn't shown it.

A couple of bulkheads down one of Luko's squad emerged, bolter at eye-level, sweeping the area for anything that moved. Three more of the fire-team followed. Luko himself would be at the far end of the ward with the rest of the squad.

'Anything, Luko?' said Sarpedon.

'Nothing,' came the voxed reply.

The squad moved into the ward in scattered formation, gradually moving down its length. There were trolleys of medical equipment standing here and there, and cabinets set into the walls containing jars of unguents and chemicals. A couple of autosurgeons were stooped over screened-off beds, their many blades tarnished, power feeds corroded to nothing.

'Luko?'

'Lord?'

'Why did they leave the equipment?'

Millions of creds' worth of medical gear, abandoned. More than that, if something untowards had happened in the warp then the crew would have tried to evacuate, probably into the quarantine decks or saviour pods. They would have at least taken some of the medicine and surgery gear with them, to treat the worst of the patients. It made no sense.

Unless whatever happened had been so sudden they had no warning before they died. In which case every bed should contain a human skeleton.

Sarpedon ran up the wall and onto the ceiling, splaying his chitinous legs to put his face close to the surface.

No scratches. No stains. He moved further, looking for any signs that something had been alive in here. Could attackers have used the air vents? Unlikely, given the number of sterile filters in the ventilation systems. What, then? And if something had taken the bodies, where had they gone?

Where were they now?

'Givrillian? I need data on the air filtration for this place.'

'Yes, commander. We don't know how old that ship is but we will see what the mem-banks can say.'

Sarpedon flicked to the squad frequency. 'Luko, stay alert. I think we've got something here.'

'Still no contacts, commander.'

The patients and crew, the Sisters of the Orders Hospitaller and the Guard Medical Corps – they were only human, and they could be manipulated like all humans. They could be herded like cattle into a slaughterhouse, and then...

'We've got something, sir,' said Givrillian. 'Hospital ships derived from that class had separate filtration systems for the wards, the command decks, the quarantine zones and the operating rooms. To prevent cross-infection.'

That was it. And it meant the attackers could still be here.

Sarpedon ran along the ceiling, the hooked talons of his legs moving him faster than even a Space Marine could run. At the end of the ward was the operating suite, where a pair of autosurgeons would have performed delicate procedures on the most badly wounded or, more likely, the most important patients. It was separated from the ward by a heavy pair of airlock doors. The edges of the doors were clean. But there was no other way.

'Luko! I want a fire-team with me, now! The rest, stay where you are, fire support pattern.'

'Yes, lord!'

The lead fire-team stomped up behind Sarpedon. Three Marines: Mallik, Sken and Zaen, with Zaen toting Squad Luko's flamer.

Sarpedon jabbed the talons of his two front legs into the gap between the doors. He forced them open, and realised they did not resist nearly so much as they should have done.

The airlock beyond was clear. The doors into the operating suite were set with glass panels but they were opaque with filth. Sarpedon drew his bolter and gestured for Vrae to take up position at his shoulder.

Sarpedon dropped a shoulder and barged through the doors, feeling them buckle under his strength.

The floor was crusted with excrement and the walls streaked with it. Against the walls were piled bones, some crumbled and grey with age, others gleaming white. Eye sockets stared blindly from the mounds of putrescence, fingers and teeth were scattered like maggots of bone. The autosurgeon arms were black with gore and filth where something had perched on them while it fed.

Warning runes were blinking at the back of Sarpedon's eye. The stench here was so strong and infectious it could have killed a normal man, but Sarpedon's armour and implants were blocking it out. For this he was grateful.

The attackers had cut off the air supply to the ward, or perhaps polluted it beyond use. The crew had moved the patients into the operating suite where the separate air supply should have kept them alive a little longer. Except that, packed into the operating room, they had been a sitting target, unable to run or fight back, when the predators came.

Herded into a slaughterhouse.

But not all the bones were that old. Some were of bodies
that had decayed thousands of years before, but others were
new. Had the inhabitants of this hulk been preying on backwater space lanes? There were tales of how treasure-hunters
would board hulks in the search for cargo or archaeotech –
but there were very few tales of them getting out again. Or
perhaps the attackers had found some way of attracting ships,
or even hunting them down?

Sarpedon took a step further into the room, talon crunch-
ing through an aged ribcage. He looked up at the ceiling,
trying to see some way they had come in. The vents had been
undisturbed, and they had not used the main airlock doors.

He realised it just before the first one attacked. It ripped
through the disposal hatch set into the far wall, scattering
sparks and debris. Sarpedon caught the flash of pulpy grey-
beige flesh beneath a glossy black exoskeleton, a pair of tiny
black eyes, a mouth like a mantrap. Claws lashed out and
knocked off Sarpedon's aim as he put two bolter-rounds into
the wall behind it.

Genestealer. A four-armed, parasitical predator – if it took
you down you could look forward to an implanted pupa and
a messy death. That was if its claws didn't tear you apart first.

Bolters chattered but the thing was fast – it picked up
Brother Mallik by the face of his helmet and smashed him
through the autosurgeon, scattering tarnished blades. Sarpedon swept up along the ceiling and stabbed down with his
staff from above, spearing the stealer through the back. He
reached down and grabbed it by the throat, hauled it up,
flicked his wrist and felt the gristle in its neck snap.

A genestealer, in close combat. Sarpedon had always
known he was formidable in battle, but had he ever been that
strong?

'Flamer!' he yelled, dropping the foul alien corpse. Zaen
was already at the opening and poured a gout of flame down
the waste chute. Something let out a gurgling scream and
thick brown smoke billowed up.

The stealers had come up from the disposal deck, where
medical waste and the bodies of those who died on the operating table were sent. That was how they had got in – it made
sense, really. Waste was ejected into space and the hatch

would be an obvious entry point for a predator like a gen-estealer. Maybe they had been there for months before taking over the ship, breeding down there amongst the automated incinerators and corpse-dumps. The hospital ship might well have jumped into the warp as it was assaulted, hoping to remove the aliens from real space. It was brave, and would have worked had the ship not become part of the immense space hulk.

'Sarpedon to control. Contact, xenos confirmed. Gen-estealers. Send fire-teams to disposal deck, form a cordon and prep kill-teams.' He glanced down at Mallik, who was struggling to pull his ruined helmet free. Blood was seeping from an eyepiece. 'One man down, request medical support.'

'Acknowledged.'

'And send Tellos in.'

'Yes, sir.'

THERE HAD BEEN a civil war. There was no other way of saying it. Chapter traditions had it that Sarpedon was judged to be in the right in the eyes of Dorn and the Emperor, by virtue of his victory over Gorgoleon. Most of the Space Marines who had watched Sarpedon tear the Chapter Master apart had sworn allegiance to Sarpedon on the spot – they said there had been a golden light shining around Sarpedon as he stood spattered in Gorgoleon's blood, and that the choirs of Terra were heard singing. Sarpedon became Chapter Master of the Soul Drinkers by the acclamation of the battle-brothers.

But there were those who had not believed. They had seen their leader slain by a half-monster, half-human psyker, and they had renounced Sarpedon as a corrupt and evil daemon-thing. They had loaded their guns and set up barricades, and fought their last fight against their brothers.

They had fought well, Sarpedon had to admit. The strange thing was, the veterans and specialists had sided with Sarpedon, while most of the novices had rebelled against him. It took weeks to reduce the most dug-in hardpoints, and to hunt down the guerrilla units striking from the labyrinthine depths of the *Glory*. The *Sanctifier's Son* had been lost entirely when rebels gained control of it and tried to flee – it had been shattered by combined broadside fire as it manoeuvred to warp jump position.

But the rebels had been rooted out, eventually. Those taken alive were rounded up and put onto the darkship, which was then destroyed with massed lance battery fire.

When the death toll was counted, between the operations on the star fort and Geryon platform, and the revolution of Sarpedon's victory, the Soul Drinkers had lost fully one third of their number. Sarpedon felt the loss of the rebels because on one level they were his brothers, but he celebrated their deaths as traitors. If they had to die to ensure the Soul Drinkers would be free of the Imperial yoke, then so be it. He had led men to their deaths before, and not regretted it. Sometimes, he realised then, a commander must be hard.

The only one that really stuck in his mind was Michairas, the Marine who had once attended upon Caeon, and who witnessed Sarpedon conducting the ceremony of the chalice. Sarpedon had faced him personally as he led a band of novices trying to flee off the *Glory* – he tore out Michairas's rebreather implants and threw him out of an airlock. For some reason that stuck with him. He could see Michairas's eyes even now, brimming with fear but tempered by defiance.

Brave boy. But he had to die. That was the price of truth, and nobody said the truth was an easy thing to follow.

When the dead were offered up to Dorn or cast out of the debris hatches according to their allegiance, the fleet had been in a grim position. An Imperial battlefleet would find them soon – if not the one led by Inquisitor Tsouras then another under an admiral hungry for the scalp of an Excommunicate Chapter. The Soul Drinkers' fleet was large and impossible to conceal forever, and the Imperial Navy could muster enough ships to destroy them in a decisive engagement or harry them to the ends of the galaxy. The Soul Drinkers were alone in the universe, with no allies or safe harbour, and it was a matter of time before they were hunted down.

It was Yser who had shown them a way. The Architect of Fate had appeared in his dreams wearing a crown of many stars – Yser had recalled the image in exact detail, and the crown had formed a star chart that led them to the hulk. Another miracle, and Yser seemed certain that the Emperor had seen the Chapter's suffering and was gifting them a new home and a new start. By now the Chaplain and Marine alike hung on his word and he was acting as Sarpedon's principal adviser. Without Yser, perhaps the Chapter would have torn itself apart completely, but he provided a spiritual leadership alongside Sarpedon's authority.

Huge, ancient, and devoid of life save the isolated stealer colony, the hulk had been perfect. It was formed of perhaps a score of other ships, crushed and fused into one – it was large enough to house the whole Chapter but, as only one ship, it would be more difficult to track than an entire fleet. With so many dead areas it could hide in debris fields or dust clouds, and the Tech-Marines had suggested that it possessed enough armament, once refitted and repaired, to create a formidable bastion. Its monstrous bulk was so twisted and deformed that it had been christened the *Brokenback*.

The *Brokenback*. The new home of an excommunicate and renegade Chapter. Somehow, it seemed fitting.

'SAD TO SEE them go, commander?' said Lygris.

'A little,' replied Sarpedon. 'But we should use this as an opportunity to start again. To refound the Chapter.'

'Perhaps.'

'Does this not grieve you, Lygris? As a Tech-Marine I would have imagined the loss of so many fine ships would be like losing a limb.'

Lygris smiled, his dead-skinned face just managing to turn up the corners of his mouth. 'With the loss of the fleet with Chapter will lose a part of its soul, commander. But we have lost so much already, it is perhaps better to destroy everything that ties us to the lies of our past. And it should not be forgotten what we have here in the *Brokenback*. We may have lost a fleet, but we have gained one of the largest space hulks ever taken intact. There must be thirty plasma reactors in the structure. The warp drive potential alone is astonishing.'

They were in one of the more recognisable parts of the *Brokenback* – a private yacht that had been owned a couple of centuries before by some rich noble or trading magnate. Whoever it was had not possessed a subtlety of taste, and every surface was covered with flowing scrollwork or gilt sculpture, now dark and tarnished with age. This was the yacht's viewing gallery, where parties of dignitaries would gather to witness some celestial phenomenon over a glass of chilled amasec – a great ocular viewing window swallowed the whole ceiling and looked out onto space.

The Soul Drinkers' fleet was drifting dark and powerless outside. Once the stealers had been cleared out – a swift and simple operation with Tellos at the fore, hand-blades slick with alien filth – the Chapter had been moved into the *Brokenback*. Now no longer needed, the fleet was a liability, large and easy to track. It had to be scuttled.

An explosion bloomed towards the stern of the *Glory*, where the fuel pods fed into the reactors. A white ring of fire suddenly burst from the heart of the ship and sheared it in two, spouting burning fuel and debris. Two of the strike cruisers were caught in the expanding disc of plasma-fire and had their hulls ripped open like foil. Another charge blew the prow off the *Carnivore* – with its structure terminally violated the ship imploded, the shock of its death spewing storms of hull fragments tens of kilometres into space.

Slowly, silently, the Soul Drinkers' fleet died. Charges carefully planted at the key points shattered power feeds and cracked open reactor cores. It took perhaps an hour for the destruction to unfold, and Sarpedon watched it all until the end.

They had saved what they could – records, equipment, the librarium and apothecarion, several serf-labour battalions. But there must have been so much lost that the Soul Drinkers Chapter that had once existed could be said to have died, and a new Chapter to have taken its place.

That was how it should be. They were not Imperial Space Marines any more – they were beholden to no one save the Emperor, who voiced His approval through the visions and miracles granted to them. At last, the Soul Drinkers were free. At last, they could begin to redeem themselves after centuries of pandering to the tyranny of the Imperium.

When all that remained of the fleet was a handful of burned-out husks, Sarpedon and Lygris watched them drift for a while, feeling the weight of history lifting off their shoulders. All these years, they had been nothing. But now they could start again, and this time they would carry the light of the Emperor into the darkness.

'Lord Sarpedon,' crackled a voice in a vox-interrupt burst. 'Sergeant Salk here, supervising labour unit secundus. We're working on a machine-spirit housing in the Sector Indigo and we've uncovered an anomaly. Requesting specialist assistance, technical and medical. And a Chaplain.'

'A Chaplain?'

'Yes, sir. I believe we are in the presence of a moral threat.'

Sarpedon snapped the link shut and opened another net-wide channel. He felt his pulse quickening. 'Sarpedon to all points. Specialists to Sector Indigo. Moral threat, moral threat.' The Soul Drinkers had done a thorough job in scouring the *Brokenback* for anything suspicious, but there had always been a possibility something had survived here. No chances could be taken.

'Lygris, with me,' said Sarpedon. 'I want to see this for myself.' His multitude of limbs gave him far greater ground speed than another Marine and he soon left Lygris behind as he hurried across the observation gallery and down along the ceiling of the corridor.

SECTOR INDIGO WAS a research ship, a squat blocky craft filled with galleries of man-sized specimen jars full of milky fluid. The markings of the Adeptus Mechanicus Xenobiologis were on every piece of equipment, and the bridge bristled with mind-impulse units for the crew. But there was nothing alive on the ship and everything had been perfectly preserved by the craft's sterilised air systems, even after the ship had been swallowed by the bulk of the *Brokenback*.

The machine-spirit was the prize here. It was held in a ceramo-plastic core just behind the bridge – a room-filling sphere of circuitry, its surface studded with valves and slots for punch cards. Initial inspection had suggested it was something beyond the scope of the Mechanicus to create from scratch, and if it could be made to work it might provide a means to control primary systems all over the *Brokenback*.

So Sergeant Salk went with labour unit secundus to open it up so the Tech-Marines could start working on it.

That was when they found the moral threat.

SARPEDON WAS QUICK but there was already an apothecary, Karendin, at the scene when he arrived, tending to the wounded serf-labourers in one of the specimen-cargo bays.

'What is our situation, Karendin?'

'Bad, sir.' Karendin was one of the youngest Soul Drinkers to side with Sarpedon – newly inducted into the ranks of the apothecarion, the Chapter war had been a baptism of blood for him. 'We've lost a half-dozen of the labourers.' He looked down at the body lying at his feet – its face had been half-scoured away by acid, which had left an ugly green-black crust around the edges of the wounds. The serf was breathing his last, and four others were lying beside the specimen containers with whole limbs, heads or torsos seared away. A dangerous, acrid smell drifted from the bow of the ship.

'And Salk?'

'By the machine-spirit core, sir. In case it tries to get out.'

Sarpedon hurried up the specimen gallery to where Salk was crouched by the sealed bulkhead, bolter ready, with two of the remaining labourers. Salk's armour was scored and pitted with acid burns.

'Bad, sergeant?'

Salk saluted hurriedly. 'We opened up the sphere and something fired. It took down half the serfs before we got out, nearly took me. It is not my place to suggest such things, commander, but I think it's possessed.'

Sarpedon glanced at the black metal bulkhead door – he could feel the wrongness beyond it, as strong as the reek of decay.

'Commander!' called Lygris as he sprinted down from the specimen gallery. 'Reinforcements are heading in. Three squads from Sector Gladius. Five minutes.'

'Too long. It's awake now, if we give it any more time it could break out or grow stronger.' Sarpedon drew his force staff. He had only just finished scrubbing the filth off it from the encounter with the genestealer, now it would taste corrupt blood again.

'Serf?' said Sarpedon, and one of the labourers hurried up. 'Open it on my mark.'

The labourer put his weight behind the black metal wheel lock. The surface of the door was creaking and bulging beside him.

'Mark.'

The serf rammed the wheel round and died, the door bursting open and vomiting a gout of grey-green acid over him. Sarpedon and Lygris were quicker by far, diving down and to the side as the billowing filth rolled over them.

The air inside would be toxic. But a Space Marine, with his extra biomechanical lung and rebreather implants, could hold his breath for many minutes. There were no excuses.

Sarpedon scuttled over the dissolving body of the serf and into the machine-spirit room, Lygris at his shoulder. The circuitry sphere was half-open, one hemisphere peeled aside. Inside, like the heart of a rotting fruit, was a pit of green-black corruption bubbling with heat and malevolence, spitting gobbets of corrosion and exuding a wave of toxic air.

Sarpedon ran onto the cylindrical wall of the room as Lygris threw a frag grenade into the corrupt core. The dripping filth swallowed the grenade and dissolved it before it could go off.

'Flamers to Sector Indigo!' voxed Lygris. 'Now!'

'Four minutes,' came the reply. Givrillian's voice, realised Sarpedon. Good.

The rear of the sphere was mostly intact, but the plates of its surface were beginning to work loose and green-brown rivulets of ichor were running from the card-slots. By the Emperor, he could feel it, the waves of hatred, the sheer malice of the thing. There was no intelligence here that could have been able to create an emotion – and yet it hated still, as if it was nothing but a receptacle for that hate.

He drove the force staff through the circuitry skin and into the thing's heart. He felt the semi-liquid machinery shredded by the staff's head, but the thing's hatred did not die.

Lygris was pumping shells into it. He must have known this was no mortal enemy that could be killed by bullets. He was trying to distract it, to give Sarpedon the time to kill it for real. Lygris, seemingly like all the Soul Drinkers, had utter faith in Sarpedon's abilities – they had seen the light of the Emperor streaming from him, and the gifts He had granted their new Chapter Master. Sarpedon hoped he could live up to their trust.

Sarpedon gripped the arunwood tight and channelled his psychic force into the staff, trying to break the thing's grip on life. The waves of malice shuddered, shifted, grew more powerful but less focused.

What was it? Alien? There were tales of creatures that could usurp control of technology. But would they project such horribly familiar, human hatred?

The arunwood squirmed in his grasp as it was repelled by the wrongness of the thing in the machine-spirit core. Sarpedon strode up the wall and onto the ceiling, dragging a long gouge in the core's surface through which bilious filth poured.

Lygris ducked to one side as a tongue of acidic gore spat out at him, lashing deep into the opposite wall with a hiss. The Tech-Marine rolled as he landed, crushing the sorry remains of the final serf-labourer before he came to his knees and pulled a wire from the back of his neck.

'Lygris, no! It'll kill you!' Sarpedon didn't want to risk using up his breath with speech, but he knew what Lygris was trying to do and he knew it would fail. He had barely survived the machine-spirit on the Geryon, and that was but a fraction of the *674-XU28* full consciousness. This was an alien infection or deliberate techno-heresy of some kind, and it would rip his mind apart.

'Hurt it for me, Lord Sarpedon!' came the reply, just before Lygris jammed the cable jack into an infoport and flopped insensible to the floor.

Sarpedon yelled, not caring if there was anything left in his lungs, and plunged his staff-wielding hand up to the elbow into the machine-spirit core. Ichor and entrail-like machinery wrapped around his arm and dragged him further in. Sarpedon twisted the staff head, felt the thing's scream of pain, and knew what he must do.

Lygris convulsed on the floor. Now it was Sarpedon's turn to distract the hideous intelligence, so Lygris might at least have a chance.

ARE YOU IN here? thought Lygris. Are you in here? For if you are not, then all is lost.

I am here, something replied through the din of blasphemous screams. *But I cannot fight it.*

It is hurting, replied Lygris. We are wounding it deeply, my lord and I. But we cannot kill it without your help, Sector Indigo.

I know. But it is so strong. When I was the research ship Bellerophon, I mapped systems unseen by man and catalogued species never even comprehended before. Now I am small and frightened. It is nothing but corruption, Tech-Marine Lygris. It is a spectre of corrosion, utterly without remorse, and it has defeated me at every turn.

But it can be beaten, said Lygris. I can show you the way. I can help you. While it is blind with pain, you can cut the primary power feed to the machine-spirit core, where its physical presence resides, and you will starve it to death.

Yes, I can, Tech-Marine Lygris. But if I do this thing, I will die too, for the core is where my mem-banks also reside.

But it will be dead. You can know that in ceasing to exist, you have destroyed a great and terrible thing. You can have revenge, Sector Indigo. Are you willing to make that sacrifice?

Tech-Marine Lygris, this creature is the enemy of everything for which I once strove. You should know, as a Space Marine, that when there is a choice between life and revenge, there is really no choice at all.

SARPEDON WRESTLED WITH the glutinous foulness that threatened to swallow him whole. He was up to his shoulders and his front two legs were thrust deep into the corrosive body of the spirit core, trying to hold his torso out of the quagmire. He held the force staff with both hands now, using both ends to gouge away while the thing fought to wrest it from him.

The armour on his forearms was mostly gone. Already his hands and wrists were burning where the armour seals had been eaten away and acid was leaking in. But the creature was angry now, focused entirely on him. If there was anything Lygris could do, it could be done now, for the monster's back was effectively turned while Sarpedon battled with it.

If it survived, it could escape and have the run of the rest of the *Brokenback*. The whole Chapter was at stake, then. That made the situation simple – Sarpedon would win or die.

Then there was something else. *Fear.*

The lights in the room guttered and died. And suddenly Lygris was beside him, the cable still snaking from his neck, slamming his bolter into the rents Sarpedon had opened up, firing explosive rounds into the core.

The thing screamed in terror as blackness opened up all around it, the bottom of its world falling away as the power drained from the core. It fought to the very end, but with its life force haemorrhaging it was no match for the combined anger of two Space Marines and its guts were shredded by bolter and staff.

Sarpedon and Lygris emerged from the machine-spirit room just over three minutes after they had gone in, covered in gore and acid burns, gasping for the relatively clean air of the specimen deck. They met the first of the reinforcements coming in, bearing flamers and plasma guns to cleanse the chamber. Karendin immediately left the dying serfs and saw to the wounds of his commander, as Salk directed the flamer troops in scouring the spirit core room.

Givrillian strode up to where Karendin was peeling the armour from Sarpedon's blackened arms. Givrillian's scar was a bright livid red and the old wound had opened up – from between folds of rent skin peered a half-dozen eyes which glanced here and there constantly. They gave the already grizzled Givrillian even more presence and importance – the sergeant's alteration was just one more of the many uncanny gifts the Architect of Fate had granted the Soul Drinkers.

'Commander, are you hurt badly?'

Sarpedon shook his head. 'A few courses of synthiflesh will suffice. I have had much worse.'

'Sergeant Givrillian,' said Lygris, his voice harsh from the rawness of his gas-burned throat. 'What we fought was in there for a purpose. I don't think it was xenos, either. If I may make a suggestion, I would have you gather the Tech-Marines and librarium adepts and find out what information remains in there.'

'Agreed,' said Sarpedon. 'If there is another force on the *Brokenback*, we must know of it.'

Givrillian saluted and moved off to prepare for the investigation.

Lygris turned to Sarpedon. 'It was trying to take over, commander. And it wasn't doing it for its own benefit.'

MUTANT.

A month had passed since the machine-spirit in Sector Indigo had been purged. In that time the exploration of the *Brokenback* had continued, the mem-banks salvaged from the fleet now being filled with information about the Chapter's new home. There had been sixteen separate component craft identified – some were rotted husks, others as clean and pristine as the day they sailed off their manufactoria docks. There was a flight of pre-heresy fighter craft fused and welded into a jagged starburst of metal, and an orbital generatorium platform that the Tech-Marines were activating and re-routing to power the hulk's myriad warp drives, and a ship-bound schola progenium habitat being divided into monastic cells. The hulk was gradually being mapped and adapted – soon, it would be as formidable a fortress-monastery as any Chapter could claim to possess.

Sarpedon's wounds had been severe but they had been quick to heal. The charred, blackened skin on his forearms had flaked away to reveal strong new flesh. The weeping acid burns that ran right up his arachnoid legs had been washed clean with the apothecaries' balms and now only tough ridges of chitinous scar remained. The sinews that had burned away grew back over a matter of days, and the rugged exoskeletal limbs were packed with new-grown muscle.

And that was, perhaps, the problem. As Sarpedon walked through the cavernous gun decks that formed a giant cavity within the body of the *Brokenback*, he knew that the strength he felt all throughout him was something not entirely natural.

Mutant. They had used the word to his face when the Chapter had fended off meltdown in the days following his victory over Gorgoleon. Michairas had gurgled it as Sarpedon strangled the life out of him – mutant: unclean, an aberration, a sinner by its mere existence. It was one of the gravest insults that could be slung at a fellow Space Marine, and Sarpedon had killed many of them for it. And yet on one level he could understand them, if not forgive them.

The gun decks had once bellowed the fiery rage of an Imperial battleship, the same craft that formed perhaps half the bulk of the *Brokenback's* forward sections. The ship's name, *Macharia Victrix*, was struck onto every bulkhead and stanchion, for this was once a proud ship which, judging by the kill tallies etched into the gun casings, had fought the misguided fight of the Imperial cause for many centuries. But at some point it had become lost and the *Brokenback* had swallowed it, leaving the guns to fall silent and corrode.

There were powdery piles of bones dotted in the shadows of the immense tarnished gun casings, where stranded crew had gathered in darkness as the madness of the warp took them. Some of the bones had teeth marks.

Sarpedon broke into a run, feeling the steel-taut tendons in the joints of his legs and the bunches of muscles contracting. Eight talons struck sparks from the iron-grated floor as he sprinted and skidded, testing the limits of his altered body. There was no pain any more – it was as if the new-grown flesh was stronger still.

To an unbeliever's eyes, he must have been a monstrous sight – a spider-centaur; half-man half-arachnid. A Space Marine was fearsome enough, but Sarpedon knew he would look truly terrifying to those who had not witnessed his triumph at the Cathedral of Dorn. Those novices had not felt the true sacred strength of the Soul Drinkers, or seen the halo of the Emperor's glory that had surrounded Sarpedon at the moment of his victory. Their minds had still had room for doubt, where a true Marine knew none. They had seen a monster and assumed that Sarpedon was a monster indeed, without feeling the magnificent truth.

But Sarpedon knew he was no monster. He knew as surely as he felt the eyes of Dorn and the Emperor upon him. For he knew what it meant to live under the taint of the mutant. He had consumed the flesh of the mutant slain by Tellos on the star fort, and remembered every detail of what he had felt – the ugliness covering him like a film of dirt, the aura of loathing that the whole universe projected towards him. The curse of the mutant was something terrible and all consuming – and Sarpedon felt none of it now. He felt only the divine strength of the Architect of Fate coursing through him, directed through his altered limbs and the newfound power in his arm.

Sarpedon hurtled up the side of the closest gun casing, talons gouging scars against the surface of the ancient metal. He reached the apex of the casing and leapt upwards, finding the wall, then the ceiling, until he was scuttling upside-down, watching the shadowy depths of the gun deck flitting by beneath him.

The battle-brothers had no doubt, either. Ever since the violence of the Sarpedon's ascendance he had not felt one echo of dissent. Many of the brothers were themselves changing – Givrillian with his many eyes, Tellos with his strangely changed flesh and keener senses. Every day brought some new gift to light – Brother Zaen was growing sharp triangular scales down his back and upper arms, while the fingers of Sergeant Graevus's right hand were so long and powerful that he could handle his power axe as if it weighed no more than a combat knife.

Sarpedon flipped off the ceiling and dropped, his eight legs spread to cushion his landing as he slammed into the floor, denting the rusted metal.

Mutant? No, his new form and those of his battle-brothers were gifts from the Emperor, a sign that they had been set further apart from the mindless masses of humanity, that they were as different in body as they were in spirit. It was fitting that the weak-stomached inhabitants of the Imperium would mistake them for unclean mutants – it was just one more symptom of their feeble-mindedness.

In a chamber towards the stern of the *Brokenback*, the Tech-Marines would be routing the shattered remnants of Sector Indigo's mem-banks to the information feed cluster they had assembled in the sensorium dome of the yacht-ship. If there was anything left to find, it might tell them something about why the foulness had dedicated itself to winning control of the *Brokenback*.

THE PLACE HAD no name. But that made no sense – every planet had a name, even if it was only a number assigned to it by the navi-cogitators mapping the area. Here, there was nothing – every field in the readout was blank. The only information available was its location. That, and the image. But that was of little use, for the world was smeared with a layer of thick cloud, a swirling grey-white mantle that wrapped the planet from pole to pole. The milky glare of the image cast sharp-toothed shadows on the walls of the captain's quarters being converted into Sarpedon's chambers.

'There is nothing here that warrants our attention,' said Sarpedon, sitting back on the haunches of his newly blackened legs.

Tech-Marine Solun adjusted the servitor's holo-array and the image drew out, revealing a shattered grid of information

– hundreds of panels of planetary data, all scarred and defaced until not one world was legible. It was the visual representation of a database that had been corrupted beyond redemption.

'The mem-banks to which the machine-spirit had access were in an appalling state,' said Solun. 'The infection had destroyed the information systematically. The mem-plates were nearly liquid when we opened them up.'

'So it left this one world. But why?'

Solun adjusted the servitor again and the image flickered into a complex map of Sector Indigo's navigational systems. Solun was, like all Tech-Marines, responsible for maintenance of the Chapter's battlegear and field engineering duties.

Unlike most Tech-Marines, however, his area of expertise was in the arcane and near-magical world of information, retrieving and storing it. Temporary mem-banks were ranged in black slabs on his armour's backpack and shoulder blades, while his servo-arm was tipped with a syringe-like data-thief probe.

'This is Sector Indigo's own navigational system,' said Solun, as a section of the map flickered red. 'It's been hooked up to the bridges of at least eight more of the *Brokenback's* components craft. Most notably, a high-capacity cargo freighter and a xenos ship currently in a quarantined sector. It is probable that controlled movement of these ships would have allowed the *Brokenback* to be flown very effectively.'

'So it was about control? It was taking over the ship and flying it to our mystery planet.'

Solus nodded. 'That would be our conclusion.'

'Very well. Good work, Tech-Marine.' Sarpedon looked towards another figure, half-covered in the shadows cast by the holo-array. 'Now, do we know what it was?'

The black-armoured bulk of Chaplain Iktinos loomed from the darkness. 'It was a daemon,' he said evenly. 'You say you felt its intelligence. It was a hatred you recognised, commander. That was no alien or man-made abomination. It was a servant of the enemy.'

A daemon. A footsoldier of the powers of the warp, a servant of the Dark Gods of Chaos. Chaos was the horror that the Emperor had died to thwart. It was the dread Horus,

Warmaster of Chaos, who had been slain by the Emperor at the height of the battle for Earth, and who had grievously wounded the Emperor in return. It had been Chaos that had corrupted the weak hearts of the lesser primarchs and brought the foul traitor legions into being.

When Sarpedon had turned his back on the Imperium it was apparent to him how Chaos might thrive in such a tyranny – there were so many corrupt institutions through which Chaos might seep into the galaxy. Sarpedon had harboured visions of the Soul Drinkers battling the pure horror of Chaos, and even dismantling the Imperium to deny the enemy a breeding ground. But now, the touch of Chaos was here, on the *Brokenback*.

A thought came unbidden – at last, Sarpedon, you can get to grips with a foe worth fighting.

But there was more. A tiny incessant voice at the back of his mind…

You have seen this place before. You have been here in your dreams, and felt the stink of what lives there. Peel back the layers of cloud and the raw, bleeding planet revealed will be more familiar to you than your own battlegear.

'It was going to this place, wasn't it?' said Sarpedon. 'The daemon-disease was supposed to corrupt the *Brokenback's* guidance systems so it could be flown to this planet.'

'That would be my conclusion, commander. The Librarians concur. The question remaining is why?'

'Because it is an evil place, Iktinos.' Sarpedon looked from the milky sphere of the unnamed planet to the Chaplain's impassive helmet mask. 'This is the place Yser spoke of. This is where we are required to prove our worth to the immortal Emperor. I have seen the evil that is waiting for us here, and now the Emperor has delivered us proof. That evil sent a daemon to bring it the *Brokenback*, but we got here before it could complete its mission. And the *Brokenback* will sail to this world, but with us as masters.'

'I take it, Lord Sarpedon, that you would have me deliver the litanies of readiness,' said Iktinos, as if he had expected this all along.

'Indeed, Chaplain. As soon as we are warp-worthy, this is where we will be headed.' Sarpedon pointed at the unnamed world – and though it was clouded and obscure, he could see burning bright behind his eyes the nightmare that boiled on its surface.

Was there any greater blessing for a warrior? Here was something utterly evil that could be brought to battle and crushed. Something wicked formed not from betrayal or greed but pure, understandable sin.

Something he could face.

Something he could kill.

CHAPTER NINE

THE UPPER ATMOSPHERE was freezing and harsh, but even there he could feel the warm pulse of unholy life throbbing thousands of metres below. Yser knew that if he looked down he would see the same sight again, the same one that had threatened to strip his sanity away these last few months – but he also knew that he could not just shut his eyes and refuse to believe. He was here for a reason – for nothing would happen to him that the Architect of Fate did not will.

There was a hideous lurch as Yser dropped into freefall. He opened his eyes and saw the yellowing banks of clouds sweeping up towards him before he was plunged into a foul-reeking soup of pollution. It was thick against his skin, heaving like a diseased lung drawing breath. But there was worse, he knew. He had been here more times than he could remember, and knew the next layer was worse.

As always, he heard it before he saw it. A saw-like hum that cut through the howling winds and the sinister bubbling of the rot-cloud, an oath hummed by a trillion tiny throats. He braced himself, but knew it would not be enough. The horror was welling up inside him a second before he hit.

Flies. A near-solid slab of fat-bodied flies half a kilometre
deep, a foul black choir of insect vermin. They burst against
his skin and became a shell of thick liquid gore, forcing up
his nose and into his ears, prying at his lips and eyelids. The
roar of millions of ripping bodies flooded his ears as he tore
deeper into the fly-layer, arms flailing.

And past that would be the worst of all. For a second he
was almost begging for the stratum of insects to hold him
forever, just so he wouldn't have to see what lay beyond. But
their slimy grip was weak and he slipped deeper and deeper
until the fly-layer thinned out and now it was heavy, clammy
air that squeezed the sweat from Yser's frail body.

He opened his eyes. He had to. The Architect wanted him
to see.

Yser knew it would not look like this. But this was how it
would feel. To his eyes it was black shot through with purple,
a mile-high bloom of dark flame. The heat billowing off it was
damp and heavy. Its massive flickering form was watching
him – Yser could feel that hard, cold, evil intelligence burning
against his mind. It was speaking to him, taunting him in
words he couldn't hear. It was laughing. It could see him, and
knew how weak and pathetic he was in the face of such evil.

He forced his eyes down. The Architect wanted him to see.

A million million corpses were piled into a wet, pale landscape of suffering. Yser knew they were all good men and
women, those whose souls the Architect of Fate wished to
seek out and introduce to His light. This hideous darkness
had taken them, enslaved them, butchered them in their millions and was living off them like a wily predator lived off
carrion.

They were the fuel for the flame. This abomination lived
by consuming their goodness and truth, and the black-hot
fire rippled over the deathscape reducing the corpses to
crumbling husks. It needed decency and honesty and purity
to survive, for it fed by corrupting their purity into something it could live upon. These men and women were the
last chance of humanity, the only ones with the strength to
face the truth of the Architect's will, and the evil force here
would consume them until there was nothing left.

One day, it would be Yser's turn to become fuel for the
flame of darkness.

Unless it was stopped. That was the message the Architect was giving Yser by forcing him to see this horror. The vision was not of the present but of the future, a universe where evil had triumphed and the Architect's flock lay amongst the heaps of the dead. A future that could be prevented if Yser and the sacred warriors of the Emperor could find the nightmare and end it before it became that all-consuming flame.

A force seized Yser like a huge invisible hand, yanking him upwards away from the deathscape, ripping through the fly-slab and through the clouds of pollution. Then faster, further, into the raw cold of space.

The last sight was always the same – a glimpse of the world they had to cleanse. Clouded and pale like an immense cataract, it festered in orbit around a star that was bloated and dying as if the hell-planet had infected it with its evil.

Then blackness washed over everything, and the vision was over.

WHEN YSER TOLD Sarpedon of his latest vision, it was in the new Cathedral of Dorn, the air heavy with a mix of ancient engine oil and burning incense, and resounding with the echoes of prayers old and new.

'It was the same?'

'No. More intense, Lord Sarpedon, More real.'

'As if you were closer?'

'Yes. Yes, that was it. We are close, I feel it.' Yser held the copy of the *Catechisms Martial* in still-shaking hands – Daenyathos's masterpiece was never far from his side now. His voice sounded small and feeble in the high-ceilinged nave that had been selected as the new Cathedral of Dorn, and though Yser was far cleaner and healthier than when he had been found on the star fort it was still very apparent that he was a frail old man.

'Are you afraid, father?'

Yser's old, watery eyes looked up from the hidebound book. 'Lord Sarpedon, it does not matter if I am. I will do what I must. We all will.'

The nave had once held hundreds of torpedoes, racked up ready for loading into the tubes of a blocky, squat warship. The torpedoes had long since been looted leaving a massive pyramidal cavity with its apex lost in the shadows overhead.

The statues of Chapter heroes had been transferred from the fleet before its scuttling and were now standing around the edges of the chamber, glaring and huge. In the centre was the colossal statue of the Primarch Rogal Dorn – his power sword was holstered but his combat blade was drawn, symbolising the potency of a compact, cunningly-wielded force like the Soul Drinkers. His noble, high-browed face was turned upwards and away from the half-formed spawn beneath his feet that represented the creatures of Chaos. Overlooked by the stone primarch was a lectern of black wood, where the Chaplains would hold their sermons, and from where Yser would preach the new, true faith to the Soul Drinkers. The Chaplains themselves were receiving instruction from Yser, so that it was with words of truth that they would inspire their men.

'Will they rebuild the window, do you think?' said Yser unexpectedly. 'The one that was broken.'

Sarpedon remembered the storm of shattered glass as he plunged through the stained-glass window of the first cathedral. The shards had been gathered from the floor of the Hall of Novices and transported aboard the *Brokenback* before the scuppering of the fleet. But Sarpedon somehow felt it would be inappropriate to reforge the window, symbolising as it did the Chapter bound to the whims of the Imperium. They had left the Imperium behind now, and every symbol of the Chapter would have to be reworked to reflect their freedom. 'The artificers will craft a new one. I shall see to it once we have returned.'

'You will be here one day, Lord Sarpedon,' said Yser, gesturing at the stern-faced statues ranged around the chamber.

Sarpedon smiled. 'I hope they include all the scars. I would hate to be remembered as a handsome man.'

'And the legs.'

'Of course.'

The silence of the cathedral was light and calming. It was hard to imagine the maelstrom of the warp that boiled around the *Brokenback*. For several weeks now the *Brokenback* had traversed the warp once more, but this time it was under human control, its massive array of warp engines linked up to the nav-cogitators of the *Macharia Victrix* and a half-dozen other semi-intact ship's bridges. The co-ordinates of the

unnamed planet from the mem-banks of the *Bellerophon* were
hard-wired into every system. Within a scant few days the
Brokenback would arrive close enough to begin preliminary
scans.

'And what about you, Sarpedon?' asked Yser. 'What have
you seen?'

Sarpedon paused, recalling the depths of the dreams he
had witnessed in half-sleep. 'Quixian Obscura again. But…
there is something else. When I am up on the battlements
and I cannot fathom why I am fighting, there is something
new behind it all. Not just in the distance – I mean it is
beneath everything, as if it was in layer of reality that I could
not see before. It is huge and dark, like a black cloud. I can
feel its hunger, Yser. I can hear it laughing at me. When I have
fought off the aliens and Kallis is dead, Caeon looks round to
me and his words are lost in the laughter coming from all
around me.'

Yser smiled. 'And when it is done, you see the tainted world
like a blind eye in orbit.'

'Yes, father. The same as you.'

'Then it is good, Sarpedon. You know what you must do.
How many of us ever really know what our true purpose is?
There are billions of men who are lost and stumbling,
unaware of the truth or how best to serve their Emperor. But
you – you have seen it. You know where you must go and you
have seen the magnitude of the evil you must destroy there.
Is this not a blessing, Sarpedon?'

Sarpedon looked up at the towering statue of Rogal Dorn.
Soon, when the serf battalions had finished dressing the
stone taken from the hold of the *Glory* and the artificers had
completed their carving, there would be a new statue behind
the primarch, towering over it. It would be the Emperor, the
Architect of Fate, as He appeared in the scrawlings of Yser's
flock and the fleeting visionary moments of the Marines –
face masked, shoulders broad, great jewelled wings of truth
spreading from His back. It would be the first properly rendered image of the Emperor as the Soul Drinkers now
worshipped him.

And he would look down on them, eyes searching, accusing if they failed and proud if they succeeded. Never would
they forget the Emperor's eyes on them.

'Yes, Yser,' said Sarpedon. 'I am blessed. Chances like ours are rare indeed. I know I can count on you for guidance, Yser and the brothers can too. But the Emperor will not have set us a simple task to prove our worth. I will be taking our finest warriors with me, and even if we are victorious you may have to counsel a Chapter which has lost many of its best to this evil.'

'I have given my life to service in the name of the Architect of Fate, Sarpedon. I may not hold a gun but I know I have my part to play.'

Sarpedon stood, flexing his legs. They were almost healed – the tightness around the joints was gone. He felt as if he could punch a talon through solid rock. 'Of course, Yser. But I would not be much of a commander if I was not sure you knew what you might have to do.'

'Don't worry about me, commander. This Chapter is my flock now, and I will give them my heart and soul if that is what they need.'

Sarpedon knew the statue of Dorn was mostly conjecture – the primarch was a legend, his deeds half-myth, and no one could claim to know what he had looked like. But a symbol of him was enough. Dorn was amongst them, watching over them, judging them, so that when the end came he would know the best of men were at his side in the final battle.

'And commander?'

'Yser?'

'Kill a few for me.'

IT WAS RAINING on the forge world Koden Tertius, which meant a total lockdown. Triple-layered armaplas shutters slid down over the viewports and doorways, and the sensoria were drawn into smooth white sheaths against the elements. The sulphuric acid rain and nuclear lightning-storms sheeting down outside would kill even the most unfleshed tech-priest in seconds, and every facility on the planet had to be sealed completely. Acid could get in anywhere and eat away essential power feeds, and any metallic contact could channel lethal shocks into the bodies of the laboratories and manufactoria. When the great storms of Koden Tertius were overhead, all manufacturing stopped, and the acolytes of the tech-priesthood withdrew into the habitats deep in the rock to contemplate their devotion to the masterpiece of the Omnissiah.

But even though a day of introspection had been declared, there were corners of the forge world where work continued. There were those for whom the desire to deconstruct the most sacred secrets of the universe overrode everything. Five of them were gathered in the reverse-engineering laboratory of Sasia Koraloth.

Perched over a bench scattered with servitor parts was Kolo Vaien – a pale adolescent with a permanent sheen of sickly sweat, he had been found on the streets outside a mechanicus lab-temple on a distant hive-city. An astonishing capacity to absorb and process reams of information at will had seen him taken in by the tech-priests and transferred to the forge world.

Beside Vaien, dwarfing him, was Tallin, once of the tech-guard Skitarii, who had been taken on as an apprentice engineer in the forge world heatsinks and had worked his way onto the fringes of the priesthood. He was scarred and scowling, his dextrous paws clenched with anticipation.

'You've seen it, Sasia? Come on, girl, show it!'

'It's not that simple, Tarrin. We never anticipated this kind of power.'

'There are ways,' said a dry, deathly voice.

They were the first words El'Hirn had spoken that day, and for many days before that. The only thing any of them really knew about El'Hirn was that he was old. He had joined the coven halfway through the study, without warning, and though they all suspected he had been watching them for several months before, none of them had asked how he had come to find out about them. 'Your laboratory is rigged with an electromagnetic field-cage, Tech-Priest Koraloth. There is very little that can escape.' El'Hirn gestured with a hand draped in the tattered strips of mottled fabric that covered him from head to toe.

'You are very observant,' said Koraloth, aware as ever that El'Hirn could be anything, including a spy for the tech-magi of Koden Tertius. 'But I am beginning to understand the magnitude of power we are dealing with. I have taken all the precautions I can, but it will never be enough if something goes wrong, or if this artefact is something other than we first believed.'

'What sort of power are we talking about?' asked Gelentian, the savant, loose-fleshed and ugly, who stood against the wall of the lab supported by a basic augmetic framework that took the place of his withered legs. 'Powerful like a bomb? Like a bullet? Something that could hurt us or something that could give us away to the priesthood? We have seen very few results, Koraloth, yet it has been almost a year. Time is running out.' As a savant Gelentian had been altered by the magi to increase his capacity for information gathering and storage, but while Vaien was raw, Gelentian was experienced and disciplined. He functioned as the coven's archivist, with all their findings sealed within his memory – it was too volatile a set of information to entrust to any mem-bank.

'Gelentian,' said Koraloth, 'have you ever seen a vortex grenade explode?'

The coven were silent for a moment. Vortex weapons had not been manufactured for thousands of years – there were theories that they had not been made since the mythic days of the Dark Age of Technology.

'He hasn't,' said Tallin. 'I have. A vortex missile on an Imperator Titan, back when we supported the Guard at Ichar IV. Just one, that was all it took. One of them great big tyranid bio-titans got hit – there was this huge black explosion and then nothing. Nothing where its head had been.'

'Seventeen thousand rounds of standard Titan battery ammunition to kill one Vermis-class tyranid bio-titan,' said Vaien with something approaching awe. 'Twelve hellstrike missiles. But only one vortex charge. Is that what we have, Priest Koraloth?'

Sasia Koraloth shook her head. 'A vortex grenade or missile creates a one-time reality-break effect, an area of null-space. Anything inside the effect is dislocated from this layer of reality and annihilated. This is all anyone really knows. You will also know that anything as short-lived and uncontrolled as an explosion is of strictly limited use.'

'Ah, Koraloth, we begin to understand,' hissed El'Hirn. 'It is not about power at all. It is about control.'

Koraloth stepped into the centre of the lab where the brass-banded cryochamber stood. She slid a finger across the clasp's print-reader and lid swung open, sighing out a fog of frozen air. The Soulspear had been measured emitting low levels of radiation, and it had to be kept completely inert to avoid detection. Koraloth slipped an elbow-length thermoglove onto one hand and lifted the artefact from inside the cask – no matter how many times they saw it, the coven who had been studying its intricacies for almost a year still felt that thrill of power when they saw the Soulspear.

It had proven remarkably resilient, being composed of alloys and high density ceramo-plastics with properties they could not find on any database. They had managed to pry off some of the outer sections and attach data-thief lines which dangled like bloodless veins from the cylindrical shaft. The tiny apertures on the grip had lit up in red shortly after the study had began and were still winking brightly, as if protesting at the invasion.

'We thought these were gene-encoders,' said Koraloth, indicating the lit apertures. 'I suspected they were something else. I think now they're measuring not just genetic information but chemical balance, acidity, even temperature.'

'And you tried to bypass them?' said Tallin. 'Gene-coders are a piece of skrok to short-circuit. Our magos commander had a gene-lock on his liquor cabinet but it never stopped any of us.'

'I tried,' replied Koraloth. 'And it almost worked. But it doesn't like being messed around with. The circuitry structure changes when you so much as look at it. Every route I found around the encoders, the Soulspear closed it. I don't have the cogitator power here to keep one step ahead of it. I had it active for a couple of tenths of a second at most, not long enough for a full reading.'

'You sound like you think it's alive,' said Gelentian. He sounded unimpressed.

'I do, savant. If a machine can have a soul, and the Omnissiah teaches us it can, then the Soulspear has a cunning and powerful one.' Koraloth turned to Vaien, who was fidgeting nervously in the presence of such power. 'Vaien, we cannot crack this artefact with raw power. We must outthink it. That is why I brought you amongst us. Do you know what you have to do?'

Vaien silently rolled up a sleeve of his simple adept's tunic and removed the prosthetic left hand. It was merely cosmetic

– beneath it was the real augmentation. Fused into the boy's elbow was a simple but elegant neuro-bionic attachment composed of two long, thin, blunt-ended metal tines. A knot of servos at the elbow chattered as the tines juddered and warmed up.

Koraloth unfolded a broad keypad from one of the lab benches, and connected its info-feeds to the data-thief lines running into the Soulspear. Immediately lines of glowing green text and numerals ran rapidly through the air above the pad's holo-projector. Vaien's eyes followed them, his pupils a blur, as the raw data generated by the sleeping Soulspear flowed into his prodigious brain.

'Ready?' asked Koraloth. Vaien nodded almost imperceptibly, the streams of numbers reflected in his glazed eyes.

'Very well.' Koraloth made a complex gesture with her free hand and the control studs wired into her fingertips activated the field-cage. A deep thrum opened up as the coils built into the lab's walls came to life and projected a web of electro-magnetic lines to contain the power generated by the Soulspear. They all knew that if something really went wrong it wouldn't be enough.

Needle-like manipulators slid from Koraloth's fingertips and she began to work on the first encoder, bypassing the Soulspear's defences to force the activation signal deeper into the labyrinthine circuitry.

At once it fought back, the crypto-electronics squirming and shifting against Koraloth's invasion. Vaien's tine-hand typed information at an astonishing rate into the keypad, firing up a data-war against the Soulspear, immeasurably ancient archeotech against raw human brainpower.

The first encoder went down, then the second as the Soulspear was blindsided by the novelty of a worthy opponent. It rallied and Vaien fought it at the speed of thought, Koraloth's activation commands breaking past the third barrier. Silver sparks were dancing around the glowing ends of the Soulspear and the air was turning thick.

El'Hirn was backing off slowly. Gelentian scribbled notes onto the data-slate hung around his neck, and Tallin stood arms folded, daring the Soulspear to defy them.

The fourth took longer and the sheer volume of processing power coursing through the interface between Vaien and the

Soulspear robbed the local systems of power – the lab's lights dimmed further; attentive servo-arm arrays slumped powerless.

Then the fifth went down and the Soulspear was activated for the first time in a thousand years.

ALL ACROSS KODEN Tertius, klaxons wailed in alarm. Monitoring stations were bathed in pulsing amber light and the menials manning them jumped into full alert mode. Any forge world was in constant danger of suffering a massive industrial disaster, such were the magnitudes of forces involved in the manufactoria and the sheer levels of power the planet had to manage, and vigilance was heightened during Koden Tertius's regular death-storms.

At first it was assumed by most that the shielding had somehow failed and acid rain had sheeted through some vital component in the power grid, or that lightning had been conducted away from the earthing towers and seared deep into some crucial control system. The first hurried diagnostic rituals showed an immense power spike at a point on the equator, in the research and theoretical engineering sector commanded by Archmagos Khobotov.

The closest tech-guard garrison was alerted and rescue/retribution teams scrambled. The history of Koden Tertius was punctuated by industrial catastrophes and occasional massive loss of life amongst the menials and even tech-priests, and it was not always entirely accidental. The sector was to be surrounded and the tech-guard were to move in around the source of the readings, letting nothing escape, and hold the position until some answers could be found.

They hurried through the tunnel-streets and across the great gantries crossing chasms of generators, until four hundred men surrounded the laboratory of Tech-Priest Sasia Koraloth.

THE FIRST THING Sasia Koraloth saw when she regained consciousness was the closest lab bench sheared in two, the edges dripping and melted. The equipment bolted to its surface had overloaded and was belching acrid smoke. One wall was spattered with black coolant spray fountaining from a severed hydraulic line – it was mixing with the blood on the floor, seeping from the bodies of her tech-coven members that had been thrown around the room.

'Tallin? Anyone?' Koraloth hadn't been out for more than a couple of seconds, she was sure, but in that time her lab had been reduced to a ruin. She tried to haul herself to her feet but the pain was making her groggy. The bones of one hand had been pulped by the violent vibrations of the Soul-spear as it tried to break free from the field-cage. She coughed and peered through the stinking smoke of burned plastic.

Gelentian must have died instantly – there was a clean, round wound right through his chest. Vaien had probably taken a moment longer, for one arm and shoulder had been sheared neatly off when the Soulspear had swung wildly in her grasp as the field-cage began to fail. All around the lab chunks had been sliced out of the lab benches, the equipment, the walls. The Soulspear itself lay on the floor, white smoke coiling off it.

'Here, girl,' said Tallin. Still a soldier at heart, he had hit the floor the instant the Soulspear had come on line and owed his life to it. 'I think it all worked a little too well.'

'Omnissiah preserve us…' gasped Koraloth with a shudder, staring at Vaien's lopsided corpse. 'Did you see it?'

It was… magnificent. Twin blades of pure blackness, two tears in reality, shearing out from either end of the Soulspear. It was as she had suspected – the Soulspear generated a vortex field just like a vortex missile or grenade, but it could maintain the integrity of that field instead of just unleashing it as an explosion. If they could unravel the inner working of the Soulspear, think of the wondrous things they could make…

'In time, perhaps,' came that sinister hissing voice. 'But for now, Tech-Priest Koraloth, our objectives are rather less lofty. We must flee.'

El'Hirn caught Koraloth's uninjured arm and pulled her to her feet with surprising strength. 'The tech-guard will be coming. If they find out you have not been working alone then Khobotov will find out our true purpose here. You understand that cannot happen.'

Tallin pulled himself upright. 'Where can we go? They'll have us surrounded.'

'There are places,' said El'Hirn. 'I have been on this planet some time. I know many of its dark corners where a fugitive might hide.'

'Not just hide,' said Koraloth, her face pale and sheened with sweat as she fought off the pain. 'We have to finish this. We know what the Soulspear can do. It is what we have been looking for all these years, it is why I gathered you and Vaien and Gelentian. We have heard the true word of the Omnissiah, and we must offer up a sacrifice in return.'

El'Hirn headed towards the lab's entrance. 'Indeed we have, tech-priest. The Omnissiah appeared to me, too, in his guise as the Engineer of Time, and told me all those things that you believe. And I know that he demanded you prove your worthiness to receive that truth. We will offer up to him the Soulspear, but first, we must ensure that we survive.'

El'Hirn took up the Soulspear in one hand and led the survivors of Koraloth's coven out of the lab. Glancing around at the sound of approaching tech-guard, he levered a panel away from the wall with his fingers to reveal the rusting hollow of a humidity shaft. Wordlessly, he dropped into the darkness. Tallin followed and, faint with pain but determined not to fall when she had got so far, Koraloth was last.

If they could find a place to hide, if they could survive, then they could complete the task that had been planted in the heart of Tech-priest Sasia Koraloth when the Engineer of Time had appeared in her dreams and begun to tell her the truth. She believed all his whisperings of how mindless and hidebound the Adeptus Mechanicus had become, of how an entire universe of arcane technology was gleaming beneath the surface of reality, begging for an open mind to uncover it. Since she had been given the Soulspear to study the certainty inside her had hardened until she knew what she must to.

She would offer the Soulspear to the Engineer of Time, and see the truth for herself.

AT FIRST, ALL the sensors could come up with was a web of contradictions. The unnamed planet was in far orbit around a near-dead star, and yet it was warm and teeming with life that showed brightly on the carbon scans even from the range limit. The atmosphere was theoretically human-breathable but, in all probability, practically near-toxic. That there was oxygen at all was an anomaly for the planet's surface was almost entirely ocean, broken only by scattered archipelagoes and island chains, and there were no forests or jungles to act as the planet's lungs. The closer the *Brokenback* got the more it seemed that there was a prosperous civilisation on the planet, but that the swarms of life were not a part of it – there were negligible artificial energy signatures, no communications net, and the one or two orbital installations were cold, ancient and corroded.

Now the *Brokenback* was the closest an unexpected craft could get and not run a severe risk of detection. The Soul Drinkers had turned to their Chapter Master for a decision.

'Even if we could be sure of landing the *Brokenback* safely, there is no land mass down there isolated or stable enough to serve as a landing zone.' Varuk, the Tech-Marine who had been supervising the scans from the multitude of sensorium spines that stabbed from the *Brokenback's* hulls, was pointing out the few islands of any size on the giant holo of the unnamed planet. The sensors had had some luck penetrating the freakishly dense cloud layers and could generate an image of the surface stripped of its pale shroud. 'We know that these are volcanic and active, they'd collapse under the hulk's weight.'

The Chapter's most able combat leaders were assembled in the audience hall of the noble's yacht that had evolved into Sarpedon's quarters and the centre of his command. Most of them, like the glowering Graevus or the ever-present Givrillian, were from the force that had been alongside Sarpedon since the star fort. They had earned his trust directly and he knew their strengths. Some others were from the rest of the Chapter who had acclaimed him Chapter Master after the victory over Gorgoleon, and were all Marines who Sarpedon had fought alongside before.

Sarpedon sat back in the throne that had once belonged to the noble whose chambers he had adopted. 'Landing the *Brokenback* was never an attractive option,' he said. 'Could we use the Thunderhawks? Or the drop-pods?'

'Not to strike directly at the enemy, commander,' replied Varuk. A section of the globe lifted off the image and was magnified. It showed an archipelago, a chain of volcanic islands strewn across the ocean. The image was misted by clouds of interference. 'The librarium believe this is the origin point of the psychic emanations,' said Varuk. 'If we are to defeat the force that holds this planet, this is where we will find it.'

Sarpedon knew even before Varuk had pointed it out – that was where the black flame burned.

'But it is also the point where the atmosphere is the most volatile,' continued Varuk. 'You can see, the scans can hardly get through it. It is thick and stormy and completely impassable from the troposphere down. There's a layer that is effectively semi-liquid. It would be like trying to fly a Thunderhawk underwater.'

'Then we will have to land them somewhere else,' said Sarpedon. 'Any ideas?'

It was Sergeant Luko who stood up, smiling. 'Commander, I believe I may have an answer for you. The atmosphere thins out in patches further across the globe, specifically here.' The view switched to a sickly scattering of islands. 'You will have been briefed that there was once a civilisation on this world, probably human. These islands formed one of its centres.'

'If they were human, are there any left? And what are they like now?' asked Graevus gruffly. Sarpedon noticed he was flexing and unflexing his unnaturally long, powerful fingers.

'It's not them I'm interested in, sergeant,' continued Luko. 'It's what they left behind.'

The scans were more accurate through the thinner atmosphere so the view could be zoomed in. Contours appeared, gnarled knots of basalt and cold, rippled lava flows. Luko picked out a section of coastline on the second-largest island and shifted the holo into a close-up of a large natural harbour.

'Commander, we have no logistical structure on this planet and the Thunderhawks cannot stop off for fuel if they are over the ocean of a primitive planet. But whoever lived on this world before it fell to the dark powers had their own ways of getting around. These.'

They could all see them. Ships, three of them, large and dark, singularly ugly vessels built for stability and resilience rather than speed. Each was big enough to have been a major cargo vessel or troop transport.

'There look to be some very basic settlements on the islands,' continued Luko, 'but it's clear they're devolved far from the people who built them. We won't know until we get closer but the ships still look intact.'

'So we sail in,' said Sarpedon with a smile. 'Well done, Luko. Trust you to come up with the must unorthodox tactics possible.'

'One which will leave us on an enemy-held planet an ocean away from the nearest support,' said Dreo from the other side of the room. 'What happens afterwards?'

Sarpedon gave him a withering look. 'It does not matter, sergeant. Even if there will be no afterwards, if there is a way we can get there we must take it. I relinquished our choice in this matter when I took the Emperor as my guide.' He turned to Varuk. 'We could refit the ships with engines from the Thunderhawks and travel under power. Can it be done?'

'We would have to take a number of serfs with us to accomplish it, and they would be unlikely to survive for long given the environment. But yes, it could be done.'

'Good. Varuk, Luko, I shall require a full tactical sermon in eight hours. If the details are sound we shall proceed. I want some better scans of the archipelago and a full survey of potential drop zones. Fall out, brothers.'

THE CHAPTER LIBRARIUM was as old as the Chapter itself, and in many ways older, for it had stemmed from the conclave of Librarians in the Imperial Fists legion in the time of Rogal Dorn. Every novice who showed psychic potential was tested rigorously by the librarium – those who passed were trained in the control of their powers, more art than discipline, alongside the combat skills of a Space Marine. What happened to those who failed was irrelevant, for failure equalled death. It was a gruelling process that none ever mentioned but none ever forgot – novices kneeled before a council of three Librarians and had to keep their mind closed against the most brutal psyk-interrogation. Sarpedon himself had gone through this process, and had passed with some distinction, for instead of just shutting his mind against the assault he had reached out and woven a web of confusion amongst the interrogators. Every novice who made the grade did it differently, some blasting their tormentors across the interrogation chamber, others building an unbreakable wall of mental power. More than one had immolated themselves with mental fire and let the pain block out the probing, to wake up in a synthiflesh incubator with the assembled librarium applauding their success.

When not in battle the Librarians acted as an independent advisory body to the Chapter Master, and it was in this capacity that Sarpedon had commanded them to build up a picture of the threat that awaited the Chapter on the unnamed planet. There were seventeen Librarians left in the Chapter, not including Sarpedon himself, who had survived the violence the Chapter had done to itself in the past months, and in their days-long meditative sessions they had carefully probed the psychic maelstrom that lay beneath the storm-laden clouds.

It was a nightmare. Aekar had died, his eyes pools of streaming jelly and his organs burst and ruptured, when he had peered with the psyker's sixth sense into the boiling mass of madness. The others suffered hideous nightmares, sometimes waking visions, of purple-black firestorms and canyons brimming with corpses. When they probed the darkness they could make out a location, the largest of a string of black coral islands forming an archipelago. There was something down there, burning bright with malice, wallowing in a pool of life. They could not give it a form or divine its powers, except that it was strong, and held the planet under its thrall by force of will alone. Its will extended from the highest wisps of atmosphere to the depths of the oceanic trenches, and every living thing was corroded until it was mindless or enslaved.

There was one thing more, gleaned even as Sarpedon and Yser were addressing the assembled strikeforce in the new cathedral of Dorn. Tyrendian had found it as he forced his consciousness deeper into the wailing madness than any had dared go save Aekar, risking his sanity in the hope he would find something, anything, that might give them a clue as to what they were facing.

He heard them, millions of them crowding the black coral cliffs, chanting. Chanting its name: *Ve'Meth*.

SOMEWHERE ACROSS THAT half-sighted horizon lurked Ve'Meth, a daemonic power of vast brutality, corrupt and merciless. Commander Sarpedon had told them of its evil and of the

Architect's wish for them to put it to the sword, but none of them had really needed telling. They could feel it, a great horror throbbing beneath the deck of the Thunderhawk, watching them. For months it had been disturbing their dreams.

Brother Zaen saw the unnamed planet for the first time through the open rear hatch of the Thunderhawk gunship as it screamed down low over the dark waves. The sky was purplish grey, like an old bruise, a massive heavy ceiling of rain-laden cloud. The sea roiled beneath in sharp waves, breaking against the scattered black rocks as the gunship roared at full tilt towards the island that formed their objective.

Zaen had made airborne drops before, dozens of times in his still-short career as a Soul Drinker. But not like this. They had always known something about the foe they were facing, even if it was only who they were – unclean hordes of orks holding the refineries on the ice caps of Gyrix, secessionists who had taken over the manufactoria of Achille XII. Here, they had only a name, and an assurance that the foe was terrible indeed.

The air swirled in the back of the Thunderhawk and Zaen instinctively checked the survivability readouts reflected onto the crystal of his helmet's eyepiece. He could breathe the air but his lungs would have filled up with phlegm and his eyes would have started streaming after half an hour – armour discipline was to be made paramount and helmets were to be worn.

Closer now, and the dead volcanic peak rose like a broken tooth from the crags of the island. Half-formed ruins, rotted by corrosives in the air, clung to the rocks. They had once been majestic, but now they were like the mouldering skeletons of civilisation.

One last check of the seals around his flamer's fuel cylinder. One last whispered word to the ever-watchful Emperor, and to the vigilant Rogal Dorn whose blood flowed in Zaen's veins.

Squad Luko would be first out, and Zaen had the point where his flamer could buy a half-second if they found themselves facing danger. Zaen had been in the same position when they dropped into the demiurg positions at the Dog's

Head River, and two aliens had died in the wash of his flame before Squad Luko's bolters had began to open up.

Was there fear? No, there was none. What lesser men felt as fear, a Space Marine felt as a high-tensile readiness, a state of rarified awareness that let him act faster, think quicker, hit harder where it counted. So were written the words of Daenyathos – for a Space Marine shall know no fear.

The razor-sharp rocks hurtled by beneath as they headed over the coast, black-grey shot through with streaks of quartz. The Thunderhawk lurched to one side and flew in a broad curve as it descended, losing speed, dropping over a ridge on the final approach.

The landing zone was a broad bowl of broken rock, a short run from the harbour but far enough away from the nearest ruins. The Soul Drinkers would have to secure the landing zone before the Thunderhawks could land, which meant the gunships would have to stay in the air while the Space Marines swept the area. The engine pitch dropped as the Thunderhawk reached bale-out level, four metres above the ground. Zaen jumped.

They were still travelling at a fair pace when he landed but he had done this many times before, rolling on and coming up on one knee, flamer braced, head jerking as he swept for contacts. For a second or two he held fast as the remaining nine Marines of Squad Luko hit all around him, the sergeant coming down halfway through, lightning claws spread like skeletal wings as he fell.

'Squad Luko down, no contacts,' he heard the sergeant voxing to the command Thunderhawk. The acknowledgement blip sounded and Luko raised a hand for them to follow.

The storm-swept island seemed devoid of life. Indeed, it seemed hard to believe that anything could survive here. Zaen could see nothing moving save the Marines and the incoming Thunderhawks, and could hear nothing beneath the white noise of the ocean, the pounding of boots and his own double heartbeat.

Squad Luko moved at a jog towards the harbour, careful to keep their feet on the cracked strata of rock. The harbour itself was like a bite taken out of the rock, and beyond it the ocean reflected the grim dark grey of the sky. The volcanic peak of the island loomed to the rear of the landing zone, the sorry ruins zigzagging up the dark rock. Everything was covered in sea spray, glistening in the weak light.

'Movement!' called Brother Griv on the squad vox. 'North-north-east!'

Zaen saw it a second after, something pale and spindly darting amongst the rocks in front of them. He knew that Squads Graevus and Dreo would be dropping some distance away to form the two ends of the Marine line. Squad Luko was in the centre, and the next squads would fill in the rest of the line. They had twenty seconds, perhaps, on their own before the rest arrived.

'First blood, men!' shouted Luko.

Griv fired on the move and missed. Three more bolters took his range and hit – something thin and humanoid flailed in pain and another shot took off what must be its arm.

The name of Squad Luko would be inscribed in the Chapter records as taking first blood of the enemy on the unnamed planet. Zaen knew Luko took pride in such things, and to tell the truth Zaen felt the same. His hands were fairly itching to get close enough to use his flamer.

'Command, this is Squad Luko. Positive contacts, repeat, contacts.'

Zaen glanced back and saw Lord Sarpedon himself disembarking with Givrillian leading his command squad. Sarpedon was majestic, his strong taloned legs carrying him swiftly over the rock, bolter barking at the figures scurrying towards the Marines.

Zaen saw the enemy properly for the first time – humanoid and perhaps technically human, but shambling, with sloped gaits and lolling mouths. Luko slid into cover behind a lip of rock and fired a burst from the bolt pistol worked into the back of his right lightning claw gauntlet. The squad followed him into cover.

'I want bolter discipline, men, and I'm counting every bullet!' he yelled. 'Fire!'

There were more now, a dozen, reaching out from deep furrows in the rock where they had taken shelter. Their eyes were wide watery saucers and their skin streaked with blood and filth.

This was what had happened to the human peoples that once called this planet home. They had perhaps been proud and noble, until Ve'Meth came. Now, maybe generations later, the daemon's influence had robbed them of intelligence and left them slack-jawed primitives, cannibals clutching clubs of human bone and chunks of sharp flint.

Bolters chattered and a dozen fell, their soft, light-starved flesh coming apart. Zaen heard their moans of pain and anger beneath the gunfire. With their dead as cover still more poured from the cracks in the ground: twenty, fifty, a hundred.

'Hold, brothers, and close on my lead!' called Luko, the vox cutting through the jabbering of the humanoids and the crackling bolter-fire.

The creatures were within a half-dozen strides, clambering over the dead and jabbering with anger, their teeth gnashing and eyes glaring wetly with fury at the invasion of what passed for their home.

Luko vaulted over the ridge of rock and three of the enemy were dead before he landed, their torsos sliced to thick bloody ribbons with a swipe of his lightning claw. A follow-up swipe tore another one into strips lengthways in the flash of a discharging power-field. The howls were screams now, the creatures a wall of sallow flesh rearing over Luko on a tide of broken bodies.

By then, Brother Zaen was at his side, and Luko stepped back, dripping with watery blood, to let him do his work.

Zaen took the split-second to check range and target density. Close and packed. Perfect. The pilot light on the tip of the flamer nozzle flickered hungrily, and Zaen issued a silent prayer to the watchful primarch as he squeezed the trigger handle in his gauntleted hand.

The blue-white cone of flame ripped through the closest bodies sure as any bullet, rending four or five hapless subhumans into shrivelling, flailing limbs half-glimpsed in the flamewash. Those further away fared even worse, coated in a cloak of burning petrochemical that ate through their skin and left screaming, flaming skeletons spasming as they died.

The closest survivors, many half-aflame, screamed in pain and shock and ran. They took their fellows with them and soon the subhumans opposing Squad Luko were in full rout, Luko himself laying into the closest with his shining claws, the squad's bolters thudding shells into the disintegrating flesh of the fleeing pack. Zaen washed the ground with flame, scouring the few survivors into burning ash, melting the flesh of those who had fallen in their flight.

'Squad to me, regroup!' came Luko's order, and the squad strode over the sticky, burning remains of the cannibals to where their sergeant stood, the power field around his claws flickering as the residue of muscle and bone burned off. Zaen knelt to the squad's fore, ready to answer another ambush with a burst of burning justice.

He could hear the crackle of gunfire as the fleeing creatures blundered into the fire zones of the other squads, and were cut down in short order. There was a flash of light as the psyker-lightning lanced out and shattered a swathe of fleeing bodies – it was Tyrendian, the Librarian, lending his mental artillery to the fire of his battle-brothers. Zaen knew the fleeing subhumans wouldn't return, not after so many of them had suffered the white heat of his flamer, the speed and savagery of Luko's claws and the massed gunfire of the Soul Drinkers.

They had taken first blood. The omen was good, one of the best, for it promised the Soul Drinkers would meet the enemy face to face and bring their superior quality to bear. But these cannibal creatures were no kind of resistance. Just looking at the bruised sky and the murderous, polluted ocean promised that the real test was ahead, and the sternest of tests it would be.

Zaen might not survive. Zaen didn't care. To die while partaking in the destruction of such evil was a victory in itself, and whatever happened, his name would be inscribed along with his brothers in the tales of the first true battle of the only free Chapter in the galaxy.

He checked his flamer tanks. They were still nearly full of fuel – the weapon had barely cleared its throat yet. But he did not need the words of Daenyathos to tell him that soon, he would need every drop.

SARPEDON SCUTTLED UP a rise of rock, watching the patrol squads cutting down the few straggling half-humans with placed gunfire. Assault squads saved ammunition and used their combat knives – Tellos, easy to spot even at a distance with his bare pale-skinned torso, was using them as practice for the complex twin-sword techniques he had found in the ancient combat records of the Chapter archives.

Sarpedon was pleased. It hadn't been much of a fight, truth be told, but his Marines had responded with every bit of discipline and sharpness a Chapter Master of the Soul Drinkers could expect of his men. Squad Luko had faced the largest mass of them and Graevus had found his unit nearly surrounded, but in each case the enemy had been broken rapidly and totally, then pursued to destruction.

That had been three days ago, in which time Sarpedon had kept up aggressive patrols against the island's natives. He knew that activity as much as rest was needed to keep his troops battle-ready, and they would need nothing less than total focus. The Soul Drinkers were heading into an uncertain enemy, who might well have control of the battlefield in the most literal sense if the librarium conclave was to believed. It was not a situation he had not faced before or that his Marines were not trained and experienced for, but they all knew those uncertainties multiplied the danger a hundredfold. This was an operation that, if it were not carried out by the Soul Drinkers, could not be carried out at all.

He could see the three ships in the harbour, lit by showers of sparks as serf-labourers fitted the power systems of the Thunderhawks into the hulls. The ships were well-made and the years had done surprisingly little to rot their hulls – they were made of some splendidly light hardwood and banded with quality iron. The sails had long since disintegrated in the foul winds but the Soul Drinkers didn't need them, and indeed the masts themselves were being felled to reduce the profile of the ships against the horizon. These craft were a testament to the sophistication of the peoples that once called this world home, and to the utter degeneracy that Ve'Meth's influence created.

Tech-Marine Varuk was in charge of the engine conversions. Under his watchful eye the Thunderhawk propulsion systems were becoming powerful waterjet propulsion rigs that would send the ships carving across the ocean faster than the winds had ever sent them. The Thunderhawks, four of them stripped down for parts, stood on the open rocks, lashed to the stone with heavy chains.

Sarpedon had brought four hundred Soul Drinkers onto the unnamed world, well over half the Chapter's remaining strength. There was a very real chance that none of them would return, a chance every one of them understood. They would be vulnerable on the ocean – they were vulnerable now, not least because the dark power they were here to destroy could well know they had arrived. And even if everything went right they would still be attacking what was in all likelihood a well-defended and fortified position, facing doubtlessly fanatical and even daemonic resistance. And there was always the problem of whether they would even be able to get back to the orbiting *Brokenback*, regardless of their success on the ground.

None of it mattered. They were here because they owed the Emperor, the Architect of Fate, for showing them the truth, because He demanded they prove their worthiness to count themselves as His divine warriors. If they had to die, then die they would. The only fear that death held was that they would die without having accomplished their life's work of service to the Emperor – but to die here, for a Marine to give his life facing such a foe for such a reason, was to accomplish more than the longest-lived of the weak-willed Imperial servants could ever hope to achieve.

The low, throaty rumble drifted across from the harbour as the engines were tested. They sounded healthy enough – no doubt within a couple of hours the Soul Drinkers taskforce would be heading across the ocean towards the lair of Ve'Meth.

Sarpedon headed down the rocky ridge to supervise the Marines' embarkation onto the ships. Soon they would be gone from the island, leaving only a handful of serf-labourers guarding the Thunderhawks, and two hundred subhuman corpses.

CHAPTER TEN

IMAGINE A MAN. Now imagine him with no skin. Muscles wet to the open air, crowded onto slabs of pulpy pink tissue. Veins snaking, arteries squirming like snakes. Take his eyes and multiply them, like those of a spider, studding the upper half of his face, translucent blue-black. For a mouth, give him a pit lined with a dozen mandibles that could open like the tendrils of a grabflower.

Hammer a chunk of pitted metal, one edge honed sharp, into the bony club of one hand for him to wield like a sword.

Armour him, but not in iron. No, in chunks of more muscle, grown into his own until his body was massive and huge-shouldered, spines jutting from the corded tendons. Mould it into a high collar of gristle and gauntlets of bone. Have him leave footprints of gore wherever he goes, and let clear grey liquid seep from his every surface.

Gelentius Vorp knew what he looked like. He rejoiced in it. Not least, his leathery seven-valved heart swelled to think of how even the mightiest chieftains of Methuselah 41 would have quailed at his very approach.

211

The peoples of the outer hills on Methuselah 41 had never been tamed. Though the men of the Imperial Guard fought them with guns and the Missionaria Galaxia battled with faith, the horsemen of the outer hills had never relented. They had made it their livelihood to raid the Imperial settlements and refinery outposts, as much to prove the manliness of their way of life as to steal weapons and livestock. They had struck like thunder and killed like lightning, and never stooped to pity the foes who fell before them.

It had been a good life. Gelentius Vorp had been proud of his people, who had raised him on the banks of the nitrogen rivers and sent him out strapped to a warrior's saddle before he had learned to walk. He had tasted a man's blood while he was still suckling mother's milk, and taken a man's head while he could still count his years on his fingers.

As he stood on the beach of broken black coral, he tried to remember – would he have loved that life on Methuselah 41 had he known what really lay beyond his homeworld's yellow-green sky? No. He would not. A thousand heads piled outside his groxhide tent would not have sated his lust to serve a power worthy of his subservience. When Ve'Meth had come to his world, he had learned so much and seen such wonders that he could never have gone back to the horse tribes of Methuselah 41.

Not that he could – as with every world Ve'Meth had visited on his travels, he had left Methuselah 41 a blighted place, brimming with poisons and inimical to human life. A beautiful world, thought Vorp, but not one where he could leave his mark upon the universe as he desired. This new planet was better by far, hard and cold. It was one of the few worlds that could both be a home to Ve'Meth, and remain survivable enough to be a base for an army of his followers. Gelentius Vorp was the greatest of those followers, leading the plague hosts deep into the surrounding star clusters and preying on the foolhardy space traffic. One day, Vorp too would ascend to daemonhood, take a world for himself, forge an empire of malice and kill until the stars died around him.

Vorp's thoughts were broken by a messenger-thing, a dried-out tangle of tendons and skin that flapped lopsidely towards him from along the beach. In the distance Vorp could see the slave-gangs hauling sharp chunks of coral to form barricades and hardpoints, and the cult-legions of Ve'Meth marching to the tune of discordant screeches from attack beasts that dogged their steps. Daemons, skin sallow and wet, malformed warp-flesh glowing faintly in the dusklight, clambered on the rippling peaks of coral and stone, befouling everything with their touch. Every living thing here was malformed, withered by disease or torn by mutation – everywhere limbs ended in clubs of bone and skin sloughed off by the handful, skeletons were racked by uncontrolled growth and mouths lolled with madness.

And beyond the beach, the ocean. Vorp's warp-attuned senses could hear the huge, mad creatures wallowing in the deeps, waiting for the call of their prince to bring them up to the surface. Shoals of malicious things swam around them, picking bites from their flesh, laughing at their agony. The planet was steeped in life, and that life was wielded like a weapon by Ve'Meth.

A wonderful world, to have taken so much to the touch of the Daemon Prince Ve'Meth.

'Gelentius Vorp, heed us,' hissed the messenger. 'Our lord would speak with you.'

Though he had been long in service – ten years, a hundred? – Vorp had rarely had the pleasure of an audience with the daemon prince himself. Lord Ve'Meth chose only those who pleased or displeased him the most – the first for reward, the second for a fate not even his own followers could divine.

'Do you know fear, Gelentius Vorp?' asked the messenger insolently.

'No, creature. I fear nothing. I serve my lord and have never failed in his eyes.'

The creature smiled – though it was hard to tell given its loose-skinned and rotting face – and flapped away.

Daemons. They had no respect for the mortal. No matter – eventually Vorp would himself wear the flesh of a daemon prince, and would toy with the lesser daemons as he wished. He knew Ve'Meth often hurt them for amusement, as he did the hapless hordes of slaves brought in from Vorp's raiding parties, and Vorp would do the same when his time came.

He headed back up the beach towards Ve'Meth's fortress, grown from the once-dead coral like a massive black stone pustule topped with a crater from which watery pus bubbled and flowed in steaming streams down its living sides. Vorp felt the shards of coral sand digging into the raw soles of his feet, and was proud that he could take the pain like it was nothing.

Onto the foothills of the fortress, through the orifice-gate and into the innards of Ve'Meth's palace, where the floors were paved with the half-living bodies of worn-out, plague-wracked slaves and the walls sweated bile. Up the tortuously twisted spiral staircases, upwards through the halls where shock troops, hardened cultists with sheets of metal nailed to their pustuled bodies, ran through the drills that had bill-hooks and morningstars slashing through imaginary foes. Through the viewing gallery where visions of the planet's pol-luted clouds scudded across the room, past the moaning huddles of disease-stricken slaves who had displeased their master, and into the audience chamber of the Daemon Prince Ve'Meth.

'Vorp. Good.' The voice that spoke was a woman's, sharp and clipped. Then, in a deep and slovenly masculine voice – 'Our world is less wearisome, for the hunting will soon be good.'

The chamber was an immense abscess beneath the pus-filled tip of the fortress-blister. And in the chamber stood eight hundred human bodies, male and female, all shapes and appearances, dressed in rags or finery or spacer's boiler suits. The only things they had in common were that they all bore the mark of some disease plain on their pasty skin, and they looked towards Gelentius Vorp as one.

'Something clean and unpestilent has come to our world, my champion,' said yet another of the bodies, for every sen-tence came from a different mouth. 'Unblessed! Cleanlisome! Four times a hundred of them, Vorp, and even now they ride the waves of our world in the hope they can face me and destroy me.'

Vorp smiled, if it could be called a smile. 'You cannot be destroyed, Lord Ve'Meth.'

All who were graced by the favour of Ve'Meth knew it to be true. The daemon prince had been blessed by the Plague God with a form most pleasing to those who revered pestilence and decay – he was a sentient disease, a colony of industrious microbes that infected the hosts of his choice and rotted their senses until they belonged completely to him. The eight hundred bodies of Ve'Meth, knitted together by the prince's infectious colony-mind, formed the blighted heart of the unnamed world, and the crusade of corruption that would one day soon sweep out from this planet and into the soft underbelly of the universe.

The eight hundred mouths of Ve'Meth scowled. 'Destruction, Vorp? Such a base, crude, unbotheratious thing! Do we fear destruction? How much of the flesh you wear now were you born with? None, I feel. You have been destroyed, Vorp. So have I, a million times over as I scaled the ladder of His pestilent Grandfathership's favour. No, I think of what they could do to the future. The potential I have created, Vorp, the bepustulated, filthificatious future! And they would make us nothing, rob us of our power, scrape our beautiful world clean of its vileness and make us just one more meaningless drop of nothing!

'Destruction, Vorp? Destruction is nothing. We will survive. But nothingness – that is something to fear.'

A little under sixteen hundred eyes glared. Ve'Meth rarely admitted to any weakness, much less fear. But Gelentius Vorp, champion of the plague god, felt it too. They had come so far, from the scattered warbands following Grandfather Nurgle through the stars to the perfection of this world, shaped by Ve'Meth's will, a seed that would grow into an empire of glorious fecundity and decay. They were so close now, but perhaps an enemy dedicated and deadly enough would have a chance of fatally upsetting their preparations.

'What do you wish of me, Lord Ve'Meth?'

Ve'Meth paused, and eight hundred faces seemed to consider this question. 'Ah, what to do? You are but a soldier, Gelentius Vorp, but one whom I have raised to be my right hand. If the enemy have lost their way, they will die no matter what they do, for my oceans are vomitorious and grave. But if they find their way here, they will surely attack with every last cleanlisome one of them. Therefore I give you, Gelentius Vorp, the task of marshalling an army on my shore, to fend off the uncorroded ones. You have the enlightened of my cults and the creatures born of my daemonhood, and the slaves if you can find a use for them.'

Gelentius Vorp felt the maggots in his entrails writhe with pride. To think that the Daemon Prince Ve'Meth himself had chosen him for such a task! He had captained daemon-fuelled plague-galleons into the cosmos to raid the space traffic foolish enough to stray too close, but he had longed to wield a true army in the field against a worthy enemy. Now he had got his wish – and on the doorstep of the fortress, under the very eyes of Ve'Meth himself!

'Lord Ve'Meth, it is a most plaguesome honour to–'

'Do not fail me, Gelentius Vorp, General of Chaos.' The voice this time was hard and commanding. 'To waste energy creating a punishment for you would not please me. Now leave, and prepare your defences.'

Eight hundred backs were turned to him. Ve'Meth was not in the habit of granting such audiences and when he did, they were short. Vorp turned and left the chamber, to feel the hundreds of eyes suddenly against his back.

'Vorp? Am I not stenchsome? Am I not the fulgurating glory of Grandfather Nurgle's joyous corruption?' said eight hundred voices.

'Yes, my prince. As always.'

One day, thought Vorp as he strode through the ichor-crusted halls of Ve'Meth's fortress, he would take on the mantle of daemon in the hordes of Ve'Meth's crusade, and this planet would bloom into a cancerous empire smearing corruption across the stars.

But first, the interlopers would die. Muscles tightened around the pitted iron of his bastard sword and the grim-worms squirmed down his spine with anticipation. Once he had been proud to lead a dozen warriors on horseback against the outposts of the Missionaria Galaxia – now he would have gibbering daemon-spawn beneath his lash, and ten thousand slave-filth crushed at his whim, all for the purpose of fending off those who would violate this world with their purity.

He found himself wishing the invaders would survive this far, so he could face them across the black coral beach and hurl them back screaming into the sea.

THE FOG ROLLED in like an enemy. Sarpedon was perched on the bow, talons dug into the iron-hard wood, the blade of the ship's prow cutting through the waves beneath him. The pulse of the engine throbbed through the hull as it powered the ship forwards at a speed even the exacting Tech-Marines had been pleased to reach.

The air was fouler the longer they travelled – it had got steadily worse over the last two days, and Sarpedon was sure it was because they were closing in on the source of the planet's sickness. Every Marine was still under orders to wear his helmet, and the serf-labourers were already developing lesions on exposed skin no matter how hard they tried to keep covered and stay below decks. The skies ended in an impenetrable ceiling of yellow-grey cloud even when there was no fog, and the waves were tipped with unhealthy foam. Fish with too many fins attached themselves to the sides of the hulls with vile round sucker-mouths, and titanic dark shapes slid into the depths in the distance.

The unnamed planet was against them. Every time one of the Soul Drinker lookouts spotted land, the damn fog swept in again. It was as if it knew they were here and blinded them as soon as there was anything worth seeing. It made it difficult in the extreme to navigate, not least because communications with the *Brokenback* had, as expected, been lost. Tyrendian, stationed on the second ship half-glimpsed through the fog, was responsible for navigation, and had filled a cabin below decks of the second ship with orbital scan printouts covered in scribbled routes and sightings. It had been hoped that Tyrendian and Sarpedon could navigate by psychic means, but the menacing darkness of the black flame burned so intensely that they feared it could poison their minds if they stared too far with their minds' eyes.

Sarpedon had put Captain Karraidin in command of the second ship – Karraidin was a respected force commander who had shown total loyalty to Sarpedon ever since the fires of the chapter war. Chaplain Iktinos was at his side, crozius in hand, along with several tactical squads and the few serf-labourers the taskforce had taken with them. The first of the three ships had been christened the *Hellblade*, after the Hellblade Pass where the Chapter had made one of its most celebrated stands.

Sarpedon's own ship – the *Ultima*, after the operations around Ultima Macharia – included his command squad

under Givrillian and rather more than a hundred Space
Marines. The third ship, hanging just behind the other two,
was commanded by Sergeant Graevus and contained the
bulk of the assault squads under Tellos. Even Sarpedon had
to consider the wisdom of putting Tellos in charge of anything – he had changed so much in body and mind that a
more hidebound commander would consider him unstable.
But his enthusiasm was such that the battle-brothers would
feel something was missing if they launched an assault without Tellos, twin hand-blades flashing, at its head. Graevus's
ship would be the first onto the shore when they reached
Ve'Meth's archipelago, and Tellos would be the first into the
face of the enemy.

Graevus had wanted to call his ship the *Quixian*, but Sarpedon had suggested otherwise. Instead, it was named the
Lakonia. This name Sarpedon approved of – it was good
omen, to name the ship after the Soul Drinkers' first true victory.

Four hundred Marines, packed into three ships. Three
arrows speeding towards the heart of corruption? Maybe.
Three pens of animals, herded into killing pens? Definitely.
They had never been more vulnerable. No matter that the
augmented musculature and the nerve-fibre bundles of
power armour made a Marine a strong swimmer – anyone
who ended up in the water would have minutes to live, and
that was assuming he could struggle out of his heavier
armour sections before he sank like a stone. A ship that went
down might take every fighting man with it.

Something huge and mindless lolled just beneath the
water's surface. Its flesh was grey and rubbery and Sarpedon
thought he could see a massive pale eye through the swelling
waves. He glimpsed great flapping things through the fog and
thought how deformed and unnatural they must be to
breathe the air here. Every Marine's internal rebreather
implant was already furring up. When they got back to the
Brokenback the apothecaries would be on constant duty
replacing the pre-lung filters.

If they got back at all.

But it didn't matter. None of it mattered, as long as they cut
out the cancer that was Ve'Meth, or did themselves the honour of dying in the attempt.

Gunfire chattered. One of the flapping creatures spasmed and fell into the sea, the sound of its death drowned by the rumblings of the waves and the creaking of the ship's timbers. Sarpedon glanced back over the deck and saw Sergeant Dreo holstering his boltgun, his squad gathered around him with guns still drawn, scanning for targets. The game was the same – any Marine who could bring down a target before the sergeant would be excused menial tasks for one day, spending it instead in contemplation and research in the archivum. This had happened twice since Dreo had been made sergeant, and that was twelve years ago.

Dreo was a hell of a shot, one of the best in the strikeforce. He had just brought down a creature that the rest of his squad had hardly been able to see. But it was guts, not a good eye, that made Dreo officer material, and it was guts that would win this battle.

Sarpedon watched Dreo turn to head back below decks. Suddenly the sergeant paused and stared back out to sea. He took off his helmet, exposing himself to the polluted air, squinting into the fog-shrouded distance.

The vox crackled and an alert rune lit up.

'Commander, we have a sighting.'

'Dreo? Give me details. A ship?'

'I think calling it a ship would be far too kind.'

'THERE, BROTHER. SEE IT?'

Zaen peered from the stern of the *Ultima* into the murk, in the direction that Keldyn was pointing. There was little more than a smudge of darkness deep into the brown-black gloom that rose and fell with the swell of the waves. It was maybe five hundred metres from the *Ultima*, and closing. 'Just,' he said.

The rest of Squad Luko was emerging from below decks to join the fire-team on the stern of the *Ultima*, even as the general alert runes were beginning to blink on the eyepieces of their helmets. The sergeant had the blades of his power claws folded back and was loading the bolter fixed to the back of his gauntlet. Brother Griv was lugging a missile launcher, one of the few heavy weapons the strikeforce had. Soul Drinkers rarely used heavy weapons, preferring to use speed and surprise, but even the proudest commanders admitted they had their uses.

'Griv, hit them as soon as they're within range. And aim low,' said Luko. Griv took up position at the edge of the stern, with the ship's wave boiling beneath him. There were several more squads up on the deck now, checking their weapons and pulling loose deck equipment into crude barricades. Captain Karraidin, resplendent in one of the few suits of terminator armour the Chapter owned, stood proud amidships, watching the Marines under his command run through the mind-drills and wargear rites to prepare themselves for the fight.

The enemy ship was close enough now to pick out some details. It was a strange bloated shape, something that should never have been seaworthy. Splintered masts stabbed up from its deck like stumps of rotted teeth, and a filmy darkness played around it as if a permanent shadow followed it. Zaen thought it might be interference in his helmet's auto-senses – but when he heard the low, dark buzzing he realised it was a swarm of insects drawn to the ship as if to a ripe corpse.

Zaen was very aware his primary weapon, a flamer, would be of no use in a long-range firefight such as one they could expect here.

'Take mine,' said Griv, who was loading the rocket launcher. He handed his own bolter to Zaen.

'My gratitude, brother,' said Zaen as he took it.

'I want that back, Zaen. And you'll owe me for the bullets.'

The all-squads vox-frequency crackled into life. 'All points, this is Graevus! We have sighted another enemy ship.'

'Understood, Graevus,' came Karraidin's voxed reply. 'You handle yours. We'll deal with this one.'

'You heard the man,' said Sergeant Luko, nodding at Griv. 'Blow them out of the water.'

Griv shouldered the missile launcher and fired.

The missile streaked over the waves and slammed into the ship, a ball of flame erupting from just above the waterline. It was close enough now to see something pouring out of the hole in the hull, lumpen and semi-liquid.

'Throne of Terra…' whispered Keldyn.

Cargo? Ballast?

No. Maggots.

The enemy ship lurched forward as if affronted by the attack. Return fire thudded from its bow, large-calibre and low-velocity. Shots peppered the sea in front of the stern and a couple impacted on the hull. The *Ultima* was made of sterner stuff than that, though.

'Sergeant Luko, give me a range,' voxed Karraidin.

'We'll be in bolter range in thirty seconds,' replied Luko.

'Good. You give the word.'

'Yes, sir.'

Griv had another missile loaded and had the launcher up to his shoulder, drawing a bead on the lower prow.

A black shadow was thrown over Griv and several Marines of Squad Luko. Too late. Zaen realised it wasn't a shadow but the wings of some immense gliding creature that had slammed onto the deck. It shrieked as bolter-rounds tore through it from underneath, its skeletal head jabbing downwards, beak seeking Griv.

Zaen dropped the bolter, tore his flamer from its holster on his back and pumped a gout of flame over the beast, hearing it howling in pain. There was a flash of near-blinding light as lightning claws sheared its head clean off. Another flying creature was diving towards the prow but bolter-fire tore it to rags as the Marines underneath the first creature hauled its body over the stern.

There were flies in the air now, turning the sky darker, a storm of tiny black bodies. The enemy ship yawed closer and Zaen was not surprised to see it was festooned with human body parts nailed to the hull. The hull bulged hugely amid ships like the abdomen of a huge insect, the splintered boards barely holding together, as the pulpy white mass of maggots poured through the missile rent and plunged foaming into the sea. Shadowy shapes flickered at the deck rail, half-glimpsed crew with no form of substance as if the horror of the ship had sucked the reality from them. They were of no consequence, Zaen felt, they weren't the threat here. It was the ship that was the enemy, bulging with malice, its hull limned with tattered mould like the rind of an old fruit, desiccated limbs and wizened heads nailed to its prow.

Bolter range.

'Fire!' yelled Zaen and the fire line assembled on the stern opened up as one, their bolters sending a layer of hot shrapnel shrieking into the enemy ship. Shells tore the deck apart, shredding the splintered wood at waist height, ripping cover apart, felling the masts like rotten oaks. Vaguely humanoid figures jerked and came apart. A great tear opened up in the wall of flies, like a dark cloud blown away by the wind.

In the time it took him to put down his flamer and take up Griv's bolter, Brother Zaen had a closer view the river of maggots and bile pouring from the hole in the enemy ship's hull. There were a dozen runes flashing warnings in his peripheral vision – atmospheric tolerance levels exceeded, lethal toxins measured, infectious agents present – all set off by the concentrated foulness inside the ship.

This time Griv got another missile off and shattered the enemy ship's hull on the waterline, so the ship would scoop up water as it advanced and be dragged prow-first downwards.

Something erupted from the new rip in the hull. Not a limb, not a tentacle, but something both jointed and flexible, tipped with a slavering lamprey's mouth, an ugly mottled grey and studded with barnacles. The pseudopod lashed out and Zaen heard, even above the massed gunfire, the crunch as it crashed through the hull of the *Ultima*.

'Damnation, what is that thing?' shouted Keldyn.

'I don't care what it is, I want it dead!' came the reply from Luko, even as a Marine from Karraidin's veteran squad arrived at the stern and fired a superheated blast from his melta-gun into the rubbery flesh of the writhing limb.

But the monster in the ship had got a grip on the *Ultima* now and was dragging itself closer. Its stench was so great it was clogging up Zaen's helmet pre-filter and the reek of rotting flesh and excrement was getting through the auto-senses. What kind of monster survived sealed in the hull of a rotting hulk of a ship, wallowing in maggots and filth?

The Chaos kind. The great enemy had many faces, and this was one of them – the monstrous and deformed, mindless and destructive. They called them Chaos spawn, and they were constantly mutating, idiot engines of destruction. It stood to reason that one of them should have made this ugly world its home.

Zaen lent his fire to those of his brothers, sending shells into the hull of the enemy ship and hopefully into the body of the monster it contained. The return fire was feeble – the humanoid crew were mostly dead or thrown off their feet by the violent lurching as their ship was dragged through the waves towards the *Ultima*. It was the beast that formed the real threat.

Above the gunfire pouring into the body of the ship there was a shriek of tearing wood. The whole side of the enemy ship was rent open and – *something* – erupted outwards, bloated and foul, its sagging flesh bubbling into new shapes. A massive spasm cast it out of the plague ship's hull, ripping the deck open, and across the closing distance between the two ships.

It was huge, the size of a spacecraft shuttle. Impossibly, the horror thudded wetly onto the starboard deck of the *Ultima*. Two squads were trapped beneath its immense bulk – some were mashed into the hardwood of the deck, some dragged themselves out with help from the battle-brothers, others were stuck fast but had the freedom to point their bolters and empty their magazines into the heaving flesh.

The beast reared up in pain, half-limbs reaching from its guts and dashing Marines aside. Zaen ducking the flying bodies and flailing tentacles, stepping round to the beast's exposed side and sending spurts of flames over its blistering skin.

He saw Luko's claws flashing and a tentacle as thick as a Marine's waist fall charred to the deck. He saw Karraidin, like a walking tank in his huge terminator armour, punching a power fist into a descending globe of flesh and bursting it like a bubble of pus. He saw Marines lining up on the opposite side of the deck and forming a firing squad that sent a sheet of hot bullets carving deep into the spawn's body, soaking the deck in something watery and brown that might have passed for blood. He saw the black-armoured form of Chaplain Iktinos and the power that fountained off the crozius he swung into the boiling flesh of the spawn.

The flesh flowed back over the wounds and the beast kept changing, horns of bone shearing out from its side and spearing Brother Keldyn through the thigh.

'Pin it down! Keep it pinned!' shouted Karraidin over the din as a mess of toothed tendrils lashed against his massive purple armour.

As the bullets poured into it and blasts of energy weapons bored deep into the spawn's hide, Zaen realised it really didn't feel pain or fear, or any of the things that might drive it back. It would soak up the bullets until every Marine was dead, and then it would nest in the hull of the *Ultima* until it drifted upon another meal. Keldyn screamed as the flesh flowed over him like water and sucked him up into the belly of the monster.

Sometimes, thought Zaen, a stupid enemy was the most dangerous of all.

The beast thrashed and knocked half of Squad Vorts into the ocean as the *Ultima* pitched wildly. Zaen's flamer and a plasma gun from Karraidin's squad razed another layer off the spawn's skin, but entrails that spilled out plastered themselves across the wound. The serf-labourers – barred by the Chapter from combat in all but the most dire circumstances – were clambering up from the hold with power spanners and crowbars, ready to die alongside their masters.

The Soul Drinkers would have to kill this creature bit by bit. Before it did the same to them.

VARUK WAS IN the hull, screaming at the Marines assisting him to swing the *Hellblade* around so they could lend fire to the *Ultima*. Sarpedon could hear him from the deck – but he was more intent on listening to the screams over the vox as Karraidin and Luko desperately tried to keep the spawn at bay. He could see the scattering of muzzle flashes and the pulse of energy weapons, and the rearing amorphous mass that had swallowed up a large chunk of the *Ultima*.

'Moving now, commander,' said a breathless Varuk as the prow of the *Hellblade* turned towards the stricken *Ultima*.

'Good. Keep us at half bolter range, I don't want it taking us down with it. And I want a ten-man reserve to take men out of the water.' Sarpedon switched a channel. 'Dreo?'

'Commander?'

'You are in fire command. It'll be mayhem on the deck but the target is large. Go for the central mass, we'll have to bleed it dry.'

'Understood, commander. Kill it for the throne.'

'Kill it for the throne, sergeant.'

Sarpedon tried the vox-channels for the *Ultima* again. Iktinos was chanting on the all-squad channel, bellowing prayers to inspire any Marine who tuned in. Karraidin was leading from the front but most of his squad were dead and only his terminator armour had kept him alive for this long. Luko was in close, too, skirmishing his squad around the monster's flailing limbs and hitting it where it hurt. Even over the static he could hear Luko's lightning claws slicing through flesh, and the growl of the squad's flamer.

But even without the vox he could pick out the tortured howls of the *Ultima's* hull as it began to break apart.

'Sarpedon to Graevus. The *Hellblade* is moving to support the *Ultima*. What is your situation?'

'One ship, closing fast,' replied the gruff-voiced Graevus. 'Full of troops, heavily armed. We're taking fire and gearing up for boarding.'

'In short, then, your situation is excellent.'

'Never better, commander. Graevus out.'

SERGEANT GRAEVUS HEFTED his power axe in his altered hand and switched to the all-squads vox.

'Here they come, lads! We don't just sit here and take it – you follow me and board 'em back!'

The assault squads cheered throatily. The Soul Drinkers had long claimed excellence in spaceship boarding actions and that included defence, where the preferred tactic was to let the enemy do the hard work in closing with you and then launch a counter-boarding action to cut down the attackers and lay into the vital crew. This would be no different in principle – confined spaces, fearsome enemy, and woe betide any man who went overboard.

The Chaos ship bore out of the mist and they saw it wasn't a ship at all. It was a sea monster, an immense shark perhaps a hundred and fifty metres long, a gargantuan living corpse with dark blue-grey skin covered with scars and bite marks, tiny blank cataracted eyes and a mouth big enough to swallow a tank and filled with sword-like teeth. The middle section of its back had been hollowed of flesh leaving the ribs exposed, between which stood the readied ranks of Chaos shock troops on a deck of desiccated organs. The shark's massive ragged tail propelled it forward through the waves towards the *Lakonia*.

The enemy boarders wore armour of black iron and carried vicious billhooks and halberds, with swords sheathed at their sides. Their bodies were misshapen and every one had its face covered, as if to spare the universe their ugliness. They would have looked like backwards savages from an evil-hearted feudal world were it not for the haloes of sickly energy that played around the power weapons of their leaders. There were perhaps two hundred of them packed onto the beast-ship.

Pistol fire crackled towards the *Lakonia*. Graevus ignored it. The few that hit were turned away by the power armour of the Soul Drinkers, one hundred and thirty of whom were ready to take whatever the enemy could throw at them and then throw it right back.

Graevus saw Tellos leaning out over the water, first in line, daring the Chaos vermin to take him on. He was unarmoured from the waist up, but somehow he seemed twice as deadly as any Marine – the determination in his eyes, the shocking pallor of his skin, the keenness of the blades with which he had replaced his lost hands.

Close now. He could see the swarms of mites living off the shark-ship's eyes and the chunks of metal and bone embedded in its raw, pink gums. The beast slewed, presenting its side to the *Lakonia* as it made the final approach. The warriors on board grabbed the polished ribs to lean out over the side, ready to catch the *Lakonia* with the hooks of their halberds and drag her close enough to be boarded.

Close enough.

'Fire!' yelled Sergeant Graevus and a hundred bolt pistols erupted. The warriors were better-armoured than they looked, perhaps clad more in infernally tough hides and resistance to pain than in mere iron. Half a dozen fell, torsos pulped by the bullets, and two more were rent open by the blasts of plasma pistols.

Tellos was the first off the *Lakonia*, as Graevus and everyone else had known he would be. He leapt the gap between the ships, whirling as he went and decapitating the closest hulking warrior with his trailing blade, shearing the arm clean off another. His teeth were bared, but Graevus felt it was through joy and not anger. Tellos loved a good fight. That, at least, had not changed.

For the few seconds that Tellos was alone on the shark-ship, maybe twelve of the enemy were cleaved apart, stabbed through the gut, sliced through face or simply pitched over the side to sink. The blades were extensions of his body as Tellos fought with a swirling, lightning-fast style, a swing that parried the blow of one attacker while taking the head off another. The Chaos troops clambered over the falling bodies of their dead to get close, and died in turn.

The shark-beast slammed into the side of the *Lakonia*, the hard wood gouging rotting flesh from its side.

'Charge!' yelled Graevus, and leapt over the side.

The Assault Marines charged as one, chainswords biting deep into the first enemy they found, slashing down the first rank of Chaos warriors like a hurricane felling a forest. The beachhead forged by Tellos let those nearer the prow thrust deep into the mass of Chaos troopers, running past their gore-drenched sergeant to lay into those warriors reeling from his attack.

Graevus landed with a dozen Assault Marines at his back, the dried loops of the monster's compacted entrails spongy beneath his feet. There was a mass of black iron all around him and a hundred halberd heads stabbing down at him. He blocked one, pivoted, swept his power axe one-handed up into a soldier's torso and clove a grimacing face-wrought visor in two. Chainblades lanced in from behind him and carved limbs and heads away. The Soul Drinkers yelled their battle-cries and the Chaos warriors howled in anger and pain, punctuated by the report as a bolt pistol was brought to bear and the hideous grinding of chainsword teeth against bone.

Graevus paused and glanced around to see a bolt of Chaos-stuff lance down from a flying figure's finger and explode deep in the seething mass of combat towards the prow. The flying creature was humanoid but cloaked in ragged shadows, and was held aloft by a near-solid halo of flies. As Graevus watched, Tellos reached up and hooked an elbow over the shark-beast's spine, using it to lever himself up level with the magician. Tellos lunged and impaled the magician on his hand-blades, ignoring the black lightning that arced into him from the magician's hands, and held him aloft and helpless.

Bolter-fire from the supporting Tactical Marines on the deck of the *Lakonia* thudded into the spasming magician's body. He was ripped apart until all that remained of him were shreds of shadow drifting feebly on the wind, and dark charred stains on Tellos's blades. With a glance of acknowledgement at the

Marines on the *Lakonia*, Tellos vaulted back down into the fray.

Graevus allowed himself a smile and swung his axe back into the iron-clad warriors, knowing that with every blow another of the Emperor's most hated foes would die.

Every Marine was brimming with the fire of battle, the white-hot glorious surge that made men into heroes and Marines into something more. Graevus felt himself becoming lost in the glare of battle, and knew that the Soul Drinkers would not take a step back until every single Chaos-loving piece of filth was dead.

ZAEN WAS BACK-TO-BACK with Chaplain Iktinos. The deck beneath them was slick with the blood of Squad Vorts, of whom not one Marine survived, mingled with the steaming foulness that poured from the Chaos spawn. The beast had extruded a huge club-headed limb which arched over their heads – from its tip barbed whips of sinew were lashing. Iktinos was parrying them with his crozius, sending showers of sparks cascading, while Zaen kept up the stream of flame into the side of the monster.

They were cut off, surrounded by walls of flesh. They had to fend off the beast themselves, for they could not rely on the battle-brothers cutting their way through to rescue them.

Zaen had been in awe of Iktinos as a novice and some of that still remained – to think that anyone could be picked for their piety and strength of mind from amongst such devoted men as the Soul Drinkers fascinated him. Now, Zaen would die alongside the Chaplain who had so mesmerised him during his novicehood, and he was proud.

He could barely tell what was happening elsewhere on the *Ultima*. The deck was smashed to pulp and the spawn's growing bulk had poured into the hull. Gunfire came from all directions, sometimes in massive walls of shrapnel, sometimes single shots from battle-brothers trapped or stranded by the beast's always-changing limbs. The vox was a mess, with only Karraidin's booming voice cutting through the yells of the dying and the howling battle-oaths.

'We will go to the Halls of Dorn together, Chaplain,' said Zaen breathlessly as he blasted at the limb arching over them with Griv's bolter, pausing to slam his last fuel canister into the flamer.

'There is no place there for me yet, Brother Zaen,' replied Iktinos, slicing through a writhing spear of tendon. 'When my task here is done, then I can die.'

The spawn reared up over them, a wave of flesh. It roared like nothing alive could, and crashed down on them like a landslide.

The flabby slabs of fat and slippery loops of entrails closed over Zaen as he tried to dive out of the way, a massive liquid weight slamming down onto him and driving him into the wood of the deck. Everything was black and hot, and foul ichor was forced through his helmet's pre-filter. His arms were pinned down, one leg folded under him in a gunshot of pain, he felt the plasteel of his armour's backpack fracturing and his breastplate bending out of shape. His shoulder pads split and there was a white-hot shock as his skull fractured.

His trigger finger spasmed and bolts from Griv's gun spun into the pressing mass of flesh. It would do no good. He tried his flamer hand but the pilot light had been smothered.

It was a rare Space Marine who retired from combat duty. In many ways they existed to die in battle. Brother Zaen had not just been trained and altered to fight the Emperor's foes across the stars – his purpose was also to give his life to the fires of war, so that his death would form a part of that monolithic legend of the Chapter, which would inspire its future Marines to their own feats of arms and sacrifice.

This is what Zaen told himself as his abdominal armour gave way and his organs began to burst under the spawn's weight.

A blue-white gash opened in front of his eyes and a black-armoured hand reached in, grabbing the lip of his shoulder pad and dragging him out onto the deck. Pain ripped through him as his mangled leg was twisted further, but he was alive – the huge inspiring form of Iktinos was bent above him, hauling him from the sucking flesh.

A thick leathery mass shot out and caught Iktinos square in the chest, hurling him backwards. Zaen glanced round and through the gauze of pain he saw a cavernous orifice opening in the wall of flesh. It was a mouth, and he was staring down the wet quivering tunnel of the spawn's throat. Iktinos had been batted aside by the beast's tongue, a thick leathery stalk tipped with a knotted club of meat.

The blubbery mass of its body slid underneath him and Brother Zaen was washed towards its mouth. He tried to brace himself with his hands but the skin was slippery and the shadow of the spawn's jaw passed over him. Past his shattered foot he could see the ribbed shaft of its throat convulsing as it swallowed, hungry to contract around him and squeeze him to crimson paste.

Teeth slid from the pulpy gums as Zaen slipped over the threshold. One speared into his groin and out through the small of his back, and another stabbed down from above through the top of his shoulder, ripping through one of his lungs and deep into his guts.

He had his left arm free. Everything else was broken. In that hand he held his flamer but he needed another hand to flick on the nozzle's pilot light. He tossed the useless weapon into the maw of the spawn, which was darkening as the mouth closed behind him.

He reached round to where his right hand dangled feebly. His hand had clenched as the nerves were severed and it still held Griv's bolter. But it was too far away. His left didn't reach.

Come on, novice Zaen. What are you? A child! A weak, useless child! So there is pain? You have had pain before. You survived. Survive it again. Move your hand, novice. Move your right hand and stop complaining like a scolded stripling.

Zaen moved his right hand and snatched Griv's bolter from it with his left before the tendons snapped. Was Griv still alive? Would he ever know how his weapon met its end?

Zaen could just see the dull glint of the flamer's fuel canister in the failing light, lodged in the throat of the spawn.

The jaws closed and the monster's teeth sliced through Zaen's body. Out of the corner of his eye he saw the right side of his body flopping away. A knee was forced up into his throat.

Everything went black as the jaws closed.

Zaen fired.

SARPEDON SAW THE collar of flame that burst out through what must have been the beast's throat. The *Hellblade* was closing fast – he was close enough to see the Soul Drinkers on the *Ultima's* deck illuminated in the flame, still spitting gunfire into the rearing spawn that now took up about three quarters of the ship mass. Already Sarpedon's men were pulling Soul Drinkers out of the sea and hauling them gasping onto the deck of the *Hellblade*. Many of them had discarded most of their armour to stop them from sinking into the black depths, and some were completely unarmoured.

They said that the whole of Squad Vorts was dead, and maybe thirty others, either torn apart by the spawn or pitched into the sea to drown.

The Marines cheered as the head of the beast was all but torn off by the explosion, burning fuel streaming from the huge wound. Sarpedon's Soul Drinkers, and those from the *Ultima* who still had their weapons, formed a three-rank firing squad in the prow of the *Hellblade*. Sarpedon took his place amongst them, bolter drawn. 'Captain Karraidin, this is Sarpedon,' he voxed. 'Tell your men to get their heads down and hold tight. We'll get them out of there.'

'Yes, lord!' came the reply through a haze of static and gunfire.

'Soul Drinkers!' yelled Sarpedon to the Marines around him. 'The beast is hurt! It is blind and confused. If we hit it now we can kill it!' He took aim at the rearing bulk of the Chaos spawn, which was now belching smoke from the massive charred wound. 'Open fire!'

This time the monster had no hope. Its nerve centre was shattered by the explosion, and all it could do was sit there on the deck of the *Ultima* and take the hail of gunfire. Before, it had been sheltered by the hull of the enemy ship or fired at by scattered opponents. Now it bore the full weight of sustained bolter-fire from nearly one hundred and fifty Space Marines, each one thirsting for revenge against the good men they had lost.

Its skin blistered and cracked against the heat from within and without. Chunks of bloody fat were thrown into the air and fountains of ichor spurted as its organs ruptured. It lost what little shape it had and reared up in its death throes, scattering storms of muscle and ragged skin, before it toppled back and dragged its massive semi-liquid bulk into the sea. The *Ultima* yawed violently with the beast's weight, the

Marines still on board clinging desperately, but as the spawn's body poured into the water it righted itself and stayed firm.

Sarpedon's Marines cheered the spawn's death even as Varuk gunned the *Hellblade's* engine to sweep in and rescue what they could.

THE SHARK-SHIP KNEW its crew were dying and it was starting to thrash, its massive tail sending sheets of filthy water into the air, its huge mouth biting at the air.

The Chaos dead were two bodies deep on the deck, and the Soul Drinkers had effectively taken half the ship. The Chaos survivors had closed ranks and were keeping the Soul Drinkers' chainswords at bay with halberds and hooked spears. The Space Marines were replying with pistol fire, keeping the Chaos warriors pinned and wearing them down. Tellos was up close, stabbing into the black-armoured mass, weaving between the thrusting blades. He was red to the shoulders in blood, and had a score of Chaos dead to his name.

'Marines, prepare to fall back! We've got to kill this thing!' called Graevus over the vox. The Chaos troops might be beaten but they were now riding on the back of a huge and angry sea monster. The *Lakonia* was locked to the side of the shark-ship and could easily be brought down if the monster dived.

Graevus pointed at the three closest Marines. 'You! Give me your frags, now!' They handed him their frag grenades and, gesturing for them to follow, he ran towards the head end of the ship, where a wall of leathery muscle pulsed. Graevus's power axe flashed and a gash opened in the thick membrane, exposing the roiling pink mass of the shark's brain stem beyond.

'Soul Drinkers, disengage and cut the ship free! Now!'

Instantly, the Marines were falling back, keeping up fire. Tellos had to be physically dragged away from the slaughter and hauled back onto the *Lakonia*.

Graevus took the bundle of frag grenades in his altered hand and thrust it deep into the shark's brain stem.

'Fire in the hole!' he yelled and ducked to the side. The explosion was deep and muffled and sent a shower of pink blubber raining down over the deck. The shark spasmed violently, throwing two of the Marines off their feet. Graevus looked up and saw the *Lakonia* was free but still close and sprinted towards it, lashing out with his axe at the Chaos soldiers who stood in his way and cutting them down in short order. The shark thrashed as it died, its brain stem destroyed, Graevus kept his feet and reached the edge of the deck.

He leapt, and found the solid wood of the *Lakonia's* deck under his feet. He turned in time to see the shark-ship rolling over, exposing its mottled white belly, before it slid under the waves.

He looked round at the Marines who were watching the monster die. He didn't think they had lost any of them. Every one of them was spattered with gore, and Tellos was thick with it, shocking red against his pale skin. Graevus looked down at himself and saw he was spattered with clots of brain matter.

'Graevus to Sarpedon,' he voxed. 'Enemy ship destroyed. No losses.'

'Understood, sergeant. The *Ultima* is lost. Return to assist.'

So it had not all gone well. But they knew it would be bad here – they knew they would be fortunate if any of them got off alive. Now they had lost their first battle-brothers on this world.

'Acknowledged, commander. Graevus out.'

CHAPTER ELEVEN

ARCHMAGOS KHOBOTOV KNEW she was here. He could hear the machines whispering to him. The rogue Tech-Priest Sasia Koraloth had chosen a poor place to hide, for there was nothing in this place but machinery, and the machines here were like his children. The forge world of Koden Tertius was falling under the archmagos's mantle, like the *674-XU28* before it, to the extent that when the Omnissiah was with him he could hear the generatorium depths like old friends telling him their secrets.

She was down here. She was wounded – the walkways tasted the blood where she had stood. She was desperate, for the coolant regulators heard her sobbing. And most importantly, every system in the sector told him that she had with her an item of such power that the energy readouts spiked wherever she went. That could mean only one thing: Sasia Koraloth had the Soulspear.

The mechadendrites slid back from the generatorium readout console and the mundane world swam back into view. Khobotov and the tech-guard strike team he commanded were at the top of the generatorium stack – a massive turbine sunk vertically into a cylindrical pit in the rock of Koden Tertius. The great silvery bulk of the turbine was bounded by a spindly network of walkways and control centres where tech-priests, menials and servitors would keep the generatorium at optimal power output. All those personnel had been evacuated, and the only living things in this area now were Khobotov's men and Sasia Koraloth.

Even powered down, the turbine's latent energy output was massive. It swelled Khobotov's iron heart to be in the presence of such power.

Captain Skrill adjusted the readout on his auspex and turned to the archmagos. 'We've got biomass, sir, but not much of it. Probably dead. Think it could be her?'

'Unlikely. Tech-Priest Koraloth had very limited augmentation, her bio-readings would be higher. It is likely your auspex sensors will be blinded by the artefact when we get near, in any case.'

'Understood. Shall I have the squad begin the sweep?'

'Proceed.'

Skrill was a good man. Blunt, simple, with an acceptable head for logic and little compassion. He and his dozen-strong tech-guard unit were clad in heavy rust-red flak-armour and carried high-calibre autogun variants. Khobotov had witnessed the effectiveness of the unit's mass-reactive ammunition in police actions against wayward menials. When Sasia Koraloth's gene-signature had been flagged up by a servitor cleaning up a bloodstain in the generatorium sector, Khobotov had personally selected Skrill's squad for the search. His tactics were crude but well-suited to the mission. There was little fear that Koraloth would be left alive, which suited Archmagos Khobotov very well.

'Vilnin, cover us with the longrifle,' ordered Skrill. 'And don't fire until I give the word. I don't want you wasting any more servitors, we're the ones have to pay for 'em.' The thin-faced Vilnin nodded, uncased a long, slim sniping rifle, and took up a vantage point at the edge of the gantry.

'The rest of you, with me. There's only one of her but she's cornered, so you stay alert. Move!'

Khobotov skimmed just above the walkway on his grav-dampeners, drifting down the spiralling gantries after the advancing squad, watching the fractals they formed as they spread out through the web of walkways. Their angles of fire were good, he noted. Most mathematical. Skrill would go far. In fact, the *674-XU28* had lost a number of security components in the unfortunate altercation off Lakonia. The ship was still short-handed, and Khobotov resolved to have Skrill and his men transferred to the *674-XU28* as soon as Koraloth was apprehended.

A gunshot rang out, sharp and illogical. Not one of Skrill's squad – it was a las weapon, power setting high.

'Shots fired!' voxed Skrill as his men dropped down. 'Anyone hit?' Eleven beacon pulses sounded. The shot had missed. 'Vilnin! Target, now!'

'Think I saw a las-shot,' replied the sharpshooter. 'Somewhere underneath us.'

Skrill waved a hand and the squad split up, scattering quickly to approach the target area from a number of angles. Below them the generatorium output had created a dim fuzz of smoke and shadows, where the exposed inductor coils bled the light out of the air. It would have been a good place to hide, reflected Khobotov, if there had been a way out other than through the advancing tech-guard.

'Found our biomass, sir,' voxed one of the troopers. Khobotov's vision zoomed in to where the trooper was standing over a pathetic bundle of rags. A thin, stringy hand reached out feebly.

Ah, El'Hirn. Of course. There had been rumours the old ghost was still alive. He had been a promising magos in his day, before he fell victim to some insane heretical notions about the Omnissiah and had been cast out of the tech-priesthood. Without the support of his Mechanicus brethren his augmentations would have failed and his flesh withered until there was nothing left. Khobotov wondered how El'Hirn had survived this long and had the energy to team up with Koraloth in her schemes, but it was of little matter. Evidently the two had had a falling-out as they fled, judging by the high-energy las-burns on his robes.

Khobotov reached out with his hyper-augmented senses and latched on to the emergency vox-caster system. 'Tech-priest Koraloth,' he said, his voice booming from a score of speakers dotted throughout the generatorium structure. 'You are surrounded and alone. Escape is a logical impossibility.

Give yourself up to us, Sasia Koraloth, deliver up the artefact you have stolen, and we will not have to risk damaging the holy machinery of this place in a firefight.'

Another shot, hitting the trooper who had found El'Hirn's corpse and throwing him onto his back. His torso armour fizzed with the heat of the shot, as bursts of auto-fire rattled down from the troopers on the gantries around him. Koraloth fired again from somewhere in the darkness below, hot las-bolts lancing up at the tech-guard.

'Suppression fire!' called Skrill, aiming his own autogun over the gantry railing and spraying fire downwards. 'Krik, you alright?'

'Think I took a lung shot, sir,' groaned the wounded trooper. Khobotov saw another tech-guard scurrying along the walkway to help him. Skrill's men might be tough, but there was still far too much flesh in them for Khobotov to truly respect them. If he had taken a wound like that he would just have shut down one pneumo-filter and switched to another one. This man would probably die, because the Omnissiah had not touched him with the same metallic blessings.

Vilnin's voice crackled over the vox. 'Think I got her, sir. There's an observation platform about four hundred metres down. I've got someone moving on the infra-red.'

'Good,' replied Skrill. 'Put a bullet through her.'

'She's got hard cover, sir, I can't get a shot. It's... there's something else down there. Looks like a shrine.'

'A what?'

'You know. Sacred stuff. Altar, bunch of books. She's got cover behind the altar and I can't take her from this angle. I can move around the turbine to the other side but it's a long walk.'

'Stay put, Vilnin. Put a couple of shots her way, get her scared. Then shut her down her if she moves.'

'Yes, sir.'

Interesting, thought Khobotov as he listened in. A temple. It seemed El'Hirn had found another convert to whatever half-baked belief system he had created for himself. 'Sasia Koraloth, your false religion can offer you no hope. Whatever El'Hirn told you was a lie. There is only one Omnissiah, and He is most jealous.'

Khobotov drifted further down, keeping gantries and girders between him and Koraloth, blocking her aim. It would not do to have his components tarnished with lasburns.

'You're wrong!' yelled a small, frightened voice from far below, audible only to Khobotov's hypersenses. 'He has spoken to me! He has shown me the way!'

'Then why did you find it necessary to kill your fellow unbeliever?' Khobotov could see the renegade tech-priest now. She was cowering behind a slab of carbon upon which were set two candelabra and a number of books, on a hexagonal observation platform hung with banners covered in scribbled equations. The place would normally be deserted apart from the occasional mindless maintenance servitor, and so it made a deceptively good choice for a hidden place of worship. Koraloth herself was pale and drawn with fatigue and fear, her tech-priest's robes torn and unclean, the barrel of the laspistol still glowing red in her hand.

'He couldn't face knowing the truth!' she shouted. 'When it came to make the offering, he was afraid! Everything we know is wrong, Khobotov! The Engineer of Time has told me in my dreams!'

Quite insane, thought Khobotov. A shame. There was a slight chance that Sasia Koraloth could have been a tech-priest of some note, and in any case her skill at reverse engineering would have had its uses. Instead, she had to die. But while the Omnissiah disliked the waste of good material, he abhorred the corruption of His sacred name far more.

Khobotov stepped off the gantry and floated downwards, the immense metallic curve of the turbine stack sliding by beside him. He rarely engaged his grav-dampeners so overtly, thinking it a rather vulgar way to travel, but he wanted a closer look at Koraloth and her temple before the tech-guard killed her.

Koraloth held up a hand, and from the sudden power-glare in Khobotov's eyelenses he knew the hand held the Soulspear. The artefact had just as strong an aura of power as when Khobotov had first seen it. He would find someone else to study it, and when they had made some headway in the dangerous and unpredictable process of unlocking its secrets, he would take over the research and add the Soulspear's majesty to the Omnissiah's masterpiece of learning. Koraloth was no loss. The Soulspear was what mattered.

'See!' she yelled. 'See how much you know!'

She slammed the Soulspear into the carbon altar, end-first. For a split second Khobotov's senses shut down in the face of massive overload, the synapses parting to prevent the surge of sensory energy coursing into the archmagos's brain.

An energy spike so vast even the archmagos's blessedly augmented body could barely cope with it. A discharge of power so far off the scale that the first thing he heard when his aural senses came back on line was the shriek of the generatorium stack coming apart beside him.

Critical mass.

There was a great disc of light where only the grimy depths of the generatorium sink had been before. It was white and blinding, the glare swallowing everything else, even the tumbling sheets of metal pouring from the ruptured turbine. Khobotov was dimly aware of a strangled vox-traffic, screams and howlings of pain, from the tech-guard somewhere above him. The normally dominant, analytical part of his brain told him their skin would be dry scraps fluttering upwards on the column of light, just as his own robes were burning away around him. But most of him just gawped at the fantastic output of power. Machine-discipline had served him so well these last centuries, but the Omnissiah's logic faltered in the sight of such madness.

Sasia Koraloth stood on the platform that floated at the heart of the light, the Soulspear a blazing thunderbolt in her hand. She was screaming something at him but the only sound was a wall of white noise.

The light rose up and began to swallow her, and beneath its surface something moved. Something humanoid but gargantuan, its features swimming beneath the curtain of light, reaching a hand upwards. Nails like jewels broke the surface, pale perfect skin. Symbols flashed in the air, numbers, letters, strange sigils that throbbed with power.

Sasia Koraloth sank into the light, taking the Soulspear with her. Beside her, the giant's face, still half-obscured by the glare, looked upwards with burning eyes. The arcane symbols solidified, and suddenly the air was full of sorcerous equations, leading rings of power around the upstretched hand.

Bright bolts of energy swirled in great circles as the hand opened and the fingers spread to surround Khobotov.

His motor systems burned out, Khobotov hung paralysed as the fingers closed around him. Scrabbling around inside his own head, he managed to disconnect his few remaining sensory inputs before he was crushed.

THE SOUL DRINKERS had lost more than fifty of their number. Over a quarter of the strike force down in a matter of minutes, trapped on the *Ultima* or dragged beneath the waves. Many of those they had pulled out of the water had discarded much of their armour and there were many Soul Drinkers who would have to fight on with parts of their armour missing. There weren't enough backpacks and without a power source others would go almost completely unarmoured, for even a Soul Drinker would struggle to move in an unpowered suit of Space Marine armour. Their augmented physiology would resist the pollution of the unnamed world's seas, but that would be of little consolation when they found what Ve'Meth had planned for them, and would have to face it almost naked.

Not unarmed, though. For not one of them had dropped his gun.

The night was clammy and cold at the same time, the brutal jagged ocean stretching out around them, bleak and endless. It was worse than the fog, for here a man might feel how small he was compared to an entire planet that knew they were here and wanted them dead. Ve'Meth had seen them arrive, of that he could be sure. The ships they encountered were probably part of a cordon thrown around the daemon's fortress island, a lifeform's reaction to foreign bodies. Sarpedon could feel the baleful heat of the black flame that Yser had described, the horrible mocking laugh he had heard in his dreams of Quixian Obscura. He was not just closer to Ve'Meth – the foul thing was watching him, scrying by some sorcery or watching through the eyes of the monstrous fish and distant flying creatures.

He looked round to see the survivors of Squad Luko taking over the watch at the stern of the *Hellblade*. Sergeant Luko and his few remaining men were some of the Marines who had been accommodated on the *Hellblade* and *Lakonia* after the shattered remnants of the *Ultima* had sunk beneath the waves.

Sergeant Luko saluted Sarpedon. Sarpedon left his vigil in the stern and picked his way across the shifting deck.

'Sergeant Luko, Chaplain Iktinos told me of what you did on the *Ultima*.'

'And I could tell you something of him, too, and of every Marine there. We all fought.'

'He told me how Brother Zaen died.'

Luko nodded slowly. 'Zaen. An excellent death. Something to remember.' Luko could put on a good face, never fazed by the fires of battle. But like every leader amongst the Soul Drinkers there had been a fair few men lost under him, and it always left him reflective. Few would recognise the fiercely joyous Luko save those who really knew him. 'Vorts gone, too, and all the serfs. I heard Graevus's mob did better, though.'

'They left nothing alive, and took no loss.'

'Just how Daenyathos would have liked it.' Luko looked round and Sarpedon saw how old he looked bare-headed. Sarpedon had relaxed the helmet-discipline, if only because so many Marines had lost their helmets in the ocean. He realised that he was old, too – ninety years, if he stopped to think about it, seventy of those as a fully-fledged Soul Drinker. But those seventy years seemed like a solid slab of memory, one long apprenticeship of battle he had to complete before his real life started. He had dreamed of living out a glorious career in the service of the Imperium of Man, but now he realised he had just been a child, making mistakes he had to learn from.

'They say Tellos took half of them down himself,' said Luko.

'They say right. It will be some time before I can give Sergeant Tellos an independence of command, though. Graevus's men had to drag him back on board the *Lakonia*.' Sarpedon had often asked himself the question of Tellos's future. He had lost the discipline that had made him a sergeant, but doubled the ferocity and bravery that had made him all but idolised by the Assault Marines around him. Grim as it may sound, Sarpedon suspected the problem would solve itself – there was little doubt Tellos would be the

first off the *Lakonia* onto the shore of Ve'Meth's fortress, and
it was unlikely he would survive forging the beachhead for
the Marines deploying behind him. It would be a good
death, one of the best.

There was the sudden flash of an alarm rune at the edge of
Sarpedon's vision. He peered through the twilight to see the
lookout in the prow of the *Lakonia*, pointing to the dim horizon as Marines gathered behind him.

'Sarpedon here. What do you see?'

It was Iktinos's rune that flashed. The Chaplain had taken
his turn in the watch, just like the ordinary Marines who
made up his congregation. 'Land sighted, sir. We're closing in.'

'Understood, Chaplain. The *Lakonia* can lead, we'll follow
you in.' Sarpedon saw it now, too – a hard black scab just visible on the horizon.

He would have Graevus prepare the assault troops, and
know that Tellos would be doing the same on the *Lakonia*.
The black flame was burning bright now, the mocking laughter loud in his head. The final run had begun, and he had
seen too much of this world to believe any of them would
survive.

TECH-PRIEST SASIA KORALOTH was dead. There was only Sasia
the child, her mind blasted backwards as she was bathed in
the sea of power that had swallowed her.

She was alone. She was afraid. There was light and noise all
around her, filling her, too much for her to cope with. There
was heat against her skin, and currents of power pulling her
this way and that, like a thousand hands snatching at her. She
opened her eyes, the white light nearly blinding her. But she
wanted to see. She wanted to know where she was, what had
happened to her, who was doing all this.

The light solidified, and the Engineer of Time stood before
her.

He was a thousand storeys tall. His skin was white crystal.
His thoughts were magic, and the symbols of that magic were
orbiting him in wide circles of sigils, spelling out impossibly
complex equations of power.

He held out a hand the size of a city and, with incredible
grace, plucked something from her grasp. It was a tiny thing
the little girl had been clutching in her woman's fist, and

dimly, Sasia remembered that she had wanted the Engineer to take it, and that perhaps now he had it he might be happy.

It held the thing up in front of his face and examined it with eyes like twin gas giants.

'Such a small thing,' said a voice in her head. 'So much anguish. Most satisfying.'

The Soulspear. It was called the Soulspear.

And suddenly she knew that the Engineer had everything he needed now, and that he had forgotten about her already.

He looked away from her and suddenly the forces he had created to hold her intact were dismissed. The light exploded and gargantuan islands of madness rolled in, oceans of tears, malicious lumps of thought looming dark like kraken.

Little Sasia was torn apart by the sudden storm of experience the human consciousness wasn't supposed to comprehend. She lost her mind a split-second before her body was dissolved by the forces of the warp.

In the faded splendour of the pleasure-yacht's viewing gallery, Tech-Marine Lygris looked out through the huge oculus. The great blinded eye of the unnamed planet glared back at him. Lygris knew Sarpedon and his battle-brothers would be down there, probably fighting, probably dying. They had been down there for several days now – probably halfway through the mission at the best guess. Communications with them had, as expected, been cut the instant the Thunderhawks had dropped through the thick layer of bone-coloured cloud. There had been nothing but static over the comms.

Part of him said he should have been down there. But, with so little known about Ve'Meth and his capabilities, Sarpedon had needed a level head to stay on the *Brokenback*. They were here to prove the Chapter's devotion to the Emperor's will, and if that was the part Lygris had to play, then so be it.

He wanted to fight. He wanted to feel a bolter in his hand and fires of battle all around him. But he was needed here, just in case.

He felt the rumble in the deck through his feet and heard it a split-second after, rolling through the *Brokenback's* cavernous body. The image of the unnamed world shuddered as the crystal of the oculus shook and somewhere a klaxon

sounded as a component ship's alarm system activated. There
was a jolt and Lygris only just kept his feet, tortured metal
wailing through the walls.

He switched on his vox. 'Engineering, what was that?'

'The sensors say it's a warp fluctuation, sir. Could be something arriving.'

'I'm in the viewing gallery, sector green. Route it to the oculus.'

The huge round viewing screen above him flashed and an
image was cast onto it, a composite of the region of nearby
space taken from the hundreds of sensoria all over the *Brokenback*. The disturbance was a boiling mass of blue-white
against the star field, pulsing like a beating heart and sending
out the pulses that shook the space hulk even now. Lygris
called up the damage report – the *Brokenback* was made of
tough stuff, though, and there had been little more than a
few nuts and bolts shaken loose.

Could it be another ship? Unlikely. But they were orbiting
a world saturated with Chaos, and everything about it was
unlikely.

'This is Tech-Marine Lygris,' he announced over the vox-
casters. 'All personnel to weapons stations.'

With so many Soul Drinkers on the surface the *Brokenback*
was effectively on a skeleton crew of Marines and serfs, and
every man would be heading to his weapons stations, ready
to launch the racks of torpedoes they had found intact, or fire
the macrocannon and magnalasers that studded the hulk's
surface.

As Lygris watched the disturbance rippled and faded, sinking back into the blackness of space. The *Brokenback* stopped
shaking, and the sensorium data streaming along the top of
the image returned to normal. Background radiation was up,
but there was little more.

Could be a simple ripple in the immaterium, to be
expected in a place as horribly linked with Chaos as this. Or
it could be something more sinister, that didn't show up on
the *Brokenback's* myriad scanners. Such a thing was, effectively, impossible, but Sarpedon had not given Lygris
command of the *Brokenback* to take needless risks. He would
keep the hulk on alert for a couple of hours, until he was satisfied any danger had passed.

He had the oculus blink back to the image of the unnamed planet, and the blinded eye kept on staring.

THE ISLANDS OF the archipelago rose all around them as they approached, midnight spires of broken black coral jabbing from the ocean. Ve'Meth's influence was so strong every battle-brother felt it and the pollution was stronger and viler here – there was a sickly rainbow sheen, like oil, on the surface of the water, and the coral was crusted with residue where the waves lapped at them. The air was heavy with toxins, the light feeble, the cloud a dirty dark slab of pollution in the sky like a ceiling. The lookouts saw islands floating in the air, and squat amphibian daemons on top of the coral spikes, vomiting gore into the breakers beneath. They glimpsed the distant fins of giant sharks and the mottled bodies of kraken.

They sighted other ships – a ghastly spidery thing that skimmed across the water on wooden legs, a bloated galleon with sails of skin – but the *Lakonia* and the *Hellblade* were hidden by the poor light and mist. Sarpedon wondered why they were not attacked again. Perhaps they had proved their valour in ship-to-ship combat to such a degree that Ve'Meth would rather face them on land than at sea again. Or maybe this place was so wholly Chaotic that the Soul Drinkers were simply too few to spot amongst all the madness.

There were flies everywhere. They got into armour joints, helmets, bolter actions. Wargear rites had to be doubled. Iktinos led the men in prayers for deliverance and strength in the face of such all-pervading corruption. Sarpedon had asked Tyrendian, the strike force's other psyker, what he could tell of Ve'Meth. Tyrendian's nightmares had been of a huge serpent, wrapping itself round a world and crushing it to death, then swallowing it whole along with billions of souls.

There was no need to navigate. Ve'Meth was like a dark beacon, shining evilly. Tyrendian, in the *Lakonia*, took them in. The engines were little more than idling as the ships swept almost silently through the shadows of the archipelago, the lumped black coral reefs becoming more frequent until they stood in rows like the ribs of something huge and dead.

Nine days after they had departed in their ships, and five after the loss of the *Ultima*, they came within sight of Ve'Meth's fortress.

It was the size of a mountain. Great pustules dotted its surface, opening and closing like dumb mouths weeping bile. Noxious yellowish steam rose in clouds from cracks in the scarred coral surface, and flocks of winged creatures flapped blindly around the fortress's distant pinnacle. Rivers of pus ran down the mountain's sides, clotted thick and squirming with creatures. Far above, thunderstorms raged in the solid black slab of flies that hung in a thick layer in the sky.

It was as if the black coral had been alive and then infected by something so terrible that it had flared up into this immense tumor. Even from here, the Soul Drinkers could see the columns of men marching out of it – armoured warriors such as Graevus's men had faced, shambling monstrous things, bent-backed slaves, daemons with flesh of pure disease.

Sergeant Dreo had been on lookout when the fortress was sighted, and had summoned Sarpedon right away. Sarpedon looked upon the fortress and wondered how they could assault such a place. It was not just a huge and well-defended strongpoint, but it would be alive – malevolent and deadly, more an enemy than a battlefield. He decided to keep it simple – beach the ships, pour out, and use all the speed and hitting power of the Soul Drinkers to break into the fortress and storm through it until they found Ve'Meth.

Simple. Like all the best plans. Of course, Ve'Meth's plan would be simpler still – throw waves of Chaos troops at the attacking Soul Drinkers until every one was dead.

Sarpedon voxed down to the *Hellblade's* hull. 'Varuk? Gun the engines. We're making our approach.'

'Yes sir!' The refitted Thunderhawk engines growled beneath Sarpedon's feet and the *Lakonia* darted forward, driving an arrowhead of rippling water in its wake. The *Lakonia* took the lead, sweeping fast through the waters, peeling off to one side as the approach began. The Marines on the deck scuttled into the hull to make the final battle-rites, leaving a couple of lookouts to spot the forces that would oppose the landing.

The two ships would land close together, but far enough apart so they wouldn't get in each other's way. The Marines from each one would act as an independent force, meeting up in the fortress if all went well but not relying on it. Sarpedon would be in command of the *Hellblade's* complement – Karraidin had command over the *Lakonia*, but he would be as aware as anyone that Tellos and Graevus would be leading the assault.

Sarpedon checked the mechanism of his bolter, letting the well-practiced motion act as a trigger to shut out the rest of his thoughts so he could think only of war. It was a trick he had learned when only a novice, when the universe had been much simpler. He switched on the aegis circuit and felt the old power spiralling around him, through the same armour that had clad his body every day of battle for seventy years.

Then he went below deck, to see that his battle-brothers had readied themselves for the fight.

'ONE MINUTE THIRTY!' called Graevus from the prow. The one hundred and seventy-odd Soul Drinkers in the hold of the *Lakonia* would be making their final entreaties to Rogal Dorn, that he might keep his gaze upon them and see the valour they would display.

The *Lakonia* was really moving now, carving towards the broad beach of black coral sand that stretched in broad crescent, beneath the shadow of the fortress-mountain above. The fortifications were crude – chunks of black crystal and sharpened bone jutting from bunkers of piled-up rocks – but they would be effective enough against a force without heavy weaponry or artillery to break them open.

But that wasn't the worst.

The worst was that there must have been five thousand of the enemy waiting on the shore, waiting for the *Lakonia*. In front were slaves, pale-skinned, sickly and chained. Behind the slaves were ranks of huge man-beasts using pikes and halberds to herd them forwards into the surf. Even at this distance Graevus could hear the screams of the drugged slaves and bellowing of the beastmen that drove them on.

'Thirty seconds!' yelled Graevus over the vox. He heard the reassuring sound of one hundred and seventy bolters cocked in unison.

The *Lakonia's* hull scraped the sea floor as the shore swept closer. Graevus could see the slave-soldiers herded into a defensive line – they were chained together by their collars, and had crude clubs in their hands. Their mouths lolled and their eyes were half-dead and hooded – the beastmen held spear-points at their backs and pressed them forward into the surf. A sick and cowardly tactic, but it would work – the Soul Drinkers would be mired in slave-fodder troops, giving the defenders more time to redeploy and fall upon the attacking Marines.

The solution was obvious. They would just have to kill them all.

'Ten seconds!'

The *Lakonia* ground deep into the broken coral sea bed, jarring to a halt a pistol shot from the shore. This close the ranks of slave-things seemed without number, and Graevus could see them drooling. They had been mind-wiped, or simply bred for idiocy and kept for food.

Close enough.

'Move!' yelled Graevus, swinging his power axe out of its backpack holster. There were twin thunderclaps as the shaped charges in the hold blew a huge section of the hull outwards in a shower of splinters, and hollered battle-cries as the Soul Drinkers vaulted out into the surf. As the gunfire started Graevus jumped off the prow, drew his bolt pistol, and started firing.

The slaves were like a wall of moaning flesh pressing all around him as soon as he hit the water, glazed-eyed and gibbering, swinging makeshift weapons at the Soul Drinkers pouring in amongst them. Graevus put a clip of bolt pistol shells into the closest, saw them reel and still keep fighting as they died, and knew they must have been pumped full of Frenzon or combat drugs.

'Forwards!' bellowed Karraidin over the vox, and the Soul Drinkers surged on, pistol shots and chainblades carving through the frenzied slaves as the surf around their knees turned frothy pink with blood. Karraidin's storm bolter chattered and the flash of the power field was like sheet lightning as he landed a blow into the press of bodies.

Graevus didn't pause to reload – his altered hand swung the power axe in great arc through the attackers, shearing through limbs and bodies. Assault Marines were at his shoulder, helping gouge through the slave ranks, forcing an opening through which the Soul Drinkers could charge onto the beach. A club rang off Graevus's shoulder pad and a heavy blade cut into the joint of his armoured knee but he stepped further into the fray, knowing that his battle-brothers would be doing the same at his side. There were mounds of dead on the coral beneath his feet, and the water was thick with gore.

'With me!' he voxed on the squad channel, swinging the shining power axe blade high so all could see it. 'Keep close and keep moving!' He risked a glance around and saw Karraidin's massively armoured form behind him, a walking bastion that sprayed storm bolter-fire into the baying hound pack being driven towards the rear of the Soul Drinkers. The half-rotted dogs bounded through the frothing waves but Karraidin was pumping volley after volley into them, then snapping off shots into the beastmen packmasters.

A good plan – mindless cannon fodder to the front to slow them down while fast-moving attack dogs surrounded them. Against any normal enemy, it might even have worked.

Tellos. He couldn't see Tellos.

Graevus tried the vox-channels and got the din of battle filtered through disciplined Space Marine comm-drills. Two Marines from Squad Hastis were down, trampled beneath the waves by a teeming mob of slaves who were cracking open their armour with chunks of coral. Squad Karvik was bogged down around Karraidin, shoulder-deep in the blood-choked water, trapped between the slaves and the hound packs. But most of the Soul Drinkers were bunched behind Graevus, jostling for a chance to get bolter muzzle and chainsword into contact with the mass of slaves, and that was what mattered now. Karvik and Hastis would have to fend for themselves – it was break out or die.

Graevus couldn't pick out Tellos and had no time to search for him – he blocked the downswing of an outsized club and slammed the butt end of the power axe into the attacker, feeling the strength of his massively altered arm driving the axe through the upper chest of the slave. He pushed forward and the pull of the water was gone – his feet were on land, on the black coral sand of the beach, and the slave line broke around him.

Tellos.

Sergeant Graevus had charged into a thousand battles in a hundred warzones, but he had never seen anything like it. Tellos must have dived into the slave-pack and writhed through the wall of bodies, despising the crude tactic of using cannon-fodder and determined to get to grips with the real enemy. He had reached the beach alone and been surrounded by the beastmen – for a soldier it was suicide, a quick and brutal death. But this was not just a soldier. This was Tellos.

By the time Graevus had reached him, Tellos was high up on a mound of the dead, butchered bodies beneath his feet, howling beastmen jabbing at him with spears whose tips shone with venom. There must have been twenty or more able to get at him and he was duelling with them all, blades flashing too fast to see, turning aside spear shafts and lashing deep into mutated beastman flesh. Where he had been cut his pale skin puckered and closed before the wound could bleed.

Sarpedon had his arachnoid legs. Givrillian had his multitude of eyes, Graevus his hand, and the other battle-brothers all manner of blessing the Emperor had bestowed on them in His role as the Architect of Fate. And His blessing to Tellos was to turn him into a man designed solely for war – reflexes like quicksilver, flesh that weapons could sail through without causing damage, a mind that yearned for one more fight.

Graevus was at Tellos's side and lent his axe to the slaughter, the grotesque equine faces of the beastmen grimacing in pain and hatred, cloven-hoofed legs and claw-fingered hands flailing. Gunfire whipped into the beastmen who tried to run as the ferocity of the Soul Drinkers' assault slammed into the Chaos line, throwing the beastmen onto the back foot and grinding them into the blood-slicked coral.

The momentum of the assault bought Graevus a couple of seconds to glance up the beach towards Sarpedon and the *Hellblade*. The *Hellblade* was still some distance from the shore, and Graevus knew for the moment the Marines from the *Lakonia* were alone on the beach.

There was room to move now, time to stop and take stock. Karraidin was still somewhere behind, fighting hard to link up with the beachhead, but most of the Soul Drinkers had made it to the shore. Losses were in double figures. A good start, thought Graevus, but through the murk and shadows beneath the immense fortress he could see the coral slopes teeming with Chaos reinforcements.

'Fire point!' he called over the vox, sprinting to a set of abandoned rock fortifications. 'Regroup on me, now!' They had to move with speed but there was no point in running headlong into a counter-attacking force flooding down from the fortress slopes. They would have to hop from one strongpoint to another, overwhelm one set of fortifications, regroup on it and strike out to the next until they reached the fortress, ran out of enemies or were all dead.

No problem. It was what they had been trained, engineered, and educated to do. What they had been born to do.

Soul Drinkers were forming fire arcs to cover those still struggling through the surf, bolters and bolt pistols barking at the darting packs of beastmen retreating in disarray. Graevus could see the goat-headed beastmen and black-armoured warriors swarming down the fortress slopes – even now the Soul Drinkers were snapping off ranging bolter-shots at them, ready to open up when they were within range. A minute or two, and then the killing would begin again.

Graevus loaded a fresh clip into his bolter. He had never been one to hold with visions and portent, relying instead on the gut instincts built up over a long campaigning career. But even he could feel the pure malice that boiled within the fortress high above him. He 'had heard that everyone saw Ve'Meth differently in his dreams – Graevus couldn't avoid getting the image of an immense parasitic insect, squatting on a throne, with bristly black skin and huge segmented eyes, mandibles filthy with blood.

He shook the picture out of his head. If they were here to kill that thing, then he would be proud to have a part in it.

THE STENCH WAS almost too much – dank, mossy, a reek of decay and death, rolling from the shore over the stricken *Hellblade*. A hundred metres beyond was the beach, obscured with noisome mist, through which Sarpedon could just glimpse half-human figures scurrying, eager to fight the invading Soul Drinkers.

The ship lurched as it tried to power over the obstacle, the engines screaming, the water behind foaming. Sarpedon ignored the stench and voxes below deck. 'What's the hold-up, Tech-Marine?'

'Hit a rock, lord!' came the short-breathed reply. 'We're taking on water. I'm sending everyone topside.'

The hatches were opening and the Soul Drinkers were clambering out as the *Hellblade* began to list. Sarpedon glanced below deck and saw the water foaming up around a massive black stone spike that had punched through the hull. Varuk was struggling through the waist-deep and quickly rising water – Sarpedon reached down and grabbed the Tech-Marine's hand, hauling him up onto the deck.

If they stayed, they would be trapped, and the defenders would doubtless have some way of reaching them given time – ships of their own, or those gargantuan sea monsters they had glimpsed during the voyage. Maybe something that flew. There was only one choice.

'Soul Drinkers, over the side!' he voxed. 'Stay together and keep moving!' With that he vaulted over the side of the *Hellblade*.

The water was about two metres deep – drowning point for a normal man, but a Space Marine could keep his head above water as he moved. Sarpedon's many legs helped keep his footing on the uneven coral rock underfoot but Marines around him were stumbling beneath the waves as they landed, helped back up by their battle-brothers. The *Hellblade* lurched brokenly and rolled onto its side as the last few Marines jumped into the water.

The sea was warm. Somehow, that made it far worse.

Steadily, Sarpedon strode towards the shore, the coral crumbling beneath his feet. He ordered the squads under him command to sound off as they made their way towards the beach. Givrillian, Dreo, Corvan, Karvik, Luko – there were a dozen squad sergeants and their men, plus the remnants of the squads who had survived the *Ultima* along with Tech-Marine Varuk, Chaplain Iktinos and Sarpedon himself.

The mists were rolling back from the shore, exposing the open wound that was the waiting force. Pale ragged skin, dark rotting flesh, hunched shoulders and singly glowing yellow eyes.

Daemons. Ve'Meth's will made solid, living embodiments of Chaotic power. The sight of them was grainy with the haze of flies that clung to them as they gambolled along the black sand or lay crouched in wait.

Would the Hell work here? They said daemons felt no fear. But then again, they had never met Sarpedon.

'Something in here with us, commander,' came the gravelly voice of Sergeant Karliv, one of the sergeants who had not gone to the star fort but who had proved loyal enough in the Chapter war.

'What do you mean, Karliv?'

'There's something moving in the water.'

'Kill it and keep moving.'

Sarpedon glanced backwards in time to see something thrashing in the water in the midst of the advancing Space Marines, and heard the yells of one Marine as he was dragged under.

'It's got Trass!'

Gunfire stuttered as the members of Squad Karvik held their bolt pistols above the water and fired shells into the body of the thing that had already swallowed one of their number. Tentacles flailed wildly, something pale and mottled rolled in the water.

There was a sudden flash and a cloud of steam rose with a hiss. The thrashing stopped, and Sarpedon could make out the slashes of light that were Sergeant Luko's lightning claws.

'Got it,' voxed Luko calmly. His voice was still uncharacteristically grim – he understood as well as any of them how little chance they could succeed here. But they had no choice. Ve'Meth represented everything that the Architect of Fate stood against, and if there was a chance to kill him then that chance had to be taken no matter what the risk.

They were close enough now to see the enemy lookouts staring at them, turning to gibber instructions to their brother daemons. Somewhere far along the shore gunfire flashed as Karraidin and Graevus's men stormed their section of the shore. Sarpedon listened in to the other force's vox for a second or two – bolter-fire, orders yelled, cries of pain and anger.

Sarpedon didn't have time for any of that now. He heard a bolter shot, saw the head of something on the shore snapping

back in a shower of dark green blood, and knew that Dreo
had found his range.

There was a roar from the beach and suddenly the daemons were charging as one, turning the water green-black
with filth as they splashed into the surf, sharp lengths of iron
wielded as swords. They weren't a random-willed pack, intent
only on violence – something was leading them.

'Mark targets and covering fire!' Sarpedon voxed to the tactical squads behind him as he strode into the shallower
water. 'Assault squads on me!'

Then he was close enough to see the loops of rotting
entrails through the rips in the daemons' stomachs, the
hideous leering single eyes glaring from their foreheads, their
lolling mouths and stumps of rotting teeth. The reek was like
a solid wall in front of him but he broke into a sprint and
pressed on for the charge, firing into the advancing bodies as
he strode within bolter range. Bolt pistol shots blazed in
from around him, blowing lumps of putrescence out of the
shambling bodies.

He could feel Ve'Meth laughing at them, peering down
from the rotting coral mountain above them. Ve'Meth
wouldn't be laughing for long.

The Soul Drinkers and the plague daemons clashed in the
shallows, chainswords ringing sparks off ugly two-handed
blades. Sarpedon whipped the force staff from his back to
block a crude downward swipe, followed up with an
upswing that ripped a leering daemon's head in two. The
daemons were rotting and deformed but they were quick,
with slack muscles unnaturally strong. The ruined face
howled and the blade swung at Sarpedon's waist, smashing
sideways into the ceramite breastplate and knocking Sarpedon onto two of his knees. The blow had left the daemon
wide open and Sarpedon lunged forward, hooking the staff
round the back of its shattered head and pulling it onto the
muzzle of the bolter in his other hand, so he could blast its
torso apart at point-blank range with half a magazine of
bolter shells.

They had an utter contempt of pain. Their bodies were
unnatural bags of disease which ignored injuries that would
kill a mortal thing – to kill them you had to dismember them
completely.

That was fine by him, Sarpedon thought.

He dodged another blade and darted his two front legs forward, impaling the daemon on his front claws and ripping it clean in two. The Assault Marines of Squad Karvik were around him and Karvik's power sword darted over his shoulder to shear the arms off the closest daemon. Sarpedon nodded his thanks – Karvik's helmeted head glanced at him in acknowledgement, then turned back to lead his Marines in the killing. All around was a swirling, brutal combat, plague daemons charging through a cloud of flies, Soul Drinkers meeting them with chainswords and battering them into the unclean surf. But the daemons were strong and there was a horde of them here – Squad Dreo had gone in on one flank and were four men down already, the spearhead was blunted and Sarpedon could see more daemons piling in from the shore.

The beachhead would fail. The Soul Drinkers would be trapped in the surf and surrounded.

Time for the Hell.

What did daemons fear? Nothing? No, they had minds of a sort, even if they were something a decent human being could never wish to comprehend. They had desires and hates and obsessions like everything else. They had fear, too. But of what?

All Sarpedon had were his fellow Marines, battling in the surf. The greatest warriors humanity could produce, proud soldiers of the Emperor's will. They were warriors worth fearing for even the most degenerate mind. That was what the Hell would be.

Sarpedon felt the aegis circuit pulse white-hot against his skin as he let the psychic power inside him flood out, a torrent more powerful than he had ever gathered before. Every day he had felt his powers reach greater heights and now he unleashed it all at once, the tide of the Hell rising up around him.

His battle-brothers' eyes glowed with righteous hatred. Their swords were flashes of lightning, their guns belched bolts of fire. They were five metres tall, twenty-five, fifty. The cloud-filled sky shrunk back from them in fear and the waters receded in terror. Sarpedon let the power rage through him, channelled into his fellow Marines. The chalices on their shoulder pads were brimming with traitors' blood, the masks of their helmets grim and forbidding. Those forced to fight without armour had skin that glowed with strength, as if it would turn aside bullets and blades like ceramite.

Sarpedon rose from the surf, power arcing off the force staff in his hand. He was a hero of mankind, venerated in the annals of humanity long after the corrupt Imperium had decayed and the enemies of the Emperor purged from the galaxy. He was Rogal Dorn battling the traitorous hordes of Horus on the battlements of Earth. He was huge and terrible, a demi-god of vengeance striding into the midst of the plague daemons.

The butchery faltered as the plague daemons' diseased minds struggled to comprehend the majesty of the warriors before them. Their blades stopped swinging for a second, and in that second the Soul Drinkers charged forwards as one, Sarpedon at their head, his staff ripping through deformed bodies. They tore through the daemon pack and sent them scurrying in shock, run down by the Assault Marines and massacred by supporting fire from the tactical squads.

Some tried to rally and amongst them Sarpedon saw the leader who had directed the daemon horde. He was a nightmare – a giant of bare glistening muscle and a face that was a mass of sharp mandibles and gleaming eyes. He had a huge slab of metal stabbed through one clubbed hand for a sword and was surrounded by baying daemon-things.

Kill this monstrosity and the daemon front would fail.

Sarpedon ran on to the beach at full tilt, outstripping the Assault Marines charging into the faltering daemons around him, focused on the champion of Chaos who dared stand before him.

GELENTIUS VORP SAW the invading commander and gave thanks to Grandfather Nurgle that he should have this opportunity. Oh, glorious decay, his hand would be slick with the blood of the clean ones and his body blessed with Ve'Meth's pestilent reward!

This enemy was tall and clad in massive purple armour trimmed with bone and gold, a chalice symbol picked out on one shoulder pad – a Space Marine, the most stubbornly misguided of mankind who refused to look upon the majestic corruption of Nurgle, a fine scalp for Vorp to present to Ve'Meth. This one was different, though – he had eight legs, like those of an insect or a spider, sprouting from his waist, which sent him bounding up the shore far faster than his fellow Marines advancing behind. The Space Marine had a long staff in one hand – he wore no helmet and was shaven-headed, and his eyes burned with anger. Vorp saw there was some trick that this enemy had used to throw the daemons into disarray, but Vorp himself was above such things, for Ve'Meth had shielded his mind against trickery.

His simpering daemon-pack of plaguebearers bounded alongside him as he strode towards his prey, their lips drooling at the prospect of the kill. Vorp swung his huge blade at the Space Marine but the enemy was quick and turned the pendulous sword with a shoulder pad, jabbing with the staff and spearing it through the head of the closest plaguebearer. The staff flicked and the daemon's gristly spine came apart.

A worthy opponent. Vorp made a note to offer up thanks to Ve'Meth and the Grandfather for such an opportunity to prove his devotion to the Lord of Decay.

Vorp stepped in close and rammed a clubbed fist into the enemy's chest, denting the ceramite and throwing the Space Marine back a pace. But suddenly the staff was entangled in his legs and Vorp was pitched off his feet, slamming into the sharp black sand on his back. The Marine saw Vorp was wide open and a massive downward swipe of the staff tore deep into Vorp's shoulder, narrowly missing bisecting his skull.

The arrogance! The nerve!

Vorp rose to his feet and slashed with the sword, biting into the Marine's shoulder pad and into his arm. The Marine stumbled back again and caught Vorp's descending blade with the staff – Vorp reached down and grabbed one of the strange arachnoid legs, twisted and pulled, and felt the leg come away with a snapping of tendons.

The Space Marine bellowed with rage as he saw the mangled stump of his leg spurting vermilion blood over the sand.

Vorp had hurt it. Now Vorp would kill it.

A WHITE-HOT PAIN flared bright in Sarpedon's mind, flooding through him from the bleeding socket of his left mid-leg. The leg itself was held in the paw of the skinless monster standing over him, triumph in its multitude of insect eyes. Even though the battle was raging all around him, the gunfire and howling of daemons was blocked out by the white noise of agony.

The pain would pass. Sarpedon had suffered worse. And he still had seven legs left, damn it.

The Chaos champion barrelled forwards, doubtless hoping to capitalise on its small victory and finish Sarpedon for good. Sarpedon dodged to the side and weaved between the huge swinging blows of the champion's tarnished sword. Sarpedon was favouring his left side but knew he could not let up for an instant – the champion was inhumanly strong and seemed as immune to pain as its attendant daemons.

The sword stabbed at head height and Sarpedon caught a huge fleshy knee in the throat as he ducked. He slashed upwards with a talon, following with the staff, and as the champion stepped back he slammed the heel of his free hand into the side of its leg. A bone snapped somewhere deep within the slimy muscle. The champion didn't notice, pivoted on a heel, brought the blunt pommel of its blade down on the back of Sarpedon's neck.

It was fast as well as strong. It had no finesse – there was no method here, only brutality and anger. Sarpedon couldn't outfight something like this, because every trick or flourish he might bring out would be beaten down by the champion's sheer relentless strength. The only way was to be stronger than it was.

There was no art in this fight. The champion made a wide arcing downward swing, hoping to decapitate Sarpedon. Sarpedon took the blow on a shoulder pad, swung back with his staff. The champion blocked the attack but Sarpedon struck again and again, slamming the staff into the champion's guard, battering it slowly backwards. With its free arm it slashed a spined elbow into Sarpedon's face and tried to close its gnarled fingers around his throat. But Sarpedon had to focus everything on attack, never back down or pause for breath, and hope it would be enough.

The force staff, crackling with psychic power, ripped downwards and the champion met it with a wide circling parry, driving the head of the staff deep into the sand beneath its feet. Sarpedon's assault was fended off, and in that moment, both combatants were wide open to the counterattack.

Sarpedon was a split-second quicker, reflexes honed by decades of training and battle outstripping the instincts of a life in service to the Dark Gods. Sarpedon reared up on his back legs and stabbed down, spearing a talon through the wrist of the Chaos champion's sword arm. Its foul mandibled pit of a mouth yawned wide and it howled as Sarpedon dropped the force staff and grabbed the monster's head, jabbing his gauntleted fingers into its eyes. With his free hand he drew his boltgun from its holster and jammed it under its throat. He pulled the trigger and blew a corona of filthy bilious blood out of the back of its head.

It wasn't dead. But it was close.

The champion reeled wildly, segments of skull flapping from scraps of skin. Sarpedon lunged into it, knocking it backwards and landing astride of it. He put the rest of the bolter magazine into its chest, blasting the ribcage open and spraying ragged chunks of organs. When the magazine was empty Sarpedon punched down and split the ruined ribcage clean open, plunged his hands into the pulpy mass beneath, tore out leathered lungs and a foul still-beating heart, knowing that a creature like this was harder to kill than anything he had faced before. But it still bellowed and thrashed beneath him, massive corroded sword swinging wildly even as brackish blood sprayed across the sand.

Sarpedon grasped the champion's ruined head with both hands and ripped it clean off the abomination's shoulders. He cast the hideous head into the black sand, its mandibles still writhing, its glossy eyes glaring.

As the thing fell still, Sarpedon took up his gun and staff again, glancing behind him to see how his squads were faring. The daemons were in flight and the Soul Drinkers were making a break for the rugged slopes of the mountain-fortress, where the broken landscape would afford some cover for the ascent towards Ve'Meth's sanctum.

He stood up, blocking out the pain from his severed leg. He joined the forward elements of the spearhead as they sprinted through the remains of daemonic defences, raking the distant Chaos forces with bolter-fire as they ran, the Hell still burning around them.

* * *

GELENTIUS VORP LAY there for some time on the black coral sand, trying to force the parasites infesting him to knit together his sundered organs. He could probably survive without his head, or with his chest cavity blasted free of organs, but maybe not with both.

Would the Grandfather help him? Almighty Nurgle blessed His followers with durable bodies that scorned injury – but as he stared up at the sky with his remaining eyes Vorp speculated that perhaps even the Ve'Meth, most powerful vessel of Nurgle, might have trouble saving Vorp now.

The Space Marine would pay, of that Vorp was sure. If the fortress didn't kill him then Ve'Meth himself would. But he had so longed to feel the Marine's naively clean blood on his hands and look into his eyes as he tore his heart out...

Dismembered on the beach of Ve'Meth's island, Gelentius Vorp died at last.

CHAPTER TWELVE

THE DIN OF death echoed up the bile-slicked slopes of the fortress to reach Ve'Meth. The screech of ended life, the low keening of pain, the roar of anger. The dim crackling of gunfire was drowned out by the delicious racket that living things made when they suddenly became living no more.

That there was so much death, however, was tempered by the fact that so much of it was of Ve'Meth's own servants. Space Marines had died, and their passing was most satisfying – but daemons had been torn asunder and their spirits banished to the warp, and slaves and beastmen had died in droves. Gelentius Vorp, champion of Nurgle, had actually been killed, which was something Ve'Meth had considered to be effectively beyond the capability of anything mortal.

Ve'Meth sent out a command through the living stone of his fortress. Every servant who dwelled within his walls snapped to attention and ran, slithered or wallowed towards its designated position within the organic warren of the fortress, ready to receive and repel the invaders in corruption's name. Even if the Imperial weaklings got within striking distance of Ve'Meth's abscess-chamber his body-guards should deal with them quickly enough.

And if they didn't? Well, then Ve'Meth would have to handle things personally.

A host-body broke ranks and strode towards the rear of the chamber where Ve'Meth kept a shrine to himself. Images offered up from cults and worlds under his domination were piled up against the sweating coral wall – crude idols of an insect-god, a beautifully wrought reliquary in the form of a golden snake, totems of shrunken heads and human bones, and hundreds more. Ve'Meth swept them aside to reveal the wooden box he kept there, burned with runes to keep the unworthy from opening it. The host lifted the lid, reached a hand in and removed Arguotha.

It pleased Ve'Meth to savour the memory again of all those centuries ago, when he still had a single mundane body. On his long pilgrimage through the Eye of Terror he had been beset by the Daemon Arguotha, who flew into a rage when he saw the suppurating marks of favour the Plague God had bestowed upon Ve'Meth. The daemon set his thousand offspring on Ve'Meth but the young champion had faced them all and won, scattering them in combat. Then Arguotha himself attacked, yet Ve'Meth had shown no fear and defeated the daemon. He wrestled it to the ground and intoned the canticle of binding, making the daemon his own to do with as he wished. And Ve'Meth had wished to bind the daemon into his favourite weapon.

Arguotha had brooded over the centuries and his anger was marked upon him. His barrel was gnarled and toothed, the metal of his casing twisted into faces that ground their teeth and screamed from time to time. In the magazine slung beneath, the thousand young of Arguotha writhed in captivity, eager to be released.

If the Space Marines dared cross Ve'Meth's threshold, they would get their wish, and Arguotha would speak once more.

'MEDIC!' GRAEVUS GLANCED up to see Apothecary Pallas ducking through the scattered gunfire towards where the Marine from Squad Hastis was trying to pile the oozing mass of his lung back into the massive rent in the side of his chest. The Marine knew he was dead, but he wanted to make sure Pallas took the gene-seed organ from his body for transport back to the Chapter apothecarion.

Brave lad, thought Graevus. They all were.

Graevus's spearhead had made it across the beach, clearing out the black stone fortifications of the mutants and cultists who were sheltering there. Karraidin and Squad Hastis had made it up there too, leaving a gory trail of the dead across the sand. Now the Soul Drinkers were at the foot of the cave-riddled mountain fortress, taking fire from hundreds of murder holes and firepoints studding the slopes above them. The weapons were crude and badly aimed but there were scores of them, pouring fire down onto the Soul Drinkers.

'Give the word, Graevus,' said Karraidin as his hugely armoured bulk clambered over the stone outcrop of the fortification in which Graevus was taking cover.

Graevus peered out at the Soul Drinkers still arriving through the gunsmoke. 'Give it a moment. If we make a break for it now we'll leave half the lads strung out under fire.'

Karraidin risked a long look at the firepoints above them, his aristocratic features profiled against the corpse-strewn battlefield. 'The fortress is teeming with them. There must be thousands.'

'It'll be in our favour, captain. Enclosed spaces, up close. Like a boarding action.'

Karraidin smiled grimly. As a Soul Drinker who had distinguished himself in spacecraft boarding actions, for which the valuable terminator suits had been designed, he knew full well the intense, half-blind butchery that the Soul Drinkers would have to wade through.

'Can't wait,' Karraidin said, and Graevus knew he meant it.

Another purple-armoured body dived into the cover of the rock, bullets snickering into the sand beside him. It was Sergeant Karvik, chainsword in hand.

'My squad's in position sir,' he gasped.

Squad Karvik had been trapped in the shallows when the spearhead had first advanced, and must have sprinted through both the regrouping beast-cultists and the fire from the slopes. 'Good work, sergeant. Captain, that's all of them. We move.'

'Soul Drinkers, with me!' called Karraidin over the vox and vaulted over the stone wall. All around the Soul Drinkers squads broke cover and ran, snapping shots at the openings overhead. Graevus saw Marines fall, some to be helped by their battle-brothers as they passed, others to pick themselves up and carry on, others to lie where they fell.

Karraidin had spotted an opening at foot-level – a ragged cavern entrance from which ran a runnel of sickly brown ichor. Through the shadows inside Graevus saw Chaos troops, hunched figures clad in rags, manoeuvring an autocannon to cover the entrance. A volley from Karraidin's storm bolter caused them to duck so that by the time they had squeezed off a burst of shots the closest Assault Marines were upon them, Sergeant Tellos in their midst. Three Marines fell, large-calibre autocannon rounds punching through their bodies, before the gun crew were cut to pieces and the Soul Drinkers were inside.

Graevus's eyes adjusted instantly to the darkness, and he realised that this was something that had not been built; it had been grown. The tunnel stretching into the heart of the fortress was ribbed and puckered, the internal organs of something long-dead or dormant, something that might wake or be revived at any moment. And this particular monster's brain was Ve'Meth.

The assault squads were fifty metres down the tunnel with Tellos and Karraidin, spraying bullets at things that dared move in the shadows.

'What do you think, Graevus?' voxed Karraidin.

In any normal situation Sergeant Graevus, with the decades of experience feeding a honed combat instinct, would have carefully weighed up the routes likely to bring them within striking distance of a tactical objective. But this was not a normal situation, and Graevus knew exactly where they had to go to exterminate the pollution that had deformed this whole planet. 'I think we go up,' he said.

THE HELL WAS still with them. Sarpedon couldn't have turned it off if he'd wanted to. It made them ten metres high, striding angels of death with guns that fired thunder and swords that slashed lightning. They lost a dozen men to heavy weapons that raked the broken ground with fire; another ten to the dripping, tentacled things that thumped down from the ceiling of the cave they had charged into.

But they had not slowed down. It was the classic Soul Drinkers' assault, fast and deadly, heedless of danger, cutting through everything that moved. Hunch-limbed slaves fled, hulking black-armoured warriors were sliced and blasted apart. With Sarpedon at their head they ran through tunnels and broad chambers packed with heaps of rotting meat, crevasses full to the brim with corpses, crossed bridges made of human bones.

The fortress was teeming with life – tunnels were knee-deep in insects and there were colonies of skeletal flapping creatures that hung like bats. Most living things fled instinctively at the Soul Drinkers' approach, such was the aura of righteous death surrounding them. Some stood and fought, directed by the fanaticism with which Ve'Meth had infected them, but the blubbery eyeless monsters and crooked-limbed humanoids that ran along the walls were shredded by bolter and chainsword, and the Soul Drinkers pressed on. Squads Dreo and Givrillian must have picked off a hundred enemies between them with snap shots. The assault elements in the lead, led by Sarpedon himself with talons slashing, carved their way through twice that number by the time they reached the huge subterranean lakes of bile with their islands of folded skin, and the towering cathedrals with pillars of coagulated blood.

Ve'Meth knew they were there and his fortress was coming alive around them. The walls quivered and oozed and the defences became more and more organised the higher they got. Slave-packs blocked orifice doorways with piles of their dead. Serried ranks of warriors filled caverns with rows of pikes. Heavy weapons were dragged by deformed pack beasts into corridor junctions, studding the walls with gunfire before the weight of the Soul Drinkers' assault slew the gunners, turned the weapons around, raked the path ahead with fire and moved on.

Sarpedon knew they were close. The volcanic cupola of boiling pus was raging above them, and the black laughter echoed through his mind. He could feel a massive responsibility bearing down on him, oppressive as the fortress's stink – they were within striking distance now, and suddenly the possibility that they might get this far and fail was bright in Sarpedon's mind.

But he must leave no room for doubt. He was a commander, responsible for the most vital mission in his Chapter's
history. They would kill Ve'Meth or they would die – either
way they would not go back to the *Brokenback* having failed.

Sarpedon rounded a corner and saw the library before him.
The cavern was as big as the Cathedral of Dorn had been back
on the *Glory*. It walls were of bleeding veined meat, and gargantuan cases of books were piled on top of one another in
crumbling towers. In a glance Sarpedon's augmented vision
and quick mind saw the millions of volumes bound in daemon's hide with pages of skin and clasps of bone, the tablets
of black rune-carved stone, and scrolls of tattoos cut from the
backs of cultists. He could hear them whispering, gibbering
their secrets in a thousand tongues, crammed mouldering
into every space and lying in great rotting heaps in every corner.

This was the accumulated vileness that every perverted
tongue had preached in the name of Ve'Meth, the vast tomb
of blasphemy that fuelled the daemon prince's influence.

Sarpedon was about to call the flamer Marines forward
when the first shell grazed a knee joint and slammed into a
Marine from Squad Givrillian behind him.

A bolter shell. Sarpedon would recognise it anywhere – but
it was different, a low-velocity mark that had not been issued
to Space Marines for thousands of years…

'Traitors!' he yelled in warning, diving to the side as the
fusillade opened up. A wall of bolter-fire tore across the
library, shredding the tainted books and thudding into the
Marines pouring in through the arched entrance. Twenty or
more life-runes winked out at the edge of Sarpedon's vision as
chunks were blasted out of the fleshy walls all around him.

Chaos Marines. The traitor legions. Those who turned
from the Emperor's light and betrayed Mankind ten thousand years before, when the Emperor still walked among
men and Rogal Dorn's Imperial Fists had yet to be split into
their component Chapters. It was a sign, of course – the
Architect of Fate had directed them to this place not just to
kill Ve'Meth but to confront a symbol of what could happen
when faith is lost and perverted, when the tendrils of the
enemy reached into men's hearts and they forgot the sacred
will of the Emperor.

He could see only the muzzle flashes from their positions hidden amongst the towering shelves and mounds of books on the other side of the chamber. They were disciplined and accurate – they had lost nothing of their martial prowess, for a Space Marine's quality as a soldier remained where loyalty and dignity did not.

'Charge!' rang the cry of Chaplain Iktinos and he led Squad Karvik's Assault Marines out into the library, hoping to rush the Traitor Marines under the covering fire of their battle-brothers. But the traitors seemed to ignore the fire tearing into the mouldering books and worm-ridden shelves around them, and Squad Karvik was cut to pieces, the survivors minus their sergeant scrambling into cover as the compacted meat of the floor erupted all around them. One of them grabbed the power sword of the fallen Sergeant Karvik. Sarpedon knew Karvik had carried the weapon for twenty years, and would have wanted nothing more in death than to know it would carry on his work in the hands of another.

'If we have to die, then we will,' voxed Iktinos on the command channel. 'But if there is an alternative, commander–'

'We need to flank them,' replied Sarpedon, thinking fast. 'Givrillian!'

'Unlikely, commander,' replied Sergeant Givrillian, who clambered through the debris to Sarpedon's side. 'They have an elevated field of fire and excellent cover. We will be impeded and exposed all the way.'

Givrillian was right. The Soul Drinkers would have to forge on right through several tottering bookcases, ten metres high or more – they would either break through them and bring tonnes of rotting debris down on their heads, or climb them which would be like scaling a sheer cliff under fire. Either way the Traitor Marines would have free rein to pour fire into them as the Soul Drinkers moved, and would probably redeploy as soon as Sarpedon got into any kind of flanking position.

But all was not lost. There was always hope, even if that hope was merely for a good death in battle with the Enemy.

'Iktinos?'

'Commander?'

'I believe we shall die. Pray for us, then lead the charge.'

* * *

GRAEVUS KEPT GOING as the rushing torrent of blood threatened to close over his head. His feet crunched through piles of bones on the bed of the channel, and there were tiny, sharp things zipping past him with the flow.

He was in the heart of his spearhead, with Tellos and the assault squads ahead of him and Karraidin in the rear. They had known the instant they entered the fortress that they were in some living thing, and had soon found themselves wading through the sludge in its intestines, shielding themselves from the noxious fumes exuding from the pulpy walls of its lungs, and now struggling through the gushing tunnels of its veins. They could feel its evil heartbeat through the floor and hear its slow breathing rumbling through the walls. And Graevus could hear the buzzing of the corpulent insect-god that brooded at its peak, waiting for them, thirsting for the prize of a Space Marine's blood.

'Opening ahead!' came the vox from Sergeant Hastis, whose assault squad was on point.

'Take it!' replied Graevus, knowing that even Space Marine power armour would suffer from immersion in this caustic, befouled gore that passed for the fortress's blood.

Ahead of him the Soul Drinkers pulled each other out of the sucking blood flow. A hand reached down and a Marine – one of the half-armoured battle-brothers, hauled Graevus's bulk upwards onto the shelf of slick rock that led into to an upwards-curving inlet.

Storm bolter-fire sounded above the rush of the blood torrent. 'Something on our tail,' voxed Karraidin by way of explanation.

The gunfire kept stuttering.

'Karraidin? Is that still you?' asked Graevus.

'Negative, Graevus. Killed it.'

Bolter fire. Bolter fire, without a doubt – but not theirs, maybe Sarpedon's…

The first Graevus saw of the Chaos Space Marines was a severed head. It span back down the inlet, past Graevus as he followed Sergeant Tellos who, inevitably, was the first to sprint towards the gunfire. It wasn't a helmet, but a head – in the shape of a Space Marine helmet but covered with skin, with eyepieces that were not photoblocker lenses but wet, cataracted living orbs.

Tellos had carved his way through the first and Graevus barrelled past him into the next one. It had doubtlessly once been a Marine, but its skin had grown outside its armour, pink and bleeding from sores and tears. Some of its organs were outside, too, loops of necrotic entrails and pulsing, sputtering valves. Its face mask had sharp stained teeth instead of a filter grille, and its bolter muzzle had a fleshy mouth that spat that mark four bolter ammunition across the room. Tattooed onto the skin of one shoulder pad was a three-orbed symbol that Graevus had seen daubed onto the vehicles of turncoat armies and carved into the hides of victims massacred by Chaos cultists.

Graevus hardly noticed the towering piles of volumes and the great drifts of rotting books. He was only dimly aware of the bolter fire replying from below, where Sarpedon's Marines were trying to engage the Traitor Marines. His whole vision was filled by the Chaos Marine as he slammed the blade of his power axe into the enemy's midriff, carving right through the dead-fleshed torso.

The Chaos Marine tried to turn his bolter on his assailant, but Graevus's hand speed had increased so greatly since his axe arm had changed that the return stroke had already sliced the Chaos Marine in two through the spine. The axe whirled and the blade slashed down, hacking the Chaos Marine through the collar bone down to the mid-chest.

Tellos was already in the heart of the Chaos Marine position, killing all around him, with the Assault Marines beside him relishing the chance to follow him in forging a trail of the dead.

Bolter fire was raining down on them but all was confusion – the Chaos Marines were on the back foot now, breaking ranks to form a new firing line, but the Soul Drinkers were in no mood to stand around and let the enemy shoot at them.

Graevus looked through the mist of blood and saw the next target – a leader of some kind, wielding a sword edged with gnashing teeth.

He brought his axe blade out of the quivering body at his feet, and charged back into the fray.

* * *

'WE'VE GOT THEM pegged back, commander! Move while they're down!'

It was Karraidin's voice, but it might as well have come from the throat of Rogal Dorn himself.

'You heard the captain,' yelled Sarpedon. 'Move!'

The fire that came down onto them was broken and panicked. The sounds of blades through power armour rang from above as Sarpedon's spearhead crossed the foetid expanse of Ve'Meth's library to where the exit in the far wall was a raw, open wound.

Sarpedon leapt over the tumbled heaps of books and into the ribbed throat that curved upwards beyond.

Losing a leg hadn't slowed him down. And the laughter was so loud now it was drowning out his own thoughts. The aegis hood's protective circuitry was white-hot against his body as it struggled to protect his psyker's mind.

'This is it, sir?' said Givrillian at his side. It wasn't really a question.

'Stay close,' voxed Sarpedon. 'Fast, disciplined, and no one runs.'

He didn't need to say it. But they needed to hear it – words that had been drummed into them as novices, reminding them that the training and values that they had extolled all their lives as Soul Drinkers would still serve them here.

They didn't know how they would kill Ve'Meth. They didn't really know what Ve'Meth was. The few of them who had seen a daemon prince on the field of battle each carried a violently different memory, for Chaos was ever-changing and never rose twice in the same form.

Ve'Meth could be anything. But there wasn't much that bolter and chainsword couldn't kill.

The throat was steep but none of them stumbled. The muscles shifted and contracted, trying to throw them off, but they dug their fingers into the rubbery flesh and held on.

At the top a clenched fist of flesh blocked their path. Chainsword slashed through it and Sarpedon ripped his way through with his talons, staff in hand, ready to shred whatever he saw on the other side.

It took a split-second for his eyes to adjust to the darkness. The whole fortress had been pitch-black but this was something else, an abysmal pit of darkness, as if the magnitude of evil here had sucked up the light and devoured it.

Then his augmented eyes forced an image out of the darkness, and he saw Ve'Meth's true form for the first time.

Ve'Meth was a multitude of bodies – between seven and nine hundred at Sarpedon's first count, standing rigid in square formation. There were men, women, in finery and engineer's overalls, primitive rags and camouflage, some squat and muscular from high-grav environments, some life-spacers with willowy limbs and thin faces. Every one had the same expression of intensity. Every one was looking at him.

Something stirred in their midst and Sarpedon saw one of them was holding a weapon – something old and crusted with runes, glowing with power. A gun.

The first bullet buzzed through Brother Nikkos's chest – and then it hit him again and again, whipping through the air in wide looping orbits to punch again and again through the Marine's armour. Nikkos toppled and came apart, armour joints clattering to the floor, slopping his sliced body onto the polished black coral.

Another shot barked from the weapon even as the return fire tore apart the first rank of Ve'Meth's bodies, riddling another Marine. Another, and another, each one singling out a Soul Drinker and piercing him a dozen times before he died.

Every mouth opened. Eight hundred voices laughed.

Marines were flooding into the chamber around Sarpedon but they were dying all around. Sergeant Dreo hurled himself to the ground as the bullet-daemon skimmed past him and dismembered one of his squad. Chaplain Iktinos strode forward, diving between two dying Marines to sweep his crozius arcanum through the three closest bodies – they were thrown through the air with a flash of the power field. More were dying with the bursts of return fire but the Soul Drinkers were dying faster and the air was filled with the hideous buzzing flight of the daemon-bullets.

A well-placed shot took the gun-wielding body in the throat but another stepped into its place in the ranks, took up the weapon and fired again. Time and time again the ancient gun barked and with every shot another battle-brother died, and every time the firer fell another took its place.

'Discipline! We have to kill them all!' yelled Sarpedon. Glancing to the side he saw Givrillian, the many-eyed Sergeant Givrillian who had been his most trusted and level-headed soldier, being speared by a tiny glowing monster even as he loosed a salvo of bolter shells into Ve'Meth.

Above the screams and the gunfire was the laughter, loud with the voices of Ve'Meth and louder still inside Sarpedon's head. He looked through the mayhem and saw Sergeant Dreo trying to form a firing line. Half his squad were dead.

They had to kill every body at once. That was how Ve'Meth ultimately defended itself – not with its soldiers or its daemon gun, but with the fact that it was formed of host bodies, hundreds of them, and Sarpedon was certain it could survive with just one. It could take more, too, and Sarpedon knew it would be pleased to take one of his battle-brothers if it could.

There was one way. He had seen it done often enough, but never like this. If enough of them stayed alive, if that discipline would hold even when every single one of them could die in the blink of an eye…

'Sergeant Dreo!' yelled Sarpedon. 'Execution duty!'

'Execution duty, line up on me!' bellowed Dreo. The surviving Soul Drinkers had all lined up for execution duty many times before, when traitors to the Emperor had been taken alive and sentenced to death, or when battle-brothers had committed some grave transgression for which death could be the only penalty. There had been enough executions following the Chapter war, when unrepentant rebels had been put to death with a massed bolter volley in the nave of the Cathedral of Dorn.

More died, a dozen at once. Gaps formed in the firing line even as it was formed. But Sergeant Dreo, the crack shot, didn't rush. He had been given charge of the execution on many times and knew full well that a clean kill needed one concentrated wall of fire. Many died in the seconds he paused. But it was one concentrated volley, or nothing.

The guns were in position, a line of bolters stretching two deep across Ve'Meth's chamber, the front rank kneeling.

'Fire!' yelled Dreo, and the front rank opened fire.

As one, a hundred of Ve'Meth's bodies fell, bodies punched open by the explosive bolter shells that ripped through them. The front rank emptied their magazines into a sheet of shrapnel that tore into the host bodies. The gun wielder fell and another bent to take up the weapon, to be torn apart in turn.

The front rank paused to change magazines and the rear rank came in flawlessly, keeping up a steady stream of fire that swept across the chamber. By the time the first rank took up the fire again they were pouring bolter shells into the mangled remains of eight hundred bodies, oozing tainted blood onto the black coral.

'Cease fire!' barked Sergeant Dreo. 'Good kill.'

The silence was shocking. Sarpedon lowered his bolter and through the gunsmoke stared at all that remained of Ve'Meth – a room full of broken bodies, blood spattered up the walls, torn limbs and bodies heaped across the floor.

A screaming began – quiet at first, but growing louder and louder. A grainy cloud of pestilence rose from the bodies. It solidified and darkened, and in its depths Sarpedon could see movement – huge shapes, filth-caked, daemon-plagued worlds, plunging away through space, falling into the darkness, hurling away from him and out of sight, faster and faster.

The screaming reached a pitch so loud Sarpedon could hear nothing else. He knew what he was watching – this was the empire of Ve'Meth, the kingdom it would have built in the name of its god, the empire that Sarpedon had destroyed before it could be forged. Unable to survive outside its host bodies, the daemon prince didn't mind dying, but its dreams of domination were dying with it, and that it could not stand.

The horror. The agony. Everything Ve'Meth had feared was coming to pass and it poured its hatred and terror out into the chamber, filling it with a screech of rage and the huge dark image of a universe cleaned of his presence. Then the scream became weak and the image pale, as Ve'Meth's lifeforce dissipated. The dark miasma dissolved and the chamber fell quiet.

The aegis circuit was calm. The vast oppression of Ve'Meth was lifted and suddenly the ugliness was bleeding away from the world – the darkness was not quite so complete, the stench was bearable, the weight of evil was lightening.

'Mission complete, my brothers,' said Sarpedon. 'Count the dead and regroup.'

* * *

SERGEANT GRAEVUS WATCHED as the Plague Marine dissolved. It was screaming, but the sound was dulled by the layers of ceramite and muscle that covered it. Graevus had been sure his Marines would battle the traitors to a standstill in the towering library, and that they would grind each other down until there was nothing left. The assault had swept through the Chaos positions but the enemy were undaunted and supremely resistant to injury, and Soul Drinkers were beginning to die. If that was the way it had to be, then that was how Graevus would have died – but then there had been a terrible keening from the otherwise silent Plague Marines and the traitors had convulsed with a sudden shock.

The Soul Drinkers had not paused to ponder their luck. Instinctively, Graevus knew that Sarpedon had done something magnificent at the fortress's peak, but most of his mind was concentrating on driving his axe blade through the enemies before him.

Now the Plague Marines were dead or dying, dismembered by the Assault Marines or riddled with bolter shells as they reeled. Some had pitched over the edge of the towering bookcases and been broken on the floor far below. Those who did not die by the hands of Soul Drinkers were dying all the same, their bodies liquefying as the Marines watched.

The Plague Marine was on his knees – his lower legs were gone. Alternate layers of skin and metal were flaking away and the skeleton was started to be exposed, gnarled and twisted, riddled with wormholes. The body collapsed, losing all shape as heavy metal implants rolled out onto the ground.

Graevus turned from the stinking mess, feeling something suddenly different in his mind. The buzzing was gone.

The bloated insect-god was dead.

FROM ORBIT, THE unnamed planet turned dark and clear as the clouds dissolved. The thick layer of flies dissipated and the banks of yellowing pollution faded. Suddenly the sensoria aboard the *Brokenback* mapped out every detail of a world dominated by oceans and scattered with rocky islands – for the first time the crew could see the towering coral stacks and blood-soaked beaches of the archipelago, and pick out the rotting ships, suddenly pilotless, which foundered and broke up in the rough seas.

Communications were back. Commander Sarpedon requested transport immediately. Lygris authorised a wing of Thunderhawks to land on the body-choked shore in the shadow of the fortress – the auspex arrays found the island completely dead, where hours before it had teemed with unholy life. Sarpedon and Graevus met up on the beach, compared scars, and embarked onto the Thunderhawks.

As on the ordinatus platform so long ago, there was plenty of room on the gunships for the return flight. Of the four hundred Marines who had landed on the unnamed planet, half were dead, slain in the assault on the fortress-island, or lying at the bottom of the great ocean that girded the planet.

When they reached the huge dark bulk of the *Brokenback*, the first welcome they received was the screaming of a thousand sensors all over the space hulk. Lygris's anomaly had returned, and this time, it was vast… and closing.

SARPEDON SPRINTED DOWN the corridor, the stump of his sev-ered leg trailing bandages where Apothecary Pallas had been dressing it when the alarms sounded. Lygris caught up to him at the next bulkhead, his anxious face picked out in the strobe of the warning lamps.

'We picked it up about six hours ago, but it faded out,' Lygris was saying. Serf-labourers ran past them, heading for damage control stations. 'I doubled the sensorium watch but it seemed just an anomaly. Now it's of a higher magnitude than most of our sensors can measure. We're using Sector Indigo to track it.'

'Where is it now?' Sarpedon had come straight from the apothecarion, which was packed with the Soul Drinker wounded. His armour was still crusted with unclean blood.

'Seventeen thousand kilometres at the last count. It's clos-ing, but it's erratic.'

'Not natural.'

'No.'

'Ve'Meth's dead. The planet died with him. I want to know what this thing is before we're within turret range, and it's going to have to be one hell of an explanation to stop me opening fire.'

'I'm with you on that, commander.'

Sarpedon and Lygris reached the viewing chamber, its lavish décor crudely inappropriate. Several of the Chapter's Tech-Marines were directing servitors to aim their image intensifiers at the great nimbus of light that filled the whole oculus. The whole room was bathed in its silvery light, and at its heart something was solidifying, lithe and serpentine.

'Targets!' called Lygris.

'Not yet, sir,' replied Tech-Marine Varuk, who had lost most of a kneecap to bolter-fire in the fortress and had yet to visit the apothecarion. 'Half the sensors say it isn't there and the other half say it's a black hole. We're aiming guns by eye but it's a fraction of what this ship's got.'

Sarpedon was well aware of the kind of offensive force the *Brokenback* could muster, wielding as it did the armaments of several cruiser-sized Imperial craft and the arcane weaponry of sinister alien craft. But if there was a foe who would only be seen when he wanted, who could get up close...

Ve'Meth? No. Ve'Meth was dead. What, then?

The shape in the light shifted and became real – smooth skin, long and powerful limbs, twin silver stars for eyes. Occult symbols flashed in concentric circles which stayed imprinted on the eye. A hand reached out towards the oculus, and suddenly the figure was much, much closer.

'Incoming-Incoming-Incoming...'

The voice, activated by early warning systems on one of the ancient component ships, boomed through the space hulk as something huge and powerful landed on the upper surface. The sensoria that should have seen it all overloaded simultaneously, burning out a hundred hard-wired servitors in a heartbeat.

The *Brokenback* shut down. The engines died, the life support systems reverted to failsafe and large areas of the hulk were flooded by hard vacuum. All helm control died and the *Brokenback* drifted helpless, as if awed by the power of the being that stood astride it. It reached down and long, graceful fingers dug into blackened metal. With a rippling of serpentine muscles, it ripped the top six decks off the *Brokenback*.

It looked down at the armoured humans that teemed in the corridors and gun decks. It shone a bright silver light down on them and opened the gate to his silver city, letting his beautiful minions drift down like falling stars onto the ship below.

'I am the Architect of Fate,' it said in a voice like music. 'I am the Engineer of Time. I am Abraxes, Prince of Change, and you are all my children.'

SARPEDON STARED UP at the towering figure shining against the blackness of space. He had seen some things in his decades as a Soul Drinker, not the least of them in the last few days. But none of them compared to this.

It was several kilometres tall. Wings of light spread out from its back, framing its beautiful face and flowing hair. Its body, muscular yet slim, was clad in a toga of flowing white silk, and arcane symbols glowed in wide circles all around it. Glowing figures were pouring from a disk of light that hung in space behind it – strange-shaped things made of pastel-coloured light and birds with feathers of amethyst.

Sarpedon had to tear his eyes away to see the desolation around him. The roof of the oculus room was gone, along with several decks of the space hulk, exposing a huge raw wound of broken metal to the vacuum of space that cut across countless sector and component ships. Gases vented from ruptured plasma conduits. Fractured capacitor spines flashed as their energy bled into the void.

The Soul Drinkers were hastily donning their helmets against the vacuum. In the distance a tiny white shape that was Father Yser convulsed as the air was dragged from his lungs and his limbs froze. Suffocated and ravaged by cold, the pressure drop tearing at his organs and with the sight of the Architect of Fate flaying his mind, Yser died in a dozen different ways at once.

Father Yser, who had taught the faith in the Architect to the Soul Drinkers Chapter in the depths of the Cerberian Field, what seemed a lifetime ago. He had been the vessel for the greatest revelation in the Chapter's history, he had guided the Soul Drinkers to the *Brokenback* and the unnamed planet. He had seen the terror that was Ve'Meth. And now he had been destroyed at the first sight of the being he worshipped.

'Weak,' said the musical voice again. 'See how weak it is? For one such as this, Commander Sarpedon, my mere presence is death. But you are different, are you not?'

Sarpedon knew the vox was nothing more than static and his voice wouldn't sound outside his own helmet. But he spoke anyway, certain that the thing that called itself Abraxes could hear him.

'What are you?' he asked. 'How do you know who I am?'

'The second question first, commander. I have watched you for so long, searched the galaxy for someone who could make himself more than the dullards who infest your worlds. You burn so bright, Sarpedon. I could not fail to notice you even from the Silver City where my lord holds court.

'And what am I? I am Abraxes, herald of the Lord of Change. I am your salvation. I am the glory that Yser saw in his dreams, and that turned him into a beacon for you and your battle-brothers. I am the one who granted you visions, Sarpedon, of the foulness I would have you destroy. I gave you this beautiful ship, and see how easily I could destroy it. And I am he who blessed your body and the bodies of your brothers, forged the strength of your mind so the daemons of the warp fled before you.

'I am your prince and you are my subjects, for you have done my will ever since you saw the folly of your Imperium. I am the Architect of Fate, the Engineer of Time. I am the glory and the essence of what the smallest of minds call Chaos.'

It wasn't true. It couldn't be. But...

The daemon prince brimmed with power the like of which not even Ve'Meth had possessed. Abraxes was the figure Sarpedon had seen daubed by Yser's flock, and carved into the statue that stood alongside the primarch in the Cathedral of Dorn. And the shimmering creatures that were teeming down onto the mangled surface of the *Brokenback* were surely daemons. Yes, this was a great and powerful prince of Chaos that bestrode the space hulk, the same one who had spoken to the Soul Drinkers in the guise of the Architect of Fate.

Sarpedon had thrown aside ten thousand years of service to the Imperium, because he saw honour in the Emperor where there had been none in the Imperium. But now he saw that what they believed to be the Emperor's will was nothing more than one more lie – the machinations of Abraxes, who had wished only to rid himself of a fellow daemon.

The knowledge was flooding over Sarpedon, and it was more than he could bear. He had been so sure they had achieved something magnificent, that they had thrown off the shackles of weak humanity and become the true soldiers of the Emperor – could they really be nothing? Could they really be worse than nothing, the foulest of traitors not through malice but by ignorance?

The star fort. The ordinatus. The Cerberian Fields and the *Brokenback*. Ve'Meth. What had the Soul Drinkers done? Try as he might, he couldn't help but remember the words of Inquisitor Tsouras's envoy and Chapter Master Gorgoleon – words like treachery, heresy, daemonancy. Sarpedon had killed both men, and now the horrible realisation was dawning that both had been right.

The Soul Drinkers had performed the will of Chaos. They were as much a part of the armies of the enemy as the Traitor Marines they had battled in the fortress of Ve'Meth. They had been pawns in the game of the Dark Gods, soldiers in the army of corruption. That they did not know what they had been doing was irrelevant. No true servant of the Emperor considered ignorance a defence. The Soul Drinkers were Chaos Marines.

'Ah, he understands,' said the voice like a thousand choirs. 'He knows what he is. He has thrown away the purity he held so dear, and done it willingly. He has turned his back on his allies, slain my enemies at my behest, accepted his mutant form as a blessing. And he has done all this without coercion. Sarpedon understands what he is, and he understands that there is no turning back.'

'It's not true,' Sarpedon heard himself gasping.

Abraxes smirked. 'You know yourself, mutant. I do not lie.'

Mutant. That word… and then Sarpedon felt it once more, the vile oppression of uncleanliness, the mantle of loathing that draped over him. It was just as he had felt when he had consumed the flesh of the mutant on the star fort, a crushing weight of the universe's loathing. His blood was impure, his flesh corrupt, his skin tainted. Every eye that looked upon him would do so with hatred. He was the lowest of the low – mutant, inhuman, vermin.

It would be falling on his battle-brothers, too – Graevus with his executioner's hand, Tellos with his heightened senses and strange metabolism. Even Givrillian, steadfast Givrillian slain in the grand chamber of Ve'Meth, was a deformed mutant. As Abraxes lifted the illusion of nobility from their minds the vileness of mutation would be sweeping over them as it was over Sarpedon.

Sarpedon sunk to the twisted deck, his unholy, unnatural insect legs splayed around him. Mutant. Traitor. Soldier of Chaos.

Abraxes was standing right over Sarpedon. He reached down and Sarpedon looked up through tears of rage – there was something in the daemon prince's hand, like a needle held between the gargantuan fingers.

'But Sarpedon, it pains me to see you so distressed.' Abraxes's face was troubled and sincere. 'Can you not see what you could be? You and your Chapter have achieved astonishing things. You have thrown aside the shackles of the Imperium, and you did it yourselves, for I merely stood back to watch. You proved your strength of mind when you turned your back on the tradition of mindless authority that threatened to make you weak. And with my guidance you destroyed Ve'Meth, who was a twisted parody of the glories of Chaos.

'Chaos is a wonderful thing, Sarpedon – it is freedom incarnate, where all things can change and the universe is subject only to the will of the strong. It is what you have been seeking all along, a release from the hypocrisy and dishonour of the Imperium. You sought the Emperor's blessing, because you were still naïve in the ways of the universe. The Emperor is nothing, Sarpedon, a corpse on a throne, to whom you were devoted only because you did not know what true Chaos could give you. But now I have shown you, and can you honestly say that you and your Chapter can truly follow anything other than Chaos and the glorious lord of change?'

It was true, all true. Had he really believed it was the Emperor who had granted him this foul mutation and the heretical visions that guided the Chapter to Ve'Meth?

The object Abraxes was holding was about the length of Sarpedon's forearm, a gleaming cylinder of microcircuitry that shone in the starlight. 'My lord is the only power in this galaxy worth fighting for. Join me, march as my soldiers across the stars, and give yourself to destruction in the name of the changeling god. What else is there? Your Emperor is nothing, your Imperium has excommunicated you. The only purpose you have left is the pursuit of Chaos, which you have executed so well already. There is no need for you to live a lie any longer, Sarpedon. You can have what you wanted at last – a lifetime spent in the service of a power you can believe in, towards a goal you can achieve. And in the name of my God, I wish to show you my gratitude for slaying my enemy.'

The Soulspear. A lifetime ago, it had been the only thing that mattered. It had torn the Chapter apart and set in motion a chain of events that had left the Soul Drinkers broken and heretic, with nothing left but to throw their lot in with the power which had shown itself to be a true god. The Soulspear – ancient and powerful, the artefact that should have cemented those Chapter traditions that had, instead, been thrown away.

Sarpedon reached up and took the Soulspear from Abraxes. It could be a new beginning. The Soulspear could be the symbol of a new Chapter, formed from the ashes of the Soul Drinkers, following a god that could reward them for their devotion. Sarpedon could lose himself in the eternity of battle, wielding the Soulspear as a mark of how he had broken away entirely from the lies of the Imperium and the corpse-Emperor. He could exult in the slaughter of the change god's enemies. He could blaze a trail of death against the stars, and have a purpose in slaughter that he had sought for so long.

From the back of Sarpedon's mind rose, unbidden, the snippets of history he had learned as a novice, when the story of the Soulspear had been one of pride and anger at its loss. It had been given to the Chapter by the Primarch Rogal Dorn, to show that he held them in no less esteem than the great Imperial Fists legion from which the Soul Drinkers had been founded. The custody of such an artefact had shown that the Soul Drinkers had their place in the grand plan of the Emperor, that they were beholden to His will.

Something stirred in Sarpedon's mind. Why had he turned the guns of his Marines on the tech-guard, and slain the envoy of Inquisitor Tsouras when he had declared the Chapter Excommunicate? Was it pride? Anger? Or something else, something he only had to realise?

He glanced across at his brother Marines. He saw Tellos, unarmoured as always, and it was somehow no surprise that the hard vacuum didn't seem to affect him. He saw Graevus and Karraidin, Tech-Marine Lygris, Apothecary Pallas and all the other Soul Drinkers who had followed Sarpedon through everything. Most had witnessed the catastrophe of the star fort and the hell of Ve'Meth, and all had fought through the horror of the Chapter war. Sarpedon could have led them through hell and every single one of his battle-brothers, he was sure, would have followed. If he bowed before Abraxes, they would follow him again. And they would follow him to the death if he did not.

Sarpedon's fingers tightened around the Soulspear. He found the row of pits in the cylinder's surface, and felt the tiny lasers punch through the skin of his gauntleted fingertips.

Rogal Dorn had resisted breaking up the Imperial Fists legion until he risked being branded a rebel. When forced to relent he had taken great pains to ensure each of the Chapters who bore his gene-seed were held in equal esteem, infused with the belief in independence and nobility that had characterised the Imperial Fists. Why had he done so? Was it just fatherly pride, for the Imperial Fists and their successors were in many ways his sons? Or was there something else?

Rogal Dorn had realised something that was beginning to dawn on Sarpedon, too. And as it did so Abraxes's spell was breaking. Would the other Soul Drinkers realise in time? Perhaps they were already lost to Abraxes. It some ways it didn't really matter any more.

His blood seeped through the pinprick holes in his fingertips and touched the gene-encoders built into the Soulspear. It was one of the weapon's secrets that it was attuned to the blood of Rogal Dorn, who had first discovered it. Only those whose veins flowed with Dorn's blood – the Imperial Fists or their successor Chapters, like the Soul Drinkers – could wield it. The weapon was hot and thrumming in Sarpedon's hand.

Abraxes stepped back. The shimmering daemons were gathered around his feet. 'Choose, Sarpedon.'

But Sarpedon had already chosen.

Twin spikes of pure vortex leapt from the Soulspear, infinitely darker than even the black backdrop of space. Sarpedon flexed his unholy mutant legs and prepared to run. He would have to be fast, and hope that the ship's gravitic field wasn't damaged. He would need to be strong and accurate, and would have to rely on his battle-brothers to do what was right.

He fixed the Daemon Prince Abraxes with a determined eye. 'This Chapter,' he said grimly, 'is owned by no one.'

Sarpedon charged. There was no way to communicate with his fellow Soul Drinkers, but he didn't need to.

Karraidin closed the fastest, barrelling into the closest daemons, shining creatures of pink and pastel blue light with serpent-fingered hands and huge gaping maws. His storm bolter chattered silently in the vacuum, shells ripping into the luminescent bodies. Tellos was right behind him and literally dived into the fray, blades swinging through daemonic limbs. Streaks of light flickered soundlessly against the blackness of space as every Soul Drinker opened fire, engaging the daemonic horde that had descended onto the *Brokenback*. Dreo waved the closest Marines towards him and was forming a firebase from which he could send volleys of fire raking across the landscape of twisted metal. Luko was charging across the broken deck, gathering Marines as he did so.

All they had to do was to keep the daemons occupied, while Sarpedon struck.

The missing leg didn't slow him. He propelled himself towards the towering figure of Abraxes, the Soulspear in his hand. The daemon prince's face showed shock and anger as the battle erupted around his feet. The rings of arcane symbols that shone around him turned to angry reds and yellows, his shining eyes turned dark, and ruddy veins stood out against his alabaster skin as he channelled his rage into strength.

'Fools!' Abraxes roared. 'You are nothing! Nothing!'

Sarpedon ignored him, and the only sound was his own breathing. He would have to be fast, and he would have to be accurate. He didn't know if he could do it. But it didn't matter if he couldn't – for if there was one thing that had not changed, it was that to die fighting the Enemy was an end in itself.

Fungus-bodied things, whose arms ended in flame-belching orifices, bounded into Sarpedon's path. Triple slashes of light darted and Luko's lightning claws felled two of the monstrous daemons, chainblades lashing out from the Soul Drinkers at his side. The daemons came apart, their shining flesh disintegrating. Sarpedon ran through them, swinging the Soulspear and carving the scattered daemons in two as he passed.

He drew his arm back, focusing on the huge pale-skinned torso of Abraxes. Silver fire rained from the daemon prince's outstretched hands, punching through Sarpedon's armour like bolts of molten metal but Sarpedon couldn't afford to falter now.

He flexed his seven mutant legs and jumped, tensing his arm. The fire was ripping through him now, shards of pain shearing into his torso. He felt one lung puncture and another leg torn and useless. The glare from Abraxes was blinding – there was bolter-fire stitching across Abraxes's chest and shafts of light were bleeding out into space.

Everything slowed down. There was nothing in the universe but Abraxes, Sarpedon and the sacred weapon in his hand. There was only one sound now, a rhythmic thumping that was getting faster and louder as Sarpedon hurtled closer. It was Abraxes's heartbeat, quickened by anger, pumping silver fire through the daemon prince's veins.

Sarpedon hit, jabbing his talons into the glowing skin of Abraxes's chest. Clinging to the daemon prince, burning with magical fire, Sarpedon drove the point of the Soulspear through the skin and into the huge beating blasphemy of Abraxes's heart.

AFTERWARDS, FOR MOST of the time Sarpedon would remember very little. But sometimes, when before he had dreamt of the battlements on Quixian Obscura, he would dream of a massive flare like the birth of a new sun, a beam of light that ripped from Abraxes's ruptured heart. The pure madness of the warp that was the daemon prince's lifeblood flooded out into space, hurtling Sarpedon away on a tide of fire, pouring out onto the shattered decks of the *Brokenback*.

He would recall the daemons of the change god drowned in liquid fire, screaming and gibbering even in the soundless vacuum as their flesh dissolved. Then, as the dream faded, the ball of white fire that had been Abraxes would implode into a ball of blackness that sucked in the many-coloured flame and disintegrating daemons. Soul Drinkers clung to the battered metal to avoid being dragged into the vortex. A gauntleted hand – Sarpedon would never discover who it belonged to – grabbed one of Sarpedon's flailing legs and hauled him down to the deck.

Then silence would fall, the light would die, and Sarpedon would awake.

SARPEDON LIMPED ONTO the new bridge of the *Brokenback*. It had been several months in the construction – a hard armoured bubble in the heart of the space hulk, which acted as a focus for all the many control systems that ran throughout the various component ships. On the cavernous front curve of the sphere was set a huge viewscreen, displaying a composite image taken from all the sensoria studding the hulk's hull.

The place was silent aside from the distant rumble of the engines and the gentle thrum of the control consoles. Sarpedon hobbled across the metal deck of the bridge and up onto the command pulpit. The prosthetic strapped to the stump of his missing leg clacked on the floor as he walked – the replacement bionic would take some time and was providing a learning experience for the Chapter apothecarion. Two other legs were badly fractured and were still splinted – a Space Marine healed quickly but it would still be weeks before Sarpedon lost his lopsided, limping gait.

The control lectern in front of him flashed with readouts and weapons runes. The Tech-Marines kept on finding new directional thrusters and weapon arrays, and it was a race to keep them all connected to the bridge as quickly as they were discovered. It would take years to explore the *Brokenback* fully, and there were doubtless places and systems aboard that would never be properly explained.

This was the home of the Soul Drinkers now – a space hulk that had been found drifting and polluted, now cleansed and made holy. It was indicative of the Chapter as a whole – they had been cleansed, too, of all the millennia of lies that had afflicted them. It had cost them terribly, with losses bordering on the irreplaceable. But that would not be enough to break the Chapter – the great harvest would begin again, where the *Brokenback* would descend on scattered backwards worlds and select the bravest youths for induction into the Chapter. It had been Sarpedon's first order when he had woken in the apothecarion, burned and broken – the Soul Drinkers would gather a new generation of novices and begin to replace all that they had lost. It would take time, but they had been lost for so many thousands of years that time was not a worry.

Perhaps some of what Abraxes had said was true. Perhaps the Emperor was nothing more than a corpse on a throne, dead and powerless. Such a thought would be the pinnacle of heresy for a law-abiding Imperial citizen, but the Soul Drinkers had long since ceased to care about such things. Perhaps the Chapter really was alone, without any power to lend them strength and show them the way.

But it didn't matter. The Emperor might be dead, but there were still principles He symbolised that were worth fighting for. The horror of Chaos was very real, and just because the Emperor didn't guide their hand it didn't mean that the Soul Drinkers couldn't follow the ideals He represented. Chaos was worth fighting, not because the Emperor was telling them to but because destroying the enemy was the right and noble thing to do.

The Soul Drinkers had been lapdogs of a corrupt Imperium for thousands of years, and then the slaves of Chaos. But they had thrown aside both these masters – and in any case, they had destroyed two terrible princes of Chaos, and was that not something they could be proud of, no matter that else might have happened?

This was the Soul Drinkers' fate – they would fight Chaos wherever they found it, spurning all masters, renegade and alone. They had been born to fight and fight they would – they didn't need the Emperor or anyone else to give them a reason to take up arms. When Sarpedon had recovered and the Chapter was rebuilt, there would be nothing to stop them. It was a lofty ambition, to be devoted to the destruction of Chaos, when they were hated by Chaos and Imperium alike and could never rely on allies from anywhere. But if that was the only way the Soul Drinkers could fight the good fight, that was how it would be.

Perhaps it was ridiculous, or ironic. Sarpedon was past caring. He would die fighting to fulfil the principles the Emperor had founded the Imperium upon, and which had been betrayed by the liars who ruled in his name.

And so on the bridge of the space hulk, the mutant and excommunicate Space Marine vowed to do the Emperor's work.

ABOUT THE AUTHOR

Ben Counter has made several contributions to the
Black Library's *Inferno!* magazine, and has been
published in 2000 AD and the UK small press.
An Ancient History graduate and avid miniature
painter, he is also secretary of the Comics
Creators Guild.

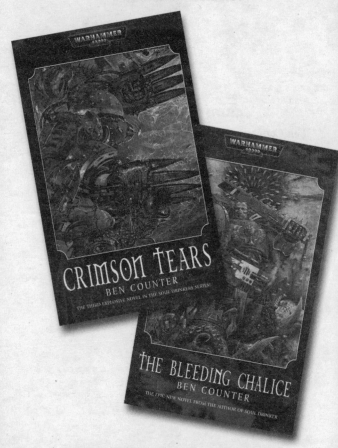